Seduced

Book Three in the Surrender Series

by Melody Anne

Seduced
Book Three in the Surrender Series
by Melody Anne

Copyright © 2013 Melody Anne

Printed and published in the United States of America.

Published by Gossamer Publishing Company

Editing by Nicole and Alison

Cover art by Trevino Creative

DEDICATION

This book is dedicated to Ray White. You are one of the kindest, hardest-working people I know. I love what a strong man you are, and how much you give to the world.

You have helped me so much, and I appreciate it more than you could imagine, even if I don't say it often enough. Thank you!

May you find your very own Ari soon, because any woman who can have you for the rest of her life is truly blessed.

NOTE FROM THE AUTHOR

I wanted to share with you all something of the way in which I come up with a story. Sixty percent of the story is from research, imagination, and thoughts that won't go away. Thirty percent comes from personal experience, some greatly embellished for dramatic effect. (Sadly, a scene in Canada with my friend left on the dance floor and trapped in a hot crowd of men was true. I did leave poor Stephy out there, but, luckily, she survived.) The remaining ten percent of my inspiration rises up while I sit on the deck at night and think about the nature around me.

Recently, when my husband and I were enjoying a cup of coffee during a family vacation, a spectacular storm flashed in the sky. I turned to him and said, "I need to write a love scene in which the characters make love during a great storm. I haven't done it yet." He said, "Oh, yes, outside in the rain." We were in Orlando, Florida, and the rain was amazingly warm. And my thoughts started to pour in, like the rain. I said, "And a waterfall! We need a waterfall!" That is how quickly one scene in this book came up.

A lot of hopeful authors, new authors, and friends ask me why I write romance. My answer? Romance is all around us. It's beautiful, it's compelling, and it will never die. Since I started writing full time three years ago, I haven't been able to stop. I pray to my Heavenly Father daily that this gift won't ever be taken from me; it's the most joyful experience of my life. I struggle with sleep at night because I lie in bed and even in the comfort of my husband's arms my mind refuses to shut down. Many times I've jumped from bed and rushed to my computer because an idea won't go away.

Why romance? Because we all need to dream. We all need to spread our wings. We all need to push for what we deserve in life. Thank you all for your support, and thank you for the joy you've brought to me and my family these last couple of years. I hope I can continue to entertain you with my dreams and visions in the years to come.

Melody Anne

Books by Melody Anne

BILLIONAIRE BACHELORS
*The Billionaire Wins the Game
*The Billionaire's Dance
*The Billionaire Falls
*The Billionaire's Marriage Proposal
*Blackmailing the Billionaire
*Runaway Heiress
*The Billionaire's Final Stand
*Unexpected Treasure
*Hidden Treasure – **Coming Soon**
*Priceless Treasure – **Coming Soon**
*Unrealized Treasure – **Coming Soon**
*Wanted Treasure– **Coming Soon**

BABY FOR THE BILLIONAIRE
+The Tycoon's Revenge
+The Tycoon's Vacation
+The Tycoon's Proposal
+The Tycoon's Secret
+The Lost Tycoon – **Coming Soon**

RISE OF THE DARK ANGEL
-Midnight Fire – Rise of the Dark Angel – Book One
-Midnight Moon – Rise of the Dark Angel – Book Two

-Midnight Storm – Rise of the Dark Angel – Book Three
-Midnight Eclipse – Rise of the Dark Angel – Book Four – **Coming Soon**

Surrender
=Surrender – Book One
=Submit – Book Two
=Seduced – Book Three
=Scorched – Book Four – **Nov 2013**

PROLOGUE

"My, my, how the tables have turned."

"I swear, by all that's holy, that if you don't wipe that smart-assed smirk off your face, I will pound you to a bloody pulp!" Rafe thundered as he looked at his best friend, Shane.

"Wow. Aren't you cranky? Did you wake up on the wrong side of the bed?" Shane wasn't the least bit intimidated by Rafe's outburst. Of course, part of that could be because his best friend was securely behind bars.

"Yeah, you've had your fun, Shane. Now pay the damned bail and get me the hell out of here!"

"I don't know if I can afford it, since this *is* the second time in two months…"

"Shut up, Shane! This isn't the time to be a jackass. They won't let me pay the bail myself, and I want to go home!"

"Maybe if you stopped picking fights at clubs, you wouldn't get locked up," Shane said as he came closer to the bars.

Rafe's hand snaked through the opening and grabbed hold of Shane's shirt in an iron-tight grip. "Get — me — out — now!"

"OK. OK. There's no need for violence," Shane said,

unable to control the laughter spilling from him. "We wouldn't want you to be thrown back in jail before you even get out."

Once Rafe released him, it didn't take long for Shane to post bail, and then he was leaving county detention with a very irate Rafe. "That wasn't amusing the first go-around, Shane, and certainly not this time," Rafe growled as he climbed into Shane's sleek silver Porsche.

"I seem to remember that you found it quite amusing when the shoe was on the other foot and *I* needed to be bailed out."

"That was different," Rafe muttered, rubbing his eyes. He hadn't slept in forty-eight hours, and he smelled like stale tequila and sweat. He didn't want to analyze the other odors drifting from his clothes.

"We need to get out of this town. One month in Italy wasn't long enough for Ari to forgive you, and you've been back for two months doing nothing but causing trouble. I think the best thing you can do is give the woman space. I'm scheduled to leave next week for South America because your unbelievably stubborn sister still won't speak to me. Let's take the hint and get away for a while."

Rafe stewed silently as he considered his best friend's words. The Gli Amanti Cove project was on hold because of environmental disputes, so they were stalled there. Rafe felt like crap, and for the first time in his life he had no motivation whatsoever to find the next big acquisition. Maybe he *should* just leave for a while. It would give him time to pull himself together. He didn't even know who he was anymore.

He hadn't seen Ari in three months and it was taking its toll on him. Every time he tried to speak to her, she would hang up the phone. He'd had gifts delivered to her new place, but she just returned his packages. The one time he'd cornered her, she'd coolly told him *he* wasn't ready yet.

Yes, he'd screwed up, but didn't people make mistakes? What was so wrong with liking sex? Was he that bad a man because he knew what he wanted and wasn't afraid to be with women who weren't intimidated to explore their sexuality? He didn't see it that way, but Ari apparently thought his actions were unforgivable. He'd even tried to enter into other satisfying sexual liaisons — not romantic, of course — but those had fizzled before they had even started.

He couldn't seem to forget one bright-eyed blond woman who'd stolen his breath away.

"I'll go with you."

Shane turned in surprise; his car swerved slightly into the next lane and almost clipped a station wagon. If Rafe had been in a better mood, he would have chortled at the look of terror on the father who was driving the old Volvo. The poor man had probably peed himself.

"Seriously?" It was obvious that Shane had never expected Rafe to walk away from the business world so easily.

"Yes. I need to get away before I do something incredibly foolish."

"Like you already haven't," Shane said with a laugh.

Rafe glared at him before replying. "I'm serious. I'm ready to do this."

"What about work?"

"I thought you were the one trying to talk me into this in the first place," Rafe said with a frustrated sigh.

"I am. *Really*. I just want to make sure you aren't going to get there and then turn around and leave in two weeks. These people are really counting on us."

Rafe knew that Shane was right. The homes and businesses they built in Third World countries changed lives. Rafe was surprised by how much he wanted to be a part of it. He'd grown anxious, bored, and frustrated with his life.

"I'll make some calls. My manager can run things from here. I'm ready to leave."

Assessing Rafe for several moments, Shane finally spoke. "Good. Pack up, because we'll be gone at least six months."

"What if you get called away?" Rafe asked.

"We'll cross that bridge," Shane said. He was used to being yanked away, and he always came back as soon as the task was finished.

This was a brilliant idea. Some hard physical labor was sure to take Rafe's mind off of Ari. He just needed to get away from this mess for a while. His infatuation with one woman was out of character; hell, it was completely insane. But it was all in his head and he'd be over Ari before he knew it!

CHAPTER ONE
Two Years Later

Ari

"ALL right, class, I want you to take out your books and turn to page one hundred and four." Ari took a deep breath as she looked out at the sea of students before her. *Don't let them see your fear. They will eat you alive.*

No matter how many times she chanted this in her head, she could feel the sweat beading on her brow, and what felt like ten-pound weights sitting on her chest. What if she messed up? What if she *threw* up? What if everything just went black and she face-planted in front of the entire room?

You will not psych yourself out! You are Arianna Harlow, a strong, independent woman who just completed a master's degree. That takes guts, determination, and stamina. Not everyone is cut out for a higher education, but you did it in the face of everything you'd gone through. This is nothing in comparison. A class of fifty students will not intimidate you.

OK, she was feeling a bit less faint as she dimmed

the lights and turned on the screen projector. This was her first job and she was grateful to be teaching.

The last two years hadn't been easy for Ari, but she'd worked hard, studying longer, jogging for miles upon miles to try to relieve the constant ache in her body, and spending what little free time she allowed for herself with her mother and friends.

The most difficult of times was being with Lia and Rachel. She loved them both so much, but they were a reminder of what she'd never again have.

Rafe.

It seemed that not a single day could pass without a thought of him fluttering through her mind. Time had lessened the ache but hadn't removed it altogether. Love for a man like Rafe didn't disappear overnight — apparently, not even after two years. She didn't regret her decision to walk away — it was what she'd had to do — but still, she missed him. Missed his smile and his laughter, missed the way his hands had caressed her body.

The few dates she'd attempted since leaving him had been a joke. No man could measure up to Rafe Palazzo. Yes, he'd been controlling and had pushed her in ways she still couldn't believe — he'd had her doing things she'd never thought she'd enjoy — but he'd also changed her forever.

She could never go back to that innocent girl she'd been. Rafe had opened her eyes to a new world, and it was a place she'd enjoyed. She would never settle for less than love, but she did miss the excitement the man provided. Missed the hunger that swelled into desire from deep within whenever he touched her.

Rafe was many things, but boring wasn't one of

them. No man had stirred her the way he had, and she missed him desperately, though she never admitted that — not even to herself. What good would it do her?

Shaking off the melancholy thoughts, Ari focused on the meticulously written out notes in front of her as she began her carefully planned-out lecture. Too nervous to focus on the students, she was relieved when class was nearly over and it came time for them to ask questions.

Please, someone have something to ask was her only hope in that moment. The next few minutes passed with several questions, and the stiffness eased from her body. Only a couple of minutes more to go and she could call her first class a success.

"Are there any more questions?" This she would soon regret asking.

"Yes. Will you join me for dinner tonight?"

Ari's body stiffened and her face flushed. She would never, ever forget that voice — it haunted her in her dreams, making her wake up aching and empty. It trailed her as she walked the streets and heard a man's laughter. It caressed her body when she lay in bed at night and ran through the various conversations they'd had.

Ari's ears were ringing too loudly for her to hear the chuckling in her classroom as she lifted her head and her eyes locked with Rafe's purple-and-blue gaze.

Sitting comfortably in the back of the classroom, he took her breath away with his confident grin. Two years since she'd last laid eyes on him, and he still looked deliciously perfect. Several students turned his way, the girls batting their eyelashes, the guys wanting to *be* him. It was obvious to anyone present that he was a man who would always get his way.

Some people you were drawn to simply because of their confidence. Rafe was one of them. There was nothing about him that shouted insecure. His command was obvious from his very demeanor.

No! She reminded herself. He didn't always get his way. He'd wanted her, and she'd had the courage to walk away because he hadn't been willing to give her what she deserved. He might have been a man in charge, but that didn't lessen who she was. She'd stood up, been strong and hadn't stopped her forward momentum for a single instant once she'd finally gained the courage.

Yes, her heart had shattered that day she'd left his home, then shattered again when she walked away from him at her college graduation. However, she hadn't let it stop her. She'd accepted the pain, had felt it to the utmost, but she hadn't let it define her. She'd moved on.

When she'd come to the realization that, yes, love could be magical but that magic was still only an illusion, her pain had eased. It took time and effort to make love last if you wanted it to go beyond that illusion, that vision. Rafe had expected to get what he wanted without putting in the effort. It was his loss.

Looking him straight in the eyes — showing him she wasn't afraid — she spoke. "Are there any questions pertaining to the lecture?" Only the slightest bit of breathlessness entered her words as she forced her gaze from his in a deliberately measured way.

The room was silent, apart from a few remaining snickers.

"Very well, then. On Wednesday, upon your return, I want the questions at the end of the chapter done and turned in. We'll be discussing the Civil War all semester, and I expect you to learn a heck of a lot more than who fought and the dates it happened. By the time you move on to your next subject, you should have a basic understanding of why this war took place, and the lives that it affected. Thank you. Class is dismissed."

Ari turned back to her desk and sat down, her knees shaky. Her hope was that Rafe would rush from the room with the rest of the students, but Ari wasn't a fool. Rafe was there for a purpose and that she'd ignored him didn't mean he'd simply turn and walk away. That wasn't *who he was.*

Rafe would have his say, and she'd just have to bear up while he did it.

Be strong, she commanded herself as she heard the din of students' voices fading. She greatly wished at that moment for another class to be entering, but it was the end of the night and she was teaching only one class a day, Mondays and Wednesdays.

Toying with the thought of running from the room, she knew she'd never make it. Plus, Rafe would get the satisfaction of seeing her try to escape. She refused to reveal how much he still affected her. She absolutely rejected the thought of showing weakness in his presence.

"I've missed you, Ari, more than you could possibly imagine."

The familiarity of his voice stimulated every cell in her body while his scent swirled around her, draining the strength in her knees even more, and she was grateful to be sitting. How could he still have such power over her? How could she have such strong feelings about a man who had shattered her heart, leaving her to pick up the pieces of her life, alone?

"You are wasting your time, Rafe. I would have

thought you'd have moved on by now. Have you had trouble hiring your next mistress?" Finally, Ari peered up at him, prepared to see irritation on his features.

When a smile formed on his lips instead, she was taken aback. What was this new game he was playing? She hadn't read the textbook on this one. Was he still upset that someone had walked away from him, even after so much time had passed?

Not even Rafe could be that determined to win.

"I want no other woman but you, Ari — and I've given you enough space. I made mistakes, and now I'm here to prove I'm a new man."

Ari's mouth dropped open. Rafe Palazzo was admitting to being *wrong* about something. Had the world stopped turning? She had to be dreaming — this was just another of her fantasies, and she was going to wake up at any moment, alone in her small room. And then she would have to fight the pressure in her chest as she took deep breaths and once again banished him from her mind.

No. She hadn't had an anxiety attack in a long time, and she wasn't going to start with them again. She was a college instructor, something she'd dreamed about for a very long time. A man wasn't going to unravel her — not even a man she had fallen hopelessly in love with.

"This is ridiculous, Rafe. We had our fling. It was great, but it's over and done with. Nothing good can come from us even attempting to come together again," she told him as she started to gather her possessions together.

She had to get out of that large classroom. Suddenly the walls felt as if they were closing in on her. She must get away from him before she did something foolish

— such as actually believe what he was saying. Or, even worse, jump from her chair and wrap her body around his just to experience one more taste of his lips.

She wanted so badly to envision a happy ending with him that her heart was thudding at the possibility that he had changed — that his interest in her was now more than just *really* great sex.

"Ridiculous or not, I've decided to woo you."

For the second time in sixty seconds, Ari's mouth dropped open. Did he actually just say the word *woo*? Who was this man and what had he done with Rafe Palazzo? It couldn't possibly be the same person who'd forced her into an affair with him. She needed to re-member what he'd done — what he'd demanded from her.

"I hate to disappoint you, but I'm not that same desperate girl who allowed you to make me go against everything I was brought up to hold important." *There, that would show him.*

Rafe came around her desk, turning her chair and boxing her in. She leaned back, but he followed, his face only inches from hers.

"I did some things I will forever regret, but I've had a lot of time to think since then. Yes, I forced your hand, but the night you walked away from me, you told me you loved me. I'm here to prove I'm worthy of that love."

Ari couldn't speak. Her eyes lowered as they took in the fullness of his lips, her ears straining to hear more of the enticing words coming from them. Of course, he was saying what she wanted to hear, but that's what Rafe did best. He got his way — by any means possible. She couldn't be so foolish as to actually believe him.

"No witty comebacks, Ari?"

Leaning in even closer, Ari breathed in his masculine scent and felt her heart race, the sound of her blood rushing through her veins echoing in her head. Finally, snapping out of her trance, Ari lifted her hand and pushed against him, shocked when he responded to her unspoken request to stop and pulled himself away.

Hoping her knees would work, Ari grabbed her briefcase and stood. So far, so good. She'd resisted kissing his full lips, and when she'd risen from her chair, she hadn't face-planted in front of him. Thank heavens for such small mercies.

"The girl who professed her love is long gone, Rafe. I'm following the path I want to be on, and I don't have time to date. I appreciate that you thought of me, but it's best if we both just move on," she said over her shoulder as she began ascending the steps to the back door of the classroom.

She could feel him right on her heels as she reached the top of the stairs and walked into the quiet hallway. It was late, the school quickly emptying as most of the kids had finished their last class of the day. Summer terms had fewer students attending the school, anyway, and the campus was almost a dead zone when evening classes met.

Ari began walking toward the parking lot; Rafe moved silently beside her. There was no use in telling him to stop — he wouldn't allow her to walk on her own, even though there were security guards patrolling the area. It was dark, and he was a man who insisted on escorting a woman to her destination, even if she hadn't asked him to do so.

It should irritate her, but it was one of those

old-fashioned actions that she actually liked. A gentleman should ensure the safety of a woman he cared
about. Not that she was going to get ideas into her head
that he actually cared for her.

Yes, she would admit that she was confused. How
was she supposed to respond when he so suddenly
popped back into her life? She obviously needed time to
think. She certainly couldn't keep a clear head with him
right by her side.

Rafe had a way of causing her body to short-circuit.
It was one of the things she both loved and hated about
him. How could she trust what she was feeling when
she couldn't think straight? She was intelligent — far
above average — but she felt like a ditzy schoolgirl
when she was around him.

Hunger was good — she would admit to that. But
with Rafe, it wasn't just hunger, it was an all-consuming
passion that took over your mind, body and soul. That
wasn't healthy. It couldn't possibly be good for you.

When they reached her car, he put his hand on
the door, preventing her from opening it. Her will was
wearing thin, and she needed to remove herself from his
presence, immediately.

"I've had a long day, Rafe. Please let me leave." Her
voice was firm, except for only the slightest shake, but
she felt like a cornered animal, and instinct had her
wanting to lash out by kicking his leg. That might have
made him move.

"I want to talk to you. I think you owe me that
much," he said.

She looked at him incredulously. She *owed* him?
Oh, she didn't think so.

"That is the most ridiculous thing I think I've ever

heard you say, Rafe. I *owe* you nothing," she snapped as she thought about reaching for the scissors she knew were in her bag and poking them into the offending hand that was keeping her door closed.

"You owe it to *us* to listen to what I have to say," he said.

"I owe it to *myself* to do what makes me happy."

"Fine," he replied, that easy smile back.

Her suspicions rose as she looked at him. He still hadn't removed his hand. With a bow, he stepped away and as she opened her door, thinking she'd actually gotten off quite easily, he spoke again.

"I'll be back on Wednesday — and Monday — and Wednesday — and when are your office hours again?"

"Fine!" she interrupted. "What will it take to make you go away?"

"Dinner and a conversation."

Simple and to the point. Now *that* was the Rafe she remembered well.

"I guess you'll be enjoying history, then. Have a nice night, Rafe." As she slid swiftly into her car, she couldn't help but glance back. Instead of seeing anger or frustration on his face, she saw a huge grin.

That couldn't be a good sign.

CHAPTER TWO

Lia

"Are you kidding me?!" Lia slapped her arm as another bug landed on her, hell-bent on doing horrendous things to her tender flesh. What in the world was she doing in this tiny cabin in the middle of nowhere?

Once the resort was finished, this area would be breathtaking, with carefully designed spa retreats, luxury cabins, and private getaways for couples wanting exclusivity, romance, and the ultimate in indulgence.

Right now, it was hard to picture what the resort would become, because the area was untouched. Some found this beautiful just as it was, and many thought it a shame Rafe's company was building the Gli Amanti Cove, but she was a firm believer in the project.

She'd witnessed firsthand what Shane and Rafe could do. There was a reason the two of them were so successful. They didn't just throw buildings together. They made dreams come to reality, and they had a line of customers anxious to enter their next paradise.

Never before had she really thought of herself as

spoiled, but as she swatted another bug trying to land on her, she admitted that she *was* used to nice things. That didn't make her shallow or unfeeling; it made her sensible. Had she been born in a different time, then she'd expect…less. She'd heard of people who shunned air conditioning, but she had no interest in meeting crazy people.

"Troubles, Lia?"

Speaking of crazy people… Her entire body tensed as she heard the laughter of his rich voice. She turned slowly, and there was Shane, only ten feet away, leaning casually on the rickety railing of her steps.

Even knowing she'd be seeing quite a bit of him didn't lessen the reaction her body was having at the sight of the man. Though she wanted this project to succeed, since it was her first one with the company owned by her brother, Rafe, she'd been relieved by the delays, needing that time to build up her armor against Shane.

She'd wanted him for so long that she couldn't remember a time she hadn't. Then he'd had to go and ruin it all. Now, she couldn't even remember why she was so angry with him, but she felt justified in accepting that he was the enemy. It was a girl's prerogative to be irrational, wasn't it?

But of course that wasn't true. She remembered quite well, and she'd ended her incredibly brief affair with him for a good reason. She'd made a simple request — that he not tell her brother about their new relationship. True, it hadn't been simple to Shane. He always told Rafe everything, and he felt he had to tell him about the two of them.

In short, Rafe meant more to Shane than she did.

And Shane's own feelings mattered more to him than hers did. No, they hadn't discussed marriage — hell, they'd just been to bed once. But what Shane had done didn't follow her rule book. It didn't count as forsaking all others. It counted as thinking that men in general mattered more than women, and in particular that everyone he knew with testicles mattered more than she did.

Here's what really pissed her off — Shane hadn't had enough respect for her and her brain to wait and consider carefully what she'd asked. No, he'd run off and squealed to her brother while the sheets were still warm.

She didn't need another man like that, another man who dismissed her, thought of her only as a nice, warm body, useful at night, but not a friend and a confidante. Maybe she couldn't do better; maybe all guys were insensitive louts. Just look at Rafe. But she could try, and she could hope to find a man who really knew how to treat a woman, really knew how to love her.

She didn't think it was too much to ask to be put first.

"No troubles at all, Shane. Why are you here so early?"

"I couldn't let you have all the fun on your own, could I?" As he spoke, he took a step toward her, and it took all her willpower not to retreat. She couldn't back down even an inch, or he'd pounce. That was who Shane was.

"The first two weeks here is a lot of surveying, and you could have been relaxing on the beach while we do this part. Don't worry, though. It's not too late. Why don't you hop into your boat and go flirt with the locals across the channel?"

The thought of him doing just that had her stomach turning, but there was no possible way she'd admit it. Eventually she would will herself to get over her extreme lust and infatuation with her brother's best friend.

Shane wasn't fazed. "I would rather stay right where I am and flirt with you."

Why had he decided too late to say everything she'd always wanted him to say? Men! They never did what they were supposed to.

"You're wasting your time, Grayson. Go find something to do. I'm going for a walk." Lia brushed past him and bounded down the steps. There was little hope that he would listen to her and disappear, but she had to give it a try.

"Good. I was in the mood for an evening stroll. Where are we off to?"

Lia sighed and made her way in a leisurely manner along the trails she knew so well. She'd been across the entire island and back again so many times, she could probably map it out. That's what it had taken to place the resort in just the right location. There was so much more involved, too, such as not disturbing the natural appeal of the island while still making the resort a place that big spenders would be willing to come to.

"I don't recall inviting you, Shane." Though she knew he wouldn't listen to her protests, she had to give it a valiant effort. If she didn't, she would soon be falling into his arms, and that would only lead to disaster, as she'd so quickly discovered while in Las Vegas. Falling into his bed had obviously been a mistake.

What the two of them had shared had been nobody's business but theirs. Even after over two years, her blood boiled at the thought of what he'd done immediately afterward.

"The invitation was in your eyes," he said with a grin. It took her a moment to realize he meant an invitation for him to walk with her, which she hadn't issued, and not an invitation to her bed, which she didn't want, either. "Besides, someone has to protect you," he continued. He grabbed her arm and wound it through his. She tugged for a moment, then gave up, unwilling to show him that he was, in fact, affecting her.

"Believe what you will. I just want to finish this job and get back to the real world."

"How can you turn your nose up at such natural beauty? Besides, we're going to be here for a good six months…at least," he said.

The excitement in his tone had her pulse racing.

Lia had no doubt that Shane expected them to pick up where they'd left off in Vegas. For so long she'd chased him, trying to prove she wasn't the little girl he'd first met when her brother had brought him home on a break from college.

But Shane was no different from any other boyfriend she'd had. He was intimidated by her brother, or worse, he cared more about her brother than he did about her. She was the odd woman out in a cozy bromance. Whatever the reason, he hadn't been willing to be with her without Rafe's permission — he hadn't even listened to her objections. Shane had just run off to Rafe, even though she'd told him what that meant. That just pissed her off all over again every time she thought about it.

"I spoke with the designer last week and we're on schedule. I don't expect you to be here the whole time," she said. She really hoped that was the case. Nobody could ever describe Lia as weak, but when it came to Shane, she didn't trust herself to keep holding out against him, especially if he decided to be charming. She'd seen the man in action through the years, and he was good at making women trail after him. She didn't want to be another in his long line of heartbreaks.

"Yes, the project is on schedule, and we have a wonderful crew to run it. Yet the problem is that I don't trust anyone to see it through. I've decided this task needs me here until the end," he said, stopping so he could turn her to face him.

The light in his eyes left no doubt that he was more than happy about their situation. Her stomach clenched as she fought her rising hormones. As Shane lifted his hand and removed a piece of hair that was clinging to her cheek, she knew she was in trouble.

Her breath quickened, and she was hot and hungry. She hadn't been with another man since Shane in Vegas, and her body was going through withdrawal. It wasn't easy to keep her distance, but she cared about herself enough to do so.

"Shane…" She attempted to warn him off, but there wasn't much heat behind her words.

"Yes, Lia?"

Oh, the man knew how to seduce, knew exactly the power he had over her. She'd just have to be that much stronger.

Lifting her hand as if she were going to caress him, she saw triumph flash in his eyes. When she slapped his forehead instead, his shocked expression made a giggle escape her previously pursed lips.

"You had a mosquito about to attack." With that, she pulled from him and turned back toward her small cabin. She felt victory at resisting him, even knowing she had a long way to go.

"This is only the first day, Lia," Shane called out to her, making her shoulders stiffen. Yes, it was only the first day.

So he'd snatched away some of her victory. She certainly wouldn't let him get another piece of it, or her, by sticking around. Not slowing her pace, she made it back to her cabin in record time, and she locked herself safely inside.

Yes, it was only their first day, but she'd still congratulate herself. If she took it only one day at a time, she might get through this unscathed. *Might* being the key word.

CHAPTER THREE

Rafe

RAFE moved toward his waiting car with a wide grin spread across his face. Had Ari been cold, distant, or uninterested, there wouldn't have been any hope.

But she was none of those things. There was heat in her eyes, and a quiver in her body. She still loved him — she just didn't want to fess up to it. Well, too bad. He wanted her, and he *would* win her back. He meant what he'd said: he was there to *win* her love this time, not force it, which wasn't an easy task for him.

His time in South America had shifted something deep inside of him. He didn't think he'd ever be the same man again. He'd let go of the demons that had held on to him for too many years. Was he a whole new man? Well, no. But he certainly was a better person — or at least, *he* thought so.

But he wasn't an entirely new man. That would be impossible. It was difficult for him to ask instead of demand, or chase instead of capture. Only one woman could make him change the way he viewed the world, and for her he would do whatever it took.

His life would never be complete without Ari. That realization had come to him when he still wasn't over her after an entire year had passed. She was his other half — the person who made him whole. It was corny, especially in his own cynical, unromantic head, but he didn't care. His arms ached to hold her, his body needed to possess her, and his heart felt empty without her. She was his — he just had to convince her of that.

Rafe hadn't felt this good in a long, long time. He climbed into the back of the car and found himself whistling.

"I take it that your meeting with Ms. Harlow went well."

"Exceedingly well, Mario," he replied happily.

"Then why didn't she join you?"

Leave it to his long-time assistant to dampen the mood.

"She will need some convincing, but I'm not worried." And he wasn't.

"Where to, then, Mr. Palazzo?"

"Home, Mario. I have some studying to do." At the puzzled look on his assistant's face, Rafe laughed aloud. If he was going to win her back, he certainly couldn't sit in her classroom and ignore what she was trying to teach. Try that, and she'd really hand him his ass backwards.

His grin grew as he pictured her in front of that class. She'd been so nervous. Though she tried to cover it up, he knew her too well to miss a thing. Her hands had trembled slightly as she wrote on the projector, and she'd tucked her hair behind her ears over and over. Teaching was a new experience for her, and she was doing excellently, but she was definitely uncomfortable.

Rafe was sure it would be a bit worse for her now that she knew he was there. As much as he wanted her in his arms again, lying naked beneath him, he enjoyed this chase with Ari. Before her, if a girl had made him chase her, she'd have been sorely out of luck. He would just move on to the next candidate.

Even with his ex-wife, he hadn't had to put forth any effort. She'd been the one chasing him. It wasn't something he'd ever thought about until Ari entered his life. His looks had developed at a young age, and with his money on top of that, he'd never had a problem in the dating department. Only once had he ever pursued a woman — and that woman had been Ari.

She was worth pursuing twice. Hell, she was worth pursuing a thousand times. He wouldn't give up on the two of them unless he knew, finally and absolutely, that she wasn't interested anymore. And that could never happen. Fire burned through both of them, and a blaze that hot didn't die down — not ever.

Arriving home, Rafe walked into his empty living room, on the one hand wishing she were there with him, but on the other, looking forward to their next encounter. Rafe knew for certain that his life was never boring when he was in Ari's company.

Doing what he'd told Mario he would, he pulled out the textbook he'd picked up the week before just so he could know a little of what she was teaching. He'd never planned to actually learn anything. It was really quite comical if he thought about it.

Two hours later, he wondered whether he'd really be able to keep this up. Rafe liked science and numbers, things that made sense. He couldn't care less about history. Yes, he had respect for the fallen soldiers, and he knew when and where the past wars had happened, but to study the Civil War for almost three months…that was almost the definition of torture for him.

Shutting the book with a long sigh, he went to his liquor cabinet and poured himself a double shot of whiskey.

For Ari, he'd do whatever it took.

Sitting back down, he opened the book again, his pen and paper next to him as he searched for answers to the questions she expected to be turned in on Wednesday. This was going to be a very long night. He was just grateful his sisters weren't around to tease him endlessly about trying to be the teacher's pet.

Oh, yeah, he'd like to be the teacher's favorite — he would make sure he was the *only* one for Ms. Arianna Harlow.

When his phone rang, he practically leapt from his chair to answer it. Normally in the evening, he answered calls only from his assistant. If there was an emergency, he would take care of it, but if it was a minor issue, he paid people well to handle it. That he'd reached for the phone without even checking the caller ID showed how desperate he was to end his impromptu study session.

"Your sister is a pain in my ass!"

Rafe laughed instantly, knowing just how his best friend felt.

"You are just discovering this now, Shane?"

"I have no idea what to do. I've been here for a week and she won't answer her door when I come calling on her, speaks to me like I'm nothing but a passing acquaintance, and has made it more than clear that she'd rather I was anywhere else in the world than with her on a secluded island. Hell, Rafe, we're in freaking paradise — the ultimate romantic destination — and she won't even look at me, let alone allow me to kiss her."

"First off, I really don't want to hear about you kissing my sister. You're lucky as hell I caved and backed off," Rafe said. "Secondly, did you think it would be easy? She's a Palazzo. *Stubborn* is her middle name. If you truly care about her, and I think that you do, you'll just have to step up your game. But I absolutely do *not* want to hear any of the details."

The thought of his little sister being romanced was enough to make his teeth grind themselves into stubs. He knew she was an adult, and he knew Shane was in love with her, just as Lia was in love with Shane, if only she'd admit it. None of that mattered, though, when he thought of her turning into a woman. He wanted both her and Rachel to stay toddlers forever — never grow up and get married.

Granted, Rafe was starting to think it wouldn't be so bad to have some nieces and nephews around. But that meant that his sisters would have sex, and that was a thought he couldn't stomach.

"Like you could stop me from kissing her," Shane replied, but before Rafe could say anything, he continued. "I almost forgot she has the same blood as you. That should have made me run like hell in the opposite direction. For that matter, I tried — for years. She's the one who chased me, and then I do one little thing that displeases her, and she completely cuts me off. I should thank my lucky stars and move on."

"Is that what you want?"

Shane sighed heavily into the phone. "No. You know that," he admitted with self-loathing.

"You had to have done something other than just tell me about your relationship. She is really pissed at you," Rafe said as he stood up and poured himself another drink.

"Nope. Just that. She mentioned something about being first. I don't know…" he muttered.

"Well, not listening could be your first problem, Shane. Women tend to get pissed off when we ignore them," Rafe said, delighted it was his best friend on this side of things. At least Rafe wasn't the only one with woman problems.

"Yeah, I've been trying to talk to her, trying to listen. She won't speak anymore!"

"Then you will have to find a way to make her talk," Rafe said. Wasn't it quite simple? No. Maybe not. He thought of Ari and the fact that she wouldn't talk, either. Definitely not as easy as he'd thought.

"She may never talk to me again. I just don't get women," Shane sighed.

Rafe laughed again. Yes, he and Shane were both in a predicament. Well, the two of them knew what they wanted and the women would have to deal with it. They'd have to get over their tempers. Both he and Shane were trying to make up with them. One thing Ari and Lia would learn was that when he or Shane wanted something, nothing would stop them. Both women had met their matches.

Or had they?

"Do you have a plan?" Rafe knew that he'd surely love to have a plan beyond stalking Ari where she worked. Hey, at least he had a semi-plan.

"I'll figure it out. I don't know why I bothered calling you. A lot of good it did me," Shane grumbled.

"You called because you know I'm the smarter one," Rafe said with a laugh.

"In your dreams, Palazzo. Fine. I'll get off the phone. I have some *plans* to make," Shane said before hanging up.

Rafe took his unfinished drink and sat by the fire. It was time to make his own plans. One thing he knew for sure was that Arianna Harlow wasn't getting away from him this time. As he leaned back, he thought about what it was that had caused such a change inside him. It still shook him to his very soul when he thought back...

A Few Months Earlier

"Damn, Rafe. I need a break!" Shane grumbled as he hefted a thick piece of wood up to his best friend.

"Quit whining, Shane. I want this place done by nightfall. Maria is going to have the baby at any time."

"I know, but she and her family are comfortable in the tents. If the baby comes, they'll all be protected until the home is finished," Shane said.

"No. I admire her. I want them to have a real home for the baby." Rafe didn't know why it was so important. Maybe because Maria and her husband, Pablo, were good people. They worked hard, and they had been so grateful for the help from Rafe and Shane and the other workers there with them.

Rafe hadn't expected to get close to any of the villagers, but for some reason this young couple had managed to wedge themselves into his heart — the heart he'd thought was cold and shriveled when he'd arrived in Paraguay.

Shane stopped complaining and the two of them

worked through the rest of the day, finishing the modest home as the last rays of the sun drifted behind the horizon. Rafe stood back, feeling a deep sense of accomplishment as he looked at what most people would consider a shack, but what Maria and Pablo would think of as a mansion.

He was humbled by the way these people lived, so grateful for the smallest of items — a bowl of beans, fresh fruit, a warm blanket. His eyes had been opened in many ways, and he would always remember this time in his life.

"You've done really well, Rafe," Shane said as he approached, clapping him on the back.

"I feel better. I didn't think it was possible, but seeing all this poverty, all this — I don't know how to say it — simplicity? — firsthand, for so long, changes a person," Rafe replied.

"Yeah, that's why I keep coming back."

"Then why are you still such an asshole?" Rafe said.

"Look who's talking," Shane answered with a glare.

"Yeah, yeah. I know I have my moments. I really need to return to the real world, but staying here has been good. I still think about Ari all the time, but it's more manageable now," Rafe had to say.

"I know the feeling. I can't stop thinking of Lia. The project is back on track, so I'll finally have her alone. That will be good."

"Should we insure you?" Rafe said, only half kidding.

"When I'm dealing with your sister, that may be a good idea. She's more dangerous than any mission I've ever been on," Shane said, before he went silent for a moment. "I'm shipping out in a few days."

Shane hated to speak about it, but Rafe was the

only one who knew. He had to have someone to turn to when it all ended up being just a bit too much.

"You'll come home." It wasn't a prayer or a wish; it was a statement of fact. Because Rafe wouldn't lose his best friend. He could lose a lot, but not his family and not Shane.

"Yes, I will."

The two men stood for a while longer before separating and going to their small campers to try to get some rest.

The happy Paraguayan couple moved into their home that night, and Rafe went to sleep with a smile on his face. It was the first time since he'd lost Ari that he'd felt like smiling. Feeling good about what he'd been doing and starting to figure out ways of winning back the woman whom he couldn't remove from his mind, Rafe slept better than he had since she'd walked from his life.

"Rafe, wake up."

The morning light was streaming in through the camper windows, and the pained look on Shane's face had him instantly sitting up.

"What is it?"

"Maria. She…she didn't make it, Rafe."

"No." If he denied the words his friend was saying, then he could make them untrue.

"I'm sorry, Rafe. I know how much you cared about her."

Shane had warned Rafe not to get attached, warned him to keep a distance. These people led a different life than they did — had a harsher reality. They were often lost at young ages and in tragic circumstances.

"No." He denied Shane's words again.

"I'm sorry, Rafe. The baby died in her womb several

days ago. Maria passed during the night from complications. Her husband found her this morning."

Rafe jumped from the bed and threw on his clothes, needing to see Maria — needing to prove that Shane was wrong. She couldn't be gone. He rushed to their new home. The home Rafe had worked nonstop to build so she could have her baby there.

Quietly walking inside, Rafe found Pablo on his knees by the bed, a bed Rafe had specially brought in for just them. Pablo looked up, tracks of tears on his face, but tears that had obviously dried hours ago. The broken man had no more left inside him.

"She left me," Pablo whimpered, his hands repeatedly stroking his cold wife's face. "She left me alone. Our baby and Maria are gone," he choked out, his voice broken, his spirit gone.

"No," Rafe whispered, seemingly unable to say anything else.

"I can't live without her. She's my world. She's my everything. How can I go on?"

The man was looking to Rafe for an answer, and Rafe didn't know what to say. He didn't have an answer to give Pablo. Never before had Rafe witnessed someone so utterly broken — so lost — so completely alone.

"Please, Rafe. Give her back to me," the man begged as if Rafe were capable of saving her. "Please," Pablo groaned as he turned back toward his wife and laid his head on her still chest.

Rafe stood in the doorway, his own heart broken, unable to move, watching the man hold on to his dead wife. Eventually, the men from the village had to drag the bereaved husband away as he cried out in agony.

That night, Pablo took his own life, leaving a short

note. *I will be with my wife and child for eternity.*

Rafe packed the few possessions he'd brought with him, and he went home. He wouldn't allow himself to be that broken. He couldn't. It was time to win back his other half, because he needed Ari. She made him whole.

He didn't want to be on his hands and knees begging for her when she was forever gone to him. He didn't want to waste another day. They'd been apart long enough, and he would win her back.

CHAPTER FOUR

Lia

PEACE at last!

Lia strolled along the shore as the water drifted slowly toward her feet before retreating like a thief escaping into the shadows. Shane was wearing her down, though she'd never admit it to him, or even herself.

He'd been there for two weeks, and he wasn't giving her a single moment to breathe. The project was starting, materials were being boated in, and she could practically see the luxurious cabins, artfully created to look rustic, arising on the hills in the thick forest.

Paths would be cleared, and suptuous facilities built, and the land would still look untouched. She was proud to be a part of it all.

"Hey, Palazzo, we need to ride over to the mainland."

Lia slowly turned to find Shane striding toward her in nothing but a pair of slacks that were riding low on his waist. Saliva pooled in her mouth at the sight of his muscular chest flexing in all its golden glory as he moved toward her.

If she hadn't been so ridiculously attracted to him, none of this would have been difficult. Damned hormones!

"You're on your own, Grayson. I have work to do," she replied cooly, turning away, and irritated with herself at how difficult it was to do just that.

"Sorry. I need your help. We have some materials to pick out that you insisted on having final approval on. I can do it myself, though, if you just sign off. You like plaid, right?" he asked with an innocent air.

Her teeth gritting together, Lia glared at him. He knew she hated plaid, but she could easily see him decorating the luxury resort in stomach-wrenching color schemes just to spite her, not even caring that it would cost him millions to replace it all as soon as his point was made. So he would win this round, because she wasn't going to let that happen.

"Fine. Give me a minute to change and I'll meet you at the docks." She'd forced those words through her teeth.

"No need to change. We won't be that long."

Shane gripped her arm and started leading her to the dock.

"I can make it there on my own, Shane. I don't need you to guide me like I'm a child." She yanked her arm free, the skin tingling where his fingers had wrapped around her.

"Touchy," he said with a smile, then took a few steps to her right after seeing the fire in her eyes. He was smart to do so, because she was close to striking him.

"I really wish they had an airstrip here. These boat rides take forever," she said as she followed behind him.

"Quit complaining. It doesn't suit you. I prefer to travel by boat, anyway."

"Well, then, I guess whatever you prefer is the way it has to be." She knew she was acting petulant, but she couldn't seem to keep the words from spilling from her mouth. His only response was laughter, which he quickly covered up by coughing.

She wasn't fooled.

Lia decided to keep her mouth shut as they reached the dock and she approached his so-called *boat*. She wouldn't exactly call the magnificent vessel a boat. It was a large, sleek gray yacht. At least she felt comfortable on it, since she'd traveled the waters many times with him before their short romance.

It wasn't as large as her brother's yacht, but it was Shane's personal vessel, and he had no desire to do any business entertaining on it. Still, it had three bedrooms, plus the master suite, which was indecently large and luxurious. She also enjoyed the upper covered deck, where she had a full view of the ocean, but was still protected from the breeze created when it sped through the water.

"Are you going to gawk all day, or board?"

"Can you be any more rude, Shane?" she snapped as she accepted his hand. "Where's the crew?"

"They're off today. This won't take long, so I'll play captain."

Lia didn't like the idea of being all alone with him in the middle of the ocean. There were only so many temptations she was capable of resisting. At least the yacht was big enough that she could avoid him. Plus, he'd be busy piloting the thing. He wouldn't have time to pursue her.

Lia followed Shane to the control area and then stood by as he checked everything before he began moving slowly away from the dock. Before she knew it, the island was becoming a small dot on the horizon, and Shane was in his element as he navigated the choppy waters.

"It seems a little windy out today," she commented, looking around at the storm clouds threatening to move in. They were far enough away that Lia didn't feel any real alarm.

"Yeah, just a small storm on the horizon. I haven't heard anything, so it's nothing to worry about," he assured her.

"Well, I'm going to enjoy the sundeck. There's no need for me to stay in here for the two hours it takes to get to the mainland. Maybe I'll spot some dolphins," she said. She moved to the top deck and got comfortable in one of the chairs.

They passed islands and she enjoyed the warm sun streaming through the window until one of the dark clouds covered it, casting her in shadows. Well, at least she wouldn't get a burn, she thought; she closed her eyes and decided to nap.

* * * * *

Shane's shoulders were tense as he navigated his beloved yacht through the aqua waters off the coast of Italy. Normally, he could spend hours on the sea without a single negative thought, but he'd been pursuing Lia for the better part of two weeks and not getting anywhere, and he was becoming a little desperate. Not that he'd ever give her such an advantage as telling her that.

She'd chased him for years, but once he'd accepted that they were going to be together, she started giving him the cold shoulder. Well, he wouldn't allow that for long. Not anymore. Lia needed a strong, passionate man, and that was exactly what he was going to give her.

They were made for each other; they had so much in common. Plus, he didn't want some simpering female. He wanted passion and fight. He wanted romance and love. He wanted what he'd never thought he'd have, and the only one he wanted it with was Lia.

When they got back to the island that night, he wasn't letting her out of his sight until they had it out — they would work through this.

The farther out on the water they traveled, the more Shane relaxed. This was his element, where he belonged. The fresh sea air, the rolling waves of the ocean, and no one for miles around them. Maybe they should have their talk *before* arriving back to the island, where she could easily hide from him.

With that thought in mind, he steered off course, and drifted further out to sea, heading toward a group of private islands he was familiar with. Finally, he had Lia all to himself, and he wasn't letting the opportunity escape him.

An hour passed and Shane started to become a bit worried as the sky darkened dangerously and the water began churning too much for his liking. Determination to get Lia alone kept him going, but he was certainly paying attention to his surroundings now.

When the waves starting acting up even further, he decided to find out how close the storm was. May- be they should turn around. He wanted to keep Lia to himself for a while, but not at the risk of their getting trapped in a storm.

He glanced at his touchscreen navigation and switched over to the weather report. Crap! He'd been so intent on getting her alone, he hadn't been paying attention. A wicked tropical storm was brewing and it was right behind them. He didn't have time to steer back to Italy, or get back to their island. All he could do was move ahead and hope like hell that he outran the bad weather. If he had been thinking with anything other than his lower region, they wouldn't be in this mess.

After another half-hour passed, things looked desperate. His radio crackled to life and the storm warning came over its line. He picked up the handset and tried to call in his position, but didn't get a response.

"What the hell?" he muttered as he pushed the buttons, trying to get a signal. The thing went dead. That wasn't a good sign — not a good sign at all. No, it would be OK. They were going to be fine.

Using every bit of concentration he had, he focused on trying to keep the boat steady as the waves picked up in height and ferocity. They were getting tossed around too much for his liking and he really wished that Lia would get back in the control room so he could keep an eye on her.

"Shane?" Lia was standing next to him, making him sigh in relief. Her skin was flushed and her hair messed as if she'd just climbed from bed. He couldn't get them to safety while she looked like that. Tearing his eyes away, he focused on the emergency at hand and cleared his throat.

"You need to hold onto something, Lia. We're right smack in the middle of two storm fronts, and they're fighting each other to see who can sink us the fastest."

She wasn't a novice boater: she'd been on the water many times in her life. Though he tried to hide his rising panic, he knew that she was well aware of the danger.

"I was worried about the clouds," Lia said. "How long until we hit the mainland? I fell asleep, but it must not have been for very long." Her voice was slightly tense, but not overly so. After all, their whole trip was less than two hours.

"I…uh…had to take a detour."

"A detour? Seriously, Shane? The clouds were building up when I fell asleep a bit ago. You had to have noticed!" she exclaimed.

"I did, but it wasn't so bad," he said, knowing he sounded ridiculous.

"You weren't thinking at all, Shane! I can't believe I fell for your stupid trick. Did you believe a nice, romantic boat ride would win my favor back?"

Well, yeah, actually, he thought, but he stopped himself from saying so. "Look, Lia. It doesn't matter. There's a group of islands not far away now. We'll take cover there, wait out the storm, and then reach the mainland before you know it."

"You're a pain in the ass, Shane! Do you have any idea what you have done?" she snapped, but he saw the way she was looking out at the rough seas. The ocean could turn from a thing of beauty to a dangerous place in the blink of an eye.

Yes, he knew what he'd done, and he wasn't proud of himself. He'd just been trying to get some time alone with her, not put her in danger. Maybe she was the smarter of the two of them. Not that he was saying that out loud, either.

A hard wave knocked against the boat, flinging Lia against his side. Shane reached out and caught her before she went stumbling to the deck. Her face was inches from his as her curves pressed tightly against his body, and Shane felt himself sinking into her eyes.

"Don't you dare even *think* about sex," she said, but the husky quality of her tone gave him hope. He wouldn't mind at all getting stuck with her overnight. The storm was now looking like a bit of a blessing — that was, if he could get to safety in time.

As the islands came into view, still too far away for Shane's comfort, the airstream picked up, whipping through the control room. "Shut the windows," he called above the screaming wind.

For once, Lia obeyed with no argument. As they came closer to the islands, the waves swelled larger, angry splashes of water rising high around them, as if on a mission to pull the large vessel deep into the ocean, to take another victim in her merciless grasp.

Just as Shane started to breathe easier, the boat lurched, then suddenly stalled, nearly knocking him off his feet. Gripping the wheel tightly, he looked out, horrified when he saw the hole in the side of his yacht. He must have hit a reef.

The boat was going down. "Lia, we have to abandon ship. Grab the emergency pack and we'll get in the lifeboat."

When she didn't answer, Shane turned to find her on the floor, knocked unconscious. Letting go of the wheel, he rushed to her side, bending down and feeling her neck. He let out a sigh of relief when he found that she was breathing.

Not hesitating any longer, he lifted her into his arms and rushed through the yacht to where his emergency raft was holding on tight. Shane carefully laid her inside and dashed to the cupboard opposite so he could grab the emergency supply bag. He tossed it into the boat, following behind it quickly before he released the safety, dropping them into the surging waves of the ocean.

The waves had been frightening when they'd been in his giant vessel; they were deadly in the small emergency boat. Turning the engine on, he navigated the waters as best he could, grateful they were so close to one of the islands.

As they moved through the storm, he saw two giant walls of water on either side of him. The small craft was having a difficult time reaching their peaks and getting closer to safety, but she was doing it — just barely.

As they neared safety, he looked back, his heart nearly breaking as he watched the last of his yacht disappear beneath the heaving black sea. So many memories had just been sucked below to the cold ocean floor. But Shane had no more than a second to dwell on it, so he faced forward and aimed toward the safety of land.

Nearly there.

"Shane?"

This wasn't the best time for her to wake up. "It's OK, Lia. We're almost to land."

Shane spoke too soon. With a jolt, the boat was thrust forward as two waves converged on them, determined to not allow their escape.

"Hold on!" Shane called as Lia was lifted into the air. This could be it — the end. Almost in slow motion, Shane watched in horror as Lia's head slammed against the side of the boat for the second time in less than an hour.

He reached out as her body was flung from the vessel. It capsized, the ocean waves greedily swallowing her in joyous victory.

CHAPTER FIVE

Ari

ARI fumbled with her computer bag as she walked toward the doors of her classroom.

"Computer? Check. Pens? Check. Sanity?... Check," she mumbled to herself before looking around and making sure no one was paying attention. She shouldn't be so nervous. They were just students, exactly what she'd been a few months ago.

Even now, as she worked toward her doctorate, she was a student, but it felt different somehow. It was a lot of work, which was why she was teaching only one course. Still, these kids didn't have it out for her — not yet, at least! — so she had nothing to be nervous about.

No matter how much she tried convincing herself of this fact, it didn't encourage or comfort her in the least. She was still shaking as she moved through the doors. Without thinking about it, she looked around the half-full room, then sighed.

Was she feeling relief or regret that Rafe wasn't there?

Relief! Of *course* it was relief. She didn't want him chasing after her. She had been just fine on her own and didn't need him in her life, messing everything up again. The first months after she'd walked away had been hell, and it had taken everything inside her to be strong. She was strong now, and she wouldn't allow him to undermine that strength.

Just as the clock struck the hour, when she faced the class, a giggle sounded. Ari didn't need to look up to know Rafe had arrived. Only one man she knew could elicit the sigh she heard coming from the front row. Rafe was simply that stunning.

Refusing to cower, she reluctantly lifted her head and locked eyes with Rafe. With an instilled arrogance, he sent her a wink before taking a seat on the aisle halfway into the room. The girls were whispering and making eyes, and a few of the men were grumbling.

It was going to be difficult to keep the classroom's attention if he was there.

"Everyone in here needs to be registered for class," she said and pulled out her newest roster. She hoped Rafe's name wasn't there so she could boot him from the room.

No such luck. When she saw his name right where it should be, under *P*, she nearly groaned in frustration. He was smarter than she'd given him credit for. Rafe didn't take *no* for an answer, and he was apparently on a mission.

She wondered. If she just bent over her desk and let him take her one more time, would he lose interest? Was this all a game for him? Did he just have to be the last one standing — the one to end their relationship?

Of course, she would never know, because she had

enough pride in herself not to strip down and beg him to take her for the rest of the night. Not that it would be a bad night if they did end up on her desk, but that wasn't the point.

She was confusing herself, and she didn't like it. All she knew for now was that he had a mission in mind, and he wasn't leaving until he followed through on it.

She knew she was defeated…for now, so she jumped into her lesson. "I hope you completed Monday's assignment. There will be a quiz next Monday, so make sure you pay attention today." With luck, he'd fail and she could tell him to take a hike.

There was some grumbling, and a few more whispers. She was sure they were complaining that she had a test coming so soon. Too bad. This was the real world, and they'd better get used to it.

Halfway through class, she was shocked when Rafe raised his hand and easily answered her questions. He'd actually read the material. Her respect was grudging, but she had to give him his due. He was taking this seriously, or at least putting some effort into her assignments.

Did she even know this new Rafe?

Pulling herself together, Ari focused on her class. "Does anyone know the date the Civil War officially began?" Silence greeted her question. Great, no one had read the material.

"April 12, 1861." Ari looked up in surprise to see Rafe smiling at her. OK, he'd gotten one more answer correct. He was a smart guy. It didn't mean that he'd actually *done* the homework. That was absurd. He wouldn't have any reason to do homework.

"Very good. Do you know why that's the beginning

of the Civil War?" She looked around the room, hoping anyone other than Rafe would answer. She was out of luck.

"This was the day the Confederate army fired on Fort Sumter, beginning hostilities. It had been occupied by the Union army in South Carolina a few days after the state had declared its secession in 1860. After the fort's surrender, President Lincoln called on all states to raise troops to retake lost forts. Within two months, four additional pro-slave states joined the Confederacy, making eleven in total."

She didn't want to admit to being impressed, but she couldn't help herself. He'd either done a Google search or he'd actually done his homework. Either way, he wasn't just sitting in her class; he was participating. She didn't want to feel any emotions toward Rafe, but she found her heart rate increasing.

"Does anyone know how long the Civil War lasted?"

Ari waited, and finally a girl in the front row quietly said, "Four years."

"Very good, yes. The war lasted from 1861 until 1865. With every war, we study it and try to uncover ways we could have prevented the bloodshed, but why is there so much more emphasis on this war?"

"Because this was where the United States tried to break apart. Had this occurred, we wouldn't be who we are today," a student said.

"Very true, but that's not all. During this war, though there *were* threats of foreign intervention, we were on our own. In four years, hundreds of thousands were dead and the South was nearly desolated. The war ended when the Confederacy collapsed, and of course we know that slavery was abolished. But we were left with a people who were told they now needed to put down their guns and all get along. There was a lot of hatred among the soldiers, and many didn't want just to lay down their weapons. The end of the war didn't mean it was over for everyone. Too many lives had been lost; too many people had been forever changed."

"How does a nation pick up the pieces after something like that?"

"Very good question. I guess the best answer would be to focus on what was most important. The South needed to rebuild, and the North needed to step in and help. This was also one of the first industrial wars. During its four-year term, railroads and steamships were used heavily. Communication was carried on through the telegraph, and weapons were mass-produced. And of course, many women stepped up and began working outside of the home since the men were at war. The same thing happened during World War I — those of you who continue in the history sequence will discuss that next semester. The point is that the destruction contained the seeds of the nation's rebuilding, because instead of brother fighting brother, the country's people now had to come back together to restore their lives."

"So they were able to just put it all behind them?"

"No, I wish it had been that simple. But — no. Some took their own lives after the war because they couldn't live with what they had done, and people seeking revenge sometimes committed murder. That the South surrendered doesn't mean all its people did. It would take years before our nation healed. To this day, some people still have hard feelings and are essentially still fighting the Civil War, though it's been almost a hundred and fifty years since the last battle. Plus, we now had a nation of free men, but a lot of prejudice left against everyone on both sides. Former slaves had trouble getting work, and they no longer had homes; and in the North, the side that had fought for their freedom, many people weren't happy when they wanted to live there. All of this would take decades to work through. It is still being worked through. These are all good reasons to study this monumental time in our history."

Ari continued teaching and before she knew it, the class ended, and the students piled from the class. Ari knew Rafe would still be there, but she went about gathering her belongings. She had a long night ahead of her, and she was unsure whether she was more excited or nervous about the upcoming conversation.

"You did a great job today, Ari. I'm impressed."

When she looked up, she saw Rafe was sitting on the edge of her desk. Why did he have to look so devastatingly handsome in his tight jeans and polo shirt? If she hadn't been attracted to him, this would have all been so much easier on her.

"Thank you. Considering you have a master's degree in business, I don't see why you're taking a two-hundred-level history course," she returned.

"Ah, it's never a bad thing to learn. I love history, especially the Civil War. You know I had some relatives who fought in it." She wouldn't know he was actually bored while reading the material. When she spoke, he was mesmerized.

She didn't want to be interested in what he was saying, but she found herself intrigued. She loved stories from the Civil War, how brothers fought each other, how lines were divided. So many lives had been lost, and so many families had been torn apart.

"I hope they made it through," she responded softly after a long pause.

"I have one of their old journals, if you're interested."

Oooh, the man was good. *Really good.* She could feel her palms practically itching to get her hands on such a treasure. Not wanting to ask, but knowing she was going to, she stopped fighting herself.

"Is it a journal from when the war was going on?"

"Yep. My great-great-something-grandfather wrote in it. He was fighting for the North and his bride-to-be was in the South. It tells of the pain and heartache that the two of them went through, a night they were together and got caught, how she was captured, and… Oh, I'm sorry, I'm probably boring you."

Rafe waved his hand in the air as he turned to look at a poster on the wall. She wanted to wring his neck. Bored? Not in this lifetime. Should she let him know how eager she was to read this? What would he expect from her in return?

"Have you read it?" she asked, hoping she didn't sound too eager.

"No, I haven't, but my grandmother used to tell me the stories in it. She was quite the romantic," he said with a shrug.

"I wouldn't mind looking through it," she said, trying to keep her voice casual, but unable to disguise the excitement she felt at poring over such a find.

"Why don't I take you to my place and you can see it?" he asked casually.

She knew the invitation was anything but casual.

Ari was torn. She *really* wanted to see that journal, but she knew it wasn't a wise idea to go back to his place — the house she'd found the most exquisite pleasure imaginable in — the house she'd had her heart broken in.

"I…um…have a lot of work to do," she hedged.

"What if I promise not to push you…for now? You can come look at the journal, pore over the pages, take notes, whatever you like, and I'll give you space…for *tonight*, at least."

She didn't miss the emphasis on *tonight*.

He was giving her the chance to see a real gold mine, and agreeing to back off, but not agreeing to do it permanently. Even if he did back off, that wouldn't make her stomach any less nervous. Though he wasn't attacking her outright, pushing her up against a wall and ravishing her, that didn't mean she didn't have the urge to rip his clothes from his body and take him right where he stood.

Ari's eyes lowered over the contours of his muscled stomach, and she found herself gazing at the bulge in his pants. Even at rest, he was impressive to behold. She desired him as if a single day hadn't gone by. Why did she have to have such urges? Life in a convent would be so much simpler — OK, OK, simpler, but not nearly as satisfying. Not that she was satisfied at all right now.

"Well…" She knew she shouldn't cave. If you gave Rafe an inch, he'd take a mile — and a hell of a lot more. If she set foot in his house, she had the feeling that it wouldn't be long before she was lying beneath him.

"There's even a part where he was shot, left alone in abandoned slave quarters. He almost didn't make it through, but by the grace of God, he was saved by a woman on the run. She fell in love with him, and… Oh, sorry, I don't want to ruin it."

Ari wasn't fooled at all! He was making this too enticing for her to resist.

Fine! He'd won this round. She waited a moment before speaking. She couldn't let him know how eager she was to get her hands on the firsthand account, because he'd be using it for leverage forever.

"I wouldn't mind taking a look at the journal. I suppose it wouldn't hurt for me to come over. I won't be able to stay long, though. I have a lot of preparation for Monday's class," she said, hoping her voice showed a relative lack of eagerness.

By the huge grin crossing his features, she didn't think she was fooling anyone.

"Right this way, Ari," he said as he placed a hand behind her back.

"Stop right there, Rafe. You said there would be no touching," she reminded him.

Rafe slowly pulled his hand away before bending very close to her face, taking the breath right from her lungs. "For *tonight*," he reminded her, then waited, keeping only a few inches of space between them.

This is a bad idea, a very, very bad idea, she thought as she followed him from the classroom.

CHAPTER SIX

Lia

SHANE'S mouth took Lia's in a kiss fraught with hunger; his hands ran up her quivering stomach, skimmed over her swollen breasts and caressed her hungry body. Why fight it anymore? She wanted him — had always wanted him. It was time to give into her desires.

There was no other man for her except for Shane. What was the use in pretending otherwise? The feel of his mouth on hers, his hands sweeping over her neglected body…

She needed him like a fish needed water. She tried to open her eyes, but they were weighted down. As he pressed hard against her chest, she fought him. No. This wasn't right. Why was he trying to hurt her? Shane would never hurt her.

"Lia!"

That wasn't a cry of passion, but of panic. "Dammit, Lia. Don't do this!"

Suddenly, she was coughing as water spewed from her mouth. *What the heck?* Her throat was on fire from the salt water; her chest felt bruised. Finally the weights lifted from her eyes, and she cracked them open, looking into the face of a very ashen Shane.

"Thank you, Lia," Shane gasped as his arms went beneath her and he pulled her against his solid chest. She finally realized where she was, what had happened.

Falling. She'd been falling, then everything went black.

"I've never been as panicked as I was when I watched your body get sucked beneath the waves. You're OK. We're both OK."

Lia wasn't sure whether he was trying to reassure her or himself. As he loosened his grasp, she looked around her in horror. They were on the sandy beach about ten yards from the angrily pounding waves of the ocean, both of them drenched in salt water, both of them apparently trapped in the middle of nowhere.

"Shane?"

She didn't know what she was asking, but he had to have the answers. This was Shane — he'd always had the answers to everything, ever since she was a teenager and he stepped through the doors of her parents' house, his dark hair just a bit too long, his roguish smile confident and self-assured.

"I'm not exactly sure where we are, Lia, but let's hope this is one of the inhabited islands," he admitted.

"We're lost? Please tell me you have the beacon so they can find us. There are hundreds of islands out here! It could take weeks for them to locate us."

"I haven't checked the equipment yet. I'm sure it's fine," he answered, but his voice wasn't full of confidence.

Lia pulled away as she looked around the lonely

beach. With the sun shining, it would be a true sight to behold with chalky sand, fan palms, and exotic plant life. With the storm angrily brewing around them, it was sinister and frightening.

"We need to take cover, Lia. We can fight later," Shane promised as he helped her to her feet, then rushed over to their boat.

As she gazed at the broken craft, she had to fight the fear gnawing away at her stomach.

They would be all right. Rafe wouldn't rest until she was found. She knew her brother well. On a good day he was overprotective. On a bad one, he'd move heaven and hell to track down his sisters, for whom he felt responsible, even though they had incredible parents who were more than capable of taking care of them.

Just as Shane returned, carrying a large backpack, Lia felt the first drops of rain splatter down.

"Let's go," he said, holding his hand out to grip hers.

As Lia looked into his strained face, she decided she'd fought him enough for the day. They were stuck, and there was nothing they could do about it, so now it was time to give him a hand. She accepted his help up, then fought the wind instead as she followed him into the protection of the trees.

Her throat felt as if she'd swallowed sandpaper, and it hurt to breathe, but she didn't complain as she moved by Shane's side. She ignored the pain, and moved quickly, knowing they had to get under cover. It was a tropical storm, but though she wasn't freezing, the elements could still cause major damage — even death.

"It's really blowing, Shane." Pretty stupid statement, considering he could feel it too, but she needed to hear her own voice. Admitting how frightened she was wasn't acceptable, so she was stuck with stating the obvious.

"We'll be fine, Lia," he assured her again as they broke through the tree line and the wind instantly lost some of its fury. Shane threw down the large pack, which had to weigh at least a hundred pounds, and then he began pulling out a small piece of black canvas.

Soon, he had a tent going up — a tiny tent — and was tossing the pack inside. She wasn't a lot of help, because he was moving so swiftly, but she managed to pound a couple of the stakes into the ground, securing their makeshift shelter.

Lia began trembling as everything caught up to her. The air was ridiculously warm and humid; being soaked through wasn't helping, and her nerves were shot. One glance at Shane told her that he wasn't holding up much better than she was; he was just working through the pain a lot faster.

"Come on, Lia. We need to get inside so we can dry off." Shane gripped her hand and sent her into the tent ahead of him, ducking behind as he joined her.

As she sank to her knees, then fell on her butt, her body was overcome with the shakes. She couldn't even speak, her teeth were chattering so loudly. She knew it was just the situation, but she couldn't manage to stop.

"I only have two blankets and one change of clothes in the bag. The pack is mainly filled with food and fuel," he told her as he pulled out a tiny contraption and within moments was lighting a candle beneath it. A small flame cast a bit of heat and light in a tent barely big enough for the bag and them.

"We need to get out of our wet clothes. Here's a shirt. I'll take the pants," he said while tossing a long-sleeve dark T-shirt her way. Lia wasn't sure she'd be able to command her seized-up muscles to strip her clothing away. She was far past embarrassment at this point — she just wasn't sure she'd be able to get a decent grip on her saturated clothes.

Shane quickly shed the clothing he hadn't lost to the ocean, turning as he used a small towel to dry his body, then covering his firm behind with the thin sweats and turning her way.

"Lia, I've seen you naked. Get out of those wet things," he said in exasperation, and he turned around to give her a modicum of privacy. "I'm not going to jump you right now."

"I…I…my fingers aren't…working," she stuttered as her eyes filled up with frustrated tears.

He turned back around with instant regret on his face at her rare moment of vulnerability.

"Oh, baby, I'm sorry," he said as he kneeled down and placed his hands beneath the hem of her shirt and began pulling it over her head. "We need to get you out of these saturated clothes. I promise that I just want to get you dry," he said gently as her shirt was tossed in the corner and he reached around to unclasp her bra.

He rubbed her upper body with the towel and gently pushed her backward while he undid her slacks, then pulled them and her panties swiftly from her body, leaving her lying naked before him. She watched the flare of heat light his eyes, but true to his word, he just dried her off, then pulled the warm shirt over her head and covered her nakedness from his view.

"Even near death you are a stunning woman," he whispered as his arms wrapped around her and he pulled her into his tight embrace.

Exhaustion was overpowering Lia as she leaned into the security of his body. She couldn't think of anything past her near drowning.

"Come on, baby. We need to hold each other beneath the blanket, keep our bodies warm since you are still in shock. Then we'll go through the supplies and figure out what comes next."

"OK." Lia felt only relief as he laid one of the blankets on the tent floor, then stretched the other one over the two of them as he held her in his arms.

Lia had shivered for what seemed like hours. But as his arms comforted her and the shock began to wear off, she started feeling a bit of warmth. She would be angry with herself for falling apart, but for now, she was just relieved to be safe. She drifted off to sleep knowing Shane would watch over her.

CHAPTER SEVEN

Rafe

RAFE didn't even attempt to hide the smile as he walked by Ari's side. He was finally getting her to come to his house. So what if he'd agreed there would be no touching? He could seduce a woman with just his words.

Confidence.

Rafe had it in spades. He wanted Ari back in his life, and he would get her. Being away from her for two years, only catching brief glimpses here and there, had changed him in ways he couldn't even explain to himself.

The word *docile* wasn't in his vocabulary — for himself, that was — but he had learned a thing or two about give and take. He would win her this time rather than force her. The prospect was oddly enjoyable.

"My driver is parked over here," he told her. He lifted his hand to place it on her back, but he caught himself in the nick of time and instead pointed. This no-touching business was going to be a real pain in the ass.

"I can follow you in my car," she insisted.

"It's late, and I would feel much better if you just came with me," he replied. He was trying to be more patient, ask instead of tell, but he was still a man, and he'd never gone out with a woman without getting her to the destination in safety.

"Well, that's just ridiculous. Then your driver will have to go back out to bring me to my car. That's un-necessary. Besides, the campus gets a bit spooky late at night and I'm not comfortable with coming here then."

Rafe thought for a minute before picking up his phone and speaking. Then he turned toward her. "Give me your keys. I will have your car delivered home for you."

The way he spoke was just like the man she'd met in the beginning of their relationship three years earli-er. Her eyes narrowed as she focused on him, ready to unleash her wrath.

"First off, Rafe. This isn't a date. Secondly, I'm not the same scared little girl who was shaking in your office three years earlier. No. I will not give you my keys. I will admit that I want to look at the journal, but if you are going to be a high-handed ass, then I will just go home and keep searching the Web for old journals."

As she stared him down with her hands on her hips, Rafe felt his adrenaline spike. Damn, she was incredible when her temper caught fire. He wanted to take her right there in the parking lot on the hood of the nearest vehicle.

Patience, he reminded himself. He wanted to win her, not break her. He wasn't lying to her when he said he would do things differently.

"Fine."

Ari looked at him with suspicion, not understanding his easy acceptance. He could see why she was so confused. She'd never won a battle with him — at least not one that he could easily recall. OK, maybe she'd won a few skirmishes, such as when she'd made him compromise in the jet so long ago. But that was still rare enough that he was throwing her off-kilter with his new ability to compromise.

"Good. Then I'll see you at your house." She moved forward, walking through the dark parking lot, several of the campus streetlights flickering. The college really needed to do something about that.

When the two of them arrived at her car and he walked to the passenger side, she looked at him with her eyebrows raised. She paused before unlocking her doors.

"I will just ride with you," he said in explanation. He could see that she was trying to decide whether this was an acceptable compromise or not. When he just stood there, she sighed and clicked the button on her key-chain twice, unlocking the doors.

Rafe slid into the small passenger seat with a great deal of satisfaction. He hadn't been able to get her to ride with him, but at least they were still traveling together. They'd both won a bit of that battle. Now, they just had about a million small skirmishes to go — perhaps he should change the word to *squirmishes* because of what they'd both likely be feeling before it was all over — and then he could have her lying beneath him once more. He took a minute to inform his driver that he was with Ari and to meet him at home.

"Do you remember the way to my house?" he asked as he buckled his seat belt. He wasn't comfortable having her as the one driving, but he'd keep his mouth shut.

"Yes."

His heartbeat accelerated slightly at her quick response. She wasn't as over him as she wanted him to believe. He wondered if she'd ever driven by his house during the night. Had he ever stood at his window as she was passing?

No. He surely would have felt it to his very soul.

The two of them had a connection, a bond that couldn't be broken. The ties might have been loosened, but every moment they were together, the bonds were growing strong again. It was only a matter of time before she realized this and let him back into her life. They needed each other. It was as simple as that.

"You do realize that red means stop, right?"

Ari slammed on her breaks, obviously flustered. The flush in her cheeks made him want to lean over and kiss her. Damn, he wanted to touch her like nothing else. He wanted to run his hand up the lean muscles of her legs, and not stop. Next, he wanted to lean over and slide his tongue along the silky skin of her neck before pulling her against him and kissing her the way a woman should be kissed.

He was making her nervous. It was time to see how in control she really was. He leaned over, which wasn't very far in her compact Toyota.

"Green means go," he whispered in her ear, delight filling him as an army of goose bumps appeared on her flesh where his breath had danced across her skin.

She slammed her foot against the accelerator, throwing him back and causing him to fight the laughter that wanted to spill forth. Knowing it would have her hackles up, he held it in, but the more she fought her attraction, the harder it was for him to hide his joy. She brought him so much pleasure, from the smallest things she did to the little quirks that belonged to only her.

What a fool he'd been ever to want to tame her, ever to want to extinguish even the smallest flame from her eyes. No. He would embrace her passion, stoke the flames of her desire, and together the two of them would soar to new heights.

The breath she let out as they arrived at his home was filled with relief, and he couldn't hold back a light chuckle, though he was quick to cover it up with a cough. She looked at him with suspicion, but didn't say anything.

His body was hard and aching, but she seemed to be in even worse shape. He would have enjoyed riding around in her tiny car for much, much longer. He'd thought the ride would be miserable, but he'd been very wrong.

Ari jumped from the car before he could say anything.

"I can't stay long, so let's do this," she said briskly as she moved toward his front door as he was struggling to pull himself from her car. It was much harder crawling out of the small thing than it had been for him to get in. He just didn't fit.

Rafe took his time walking up behind her, enjoying the view of her hips swaying as she marched up the front steps. He wished she were wearing a skirt so he could see the muscles flexing in her toned calves. Why a woman's calves were sexy, he didn't know, but everything about Ari was sexy — absolutely everything.

"I have all night," he said, standing only an inch behind her and one step below, aligning the two of them perfectly. Her body jerked, and for a moment the back of her pressed against him, her delicate behind rubbing against his hardness.

The satisfaction of her quickly indrawn breath wasn't enough to relieve the ache. What he wanted to do was wrap his arms around her and pull her tightly against him, while his hands moved up her flat stomach and caressed her impressive breasts.

He had to get some control over himself. He wasn't a horny teenager.

"No touching," she snapped, but it came out too breathy to have any effect.

"You did that; I didn't," he said as he stepped around her with his arms raised in innocence and proceeded to unlock his door.

She didn't say anything as he opened the door wide for her to go in ahead of him. This night might test the very limits of what he could handle, but he didn't care. The torture was worth it just to be close to her.

"Would you like a drink?"

"Yes. A glass of wine…please," she said with a hint of desperation. He was sure her nerves were raw.

Rafe led her into the parlor and poured her a glass of red, then waited for her reaction.

"This is fantastic," she said as she took a sip, then placed her beautiful lips on the rim of the glass and sampled more.

"I hope so. That's a 1945 Château Mouton Rothschild. I've been waiting to open the bottle until the day I could drink it with you."

Ari's eyes widened as she looked at him, and then moved closer to examine the venerable old bottle. He'd taken her by surprise, which pleased him greatly.

"Rafe…"

"No. Don't say it. Let's just enjoy the moment."

"I didn't mean to mislead you, Rafe, but I only came here to look through the journal. I'm not interested in resuming our relationship."

She wouldn't look him in the eyes while she spoke. She just wasn't the type of person who told a lie very easily. He could call her on it, but he knew that would cause more harm than good. He was much better off to just ignore the statement — get her mind occupied on something else for a while.

"Please get comfortable while I find the journal."

He didn't want to hear her tell him all the reasons this was impossible. They would be together; it was only a matter of time. It wasn't easy for Rafe not to push her, but if it meant that he got to be with her for the long haul, he would put his immediate needs on hold even if that meant his body was on fire 24-7.

Returning to the room with the carefully preserved journal, he felt a thrill at the rapture on Ari's face. He could even overlook that he might as well have been invisible at that moment. She had eyes only for the journal. Never had he been so happy to own a piece of leather and a bunch of yellowed paper.

This was a beginning and he was taking full advantage of it. *Thank you for my in, Great-Great-Whatever-Grandpa*, he thought silently.

CHAPTER EIGHT

Rachel

RACHEL Palazzo dived into the water, reaching down farther and farther until her fingers touched the silken sand on the bottom. She'd been practically born in the water and had frightened her family many times over by showing off how long she could hold her breath.

Rafe had accused her on more than one occasion of being a mermaid, more suited for living underneath the sea than on dry land. Yes, she liked the sea, and she'd never had a problem before, so she would allow herself to indulge in her mermaid fantasies now.

Just as she was feeling the first stirrings of discomfort in her lungs, and she changed direction to begin her ascent, she suddenly felt thick arms wrap around her waist and torpedo her body to the surface of the water.

Her surprised gasp allowed water to enter her lungs, making her begin to choke as they reached air. The person gripping her didn't let go, but swam strong and sure toward the beach.

Too shocked to think about screaming or trying to

fight the man, Rachel was stuck being pulled to shore. As soon as they reached dry land, he gently laid her on the sun-warmed sand, and then his head was descending.

She had about one second to choose whether to allow him to attempt CPR on her when she clearly didn't need it. Just as his mouth reached hers, she began laughing. Yes, she could see why he'd thought she'd been drowning. If he'd seen her go in, he would think she was hurt, since a normal person couldn't last so long beneath the ocean waves.

"I'm fine, really," she managed to gasp as the man pulled back.

That was when she got her first good glimpse of her rescuer. Damn! Her breath was knocked out of her again as she gazed into his nearly black eyes. Looking at his soaked black hair, and tanned olive complexion, chiseled cheekbones, and full mouth had her body instantly responding.

"You were under too long..."

Oh, his voice matched his features to perfection. Deep baritone with a slight accent. Rachel was in instant lust.

"Yeah, I've been swimming since before I could walk. Thanks for the rescue, though," she said, giving him her most flirtatious smile. "Now, about that CPR..." she added, then giggled when his eyes widened.

She could see that he was trying to figure out whether to be incredulous or laugh with her. Finally, his eyes crinkled at the corners, and a beautiful, deep-throated chuckle emerged. Yes, she was definitely in lust!

"I guess I reacted too hastily," he admitted as he placed his strong hand beneath her shoulders and helped her up.

Dang! She'd been hoping for some lip action first. She shouldn't have stopped him from his attempted resuscitation.

"Nah. I've always wanted Prince Charming to rescue me from certain death. Isn't that the fantasy of most girls?"

For just the briefest of moments, he tensed while looking around. "What is your name?"

"Rachel."

"Do you have a last name?"

She almost answered his commanding voice before she stopped herself.

"Nope. Just Rachel for now." She felt bold and daring, and decided she needed a vacation, and she could certainly see herself having a great time with Mr. Tall, Dark and Handsome. Never before had she even thought of having a fling with a stranger, but as she looked into his intense gaze, it was all she could think about. She wanted to be lying beneath this man in the worst possible way. Or the best possible way...

"Well, Just Rachel, my name is...Ian."

"And do you have a last name?" she asked, hoping his answer would be the same as hers.

He gazed at her for several heart-stopping moments before his full lips turned up. "No. Not today."

This was good, so *very* good. It seemed he wanted to play just as much as she did. "How long are you here for, Ian?" *Please don't say you're leaving today*, she added silently.

"Only a week. Then I must return home." He didn't

seem happy about that.

"And where is home?"

"It doesn't matter. I want to forget about duty for the moment. Since I did 'rescue' you, may I escort you to dinner?"

"Yes." Rachel didn't even pretend to hesitate. She was on vacation in Florida, renting a perfect little beach house, and if she was lucky, having a weeklong affair. She needed this badly, because next week she began employment back home in Italy.

It was time for her to grow up, and to do that, she needed to work. She now had a great internship at the American embassy in Rome. It was boring, but she didn't want to work for her big brother. She was too much under his thumb as it was. She had to prove that she was capable of making it on her own — though she had doubts that she could actually do it.

Being the baby of the family, she knew she was spoiled and had never before thought that was a bad thing. But Lia was now working for Rafe and Shane and was out of the country for a while. Rachel's parents were on a six-month cruise around the world, and even Ari was teaching at a community college.

Rachel felt like a spoiled brat for the first time ever, and she'd decided that it was time she proved herself. However, she didn't see anything wrong with having a smoking-hot affair before she became distressingly responsible. This man seemed the perfect person to devour for an entire week.

"Good. May I escort you home to change?"

Whoa! She didn't think that was a great idea. An affair was one thing, but she didn't need to lead this guy to her place, where she was staying all by herself. Hot men could certainly be killers, too.

"No. You name the place and I'll meet you there," she suggested.

Assessing her for a minute, he turned up the corners of his mouth as he leaned back, pulling that delectable body farther from her gasp. She barely held in her groan of disapproval. Too many years with her siblings had taught her to be cautious, but she didn't want to be cautious right now. Still, she had her mother's voice in her head telling her to tread carefully.

Rachel didn't get any "serial killer" vibes off the man, but still…

"You are a smart woman, Rachel, but I assure you I mean no harm."

"I'm sure that's what all the nice womanizing murderers say before they cut their victims' hearts out and boil them up," she said with a grin. When he burst out laughing, she felt her thighs quiver. To hell with her last vestiges of caution. She wanted this man.

"Ah, then. I guess you will never know if I'm a hunter or a lover…"

Oh, my goodness, his accent was melting her. "I didn't say I wouldn't join you for dinner. I simply said I don't want to bring you to my place," she replied as she leaned toward him and ran her short fingernail down his arm.

Feeling like a sex goddess when he shivered, Rachel licked her lips as she gazed at his full mouth. She had a feeling the man could take her to the farthest reaches of heaven and then back over and over again. Maybe she'd never drop back down to earth after a night, or hopefully a week, with the man.

"Let's have dinner at my hotel, the Mandarin

Oriental. Do you know how to get there? I would feel better to send my driver for you."

As Rachel tore her gaze from his lips up to his eyes, she decided in a split second to be a fool. "Yes, I know where the hotel is located, and I will arrive on my own."

His eyes narrowed the slightest bit. She had a feeling that Ian was rarely refused. The added danger brought on more excitement for her. What was she thinking?

"Fine. I hope to see you tonight, then," he said and held out his hand.

Rachel took his offered hand, only to find her breath forced from her lungs as he pulled her against his chest. Without pausing, he bent down and captured her lips, barely giving her a chance to inhale a bit of needed oxygen.

She should be furious at his assumption, but since she'd been flirting openly, that would be hypocritical. Besides, who was she fooling? She wanted his kiss from the second she'd opened her eyes.

As flashes of heat invaded her core, her shock wore off; Rachel was consumed by pleasure as he teased her willing lips. His tongue quickly pushed past the barrier of her teeth and she sucked him deep inside her mouth to taste his exotic flavor.

Just when she was ready to wrap herself fully around him, he pulled back, his dark eyes black with hunger. "Until tonight," he whispered before turning and walking down the beach.

Unable to move, Rachel stood, shivering on the warm sand. There was nothing cold about her; she was just in terrible need of what she knew he could give. OK, maybe she didn't know, but from that kiss, she was pretty dang sure.

When he was out of sight, Rachel was finally able to pull herself together. Desperate to expend some of the energy built up inside her, she began jogging toward the trail that led to her rented home.

The jog didn't help. She was still agitated as she threw off her skimpy bikini and jumped into the shower. Only then did she realize that they'd never set a time for dinner. Well, she didn't want to wait too long.

Even knowing a lady should make a man wait didn't help her to slow down. They both knew how this night would end, and she was in a hurry to get it started.

CHAPTER NINE

Lia

It was just too hot.

Lia nearly panicked as she woke, burning up. She started moving around, her hands flinging the covers away, when she came into contact with virtually smoldering flesh. Her legs were wrapped around solid calf muscles that were lighting her toes on fire. Her stomach trembled, and her body turned stiff as reality came crashing into her conscious brain.

"Good morning."

She froze once her hand came into contact with something delectably hard. Only her neck moved, barely, and she found herself looking into Shane's dark chocolate eyes.

With a gasp she realized she was holding onto his thick manhood, and it took a second before she was able to get her fist to unclench and then she released him while she quickly tried to scoot backward.

"Where are you going? I thought things were just starting to heat up," he said lazily as he turned, not releasing her from his arms.

"Uh, sorry about that," she muttered, not daring to connect their eyes again. It wouldn't take much to send her over the ledge she was on. They were lying nearly naked together and she was one second away from saying *to hell with it* and climbing on top of him.

She couldn't do that.

They'd never crawl from the tent if that were to happen.

"No need to apologize. I love your hands on me. I can remember your touch like it was yesterday," he said in a low, smooth voice that was melting her from the inside out.

"I need to go outside."

"No need. We have all we could ever want right in here," he told her as his lips nuzzled her neck. Oh, that was good, very, very good.

"No. I really need to go outside," she said and wiggled uncomfortably.

Shane finally realized what she needed and chuckled.

"Well, that will dampen the mood. I guess I need to find a bush myself, now that you've put the thought in my mind."

Lia was horrified that he would say such a thing. It was just something you didn't talk about — not ever.

Shane lay back and looked at her; she clutched the thin blanket to her chest and wondered how the heck it had not only kept them warm, but also overheated her. Well, it wasn't the blanket; it was his scorching body that was turning up the temperature in the tiny tent.

"You can at least be a gentleman and turn around," she snapped when he didn't appear to have the slightest inclination to do so.

"Nah. I'm comfortable just as I am," he answered with a wicked grin — the same grin that had made her chase after him for so long.

"Fine," she huffed. If he wanted a show, then he was going to get one. He'd better enjoy it because looking was all he was going to do.

Seeing her clothes lying in the corner, she sat up, exposing her backside to him as she snatched up her own shirt, which was thankfully dry. She pulled off the borrowed shirt from him, giving him a nice long glimpse of her smooth back. Right before she got it over her head, Shane's finger trailed from her neck, all the way down the length of her spine, then slid over the curve of her soft derrière.

A chill rushed through her as she moved away, unzipping the tent with one hand and grabbing her pants with the other. She darted out, no thought crossing her mind that someone might be out there. They were on a deserted island, after all.

Luck was with her when no one spotted her streaking outside. That was a good thing, since she was half naked. Struggling into her still damp pants, she moved into the trees a short way and made sure not to be gone too long.

The area *creeped her out*. She'd never been anywhere where she was this alone. As much as she was afraid of her reaction to Shane, she was glad he was there. She wouldn't do well by herself — she was terrified of the slightest sound.

When she heard the bushes move near her, she let out a loud gasp, and went running back toward the tent.

"It's only me, Lia. Don't worry," Shane called.

It still took several moments before her heart slowed its frantic beating.

Shane returned and climbed back into the tent. Lia decided it wouldn't be wise to go back inside with him. The space was just too small. Besides, they should be looking for a way out of this mess. Maybe they'd build one of those rafts like the one Tom Hanks had made in the film *Cast Away*, and someone would rescue them in the middle of the ocean.

OK, that wasn't the brightest idea, but she was desperate here.

"Are you hungry?" Shane asked as he stepped back outside, the sight of him in his low-slung pants and nothing else causing near cardiac arrest. He was muscled and dark and beyond scrumptious looking. She could seriously dine off his abs alone. *Chomp*.

"Yes," she replied, hoping he had something and wasn't just taunting her.

"We have a few supplies, but they will only last a couple of days. We need to conserve what we can. There should be fruit and possibly nuts on this island, so we'll have to go on a hunt," he said as he cut open a bag and passed it to her.

Lia was elated when she looked inside and found a large amount of trail mix. This would be plenty for the both of them for a good breakfast. Next he pulled out a water bottle. Water had never looked more beautiful.

"We only have three bottles, but I have water purification tablets, so this isn't our limit. Still, we need to take it easy. Hopefully, we can find a fresh-water supply deeper inside the island. I don't want to go too far and risk getting lost, though. We also need to keep our belongings with us. This tent is the only thing that will keep us protected from the weather at night."

"It sounds like you've been stranded before," she murmured after she chewed and swallowed, being careful to take only small sips of water.

"I haven't ever been shipwrecked, but I've…" he trailed off.

"You've what?"

"It doesn't matter," he said, clearly wanting to change the subject.

Now Lia had to know. She couldn't stand mysteries; she refused to read anything that had suspense in it. If she did accidentally pick up a book like that, then she'd flip to the last chapter to find how it ended before going back and reading it from the beginning.

The stress of suspense was just too much for her. It wasn't pleasant in the least.

"Please tell me." See, she could ask nicely.

"Maybe sometime," he said.

She knew that was all she was going to get out of him for now. Dang it!

"Let me pack this up and then we'll be on our way," he said and began taking down the tent.

"Why are you taking it down?"

"We don't want a creature taking off with it, or a freak wave dragging it into the ocean. This is our bedroom for the next day or so. Hopefully only that long," he said, looking out across the water. Not a boat in sight.

"I'm glad I'm with you, Shane. I would never think of any of this," she said. Their eyes connected as he stuffed the tent into the pack and hefted it onto his shoulders.

"I'm glad to be here with you," he replied, grateful

that she'd forgotten that it was his fault they were stuck on the island in the first place.

The heat in his eyes had her stomach tensing. Why did he have to decide to give her his full charm now? She'd wanted him forever without it being reciprocal, and now when she'd decided to not have him be a part of her life, he was giving her his full arsenal of charm.

Men!

"We're losing daylight, Grayson," she said as she began moving, having no idea where she was supposed to go.

"We just woke up, Lia. There's plenty of light left," he said with a laugh, but he didn't complain as she began moving.

She must have been on the right path because Shane pushed ahead of her with a long stick as he moved bushes and they wove their way a bit deeper into the island. If she had to be trapped, at least she had a fantastic view, she thought as she watched the muscles in his butt flex with each step he took, and the twist of his upper torso while he worked on the brush.

"The good news is that this island isn't too big or too dense. I think it would be very difficult for us to get lost," he said as they moved along. After walking for about an hour, they both heard a noise and stopped.

"Is that a…?"

"Yes, I think it is," he said with a smile as he moved forward.

Now elated, both of them quickened their pace. Coming over a small rise, Lia stopped, her breath being taken from her.

"That's stunning," she whispered.

In front of them stood a pristine body of water with

a twenty-foot waterfall flowing into it. Lia rushed forward, excited at the thought of washing the layer of salt water from her skin. She had no thoughts of safety, just pure refreshment.

"Lia, let me check the area first," Shane said as he gripped her arm.

"I'm itchy, Shane. I need to bathe," she said as she looked at the crystal-clear water.

After a few moments of looking around, he deemed it safe, which made her roll her eyes. Yes, she'd led an easy existence, cosseted and cared for, but she was capable of ensuring her own safety. However, it would take longer to argue with him than to just let him do a small security scan. As soon as she got the green light, Lia ran to the edge, where she discarded her clothes without a thought of modesty and smoothly dived into the water.

Shane stood back watching the enticing curve of her backside, feeling his body's natural reaction. She wasn't trying to injure him, he didn't think, but she was surely causing permanent damage anyway.

Well, if he couldn't beat her, he sure as hell was going to join her. Without any further pause, he moved down to where she'd thrown off her clothes, and stripped off his own, then dived into the water and came up right in front of her.

Without giving her time to react, he pulled her close to his naked body and kissed her. He was done with letting her thrust him away.

CHAPTER TEN

Adriane

PRINCE Adriano of Corythia, or Adriane, as he called himself in the States, or even Ian Graziani when he wanted fewer people to figure out who he was, turned the corner before pausing. Taking a deep breath, he heard his trusted adviser approaching and quickly masked his face, knowing what was coming.

Adriane was never truly alone. There were bodyguards following him, his assistant right there, and when he was in public, cameras. So many cameras. Since this visit wasn't announced, at least the paparazzi weren't present, but he could never ditch his bodyguards. They'd have a heart attack.

At least they gave him the semblance of privacy, though, standing out of the way, not making their presence known, but they were always close.

"Your Majesty, should you really be entertaining this American?"

With a deep sigh, Adriane turned toward Amedeo, giving him a look that made the man back down immediately. "I am *only* having dinner with the woman, Amedeo. It's nothing for you to concern yourself about."

"Of course, Sire. It's just that we need to get back home. You know your brother is causing many problems."

"Yes, and the problems will still be there next week. I promised my mother I would return home, and I will. I just need this time. The American girl is nothing more than a distraction. Do not assume it is more than that."

Adriane had no difficulty whatsoever reminding the man who he was. Since age seventeen, he had been the crown prince of Corythia, knowing he would one day ascend the throne. That day had just come sooner than he'd planned. He wanted to be free a while longer, build something in this world before he settled down, married and ruled his country.

His father had passed away too soon, only a month ago, leaving a world of burdens on Adriane's shoulders. His mother, an American actress his father had fallen in love with, shocking the country when he'd brought home his foreign bride, had adapted amazingly well to his father's country. The people revered her, would even die for her. She knew his need for freedom, but even she was pressuring him to return home.

He'd been thrown so much at once, and had needed escape. Yes, it was selfish on his part, but soon the people would own him, and he needed this time to himself — needed it to accept the reality of what his life would be like now.

As the crown prince, he'd had a lot of responsibility thrust upon him, but he'd still managed to come and go as he pleased, to a large extent. He'd made many successful deals with business leaders in other countries, bringing a steady stream of income to Corythia. His father had been a proud man.

Adriane loved his father, but respected him more. The loss had been great, and Adriane needed time to heal, needed to get his mind off of the pain of losing him. The American girl would be a good distraction from his worries.

"Make sure Ms. Rachel arrives to her home safely. I don't think anyone has spotted me here, but if they did, I don't want her to become a target. Keep two of the men posted on her at all times."

"I will get on that right away, as well as have a background check done on her," Amedeo stated as he spoke into his microphone.

"No. There's no need. She doesn't know who I am. I like the mystery of the situation," Adriane said with a smile.

"Sire, I don't think that is wise," Amedeo gasped, obviously shocked by Adriane's unusual behavior.

"I don't want to be smart right now, Amedeo. I just want to live a little before I am ruled by the people of Corythia," Adriane said with a sigh.

He did love his country, but he had so much more living to do. At only thirty years of age, he wasn't ready to be king. But ready or not, he would be crowned next week.

"Yes, Sire." Amedeo wasn't happy, but he would obey orders. It would be unacceptable to do anything less.

With that, Adriane turned and walked up the small dune to the parking lot and toward the awaiting car. Climbing into the back seat of the Jaguar limo, he grabbed a bottle of scotch and poured himself a generous drink. He'd tried to deny it, but he knew he was excited about dinner with his mysterious woman.

Her reaction to him was expected. Women tended to fall at his feet, willing to do anything he asked of them. But his reaction to her was what startled him. He had felt an instant attraction to women before, but as he'd pulled Rachel against his chest, it had taken massive restraint on his part to let her go again.

She'd caused a stir in him that he definitely wanted to explore further. With her compelling green eyes and luscious pink lips, not to mention her perfect curves, he'd felt weak in the knees. It was unusual, though not impossible.

With all the stress he was under, this Rachel would be a welcome distraction in his turbulent life. A few nights with her and he'd be ready to leave America behind and go back to Corythia to do his duty to God and his country.

At thirty years of age, he would be the youngest king in his country in the past two hundred years. The thought made him miss his father again. What a great king and man he'd been. Adriane was confident in himself, but filling the shoes of his father wouldn't be easy. He was sure the people had their own reservations about him, as well.

As they pulled up to the hotel, Adriane's phone rang, and one look at the caller ID had his eyes narrowing dangerously as he received the call.

"What do you want, Gianni?"

"Is that any way to greet your brother, Ian?"

"You should not speak so disrespectfully to your king!" A mixture of bitterness and sadness filled him at how far apart he and his brother had grown.

"You're not king yet, Ian. Don't get too comfortable.

After all, a lot can happen in a week's time," Gianni remarked as he laughed bitterly over the phone.

"We've been through this, Gianni. I would have gladly given you the kingdom if you'd been worthy to take it. I never wanted to be tied down to one place. You threw it all away with your greed."

"You are so quick to judge me, little brother, but the throne should have been mine and we both know it. The oldest son inherits the title," Gianni spat.

"Father wanted you to rule — it was expected from the moment of your birth. You were the one who chose to disinherit us!"

"I wanted change. Was that really such a crime?"

Adriane took a deep breath as he forced himself to calm down. He'd been through this many times with his brother. The two of them had been inseparable as children, only eleven months apart. Then Gianni had run away from home at eighteen, seeking adventure. The people he'd chosen to carry on with had been political enemies, convincing him that their father was Satan resurrected. He'd denounced the throne and they hadn't heard a word from him for five years. When he'd come back, it was too late.

"I refuse to continue trying to appease you, Gianni. I hope one day we can call each other brother again, but it won't be today. I tire of your fits, and I will not indulge your games. Please, take care."

With that Adriane hung up the phone.

He inhaled deeply several times and released the breath slowly, and the anger had dissipated from his aching stomach by the time he arrived at the hotel and entered through the back door. The media hadn't been alerted to his presence and he was hoping to keep it that way. If Gianni knew where he was, his brother would sell him out in a heartbeat.

Someday, they might mend fences, but Adriane wasn't holding out much hope. His brother was too bitter, too changed to accept the way the cards had fallen — the way Gianni had made them fall.

Entering his suite, he called his assistant and had dinner ordered. As he went to shower and dress, a smile flitted across his lips. Tonight would get his mind off his responsibilities and his troubles. Tonight was about sating desires, and nothing else.

Whistling as the hot water streamed down his muscular body, Adriane smiled genuinely for the first time since his father's burial. Rachel was just what he needed before he became fully owned by his people. For the next few days, it was OK to be selfish.

Well, he thought, *I won't be completely selfish. My lover will be well satisfied.*

CHAPTER ELEVEN

Ari

"Have you read this, Rafe?" Ari exclaimed.

Rafe jumped at the sound of Ari's excited voice. Then he looked up from his computer to see what had her so animated. She'd been poring over the pages of his ancestor's journal for two hours. The bottle of wine was almost finished, mostly by her, and he'd decided his seduction skills were decidedly lacking.

Such a fine vintage wine, and it had been wasted, in his opinion. Once she'd opened the pages of the journal, he'd ceased to exist for her, leaving him to grab his laptop and get work done.

He'd whispered in her ear, brought her a plate of fruit and cheese, *accidentally* brushed his leg up against hers, and he might as well have been a cardboard box. She hadn't so much as glanced at him. After a few attempts at speaking with her, he'd discovered that she was simply mumbling, not hearing a word he was saying. So he'd given up.

She was fully mesmerized by a man he shouldn't be

jealous of, but actually was. The man had been dead for over a hundred years, yet still had her full attention.

"No. I haven't read it, just learned of the stories through my grandmother. Why don't you read to me?"

"Oh, it's beautiful, just beautiful. He loved Saphronia so much. I can feel every emotion he was feeling, the pain, fear, devastation; it's all here!"

"It was a frightening time for many in those days," he said, trying to keep her talking. Setting his laptop aside, he moved closer on the pretext of leaning over so he could see the book. He knew he was a bit pathetic when he had to use the excuse of reading just to get close to her. If only he hadn't promised not to touch her.

"It's not just his words, Rafe, but hers as well. She wrote to him, and he kept the letters from her in the journal, tucked away right next to his personal thoughts and feelings about what he was dealing with. I'm so grateful that your ancestor was smart enough to have the pages protected or all of this could have faded away by now."

"Yes, some of the old letters have weathered the test of time, and others haven't. My grandmother loved the journal so much that my grandfather didn't want to take any chances, so he protected it. That way she could flip through the pages as much as she wanted without fear of ruining it."

"Oh, I would love to hear the story of your grandparents' romance, too. It sounds like you come from a long line of romantics," she said, gracing him with a beautiful smile.

In her excitement, she reached out and grabbed his arm, her fingers searing his skin. Since she was the first to touch, would it be breaking the rules if he hauled her

onto his lap and finally took her lips? Yes, dammit. He
knew it would.

He gritted his teeth; he didn't dare move, for fear
that she would pull away.

"Listen to this:

> *My dearest Saphronia, the nights grow ever
> darker and colder without you near me. I miss
> the feel of your fingers in my hand, the soft tilt of
> your lips when you smile, the sparkle in your eyes
> when you laugh. There are times I think our God
> might never call an end to this terrible war, and
> I'll never find comfort in your presence again.
> My life as a soldier is grim, but I am saved from
> despair by thinking of those few days of felicity
> with you. The thought of kissing your sweet lips
> one more time keeps me going. The only thing that
> gets me through these long nights is the knowl-
> edge that you are waiting for me. Just know that
> if anything ever happens to me, you were loved
> to my last, dying breath. You are my light, my
> world. They can say you are the enemy, because
> you live in the Rebel South, but I will never be-
> lieve it. And though I cannot regret a war waged
> against slavery, I am cut to the quick that you
> and I must be so cruelly kept asunder.*

> *Self-slaughter has been treated as a horror
> and a shame by the church and by many who fol-
> low our Lord's tenets. And yet I witness it more
> and more, and with more understanding. Today,
> a young man in our company, a child of seven-
> teen, took his own life after looking upon a man*

he'd just killed, a Confederate soldier of similar age and aspect to his. My God! The body before him, the life taken by his hand, was his cousin, with whom he had engaged in the delights of boyish play only two years before. I am consumed by horror at the thought that such could happen to me. What if my weapon were to send one of your loved ones to the grave? How could I endure?

My love for you has no end. Please, know this and never doubt.

Yours always,
William

"That is the most heartbreaking thing I've ever read," Ari said as a tear fell down her cheek. She quickly wiped it away before it managed to reach the pages of the journal — before realizing that the pages were protected against her tears. Then her fingers stroked the page where an obvious teardrop from long ago had fallen and smudged the word *love*. It was so fitting.

"That *is* sad," Rafe said softly, not knowing what else to say. He wasn't a cold man, but it was hard to feel heartbreak over a couple of people who were long gone.

"I have to know what happened. Did they make it back into each other's arms? Do you know?" she demanded.

"I can't tell you that. It would ruin the story for you," he said, not wanting her to lose interest in reading the journal. It was the only thing he had right now that would keep her coming back to his home.

"Yes, you are right, of course. I'm just so afraid of

what is going to happen. I've never been patient when watching a movie or reading a book, especially if I can't guarantee there's a happy ending. This was your father's family, right?"

"Yes. My mother is from Italy," he reminded her.

"Yes, of course. I forgot that, probably because your father, though an American, also has an Italian name. I just — what if she was pregnant and he never made it back to her? What if he never saw his child?"

"All romances have their share of ups and downs, Ari. If the battle was too easy, then how could we appreciate what we have?" he asked. He wanted so badly to hold her, to rekindle their romance.

For several heart-stopping moments, Ari looked at him, then she glanced back down at the journal, and soon she was lost again in the story of William and Saphronia. Her hand was still gripping his arm as if it were so insignificant, she didn't even notice. He sure as hell noticed.

Rafe didn't move until her hand drifted away as she turned another page; yes, her attention was once again diverted and he was bested again by the journal. He'd wanted to get her to his home, but he had hoped to have seduced her by now.

That most likely wasn't going to happen this time around. Looking at the clock, he noted that it was nearing midnight. There was no way she could drive home, not with the amount of wine she'd drunk. He could have Mario drive her, deliver her car for her, but he didn't want her to leave. Having her in his home again, though torturous in some ways, also grounded him.

To his complete and utter astonishment, he discovered that even though his body was on fire, he didn't care. He was satisfied with sitting in the same room with her. Yes, he wanted her like nothing he'd ever wanted before, but just being with her eased the ache that had been with him for the past two years.

She completed him in a way that was beyond his capability of imagining. Leaning back, he lost all interest in work as he watched her move through the pages. The expressions on her face were a sight to behold, and he could almost read the story through her eyes alone.

It was obvious when a more lighthearted letter appeared, or when something tragic happened. Her chest would rise and her breath hitched as she carefully turned the pages of the journal to see what was happening next.

Ari was a romantic. Why hadn't he realized this before? If he wanted to win her, he had to treat her the way a woman should be treated, spoil her with priceless gifts or, better, with gifts that cost little but meant much, bring her flowers, take her to historical places. He needed to know her beyond the bedroom.

He'd thought he had known Ari, thought he'd known what she wanted, but he hadn't known her at all. He hadn't taken the time to learn what would truly make her happy, hadn't tried hard enough to win her. He would now.

He watched as her eyes closed, her fingers still holding on to the journal. Within a few moments, her breathing deepened and she was asleep, her body leaning toward the protection of his.

Rafe sighed in happiness as she floated into his arms; with his hand holding her shoulder, she murmured in her sleep, and then her head drifted to his chest. He spent the next several moments running his fingers through the silken strands of her hair as he leaned down and inhaled her floral scent.

"I can't set you free, Ari. I just can't," he said in apology; he reached beneath her and gently lifted her into his arms.

Should he let her go?

Yes, most likely. He was broken in so many ways. He'd mistreated her, broken her heart, and shattered her innocence. A better man would let her live her life free of him.

He couldn't be that better man.

Rafe slowly moved through his house and into the master bedroom, where his massive bed didn't even dominate the room.

There was so much space in his home, and he had been living there alone for so long. He hoped that wouldn't be the case for too much longer. With luck and extreme effort on his part, Ari would soon share every night with him, and the days, too.

Laying her down on his bed, he looked at the sight she made, her golden hair spread out on his pillow, her mouth turned up in a slight smile.

Being careful not to wake her, he undid her pants and slid them from her slender legs. Because he hadn't had enough torture, he leaned down and pressed his lips to hers, just a brief touch, a chaste kiss.

"Rafe…" she sighed, but didn't wake.

Yes, they would make it through. Even in her dreams, she called for him. He wondered what she was dreaming at that moment. Most likely she was somewhere in the South while waiting for her hero to find her. Rafe could picture himself as that man.

Wanting nothing more than to crawl into bed with

her, it took every ounce of willpower he possessed to cover her up and then turn away.

"You're in this for the long haul, Rafe, the long haul. If you blow this now, she will run away scared and another couple of years may pass." As much pain as it caused him, he turned off the lights and left the room. There wouldn't be much sleep for him that night.

CHAPTER TWELVE

Rachel

As Rachel arrived at the hotel, she realized she didn't have a last name for Ian or any way to let the maître d' know the person she was looking for. Stepping from the taxi, she was less than a second away from turning back and forgetting the entire evening.

It was foolish, after all. What would her parents say? What would Rafe say! Her parents, she could handle; her big brother, not so much. He'd come unglued if he knew what she was planning to do. She and Lia would never be adults in Rafe's eyes. They'd continue to be pigtailed little girls whom no man was allowed to touch — not as long as that man wanted to live.

Hypocrite!

"Good evening, Ms. Rachel. If you will follow me, I'll show you where your date is waiting."

Rachel jumped, her hand still on the door of the cab. Turning around, she spotted a very large man who looked more suited to guard the president than escort women to a one-night stand. Well, hopefully a one-week stand.

When she looked up at him, the man didn't show a single expression on his face. Was she a fool to follow through on this? No. She didn't think so. What could happen in a nice hotel where people could see her enter? OK, so maybe she *was* as naïve as Rafe thought she was.

The thought caused her shoulders to stiffen in defiance. It was her life, and if she wanted to be a fool, that was her choice. She wasn't a little girl anymore, and soon she'd be working, earning her own way in the world without the help of her parents or her big brother.

"Thank you," she replied after the silence had stretched on for an awkward amount of time. Her nerves fluttered in her stomach as she walked by the giant man's side through the elegant lobby of the Mandarin Oriental.

It didn't take long to reach the bank of elevators, and soon she was riding to the top floor. She'd expected that they'd eat in the dining room, but wasn't this better? If she wanted to act like a woman of the world, she certainly needed to arrive at his room eventually.

The thought entered her mind that she should be offended he was presuming so much, but she brushed it away. It was time she took her own pleasure into her hands, and that meant a night with the very sexy man who'd "rescued" her from the sea.

"Right this way."

They stepped up to a door, where the man inserted a key card, then held the door open for her. Walking through the entrance, she was well pleased by the elegant foyer. She didn't notice the door closing behind her with a soft click, locking her securely inside.

Approaching the spectacular floor-to-ceiling windows, she smiled at the splendid view of the Biscayne Bay and Miami's impressive skyline. Not far out was the deceptively peaceful Atlantic Ocean. She knew how violent those seas could become, but at the moment, everything was quiet and…romantic, as if Ian had commanded the perfect setting.

"I'm glad you came."

For the second time in a short span, Rachel jumped as a man's voice startled her from her thoughts. Turning slowly, her heart picked up speed at the sight of Ian standing before her in a crisp white shirt and dark slacks.

She couldn't decide whether the man was better looking with or without clothes on. No. His chest dripping with water in the hot sun was certainly a sight she wouldn't mind seeing more of. However, he looked quite debonair in his evening clothes.

"Of course I came. I couldn't resist a dinner here. I've heard they have a wonderful wine selection," she said, surprised by her smooth tone of voice. Her nerves weren't showing at all though she was shaking like a fall leaf on the inside.

"I have a table on the balcony. You'll like the view." He offered his arm, and Rachel accepted it, allowing him to lead her to the open French doors.

A native of the West Coast, she doubted she could ever adapt to the humidity of Florida, but it was more bearable in the evening. A slight breeze was blowing in off the bay, making the balcony the perfect place to dine.

Her tall, dark stranger was quite adept at seduction. A beautifully presented table was before her with a bottle of wine chilling and candles emitting a soft glow. When he held out her chair, she sat and watched his sure moves as he rounded the table.

As they sat down, he gazed at her with his dark eyes, and her nerves left her. She wanted this man too much to let them get the best of her. Maybe she'd come to regret her impulsive act, but it wouldn't be tonight — that was certain.

A man quietly approached and set down a plate for each of them before retreating. Rachel was glad to have a waiter there. One more witness to her presence couldn't hurt. At least Ian wouldn't be able to murder her without some serious questions being asked.

The thought made her smile. If she'd truly been afraid of being hacked to pieces and fed to the sharks, she never would have set foot inside the hotel. No. She was just used to her parents' fears. She wouldn't allow any of that to ruin her night.

Their first course of Aleppo Stained Swordfish was accompanied by a beautiful French Chardonnay. The man certainly had good taste in food, and she took a bite of the fish, relishing the flavors dancing on her tongue.

"Where are you from, Rachel?"

"I thought we agreed to be strangers," she replied, not sure whether she wanted them to know much about each other. If she got to know this man, there was a chance of getting attached, and that wasn't in her game plan.

"Ah, keep the mystery alive," he said with a twinkle in his eye.

"Yes. It's not every day I get rescued from certain death. I have created my own version of who you are."

He looked at her for a stunned moment before bursting into laughter. "You are quite the treat, my lady."

"As are you."

"What would you think about this? We could play a game — make guesses about each other's lives."

Rachel considered his proposal, looking for anything that would end up biting her in the behind. She didn't see how it could.

"I think certain *games* can be quite fun," she responded with a wink. Rachel was shocked with herself at her boldness. She could almost picture Lia in the corner with her mouth gaping open. Rachel had never been a wallflower, but she'd also never been so forward with a man, either.

Watching as Ian's eyes flared with delight, she couldn't help but to glow inside. He wanted her, and it was great for her ego.

As they moved on to their next course of D'Artagnan NY Striploin, with green and white asparagus, pickled mushroom, short rib ragout and béarnaise sauce, and served with a cabernet sauvignon, she looked into his eyes as she tried to guess his story.

"With your slight accent, you are obviously not a native Floridian. The golden complexion of your skin possibly makes you Italian, my mother's home country. You are obviously educated, confident, and used to getting your own way..." she began.

His eyebrows rose, as if surprised by her perception. She would have to be a bit careful, she told herself. A ditzy college student wouldn't know quite so much. Plus, she'd given a little too much information about herself by telling him where her mother was from.

"Please go on. You have my curiosity piqued as to

who you think I am," he said as he took a bite of the succulent steak and waited.

"Well, you are staying on the top floor of a nice hotel, having a fairly pricey dinner catered, and your clothes are hand-tailored, or bespoke, so you aren't poor by any means. I say you are an international banker who travels to different countries, fattening your wallet and rescuing damsels in distress before seducing them — and then jetting away."

Her words could have sounded harsh if not for the laughter in her tone. Ian gazed at her with deep, assessing eyes for a moment before leaning back and picking up his glass of wine.

The waiter cleared their plates before coming back a few moments later with a glass of Château D'Yquem Sauternes. As Rachel took a sip, she knew she was drinking only the best. He was pulling out all the stops.

Their dessert of Pistachio and Lavender Honey Panna Cotta was placed before her, and she didn't hesitate to take a bite. There were no complaints from her about the delicious meal.

"Sadly, you are wrong, so I have to admit nothing of my true identity," he said as he began eating his dessert.

"Ah, well, my next guess is that you're a top-secret superhero commissioned by the government to rescue damsels and fight crime."

"I'm afraid that you have caught me. They call me Aquahero, and I fight crime only along the oceanfront, my true nemesis being the Great White Shark."

Oh, Rachel liked him — liked him a bit too much for someone she intended only to sleep with and then never see again. There would be no exchanging of phone numbers. She had plans, and they didn't include Mr.

Sexy and his dark-as-night eyes.

"It's my turn. You are obviously educated and well-traveled. You know fine wine and good food. Confidence oozes from you, and I would wager that you're very used to getting your way. Yet as much as you want me to believe you're a woman of the world, I see a hint of vulnerability beneath your impressive act. That leads me to believe that you're from a good family, and I wouldn't be surprised if you had a coming-out season. Since you've already told me your mother is from Italy, you most likely spend a lot of time doing international travel… I say you are a shipping heiress who flits from country to country trying to win new customers."

Rachel was impressed even more. He was doing very well, though she didn't appreciate his vulnerability comment. She wasn't a weak little girl who needed protecting. And she was sick of people thinking she was such an innocent, the Palazzo daughter who would never do wrong. She'd always been aware of what people thought and had been careful to maintain a good reputation. But sometimes a girl just needed to be a little bit bad to have a whole lot of fun.

"Will there be anything else, sir?"

She'd forgotten that the waiter was even there, but as he brought a bottle of rare Rémy Martin cognac to the table and poured some into two snifters, she looked up, impressed by the man's professionalism. How hard it must be for him not to laugh at their ridiculous conversation.

"No. Thank you very much. The meal has been quite pleasant," Ian said, and the waiter disappeared, leaving them alone.

Rachel picked up her snifter and sipped the smooth

liquid, feeling just the slightest effect from the evening's alcohol. She in no way wanted to become drunk. She wouldn't allow herself to blame her decision to sleep with the man on alcohol. She wanted to remember every second and have no regrets about it.

"You have guessed wrong. It seems that neither of us has a gift for reading other people," Rachel said as Ian stood from the table and held out a hand to her.

"I think we will be much better at other things," he replied as he slowly pulled her into his arms.

Here was the moment of truth. Was she really going to follow through on her plan? He was giving her plenty of time to change her mind as he looked into her eyes. She either lifted her mouth to him, or turned and walked away. She could do that.

The night could be about nothing more than a great dinner and some amusing conversation, or she could take what she wanted.

The moment seemed to stretch on forever as he waited for her cue on what to do next. She respected that he was a man of honor — that he wasn't going to just take what he felt he deserved.

To stay or not to stay, that was the decision.

CHAPTER THIRTEEN

Lia

SHANE's perfected dive barely left a ripple in the crystal-clear water as he surfaced, droplets pouring down his face as he pulled Lia tightly to him. The only thing on his mind was the fact that they were both in this cool paradise, and they were both naked. He grabbed hold of her tightly — no hesitation on his part as his mouth met hers.

His lips coaxed Lia's open and devoured her. This was no chaste meeting of mouths; it was a possession of the highest, and she was powerless to stop it. Who did she think she was fooling, anyway? He left her breathless.

She wanted him, even after all this time. She had tried dating other men, had even tried to sleep with one of them, only to find herself feeling absolutely nothing. Nada. Zip. Zilch. She'd called a halt.

Only one man turned her blood to lava, made her desire him from deep within her soul, and that man was Shane.

His hands slid slowly around her back, and she didn't even feel the movement as he led them toward the surrounding land, where he could stand and then use his hands to glide across her body. She should at least try to stop this, but why?

They both wanted it more than they wanted rescuing, so what was the use in pretending otherwise?

"You are mine, Lia. I have given you room, I have been patient, but you want me just as much as I want you, and my patience is finished," he growled low in his throat before his lips covered hers once again.

She should protest his high-handedness, and she would — in just a few minutes…

Shane's hands slid from her waist and gripped her round behind, pulling her up his body so his straining erection was pressed just outside of her core.

She wanted to wrap her legs around him and feel the sweet bliss of him deep inside her. She was a fool to deny both him and herself. The real world would still be there tomorrow, but right at this moment, she was with him, with the man she'd wanted for so long, and hadn't had nearly long enough in their brief fling in Vegas two-odd years ago.

"Tell me you want me, Lia!" he demanded of her.

No. She wouldn't go that far. She was still waging war within herself and she wouldn't give Shane the satisfaction of submitting to his will. She did want him — wanted him so much that she ached all over — but she wouldn't tell him that.

"I won't sink inside you until you admit that you want me," he said, leaning back, his intense gaze not relenting.

"No." The word tore through her. Why did she have

to be so stubborn? Why couldn't she give in just one small inch? Was there no reason for it? Did she want to see how far she could push him and still have him come back for more? So many people who knew her would think she was that frivolous and self-absorbed. No, it wasn't that. She was simply trying to protect herself from another devil-may-care lothario who couldn't see beyond her looks and her spirit.

"What?" his expression was unreadable as he gazed at her, his hands still gripping her backside tightly, her body still pulled flush against his. One little word and he'd sink inside her.

She couldn't make herself say it. She stubbornly looked back at him as she rocked her hips. She was saying yes with her body; wasn't that enough?

"You would rather suffer than admit you still want me?" he asked incredulously.

She kept silent.

When he let her go, she couldn't stop the whimper from escaping her throat. She wanted him so much, her body felt like it was going to go up in flames. *Just tell him*, she screamed at herself.

But she couldn't.

"You will cave, Lia. I have no doubt," he said, using a practiced confident grin to mask his disappointment.

The tip of his finger moved from her throat to down between her breasts, and then disappeared in the water while it circled her stomach. She couldn't breathe as she waited for him to touch her where she most needed it.

Instead of lowering, his hand rose again and skimmed her breasts, barely running over her achingly hard nipples before lifting and rubbing along her bottom lip.

"When you finally come to me and admit what we have, I will lay you down and nibble every inch of your skin. I will suck those taut nipples into my mouth until you scream, and then I will sink inside you and make you come over and over again."

Lia felt herself *sink*ing at his words. She was grateful to be in the water because her knees would no longer lock together. One word and she could have all of that. Shane smiled at her, knowing the torment she was going through.

Without another word he dived into the water and swam to the other side of the natural pool, swimming beneath the breathtaking waterfall and disappearing from her view.

Anger filled her as he left her trembling and unfulfilled. Who in the hell did he think he was?

"I hope you're having a great time pleasing yourself!" she yelled before climbing from the water.

All appeal in her swim now lost, she climbed onto a rock to dry off, not even attempting to cover herself. To hell with him. It would be good for him to see what he'd just turned down.

Of course, she'd been the one to turn him down. But that was just a technicality. She'd been saying yes — just not out loud.

When her body was dry and she still didn't see Shane, she got up and dressed. She wasn't waiting around for him. Her stomach was growling, her body still on fire, and she thought the best thing possible for the two of them was some time apart.

Too dang bad they were stuck as the only two people on this small island.

Even knowing she was a bit of a fool to wander off

into the foliage alone, Lia didn't care. She had her temper to protect her. She hadn't seen any signs of predato-
ry animals so far, so she was sure she was fine.

She left the bag as she made her way back down
the trail they'd come in on — well, the trail that Shane
had cleared. Her stomach was complaining and she was
in desperate need of something sweet. She didn't care
at this point what she had, though, as long as she got
something into her empty stomach.

It seemed that all her hungers were going unsatis-
fied at the moment.

Walking around, she didn't know how long she'd
been away from the waterfall, but she managed to
stumble upon a few fruit trees. Excitement filled her as
she reached for the ripe mangoes. The day was already
turning around.

As she took her first bite of the fresh fruit and the
juice dripped down her chin, a big smile crossed her
face, and she sighed. Yes, things were certainly looking
up.

At least that's what she thought until she heard the
resounding clap of thunder. And then the skies opened
up on her.

CHAPTER FOURTEEN

Rachel

RACHEL clutched the chilled bottom of her cognac glass as she leaned against the balcony — was her hand imparting any heat to the crystal? Probably not, and if she wasn't careful, she'd shatter the thing.

Her eyes were frightened as she struggled with her choice. Or was she really struggling? She'd drunk a little too much, but it was giving her the courage to do what she wanted to do in the first place. She knew it was foolish, but she also knew that when the morning light hit, she would only have regrets if she were to walk away from the invitation in Ian's eyes.

She wanted this man she'd met just that day — wanted him with a desperation that bordered on obsession. She'd never before felt such intense desire for a stranger, but as her evening with him had continued, she'd found herself enamored with his words, his accent, his beautiful obsidian eyes — everything about him.

Wanting to feel his body against hers, she gave him a look that was sure to let him know what her decision was. Thankfully, Ian wasn't a stupid man. But then, if he were, would she be so attracted? Of course not.

Setting down his cognac, he closed the distance between them in a heartbeat.

"You are trouble, Rachel," he said as his hand lifted and he ran a finger across her lips. Her breath rushed out in a heated sigh, and his eyes darkened even more, making her think of a starless midnight.

"I can be," she whispered as she arched her back, pressing her breasts against the hard contours of his chest. *Yum* was all she could think as her body went flush against his, her softness meeting his steel-like musculature.

"Are you sure this is what you want? I don't think I can stop once we start," he said, his gaze boring into her widened eyes.

Was she sure?

"Yes, this is exactly what I want," she said with a confidence she hadn't known she possessed.

Without a further word, Ian wrapped his arms around her and lowered his head. Rachel had been expecting heat, hunger, passion — she got all of that and more.

He was like a man possessed as his lips claimed hers, taking ownership and telling her with nothing but the whisper of his tongue that she belonged to him right now. For tonight, she was all that he was focused on, and she hoped the clocks somehow froze and this would never end.

When Rachel was about to melt at his feet, Ian pulled back, his eyes blazing. Lifting his hands, he traced a finger beneath the collar of her shirt, the soft pad of his index finger lightly tracing her collarbone and trailing across the top of her chest.

Still looking into her eyes, he lifted his hands and slowly began unbuttoning her blouse, one button at a time, as if he weren't in the least bit of a hurry. It was torturous. She wanted his hands on her skin, not on her clothing. She reached up to assist him, but he caught her hand and shook his head with only the slightest tilting to his lips.

Not knowing why she was obeying him, Rachel dropped her hands and leaned back against the tall railing, allowing him to continue with his achingly slow removal of her clothes.

Finally, the last button was undone, and instead of instantly removing the shirt, he parted it only a couple of inches, then placed both of his hands on the shirt and ran them downward, his knuckles rasping against her skin, brushing the edges of her breasts for only the briefest of moments.

"Please, Ian," she begged, wanting his hands on her bare skin, his mouth tasting her flesh.

"What do you want, Rachel?"

Oh, the low timbre of his voice sent a thrill to her core, heating her body, and demanding satisfaction.

"Please touch me," she cried as he ran his knuckles against her skin again, still not taking hold of her peaked nipples.

"I am touching you, Rachel," he said as he gripped the edges of the shirt and pushed it back, sliding it down her arms, and letting it drop to the deck.

"Touch me more," she demanded, feeling the warm wind blow against the lace of her bra, making her nipples harden even further, stretching out against the delicate material that barely covered them.

Rachel felt a woman's power as his eyes flared while looking at her body. He wasn't as in control as he wanted her to think.

Impatience taking hold, she quickly lifted a hand before he could stop her and unclipped the front clasp of her bra, freeing her aching breasts, and groaning as his gaze and the wind rolled across her nipples.

"You are unbelievably perfect," he said in an awed voice, making her knees shake. She wasn't ashamed of her body, but the reverent way he was gazing at her made her feel like a goddess.

"I would really like to give you my opinion on how you look, but you're wearing far too many clothes," she said huskily, hoping her voice was teasing, but knowing she sounded too aroused to pull it off.

Ian grabbed his shirt and ripped the material, not taking time to unbutton it. The sound of material tearing only heightened her arousal. Then, in an instant, all that was hiding him from her view was a pair of tight black underwear that he looked good enough to model in.

"Oh, yes, Ian, you are most certainly beautiful," she gasped as she gazed at his impressive manhood straining through the material.

She reached out her hand to remove that last barrier, but he grabbed her and smiled. "Ladies first."

Rachel wasn't going to argue. She unzipped her skirt and slid out of it, then lifted her fingers to take down her panties, but he stopped her again.

"No. You are astonishing just as you are," he said, his gaze slowly caressing her body.

He grabbed her hips and pulled her to him, the sweet sensation of his hardness pressing against her

stomach. Then, with no effort at all, he lifted her, setting her on the wide ledge of the balcony with her back
against the high railing and tugging her hips forward
as he pressed tightly against her, his long, thick staff
resting against her heat.

She wiggled against him, her breasts brushing his
chest, her nipples pulsing with the need to be touched.
She didn't know whether she asked him aloud or not,
but his head moved, his lips trailing down her jaw
and then lower, his tongue going in circles around her
breast.

"Please," she called, needing him to end this torment. Why wouldn't he give her what she needed so
badly?

He circled his tongue around her dusky aureoles
several times, wetting her skin, then moving back as the
warm wind blew across her, making her stomach tight-
en.

Finally, when she was ready to grab his head and
force him to do what she wanted, he opened his mouth
and sucked her nipple inside, his tongue sweeping
across the hardened peak, making her head fall back as
she groaned in pure bliss.

"More!"

She couldn't ever remember feeling so much pure
lust and yet ethereal passion, and she couldn't help but
wrap her legs around his waist. She couldn't have ever
imagined wanting a man so badly. She didn't take sex
casually, ever! But she was grateful in this moment that
she was breaking her rules, because she was on fire.

Moving his head, Ian gave her neglected breast
equal attention, then lifted his hands and gripped them
both tightly as he tweaked her nipples, causing the

slightest ache, but soothing them so quickly, all she knew was pleasure.

"Lean back," Ian commanded.

Rachel didn't even think of arguing with him. She leaned against the safety rail, gripping it with her hands as Ian's mouth traveled down her stomach, his tongue making lazy circles against her quivering flesh.

When he reached the top of her panties, she waited for him to remove them, but he kissed her right over the top of the material, his wet tongue swiping the revealing lace. She'd never imagined something feeling so good, but when he reached the apex of her core, and sucked her swollen flesh through the lace, she jumped, her body nearly exploding with one touch of his masterful lips.

Pushing her thighs apart further, his tongue ran along the smooth flesh between her thighs and her core, slipping beneath the edge of her panties and rubbing along the smooth lips that protected her core.

After his hand shifted the lace, his skillful tongue finally touched her where she craved it most and ran along her hot pink flesh, making her body orbit to a whole new realm of pleasure. "Yes," she moaned in praise, her fingers holding on tightly to the rail.

His tongue sank inside her, pushing against her flesh, rubbing her in ways she never imagined wanting to be rubbed. He lifted his other hand, and with a quick rip, her panties fell from her body, leaving her completely bare and vulnerable before him.

"You taste more exquisite than the finest wine," he said before his lips closed over her heat and sent her soaring. Her body quivered over and over again, for seconds, minutes, hours — she didn't know. All she knew was that she was flying, and she hoped she never had the misfortune of landing.

Not pulling from her core, he squeezed her buttocks as his tongue continued flicking against her flesh, and instead of dying down, she felt the sensations in her body building again as it reached for pleasure once more.

What was this? She didn't understand. She'd never been able to come more than once. It always hurt to have this area stroked after she'd already been pleasured. But here she was, lifting higher and higher.

Before this moment, she'd fooled around with men, gone far enough that she'd been pleasured, but never to this extent, never to where she felt as if she had lifted off the ground, and would never land again. Yes, it was time to let go, time to experience what so many others had spoken of. Why would she have waited so long to experience something like this?

Because she hadn't found the right man to set her free.

"Yes, Rachel, let go," he called, lifting his head for only a second.

When he plunged two fingers deep inside her core, she flew again, her body gripping his hand as she shuddered at his touch, feeling as if she had been stripped bare.

"Oh, Ian…" she moaned as he pulled back, his lips red and moist from his thorough attentions.

"We have all night, Rachel, but I must feel your sweet flesh gripping me right now," he said as he stood and quickly thrust inside of her. A sharp pinch ripped through her, but she wouldn't allow him to know that. She was through being a little girl, and this couldn't stop.

Somewhere along the way he'd lost his underwear, and for a brief second, she was disappointed to not have seen him in all his glory, but then he pulled back and re-entered, and all her disappointment was washed away.

She gazed at the glittering stars high above her, the sound of the ocean way below washing across her. No one could see them, but she still loved being out on the open balcony, loved having only the slight rays of the quarter moon cascade across her.

"Oh, my sweet Rachel," he called out, groaning as he continued his slow and magical movements.

Rachel lifted her legs, wrapping them around his torso as she leaned back a little more, her breasts being pushed up as he quickened his pace.

"Yes, hard like that," Rachel cried as his hips thrust against her, his manhood filling her to the utmost, heating her body toward another earth-shattering orgasm.

"You are so damned beautiful," he growled as he sped up, one hand gripping her hip while the other lifted to caress her breast, his fingers pinching her nipple gently and rolling it between his fingers.

Rachel went over the edge and cried out at the same time she felt him shaking, then heard his growl of pleasure as he let go.

Several moments passed before either of them felt the last tremors of their orgasms, both of them groaning as wave after wave washed over them.

When she felt him withdraw from her, she whimpered, but couldn't find the strength even to reach out and grab him. She didn't need to worry — he lifted her into his arms and carried her to his bed, where he pulled her close, laying her head against his chest while he began stroking her back.

She expected him to fall instantly asleep, sated — having gotten what he wanted. But his hand curved around her backside, and his movements became more aggressive. To her shock, she felt him harden.

Rachel came fully alive again as she lifted her head and looked into his burning eyes.

"You didn't think we were finished, did you?" he asked.

Ohh, this was a good, good night.

CHAPTER FIFTEEN

Ari

You are welcome to stay and look through the journal. There is cereal in the cupboard, fruit cut up in the fridge, and coffee brewing. I have to be out the rest of the day on business, but here's my number in case you need it. I will drop everything for your call.

By the way, it took every ounce of control I possess not to slowly strip you of your clothing and sink my constantly hard body deep inside your moist folds. I could practically taste you on my tongue as I pictured your beautiful hot pink flesh. I want you — need you — am incomplete without you.

Just a simple yes from you and I will make you scream in ecstasy beyond anything you've felt before. Thinking of you right this minute. Hard for you. Ready to take you.

Any time. Anywhere.

Rafe

Ari did not see that letter from Rafe. She didn't know what he'd written in a growing frenzy driven by his immediate thoughts of her. His second thoughts had intervened. Here he'd just been telling himself that Ari was a romantic, that he should treat her as a woman should be treated, not as just an ornament for his bed. How had he screwed up so royally? That letter would probably have gone over like a lead balloon. It was crass and coarse and it treated Ari as little more than a much-desired body. So he'd put it through the shredder and started again. His second draft began with breakfast and business matters. And it continued —

> *I will drop everything for your call. You must know that it took every ounce of control I had to obey your request that I not touch you. You know that I ache for you in every fiber of my being. I want you — need you — am incomplete without you. Being in the same room with you last night was gloriously painful, and I hope that we can repeat it. Any time. Anywhere.*

Love, Rafe

Ari looked at the handwritten note and single orchid lying on Rafe's unused pillow and her gut clenched with need. No. No. No. What was he doing to her? She'd been down this road and it had been a complete disaster.

She couldn't cave in to her desire. If she did, she'd be right where she was before and she'd never be free. But a voice in her head argued that this was different. *He* was different.

"They always say they're different!" she shouted at herself, then looked around the empty room feeling like a fool. Now she was speaking to voices in her head. This wasn't healthy, not healthy at all.

Ari rose from his bed, having known exactly where she was from the moment she'd awoken. Once you slept with a man like Rafe, his scent washed through you, never left your consciousness. Without opening her eyes, she'd known she was in his bed. She just hadn't known whether he was in there with her.

Ari didn't want to admit it, but she was slightly disappointed that his side had been vacant and unrumpled. She was so indecisive, and that angered her. She'd been strong two years ago — strong enough to walk away from him. But he'd been demanding and arrogant. It had been hard to leave, though clearly not impossible.

This new Rafe, intent on seducing her in a civilized way, was zapping her of willpower. She wanted to say yes and fall into his arms. It shamed her even to think this way, but she wanted him to take the choice away from her so she wouldn't have a reason to feel guilty about what she'd chosen.

That made her weak — that alone should have made her feel guilty.

Ari found a change of clothes in the bathroom, in her size and something she was sure to love. He wasn't holding anything back in this quest he was on. Her favorite shampoo and body wash were there, along with her well-loved lotion.

She should leave, gather her purse and briefcase and just go home, she told herself. But an evil grin spread across her face.

She'd been so busy playing defense, the thought of playing offense hadn't even occurred to her. Rafe said he was intent on seducing her — OK, she'd just have to see how intent he really was. If she pushed him, would he become the same ruthless man she'd first met? Would he show her he hadn't changed, and make her decision so much easier?

It was time to find out.

Stripping off her clothes, Ari let them fall to the ground, her panties billowing out as they floated on top of her skirt and blouse. Leaving them there, she turned the shower on, making it steaming hot, almost to the point of scalding her, then climbed in and used a generous amount of the shampoo and body wash that Rafe had provided.

By the time she'd climbed from the shower, her skin was red and his bathroom was filled with her scent. She applied lotion generously to herself, and even placed a touch of it behind the faucets to make his bathroom really smell like her, then she put on the clothes he'd left out.

With only a glance at her discarded clothes, she walked from the room and entered his living room. She wished she could sit down and pore over the pages of the journal once more, but she didn't want to take a chance that he might show up early. With a longing look at the old leather cover, she walked out his front door.

Let the games begin.

* * * * *

Should he call or shouldn't he? He could email. No. He'd said the ball was in her court. He'd left her a nice message, clothes, her favorite bathroom products, even food. It was only fair that she call and thank him.

Right?

Yes. Anyone would say thank you. He'd been considerate and kind — not demanding anything of her. Holy hell, he should receive a giant gold medallion for not touching her the night before. He'd certainly earned it. She wasn't easy to resist, but he'd walked from the room.

He wanted a damn award!

Rafe continued gazing at his phone as if his will would make the electronic device ring. This was ridiculous. He paced his office, irritated that he was allowing this woman to affect him so much — to completely throw him from his normal cool, composed self.

"Mr. Palazzo, you have a call on line three."

Rafe's heart sped up as he gazed at the phone. He'd given her his cell number, not his business line. Not that his cell had changed in the last two years, but he didn't trust that she still had it on her. He was sure that was the first thing she'd deleted from her phone when she'd walked away from him.

Maybe she had called him on the office phone.

"For criminy's sake!" Rafe grumbled as he walked to his desk and picked up the phone. "Rafe Palazzo," he snapped.

It wasn't Ari. It was his business manager and Rafe leaned back as he prepared himself for an hour-long call. Work. This was good. This was the distraction he needed.

His cell phone shook against his desk and he glanced at it briefly without thinking much about it. Suddenly, he did a double take, because there was a message and it was from Ari. Heart thundering, not hearing a word his manager was saying to him, Rafe picked up his cell and opened the message.

Love the panties. Teal has always flattered my skin complexion. Wearing them now. Thanks.

Rafe hit mute on his end of the line as his manager droned on. What did this mean? Was she saying *thank you*? What did it mean?

"Steve, I have to go!" Rafe said as he unmuted the phone, quickly hung up on his manager halfway through a sentence, then called his secretary into the room. Since she'd been with him for more than ten years, she was used to his unorthodox questions. She was like a second mother, or at least an aunt. He could trust her.

"Yes, Mr. Palazzo?"

For the first time he could ever remember in his life, Rafe felt his cheeks heat. He was actually embarrassed. When he stared at her at a total loss for words, Nina looked at him as if he'd grown a second head.

"Is everything OK, Mr. Palazzo?"

Great. Now she looked ready to call an ambulance. Did he look so far gone that she didn't know whether he was having a heart attack or some other affliction? She was turning to make the call, or so he feared, when he finally gained his voice.

"No. No! I'm fine," he called, and she turned and

raised an eyebrow.

"OK…" she said, drawing out the word as if she didn't believe him.

"I just need some advice from you," he muttered, then shook his head. Rafe didn't mutter. He wasn't indecisive in the way he spoke. He was a man who made a decision and then went through with it no matter what. Not knowing how Ari felt about him was changing who he was, and he didn't like that at all.

"What advice?" He could understand her confusion.

"I got this text message from Ari, and I don't know how to interpret it." He spoke firmly, hoping to convey confidence, but from the knowing look in Nina's eyes, he had a feeling she wasn't being fooled.

"I would be happy to give it a look," she said as she strolled over to his desk; he handed over the phone.

She was looking at the message for so long that Rafe began to feel a need to yank his phone back, but he'd asked for her advice, so he would see it through. Finally, she looked up; the corners of her eyes were crinkled with laughter.

"She is flirting with you," Nina told him.

"Flirting?" He said the word as if it were a foreign concept.

"Yes. Flirting. You need to flirt back."

Nina had been there when his wife cheated on him and walked out the door. And she'd also been there as he'd conducted his relationships like business transactions. She understood him more than most. He knew she'd been disappointed in him, but he hadn't cared. It was his life, and he was the one who was living it. If she didn't like it, she knew where the door was.

However, she had liked Ari. Everyone liked Ari, including his parents and sisters. Ari just had a way about her.

"Well, what do I say?"

"Are you kidding me, Rafe? *You* don't know how to *flirt*?" she said with exasperation. In her surprise, she called him by his first name, something she never did. Nina was always professional — to a tee.

"Of course I know how to flirt! Hell, I can have just about any woman I want. One look and they're mine," he said almost with a smirk. Ari seemed to be the exception, and though they both knew this, neither of them said it.

"If you can have any woman you want, how do you get them?"

Rafe was at a complete loss for words. He didn't know the answer to that question. It had never taken him any effort to get a woman. Women were just naturally drawn to him.

"I'm just a likable guy," he said with a cocky grin.

"Please!" she snapped, then pursed her lips.

"I am," he insisted as he leaned back in his chair and glared at her.

"Fine. Then it looks like you don't need my assistance," she said, then turned and began walking from the office.

"Nina, I'm sorry," he called, not exactly admitting that he needed her help again, but hoping she wouldn't leave him in the lurch.

She turned, but she didn't look to be in the most helpful of moods. She crossed her arms against her chest and waited with one eyebrow slightly raised.

"How should I reply?" he asked.

Her irritated expression evaporated. "Rafe Palazzo,

I will not help you snowball this woman. I actually like Ari. If you can figure it out and win her back, you will be a better man for it."

With those words, she walked from the room. Rafe listened to the quiet click of the door shutting, then stared down at his phone.

Flirting. OK. He could do this. She wanted romance; she wanted words. Well, he was a master at that.

> *All I could picture was stripping that bit of lace off of you when I bought them. And, yes, I personally picked them out, ran my fingers across the fabric, and closed my eyes, imagining how you would look wearing them…and nothing else.*

> *Come see me tonight and I'll undress you slowly as I run my fingers over every delectable inch of your skin.*

There. That was good. Surely she didn't want any mushy stuff. Of course not. So he leaned back as he waited, all thoughts of work forgotten. His phone rang, and he quickly clicked the button, rerouting the call, and then shut it down. His sole focus right now was this new game that Ari wanted to play.

I thought you agreed to no touching.

Rafe grinned.

That was only for one night, Ari. I plan on touching every inch of your body — again and again and again…

Rafe's body hardened as he closed his eyes, recalling the smooth curve of her breasts, the sweet angle of her backside, her defined legs. She was a vision, and he had to have her soon. Several heartbeats passed before his phone beeped again.

Thanks for the gifts, but I have a date tonight. Maybe some other time…

Immense jealousy wrenched Rafe's gut. His first instinct was to demand she break the date right now. She belonged to him, and no other man was allowed to touch her. He would pound anyone who tried to a bloody pulp.

He began typing exactly that, but he came to his senses before he hit send. If he said those words, he would surely lose her all over again.

No. If Ari wanted to play games, he'd just have to prove that he was always the winner. Instead of sending a response, he picked up his other phone and made a call.

His plans for the evening had just changed.

CHAPTER SIXTEEN

Lia

THE rain wasn't just coming down; it felt as if the heavens had opened up and God was unleashing his fury on the small island. Lia could see only a couple of feet in front of her as she staggered through the bushes and trees, fear starting to escalate.

What if she was completely lost? What if she broke through the bushes just as a tidal wave was surging from the ocean and it carried her back out to sea, where she'd never be found again?

Her temper was going to end up causing her untimely death. There was a point when stubbornness was just plain stupid, and she'd crossed that line, and then redrawn all new boundaries.

Staggering along, hoping she was headed in the right direction, Lia prayed to make it through this somehow. As another horrendously loud clap of thunder sounded right above her head, she felt as if she'd gotten a big fat *no* in answer to her prayers.

* * * * *

Shane had sulked long enough. Emerging from the surprisingly deep cave, he came up out of the water and immediately searched for Lia. Looking up at the sky, he grew worried. It was going to pour at any moment. He'd stayed inside the small cavern for far too long, a couple of hours, perhaps. Maybe more.

"Lia!"

He couldn't see her anywhere. There was no way she'd be so irresponsible as to wander off alone — not with a storm brewing. But what if she'd gone off far earlier, after their tiff, perhaps to get food? After all, that had been a major point of this expedition, and he'd blown off thinking about what had to be done because he was pissed off. All in all, this was a disaster ultimately of his own making.

Shane quickly climbed from the water and grabbed the bag, rushing it over to the cave behind the waterfall so it would be safe.

Then he hurried back and dressed, his temper flaring when he realized that she had indeed wandered off. Part of it was her fault, her stubbornness, but he couldn't absolve himself of all blame. She could be anywhere and the sky was about to unleash its wrath. He hoped Lia hadn't gone back to the beach. He had no idea what the swells would be doing right now.

As the wind picked up, he made his way through the brush, shouting her name every minute or so. Suddenly, the rain came down, and it wasn't showing the least bit of mercy as thunder boomed and lightning slashed across the sky. He had to find her and get back to the safety of the cave.

Passing a fruit tree, he almost didn't stop, but knew they could be stuck for a while. He took less than thirty seconds and filled his pockets, then continued his search.

As the torrential rain poured down, Shane pushed ahead, feeling the sting on his face as the brush and low tree branches whipped past him in his fervent pursuit. Not giving the sting a second thought, he continued on. Unsure how he was going to find her, but knowing there was no way he'd give up, he continued calling for her as the light faded.

Just when he thought he would be wandering the woods in the thick of night, he spotted a flash of pink ahead. It had to be her shirt. His heart stalled as he made his way in that direction. *Please*, he prayed.

It had to be her. When he got closer, he found Lia hunched down on the ground. Terror gripped him at her stillness, but then he saw her move and his temper flared. How dare she frighten him so badly!

"What in the hell were you thinking?" he shouted.

Lia's body jerked as she turned to look at him. Defiance shone in her eyes — she wasn't going to back down an inch.

"I was thinking about getting away from you, you overgrown pig," she replied, her words slightly garbled as the pouring rain dripped into her mouth.

"We need to go now. This storm is only getting worse," he said as he gripped her arm and lifted her to her feet. They could fight once they were in the safety of the cave.

Shane was astonished when she dug in her heels. "I would rather stay out here in the rain than have you dictate to me, Shane Grayson!"

This was pure insanity. Maybe she'd eaten some of the inedible plants and was having a reaction. It was the only thing that made any sense to him. Whatever it was, this was ending now.

"Lia, I'm giving you to the count of three…"

"And what exactly are you going to do then?" she snapped as a streak of lightning flashed far too close for his comfort.

"Try me and find out. One, two… Screw this," he snapped as he grabbed her by the waist and threw her over his shoulder, her head hanging down his back and her ass high in the air.

"Shane Grayson, you put me down this instant," she demanded as he began quickly moving back the way he'd come. All he could think about was the dryness of the cave and getting food in his stomach. Well, that was all he could think about until he noticed her tight rear end so close to his face. His temper was evaporating as lust began to fill him again.

"I'm not putting you down, so just shut up and enjoy the ride," he said.

"Shane!"

"Ah, baby, your thrashing around is only turning me on more," he called, his mood changing as he carried her through the woods, walking down the path he'd forged earlier. He felt a bit like a caveman who had just claimed his prize. Thunder boomed, and he picked up his pace.

When he turned the corner and saw the path down to the water and the cave, he breathed a sigh of relief. Shelter was needed. Even though he knew that the moment he set Lia down, she would fly at him with her claws extended, it was worth it.

She was light as a feather, and he'd enjoyed feeling the warmth of her body as he carried her through the storm. It was all leading up to one hell of an explosive night. Having had a couple of hours to think on it, he would take her any way he could get. She'd soon be begging him — he didn't need her to make the first move this time.

Shane reached the cave, and he could have gone around the waterfall, but they were already soaked, and that was the quickest way in. So, without warning, Shane stepped down into the waist-deep pool and walked through the thick stream of pouring water.

Lia's shouts turned to a gurgle as she inhaled a little of the sweet water. Setting her down on her feet, he backed up quickly, hoping to get enough time to brace for impact.

"I'm going to bloody you," she snapped as she flew at him.

With her eyes flashing in the fading light that was seeping through the veil of water, and her T-shirt molded to her heaving breasts, Shane was more than ready to play.

He easily caught her in his arms and didn't give her a chance to slap him. Spinning them around, he pushed her up against the smooth cave walls, and captured her mouth, stopping her words as he plunged his tongue inside, demanding a response from her.

Holding her hands firmly against her sides, he deepened the kiss, not giving her a chance to retreat, not giving her a single moment to think. They both needed this. It was the only way to move forward. What they had together was unstoppable, and the sooner she realized that, the better off both of them would be.

"Shane," she cried as her rage quickly turned to passion. She might have thought that she despised him, but her body was telling him something entirely different.

"Are you going to behave?" he asked as he pulled back.

Her hand quickly escaped his hold and he felt the sting of her slap across his cheek. He might have deserved that. He really shouldn't have been mocking her. In fact, when this night was over, he owed her several apologies for his behavior during the day. He'd been less than a gentleman from start to finish. But he just couldn't seem to help himself when in her presence. She elicited emotions in him unlike any other woman he'd ever met. He certainly couldn't help himself now.

"Not ever in this lifetime," she said through gritted teeth. Her heaving chest was still brushing his as he leaned in closer.

"Oh, Lia, darling, we are going to make our own thunder tonight," he promised her as he lifted a hand and rubbed his jaw. She'd really put some effort into that hit.

"You are so full of yourself, Shane. The only thunder you'll be hearing is outside of these walls," she said, but the tremor in her voice let him know that she was very aware of where this was going.

They were quickly losing their light, so Shane released her, moved to the bag and pulled out their tent — the tent they'd be making love in all night long. His body hardened in anticipation. *Just a little bit longer,* he thought.

Shane, ever the romantic, threw Lia a bag of beef jerky as he quickly set up their Home Sweet Home.

She'd need her strength.

"What's the point of a tent? We're in a cave," Lia said.

"You can sleep outside it if you want, but I prefer not to have spiders crawling all over me," he said with a grin that was difficult for her to see.

Lia shut up as she looked around and began scratching her arms. Shane felt the slightest bit of guilt, but he was so worked up right now, his hands were trembling as he put the tent together.

With only a few candles in the emergency pack, he decided to light only one. With luck, they'd be rescued soon, but they were stuck in this cave until the horrendous rain stopped, and no one was going to find them there. Hmmmm.

Yes, he wanted to be rescued, but having Lia all to himself for a couple days wasn't a bad thing, in his opinion. She'd have no choice but to admit where this was going between the two of them.

When he was finished, he stood, and looked her way, her face barely discernible in the fading light. "Damn, you are stunning," he gasped, loving the silhouette of her body against the dark interior of the cave.

Her eyes widened, but it wasn't a line, it wasn't a way for him to gain her submission — she just took his breath away.

"Shane…" she began, her voice barely a whisper, need pouring through it.

"Time to get out of those clothes, Lia. We don't need you catching pneumonia," he said as his eyes raked across her chest.

She narrowed her eyes, seeming to gain just a little bit of her temper back. "I'm not getting naked in front of you again, and in this heat, I don't think I have to worry about that," she told him as a shiver passed through her that had nothing to do with her body temperature.

He just smiled as he moved forward. Holy hell, he liked it when she played hard to get.

CHAPTER SEVENTEEN

Rachel

"No. You are doing it all wrong," Rachel cried, emitting a flood of giggles.

It had been five days of utter bliss, and though she knew their time was coming to an end, she refused to think about it. She was growing attached, but she pushed that to the far recesses of her mind as well. She couldn't focus on what tomorrow would bring; she allowed space in her brain only for what the two of them had right at that moment.

Ian was spectacular in every single way, even in his imperfections, which she liked about him. He had a cowlick that wouldn't behave no matter how many times he brushed his hair. There was also a small scar on his forehead; she really wanted to know how he'd gotten it, but she didn't want to ask, didn't want to get more attached.

Their days and nights of lovemaking were more than she could have ever imagined, and he was also funny and sexy and made her never want to leave this penthouse suite.

But she would.

After their time was over, she would walk away with her head held high, and she'd have an experience that she would most likely carry with her for the rest of her life. She'd gone into this with her eyes wide open, and she refused to have regrets about it.

"I don't see how I'm doing it wrong. This is just ridiculous," Ian said with a scowl.

"Obviously you don't know how to just let go. The whole point of Pirate's Cove is to battle for rights so you can become the most feared and famous pirate the world has ever known. You aren't even trying," she said as she collected more gold. She'd won again.

"I have better ideas of games we can play," Ian told her as he flicked the board away and grabbed her quickly, pulling her into his lap.

"I thought you said I was wearing you out," she said with a grin as she kissed his square jaw.

"When would I ever have said such a thing?" he asked in horror.

"Oh, I don't know. I think it was right after our shower a few hours ago."

"Then I was a fool. I could never get enough of your delectable body," he said as he began kissing her neck.

"Mmm. You can do that for about a million more years," she offered, leaning into his mouth, enjoying the trace of his tongue along the sensitive skin of her neck.

He took her right there on the couch, and then she lay in his arms, sated...

"You'd better not go to sleep or the walls will rattle," he said with a laugh.

"What?"

"The people in the next suite over were pounding on the walls because you were snoring so loudly."

"I do not snore," she gasped in horror as she glared at him.

"Oh yes, you do," he teased as he kissed her neck.

"That is an absolutely terrible thing to say, Ian," she said with a pout.

"I'm just teasing you. Your snore is really quite cute, very delicate like you," he said.

"I do not snore, and I warn you that I am anything but delicate," she said as she sat up and climbed on top of him, already forgiving him and feeling a stir in her body.

Ian had opened up something inside of her, and she couldn't get enough — was greedy for more all the time.

"We need to leave this room for a while. I think I've forgotten what the rest of the world looks like," Ian told her as his hands gripped her hips and he pushed his wakening arousal against her heat.

"I'm happy to stay right here," she countered, pushing down against him in temptation, not wanting for him to let her go. They had only two days left, and she was battling sadness at the thought. She wasn't ready. A week just wasn't long enough.

"I am, too, but I have a surprise planned for you," he said, piquing her interest. Rachel always had loved surprises.

Though he was saying the words, he was now hard and pushing against her core.

Rachel moaned as he surged inside of her. Yes, she would certainly miss this.

Ian made slow, sweet love to her, almost bringing her to tears as he looked deep in her eyes while his body moved within her.

Her pleasure overtook her in a sweet wave, and she collapsed on top of him, feeling drained emotionally and physically.

An hour passed as she lay there in his arms, on the cusp of sleep and consciousness. His hand held her behind and squeezed as he kissed her lips, and then he sat her up.

"We are leaving this room," he said with a laugh. "Go and take a shower…alone." He added as he set her on her feet.

Rachel practically floated into the bathroom; she stepped beneath the shower spray and quickly lathered herself with sense-entrancing body wash. As much as she didn't want to leave their small haven, she was looking forward to whatever he had planned. It would be one more memory for her to carry with her when her mysterious lover disappeared forever.

They didn't talk of exchanging numbers or speaking again after their week was up. This was a fling only — they'd both made a firm agreement on that, and she considered it the smartest course. Even if he asked, she'd have to say no.

Her thoughts burst forth in a jumble. Her life was moving in a new direction. She was going back to Italy. They didn't have a future together. All they could possibly have was meeting once in a while in foreign places. Though that idea was appealing, she could see only heartbreak coming her way if they went that route.

It was going to be hell on her to let Ian go after only a week, but meeting with him every few months would make her crave him more. She wouldn't do that to herself.

When she stepped back into the living area, dressed and ready to go, she was happy to see him in a pair of fitted trousers and a tucked-in dark blue dress shirt. He looked incredible no matter what he wore, but in that attire, his appeal was sinful indeed.

"That was quick. I guess you are eager to get started," he said as she walked up to him and looped her arms around his neck.

"I can't seem to get enough of you," she replied, and her lips found his. Ian didn't hesitate, but took her mouth in a possessive kiss. Oh, how he could kiss, stirring low in her midsection, and making her melt against him.

"Yes, you have me quite bewitched, Rachel," he said, pulling back and looking into her eyes. His dark pupils dilated and she wanted to crawl back into bed with him. "What a spell you have me under, woman. We must leave now, or we'll be late," he said as he gently pushed her from him, then took her delicate hand in his, placing a gentle kiss on her fingers so she wouldn't feel rejected.

The two of them walked from the room and took the elevator down, then slipped out the back door, where a limo was waiting. She found a bit of guilty pleasure in the ride, but was frustrated since she was trying to ease away from such an extravagant lifestyle, trying to fit in more in normal society. Ian was really pulling out all the stops on this adventure, though, and she couldn't fault him for showing her what he considered the ultimate in romance.

"Where are we headed?"

"That is a surprise," he said as they drove through the city.

When they arrived at the heliport, she raised an eyebrow but didn't ask any more questions. He wasn't going to tell her, so it wouldn't do any good.

She'd flown many times with her brother in a helicopter and felt no fear as Ian helped her get situated before speaking to his pilot. Then he sat next to her in the luxury machine, and she sat back and waited for the fun to begin.

Yet they were flying out across the ocean, and Rachel was thoroughly confused. She'd expected him to be taking her somewhere in Florida, but they went instead farther and farther out to sea.

Lights appeared on the ocean surface, and her eyes widened in pleasure as the chopper began making its descent. She turned to grin at him as they landed on a giant yacht in the middle of the ocean. The vessel they'd just landed on made her brother's boat look small.

"Is this yours?" she asked. She'd known Ian was wealthy, but this was a whole new level of wealth, at least equal to that of her brother's, and she found that hard to believe. Ian had a certain arrogance about him, but he didn't seem like others she'd met in the billionaire class she'd been around her entire life.

"No. It's a friend's," he replied.

They'd agreed on not asking personal questions, but curiosity was eating her alive. But caution dragged her more firmly into the opposite direction. If she asked him questions, she reminded herself, Ian might answer. The problem? The price would be her own story, and she didn't want to tell it. So she kept quiet.

"It's beautiful," she said instead.

"Yes, she is a beauty. My friend has excellent taste. Right this way." He leapt from the craft, then reached for her hand to assist her, and led her from the landing to an elevator that took them down a couple of levels.

When the doors opened, she laughed in delight at the dim room with a candlelit table set up in one corner, and a small group of musicians on the opposite side playing classical music.

"You are quite the romantic, Ian," she said as he led her to the table.

"Only when I'm inspired," he whispered in her ear. Chills traveled down her spine.

If she had only two nights left, then this was the way to end things.

"Do *I* inspire you?" she asked, knowing she shouldn't fish for compliments, but unable to help herself.

"Oh, yes. You have greatly inspired me, Rachel. I fear letting you go won't be such an easy endeavor."

The serious look in his eyes had her heart racing.

No. She had to change the subject. They must keep their affair light and brief. It was the only way. Looking around, she saw that no one else was in the room with them yet, making her bold.

"Well, then, you'd better hold on tight while we still have time," she said as she rose from the table, and slowly walked to him, sitting down on his lap.

"I will learn your secrets, Rachel. I have decided I want to know them."

Rachel leaned in and kissed him, needing to distract them both before she made a fool of herself.

CHAPTER EIGHTEEN

Ari

"...Then my wife took all the furniture and I walked into the house to find nothing but dust balls all over the place. It wasn't bad enough that she had to clear me out, but she was a slob on top of it. I can't stand filth. A woman should care enough about her home to want to keep it clean."

Ari had to fight to keep from chewing out Dr. Lynn Sherman, the world's most boring podiatrist, who just happened to be sitting across from her at the nice Italian restaurant. She was thankful for the decent wine, because if she hadn't had it, she might not have been able to hold her tongue. Not that she should have had to.

She was also ready to kill her friend Amber, who had set her up on the date. Paybacks were definitely in order!

"I'm sorry to hear that," she finally replied when she was sure she could say it with as little sarcasm as possible.

"Do you cook, Ari?"

"Um, well, I guess I cook. I wouldn't go so far as to say that I cook well, but I know the basics," she said with a chuckle.

His mouth didn't turn up even the slightest.

"Don't worry too much about it. There are classes you can take. Any woman can learn to cook well with enough training," he said as he reached over and patted her hand.

Did he seriously just say and do that? She was ready to punch this man in the face.

"I wasn't worried," she said through gritted teeth.

"I know. I know. You can learn. So, you said you are teaching a class at a community college. That must be a nice pastime. Of course, when you have children, you will want to focus on them, right?"

"Pastime?" Ari said, her eyes rounding in anger. So far she'd put in six years of college, maintaining a perfect GPA, working hard, and achieving her dreams. She still had a doctorate to complete, and was working her tail end off on it. For him to call that a pastime completely infuriated her.

"Well, yes. I think it's cute that you want to teach, but it's not a real job. For women, work isn't necessary, though. Your husband will take care of you."

Dr. Lynn returned his attention to his plate, cutting a piece of salmon and taking a bite. She wanted to shove the fish down his throat — too bad there were no bones in it — then push him to the floor while she impaled him with her three-inch heels.

"Look —"

She was about to lay into him when his pager went off. Who the hell did this guy think he was? At first he'd just been boring; now he was downright insulting.

"Sorry. I need to return this call. You are never off work when you're a doctor," he said, his satisfied laugh slaughtering an already sad attempt at self-depreciation.

She wanted to yell at his back that he was a flipping foot doctor. The world wasn't going to end if he took a night off. How she held her tongue, she would never know.

Several moments passed and Ari sat there toying with her food. She was seriously considering sneaking away from the restaurant.

"I apologize, but I have an emergency at the hospital. I need to cut our date short," he said as he returned.

"What possible emergency is there with feet?" Ari clamped her mouth shut too late. In her defense, he'd been rude first.

"Feet are very important, Ari," he scolded her as he stood there looking indignant.

"Yes, of course," she responded, trying really hard not to laugh. She wasn't in the least apologetic, but she was afraid that if she didn't seem at least a little repentant, he might feel the need to lecture her. She would lose it completely then, and end up screaming at the man, making a spectacle of herself and getting hauled from the restaurant.

"You enjoy the rest of your meal. I will call you tomorrow. The evening went exceedingly well, and I look forward to doing it again," he said. To her surprise and horror, he leaned down and kissed her before she was able to stop him.

As he turned and walked away, Ari lifted her arm and attacked her mouth with her napkin, wanting to get any trace of his flavor off her lips. Picking up her wine, she took a big gulp, then licked her lips, seeking out and destroying any remnants of the taste of that pathetic man.

It took her a few moments before she realized that he'd left her with the bill — after ordering a two-hundred-dollar bottle of wine.

Crap! That was a bummer, to use language that she'd left behind in her teens. It would seriously hurt her budget. She couldn't bring herself to care too much, though. It was worth it to be rid of his company. She might as well drink up, finish her meal and then order a decadent dessert to drown out her woes.

"Good evening, Ari."

Her heart sped up at the sound of Rafe's deep voice behind her. This couldn't have been a coincidence.

"Rafe."

She hoped he hadn't heard the excitement in her voice. She didn't want to be happy to see him, but she was anticipating her first glance. She didn't turn — she'd wait for him to come around her. It didn't take long, and her breath became erratic as she gazed at him in his dark Armani suit and the bright blue-and-purple tie, which matched his eyes to perfection.

"It looks as if you could use some company," he said as he sat down, lifting his hand to summon a waiter, who rushed over and cleared away the poor doctor's setting before placing new dishes in front of Rafe.

Ari wondered what the other patrons of the restaurant were thinking. Maybe they thought she was on a speed date, going through as many men as possible in a two-hour block. At least this one was a vast improvement over the last, even if she would never admit that to Rafe.

"I'm on a date, Rafe," she said. Technically she was, even if she'd been ditched.

"Not anymore, Ari. He was paged to the hospital."

Her eyes narrowed as she watched the satisfied smirk on Rafe's face. She had no doubt that the page had come from Rafe. She hadn't realized Rafe's determination — which made her the fool. She should have known this man better by now.

If she weren't so darned happy to be rid of her date, she'd be seriously pissed off.

"Though my dinner companion is no longer here, I don't necessarily wish to dine with you, Rafe," she said as she took another bite of her pasta. Suddenly her appetite had returned. She could at least say that she was never bored in Rafe's presence.

"Ah, but I couldn't let such a beautiful woman dine alone, could I? What kind of gentleman would I be?"

The waiter approached and Rafe ordered for himself, including another very nice bottle of wine.

"I am perfectly happy to eat on my own. I've been doing it a long time," she countered as she sipped the last of her wine, then reluctantly accepted as the waiter offered a glass from Rafe's bottle.

When she took a taste, she was disappointed to like it so much. Rafe knew what she liked a little too well. For that matter, no other person knew her as much as this man sitting before her. No one else, that is, but her mother.

Of course, during her mother's drawn-out illness, her mother had missed a lot, but it wasn't Sandra's fault. She'd been trying to get better, and Ari had doubted the bond they shared, or at least that's what it felt like she'd been doing, since she hadn't trusted her mother with the truth. Had Ari not doubted her mother, she never would have felt a need to lower herself to become what Rafe had demanded of her.

Though she'd somehow managed to fall in love with Rafe during that time, she still hadn't forgiven him for what he'd asked of her. She'd given him a piece of her soul when she complied with his commands, and she didn't know if she'd ever get that back.

That was a big reason that she couldn't understand her attraction to him now. How could she still desire this man? Probably because she had made a choice to follow him. Though his methods had been abhorrent, he hadn't abused her — hadn't followed through on what he'd commanded in the beginning.

He'd never been cold with her, just demanding. The sad thing about it was that she liked Rafe strong and taking charge. She just needed to be able to say no, and she needed to be able to take charge, too. He'd been weaker on the second point, but she'd always been able to say no. He'd told her he wanted a puppet on strings, but he'd never actually made her his toy.

"Yes, you are strong and independent, beautiful, and smart. I am very impressed with you, Ari. It is my honor to dine with you," he said as a bowl of soup was set before him.

"You have become smarter, Rafe. I am almost curious to learn what has happened to you," she said, her guard dropping as she gazed at him.

"Oh, I'm the same man, Ari," he told her with a wink and a confident grin. "I've just realized that I can't live without you. It changed me in some ways — I know where I went wrong, and I know I can never let you go."

"That's not really your choice, is it, Rafe? I choose the people I want to be with. I am not a frightened child who must do your bidding. It may only be three years after the first day I was in your office, but I've grown in that time. I won't bow to you or to anyone. I will never be blackmailed again or forced into a situation I don't want to be in. I will never be your mistress."

Her shoulders stiffened as she looked steadily into his eyes. If she couldn't get anything else through his thick skull, she wanted him to understand that she wouldn't be a kept woman again.

"I don't want you to be my mistress. I want you for my wife," he said almost casually as he lifted his glass and took a sip.

Ari choked on the bite of food she'd just taken. The waiter rushed over, looking at her with concern while she gained back her breath and then picked up her water glass. Sending the waiter away, she glared at Rafe.

"You're not amusing, Rafe," she sputtered.

"I'm not trying to be humorous, Ari. I intend on marrying you. When the time is right, I will ask — and you *will* say yes."

He spoke as if they were talking of nothing bigger than next week's dinner menu. Confidence radiated from him and his eyes sparkled. He was so full of himself that he actually believed the words coming from his mouth.

"We'll just see about that, Rafe," she said as she angrily picked up her fork and speared a chunk of asparagus, clenching her teeth on the vegetable.

"You are so good for me, Ari. If ever I think I'm in control, you remind me that I am powerless in your presence. Why would I ever have let you go? I was a fool once — it won't happen again."

"You haven't changed, Rafe. You are still the 'control freak' I met three years ago. You have just gotten much better at masking the commander beneath seductive smiles and come-on lines. I am not fooled," she told him.

"You are right, Ari. In some ways I will never change. You are also wrong. I said I won't force you, and I won't. But I have never said I won't seduce you. I know just what it takes to heat your very core. I know how to make you come alive, with your body straining against mine for my touch only. I will use every weapon in my arsenal to win you over, and I will feel tremendous pleasure while doing it. You wanted to play a game with me with your text messages. Well, you started it, and I'm not conceding defeat. I do hope you're still wearing the teal panties. I'll enjoy removing them with my teeth."

Ari felt heat pool inside her as he gazed into her eyes. She couldn't get the image from her mind of his teeth scraping along the delicate lace of her panties. Would it really be so bad for her to give in for one night? Perhaps the lovemaking would be terrible — perhaps time had loosened his hold.

As he lifted a hand, reaching across the intimate table, to caress her hand as she reached for a piece of warm French bread, her stomach quivered. When he softly caressed the top of her hand, running his fingers over her flesh, she melted, though she knew it was quite foolish of her to do so. Being with him would be even better than she remembered — she had no doubt about it. He'd make her body sing in ways no other man ever could.

"You want to play games, Rafe? Fine. I'll play some

games," she said, and she stood up.

His eyes never left her as she moved over to him and leaned down, her mouth an inch from his. Oh, he smelled so unbelievably good.

"When I go home tonight and lie naked in my bed…" Mmm, she enjoyed the quick intake of his breath and the narrowing of his eyes.

"It will be all alone."

With that, she turned and walked from the table, a huge smile on her face. It wasn't easy to best Rafe, but she'd just done it. And to top it off, he'd have to pay for that two-hundred-dollar bottle of wine.

CHAPTER NINETEEN

Lia

HEART racing, rage and excitement boiling inside her, Lia knew she had about two seconds to make a decision. Was she going to go down this road again with Shane? Because she knew if she did, all bets were off.

Shane wouldn't force her, but then he wouldn't need to, would he? One touch and she'd go up in flames. The way she craved him was what scared her the most. What if this was nothing but a game for him, with her as the prize?

Trust was the hardest thing to gain back once it was stripped from you. He'd broken her trust, and she was afraid to give it to him again.

The hunger for him would never diminish, but was it worth surrendering to her own desires when she knew she'd have to deal with his betrayal? And she was sure he would betray her again. It seemed impossible for him not to.

She did believe he cared about her. Just not enough. Survival kicked in and she turned to make a quick retreat, slipping from the cave and dashing back out into the raging storm. If he touched her, she would lose all willpower, and then she'd never get him out of her heart.

Though she really believed she could protect herself by not having sex with him, inside she knew that she was lying to herself, because he was already lodged so deeply inside her soul that she'd never be free of him. But her pride and stubbornness were the only things holding her together, and she was afraid to let them go.

Not making it very far, Lia gasped as Shane's arms wrapped around her, swinging her to face him, his eyes boring into hers.

"The time for running is over, Lia," he said above the roaring of the storm.

There was a pause as his face illuminated over hers with the flash from lightning overhead. The heat in his eyes was enough to melt her from the inside out.

As her body betrayed her and fused against his, his lips latched on to hers, and the fight was over, just as she'd known it would be. It was inevitable.

With a deep moan, she submitted to his hard body, giving back as much as she was receiving. The warm rain emptied over them as he hungrily captured her mouth, his hands molding her wet skin, touching her back, gripping her sweet backside as he pulled her tightly against his stiff arousal.

"You have been mine for a long time. I was just a fool for fighting against it. Now, you are the fool for running away," he said, pausing for only a moment in his kiss.

"Yes, we're both fools, Shane, and this can't lead any-where," she gasped.

"That's where you're wrong, Lia. I don't intend to let you get away this time," he said, and he ended their conversation by sealing their mouths together.

His tongue pressed against her lips, demanding entrance, and she opened to him, no longer desiring anything other than their bodies joining together. She had to have him fill her, needed him to take away the constant agony she'd been in since walking from his room more than two years earlier.

Shane lifted her in his arms, moving to the wet grass next to the lake, the warm rain coating their heated bodies.

"I wish I could see you better," he said as his lips skimmed across her cheek, then moved down to her neck.

Another streak of lightning flashed through the sky and on his face was an expression of such complete adoration that she was overwhelmingly undone. It was an emotion she had yet to see in him before this moment. It was as if in the dark of the night he felt safe enough to let down the hard shell surrounding him and was completely unaware of his vulnerability.

The rest of her fight with herself was lost as she pulled him closer, needing to comfort him, to love this vulnerable side of him. Yes, she most likely would be hurt, but this was Shane, this was the man she'd loved for so long. She couldn't imagine loving anyone else.

Not letting him know what she'd just witnessed, she said, "I guess we'll just have to remember each other's bodies by touch alone."

A groan escaped his throat, barely discernible above the raging storm around them. He grabbed her shirt, pulled it off and tossed it aside.

The rain continued to fall, but it was only a drizzle now, just enough to make them slide against each other as the lightning streaked across the sky, giving Lia glimpses of Shane's perfect form, his enraptured expression.

"I can't touch you in enough places. It's been so long. I need you, Lia," he gasped as he struggled to pull off the rest of her clothing, which was plastered to her skin.

"Yes, way too long." She helped him with the removal of their clothes.

Within moments, they were both naked. Her back was cradled against the soft grass; he leaned against her, his mouth roaming across her neck while the rain pulsed against her skin.

When his mouth captured her nipple, Lia arched off the ground, reaching up to grasp his hair and tug him closer. Why had she thought she could resist this?

Shane's mouth moved down her stomach, and the sensation of his tongue swirling along her heated skin while the rain hit her nipples was building her pleasure in an unimaginable way.

"You taste so sweet," he growled as his mouth reached her hips and he spread her legs apart. His hands ran across her thighs, pushing them farther and farther apart, opening her to him.

Lia's head fell from side to side as she groaned in need. His tongue lapped at the outside of her core, teasing her to madness as she waited for him to take her to a higher place.

"Please, Shane, please make me come," she cried.

"Oh, Lia, I'm going to give you pleasure long into the night," he promised, making her shiver as he clasped her sweet spot with the warmth of his lips and sucked her into his mouth while feverishly flicking his tongue.

Her hips arched into the air as she pushed into him, reaching…reaching…almost there…

"Yes," she cried, her voice being carried away on the wind, rising in the sky to mix with the storm clouds. Thunder echoed, shaking through her body, and making her orgasm go on endlessly.

As Lia started to descend from the high of a spectacular orgasm, Shane made his way up her body, taking his time as he licked away the rain still washing across her. When his face came into view and blocked out the downpour, another flash lit the sky, and the look in his eyes took her breath away.

"I'm right where I need to be, Lia. Your beauty, strength and passion overwhelm me. You're strong and brave, talented and kind. You mean everything to me. Yes, I love how my body feels as I sink deep within you, I love the taste of your release on my tongue, but more than that, I love everything about you — from the sweet taste of your skin to the fire that lights your eyes. I can't ever let you leave me. There are those who say that if you love someone, you must set the person free, but they have never been with you, because to set you free would be to lose myself."

He entered her body, slowly and sweetly — wondrously — and Lia flew again, but not away from him. She flew higher than she'd ever been, her body clutching him, holding him deep within her.

Safe.

Warm.

Loved.

Lia didn't want to be set free. She wanted to be right

there in Shane's arms with the rain blanketing them, the thunder rumbling in the sky, and the lightning giving her flashes of the passion and love on Shane's face.

"I don't want to go," she whispered when she could speak again.

Shane began moving, and all she could do was cry out as he brought her to the peak again and again, as he'd promised, while he surged deep within her body.

She loved him. She had for more than ten years, and no matter what had parted them, she had a feeling that nothing would separate them again.

CHAPTER TWENTY

Adriane

ADRIANE was shocked at how much he was enjoying his time with Rachel. He still hadn't learned anything about her, because she was much better than he was at this game of Don't Ask, Don't Tell. He found himself wanting to lie in her arms and speak of the throne, of his brother, of his duty. He was barely able to hold himself back.

This was supposed to be nothing more than a fling, just something to ease his stress before he took on the responsibility of his position — a responsibility that he didn't even want. But somehow this American girl had slipped past his defenses.

It wasn't love.

Adriane wasn't such a fool as to believe in love at first sight. He knew the fragile emotion existed, but he chose not to fall into its merciless grasp. Once love got its talons into a man, it would never let go, never let him think objectively again.

No. He would marry a proper woman when the time came, and his wife would produce heirs for his kingdom. That was what a king did. That was what was responsible, what he'd known he must do from the time he was seventeen and discovered he'd inherit the throne one day.

Still, though he didn't want his affair with Rachel to end, duty called. He must return to his homeland and perform as king of Corythia.

"I can't believe how virile you are. Do you ever get enough?"

Adrian turned to look into Rachel's gleaming green eyes, and he almost gasped, as he always did, when confronted by her beauty. Instead, he reached upward and tweaked her hardened nipple.

"Look who's talking, wildcat. You're always just as eager," he reminded her as he crushed her smooth body against him, allowing her scent to engulf him and inhaling it deeply. Desire, sure and strong, thrummed inside him as he lay over her, his arousal pulsing as he moved it against the hot folds of her core.

This was their last night, unless he made an excuse to keep them together longer. He wanted to…

"You are distracted, Ian. Don't be. I want your full attention," Rachel demanded as she grabbed his hair and brought his mouth down to hers, taking his lips and pushing her tongue forward as she entered his mouth.

He was torn between lust and confusion, and lust won out as Adriane's tongue followed her retreat and he deepened the kiss, tightening his lips on hers as his hand smoothed down her side to slide beneath her derrière and pull her more tightly against him.

Her responses to him were always so deliciously open and honest. She groaned with pleasure as her hips rocked forward, encouraging him to press inside her.

She demanded satisfaction, and that was one of the things he loved most about her.

Not proud of the many women he'd lain with, he could safely say none had made a place inside his head — none but Rachel.

She made him lose his mind — made him forget everything except for her.

Pulling back, he smiled when she growled at him, light flaring in her eyes as she reached for him. She was always so eager to have them join together, but Adriane loved to play with her lissome body, loved to make her cry out over and over again.

Grinning at her for only a brief moment before bending down and kissing her ear, his warm, wet tongue slipped along the outer edges, making her break out in goose bumps. Her nipples strained toward him, aching with a need to be touched.

As if reading her body's yearning desire, he reached down, taking her peaked nipples between his fingers and pinching down, elongating the sensitive flesh, bringing such intense pleasure that she called out.

His hand moved down her quivering stomach; he circled the sensitive flesh between her legs, and then teased her swollen little bundle of nerves, not quite giving her what she wanted, but touching her just enough to keep her on edge.

When he slipped inside with two long, supple fingers, then rubbed her in just the right place with his thumb, she cried out her encouragement for him to continue.

Lowering his head, he sucked the puckered flesh on her breast into his mouth, gently clamping his teeth down, rubbing the hard skin lightly before releasing one pink bud and moving to the opposite side. Her hands tangled in his hair as she guided him, showing him exactly what she wanted.

He moved both hands upward, abandoning her principal pleasure point, and he cupped her twin peaks, squeezing the wet flesh and running his thumbs across it before his mouth descended again and teased her breasts even more.

"I want you inside of me now, Ian. Right now!" Little did Rachel know to whom she had issued that command.

Who was he to argue? Adriane offered a pained smile as he reached over to the nightstand and grabbed protection, slipping it on before moving over her body and positioning himself just outside of her heat.

He wanted to plunge in, but he loved making her wild, loved the thrust of her hips upward as she demanded completion. Yes, he was in agony, but the fire igniting in her eyes made the pleasure so much better.

"Now!"

"Yes, now," he said as he surged forward and drove his full length inside her glorious body.

"Oh, Ian, what you do to me," she cried as her hips lifted off the bed and her nails scraped down his back.

"I can't get enough of you," he groaned, thrusting deep inside, over and over, pressure building in his loins.

"You make my head....spin," she said, almost unthinkingly, as her orgasm drew near. He felt her silken folds tighten on him, felt her body stiffen as she readied to fall over the edge.

"Now, Rachel. Come right now," he demanded as he loved her hard and fast, his hips in sweet collision against her smooth, soft skin.

She exploded around him, screaming in her passion; her eyes closed and her head fell back, her body stiff as she shook beneath him.

"Yes, baby," he groaned as he followed her into the abyss of pleasure. He also shook, trembling with the strength of his release.

When the final tremors faded, Adriane barely had the strength to free her of his weight. Quickly pulling off the latex protection, he tossed it aside before taking her into his arms, and sighing with pleasure as her head lay cradled against his neck.

He stroked her hair as his brain whirled in circles and his heart felt…lost? This was their last night.

"It's OK, Ian."

"What is?" he asked. Could she read his mind?

"Tonight is our last night. I've seen the turmoil in you all day. We both knew this was for a week. You really need to quit worrying that I am planning on taking it further than that," she said with a laugh as she rubbed her fingers against his chest.

Exhaustion filled him, but unbelievably, he felt himself growing hard again. But he forced himself to repress those baser urges; he needed to speak to her.

"What if I don't want tonight to be our last night?" Adriane was a little surprised by his words, but not enough to take them back.

"We aren't going there," she said.

"Why not?" He was thoroughly insulted that she wasn't jumping at the opportunity to see more of him. He couldn't remember that ever happening before.

"Because we know nothing about each other — and before you interrupt, I like it that way. I do know that we are both heading in different directions, moving forward with our lives, and I won't change my plans over a weeklong affair that would burn out within a month if we decided to lengthen it. Just hold me tonight, and let me remember this week always," she said, almost pleadingly.

Adriane didn't like her idea of a compromise, but he said nothing as he listened to her breathing. Soon, she was asleep within the safety of his arms.

Extracting himself from her sweet grip, he rose and did something he'd never done before. Finding her purse, he called his assistant and had him copy her information.

It was just in case, he told himself, not looking at any of it. It was a matter of honor. He himself would invade her privacy only if absolutely compelled.

The next morning they returned to the hotel, and when he came out of the shower, he found Rachel gone. Confusion filled him when he looked around and didn't find anything of hers. It was almost as if she'd never been there, as if this was all nothing more than a dream.

A very, *very* good dream — but only a dream, nonetheless.

When the shock wore off, fury overtook him. How could she have just walked away so easily?

The two of them had been careful, but he always kept an eye on the women he was with sexually. If something were to happen, he wanted to be the first to know about it.

Making himself calm down, he paged his assistant to the room. Amedeo was there within a minute.

"Amedeo, make sure two men are aware of Rachel's whereabouts for the next three months," he demanded.

His assistant didn't blink and didn't ask questions;

he just followed orders.

After Adriane had given more orders for packing the things in his hotel room, he mentally prepared himself for what was to come. He tried to push Rachel and his impromptu visit to Florida to the back of his mind, but for once, it wasn't easy. He took a final look around the room that he had spent so much time in for the last week, and then just shook his head before he firmly closed the door behind him.

Adriane made his way to his jet, focused on what was ahead of him. It was time to return home and fulfill his duty.

CHAPTER TWENTY-ONE

Ari

ARI was feeling quite smug as she left the restaurant.

Yes, she would be aching all night, but at least she'd been strong. At least she'd been able to get the upper hand and walk away from Rafe's invasion of her space with her head held high and a smile on her lips.

If the dismally dull doctor had stirred her in any way at all, she might have called him up to see whether his emergency was finished. Of course, in reality, he most likely hadn't had an emergency. He'd probably arrived at the hospital only to find it had been a false alarm. Yep, Rafe and that page…

She was vaguely curious to find out whether Dr. Foot in Mouth would call *her*. She knew she wouldn't take the call, as she wasn't so desperate for attention that she would endure that man for even another thirty seconds, but it had been the first date she'd been on in months.

It didn't please her that she had found much more pleasure sitting with Rafe for an hour than she'd found with any of the men she'd attempted to date. None of them stirred her; none of them piqued her interest. She was afraid that she was ruined for any other man after having Rafe in her life.

As she approached the curb to hail a cab, she felt a hand on her arm. Alarm zipped through her until she realized that it was Rafe, then excitement rose unwanted in her stomach. She should have known that getting away from Rafe wouldn't be *that* easy. Turning to give him a snarky comment to cover up the pleasure she felt, she never got the chance — she was suddenly being pulled forward. A squeak escaped her tight throat as she was thrust into the backseat of a limo.

Getting her voice back quickly, she turned to him in a rage. "What the hell do you think you are doing?" she demanded as the vehicle pulled away from the curb and she punched Rafe in the arm.

"You know that I always escort my date home," he replied, not even flinching from her hit.

"This wasn't a date — at least not with you, Rafe!" she said between her teeth as she glared at him. She retracted her hand; she had hurt it far more than she had him by her punch.

"I had a good time, bought you dinner, and watched the sexy sway of your beautiful derrière as you walked from the table. It was a date," he said with a satisfied smile.

"I guess you haven't changed, have you Rafe? You still must get your way," she snapped as she leaned back in irritation, both from his words and the perverse pleasure they brought her.

"I've changed, Ari. I have just discovered in the last week that you have, as well. I'm not going anywhere, so a little…persuasion is needed."

"Persuasion? This is downright force, Rafe."

"No, Ari. You would know if it were force," he said as he slid closer.

She moved away, squeezing against the door on the opposite side of the car.

Rafe followed.

"I have papers to grade," she said as his leg brushed against hers.

Please don't betray me now, she begged her body.

"It's Thursday night, Ari. You don't have class again until Monday. I think the papers can wait."

"You aren't the one who gets to decide that."

"Of course not, but I thought you would like to see more of the journal."

He was dangling the carrot before her, and she really wanted to take a bite.

"I don't think I should. Your behavior has been reprehensible," she said.

"It's your choice, of course." He knew how badly she wanted to lose herself in that journal again. He knew it was his ace in the hole, so to speak.

"Can you keep your hands to yourself?" she asked.

"Nope. That was a one-time deal."

Oooh, the man was a rogue. He'd given her a taste and now all bets were off.

"Fine. Then, I want to go to the library to read it. That's a nice and safe place where it won't get hurt."

Rafe looked at her with a new light in his eyes that had her worried.

"Do you really think that you would be safe just because we'd be at a library, Ari? With a connection like ours, it doesn't matter where we are."

"I can control myself, Rafe. I will admit that I still feel *some* attraction toward you, but that doesn't mean I want to jump your bones. I can control myself, and I would expect a man of *your age* to be able to do so as well," she said primly.

Rafe laughed as he looked into her eyes. "Did you just call me old, Ari? I'm barely over thirty. I don't think I have a foot in the grave quite yet."

"Well, you act like a teenager, so you may be safe. I would think a respectable businessman would act with more…decorum," she said, taking a moment to think of the right word.

"I don't care what anyone thinks. I want you, and I refuse to hide that fact. You're a stunning woman who makes my head spin and my body hard. I will give you the moon and stars if you just let me."

She wanted to snort at his language, but he was serious. She could see it in his expression. And yet she was afraid. He'd hurt her in ways she didn't know a person could be hurt. If she surrendered to him again, he would take her soul, and she might never get it back.

Wasn't it all about the chase with Rafe? Once he had her, wouldn't he lose interest and want to move on to his next conquest? She was sure that she was the only woman ever to have walked away. Offering him her heart hadn't been enough for him — he'd wanted only her body — her submission. Well, that wasn't good enough for her. It wasn't then, and it certainly wasn't now.

"We aren't going to agree on this, Rafe. I've moved on, and you need to accept that. I would, however, like to see more of the journal," she said, hating that he had something she wanted so badly.

He sat back, not looking the least bit affected by her words. Was he hearing only what he wanted to hear?

"I will meet you at the public library tomorrow."

She was so surprised, she didn't realize at first that her mouth was hanging open. Rafe didn't compromise — not often, anyway — so his agreeing to meet her with his treasured item in public left her reeling.

That was obviously the good news; what was the bad news? She knew the other shoe had yet to drop, but she couldn't figure out the negative to the situation.

"Good. I'm glad you are giving in a little," she said slowly.

The car stopped and she reached for the door.

"Here's something to think about while you're lying alone…naked…in bed," he whispered. His arms snaked around her and she found herself crushed against his chest.

Before she had a chance to utter a protest, Rafe's head descended and his mouth captured hers. She remained stiff in his arms for all of two seconds before her traitorous body began pressing into his, unable to get close enough.

Ari tried to stiffen against him again, but it was of no use. As his tongue slid across the seam of her lips, her stomach turned to liquid, and fire ignited on a traveling journey through her veins. Though she fought her attraction to Rafe, her body knew it was where it wanted to be.

He'd placed his mark on her, and her body hadn't forgotten.

Her nipples tightened, poking against his chest, as her core heated and she felt her thin panties become wet with her desire. Rafe's hands slid along her back;

he coaxed her mouth open, then devoured its sweetness with the hunger of a starving man.

Giving in to what she'd wanted for so long, Ari's hands slowly lifted, her arms wrapping around his solid shoulders as he pulled against her, molding her body to his. Her tongue followed the retreat of his as they twisted and tangled against each other.

"Mmm." Ari's body ached at the low murmur from deep within Rafe's chest.

Knowing she was making this powerful man tremble was like throwing gasoline on the fire already consuming her. She ground her hips against him, seeking relief from her sensitive pink pearl against his stiff erection, forgetting about all the reasons that she shouldn't be doing this.

He was controlling, took what he wanted when he wanted it, was uncompromising, unforgiving.

But was he these things?

She couldn't think. It had been so long…she could focus only on feeling.

When his hands gripped the soft flesh of her backside and tugged her against his stiff manhood, which was obviously trying to break free from his clothing, the last thought of willpower dissipated.

She could remember the sight, feel, smell and taste of him as if they'd just made love yesterday. She hungered to take his arousal between her teeth, taste his pleasure on her tongue. She just…hungered.

When she was ready for him to lay her back on the seat of the limo and take her right there, he pulled back, his eyes nearly black with lust as he looked at her.

"Invite me in, Ari…please?" he asked.

Her brain couldn't process what he was saying.

Invite him in? Where? She could barely even remember her first name, let alone where they were.

She gazed at him in confusion as she tried to clear the cobwebs from her brain.

"Let me pleasure you," he said as his hands drifted up her back, then around her sides, where his thumbs rubbed across the edges of her breasts, not quite touching her sensitive peaks.

There was a reason she needed to tell him *no*, but for the life of her she couldn't figure out what it was.

"I see you want to finish this, Ari. Don't be stubborn. Don't let your pride leave us both hurting," he said, his lips drifting along her neck, his hot breath deliciously inviting.

A horn sounded outside of the car, and it was just enough of a distraction to begin pulling her from her haze.

No. She couldn't do this. Without a doubt, she'd regret it in the morning. Yes, her night would be passionate and her body fulfilled, but then her heart would begin breaking again, and she'd have to start the healing process all over.

Getting over a man like Rafe once had nearly destroyed her. She wouldn't live through that kind of heartache twice.

Rafe sighed when he saw the determination begin to shine in her eyes, but to her complete surprise, he released her, then moved around her to open her door so she could exit on the sidewalk.

Stepping from the vehicle, he reached inside and took her hand, helping her out.

"I should just kiss you senseless and let your body decide," he said as they reached the top of her steps.

She almost wished he would. Almost.

"Goodnight, Rafe." She inserted the key in her door.

As the door swung open, Rafe gripped her arm, turning her. Her eyes wide, Ari waited for his next move.

"Sweet dreams, Ari," he said. He leaned down and brushed his lips chastely across hers. Then he pulled back, placed his hand on her lower back and nudged her inside the door.

The door shut behind her. Ari went on autopilot as she locked it, then leaned against the solid wood and listened to Rafe's retreating footsteps.

It took everything inside of her not to yank the door back open and call out to him.

Her game had backfired on her in a big way. He might be hurting, but she had a feeling that she was the one in much worse shape. She ached all over, and she knew the fire wasn't going out any time in the near future.

Walking almost in a trance, Ari moved to her bathroom and drew a scalding hot bath. She'd simply try to burn the ache out. After an hour, she knew nothing was going to help. She certainly wasn't going to attempt an ice bath. Leave that to the men.

Damn Rafe! He affected her whether he was dominating her or seducing her. She couldn't seem to win either way.

CHAPTER TWENTY-TWO

Lia

LIA woke up as sunlight began streaming in through the thin line of the waterfall, lighting up their tent.

After their lovemaking last night in the rain, Shane had lifted her in his arms, carried her inside, and gently set her down while he got their tent ready for bed. There, they'd made love again, slowly and long into the night.

It felt like coming home.

"Don't try to pull away again."

Lia turned her head to look into Shane's worried eyes. He was drawing her naked body close to his as he kissed her neck.

"I'm not going to."

She could try to fight this all she wanted, but she was right where she wanted to be, so what would be the point?

She was in love with Shane. She always had been and always would be. Being without him took away a piece of her.

Fear that he would walk away tore at her, but Lia was tired of living in fear. She was ready to let it all go and just relax in his arms. Who knew what would happen when they got off this island? But for now, they had each other, and that was all that mattered.

"I'm not going anywhere," she said as she snuggled closer.

Surprisingly, her desire was tamped down. She was content just to lie there with him, feel the stroke of his hand on her flesh as she basked in the warmth filling her heart.

"Good. I was afraid you would retreat once you woke up. I need you, Lia, more than I can possibly ever describe."

Oh, the rapture that his words aroused in her. They were the words she'd always wanted to hear coming from his lips. She needed him, too. She had for so long that she couldn't remember a time she hadn't needed him — wanted him — *loved* him.

"Why don't you ever talk about your childhood, Shane?"

She felt him stiffen in her arms and worried that she'd crossed a line. He always closed up when anyone mentioned his past. All she knew was that he'd gone through hell. Neither he nor Rafe would say anything about it.

"It's not worth speaking of," he said as she felt him force himself to relax with a deep exhaling breath. He wasn't able to fully unlock his muscles.

"I want to know you — know why the exterior that you present to the world is so tough, so untouchable. Please tell me," she said, her fingers trailing across his back in a comforting way. If he could open up to her, then maybe they would have a real chance.

"You don't want to know, Lia," he warned her.

She could tell he wanted to speak to her, though. He needed to let it out.

"I honestly do, Shane. I want to know everything about you — the good and the bad. I promise not to ever judge. I promise to listen."

"Do you want to know the ugly, too?"

"Everything, Shane."

Shane hesitated as a deep sigh rose from his chest. When he began to speak, she was completely still.

"I didn't have parents like yours, Lia. My father — well, he was…not a good man. Far from it."

"What about your mom?"

"She was weak and pathetic. I hate to say that about my mother, but it's true. The things she let happen to me were things a mother should never allow. She went through her own trauma, and I'm sorry for that, but she had a child to think about. If I had children, and I can't imagine I will, I would never let someone hurt them the way that my father hurt me."

There was so much pain in his voice, stiffness in his body. Lia wished she could take his pain away, erase the memories from his brain, and help him to heal. She did all she could, by running her fingers along his bare skin, by letting him know that she was right there with him, that no one would hurt him again.

"My mom was young and in love, bright-eyed with the world as her oyster. She was such a beautiful teen-ager, with dark hair and eyes, olive skin and a laugh that could bring a smile to the most wretched and the most irascible person. She met my father her junior year of high school, and she fell instantly and hopelessly in love, if you can call that love. He was twenty-one, and the typical bad boy. Driving up to their local hamburger shop, he'd taken one look at her and decided she would be his. She'd been flattered that such a handsome older guy took an instant interest in her. She'd followed him like a puppy dog, willing to do his bidding."

There was so much bitterness in Shane's voice, but his touch against her skin never changed. He was gentle as he held Lia while he dived back into his past. She almost told him he didn't need to continue, but she knew she might never get another chance to hear, so she remained silent as he paused, as if he was drawing the courage to go on.

"Their first time together was…" Shane stopped for a minute. "It wasn't consensual. She'd been dating him for a few months, and she always put the brakes on when he tried to have sex with her. Finally, one night he'd taken her back to his crappy apartment and had a couple too many beers. She said *no*, but he didn't stop. I'll never forget the day she told me about that moment. I was so furious with her. Why didn't she turn him in? He'd raped her, and she still kept seeing him. And when she found out two months later that she was carrying his child, her parents were furious and kicked her out. What did she do? She moved in with him."

"She told you all of this?" Lia was horrified that a mother would burden her son with such awful knowledge.

"Yes. They both hated me. She hated me because I was the product of a very unpleasant experience in her life. I was also the reason she was forever locked to this man. She told me on more than one occasion that she should have just aborted me — that she would have if she'd only had the money. Her husband, the man who fathered me, hated me because — oh, probably because he was just an evil bastard. I can't get inside the brain of someone like that. He liked having such a pretty wife, someone who was so malleable to his will, but he also liked having a lot of women on the side. He would even bring one home on occasion, kicking my mother out of their bedroom so he could use it with this new 'girl-friend.' A few times, he made her, his *wife*, participate with them. She put up with it, never fighting him. She said it wasn't worth the beatings he would lay upon her if she disobeyed him."

"Why in the hell didn't she just leave, go to a victim center?" Lia was horrified. She'd never imagined that his story could be that bad. "Or why didn't she call in Child Protective Services?"

"She was weak. She blamed her woes on me, on him, on everything and everybody except for herself. He was unforgivable, but she was just as bad for stay-ing. The first time he punched me so hard that I got a concussion, she should have realized it was too much. Hell, the first time he'd laid a hand on me, period, she should have left him. If she was OK with getting the shit kicked out of her, that was one thing, but when he was knocking around his toddler son, she should have gotten me out of there. But she didn't, and it wasn't until I was older that I realized that what they were both doing was wrong. I was so used to the abuse that I thought everyone got smacked around."

"Oh, Shane," Lia moaned. She pulled him closer into her arms and held him close. Her tears fell against his shoulder as she cried for the frightened boy he had buried inside himself, and the man who still had to endure those memories.

"At sixteen, I finally had enough. I beat him nearly to death, then left the house and never turned back. I was done. The sad thing was that I didn't even care when I found out my mother had killed him. One day, I guess she just had enough, too. She stabbed him in his sleep, then waited for the police to come. She didn't even try to hide what she'd done. They asked her if it was self-defense, and she said no. She could have gotten off. He beat her constantly, especially after I left, but she still pleaded guilty to the authorities. She told the prosecutor that she'd just decided he wasn't worthy of living another day. She'd grabbed a kitchen knife, stood over him with a crazy smile on her face and plunged the knife deep into his chest. She told them that she'd laughed as his eyes popped open and he struggled to catch his breath."

"Oh, my gosh," Lia gasped, unable to imagine what he was saying.

"I went to the trial. She didn't know I was there, but I wanted to see what happened. I sat in the back row. It was odd, the emotions I felt. It was as if I was a different person, just a journalist there to take notes. I felt nothing when she was deemed crazy and the judge had her locked up in a mental institution. I felt nothing for the man who had been killed. No…that's not true. The only thing I felt at knowing he was dead was regret — regret that I hadn't been the one to plunge the knife into the coldhearted bastard's chest."

"You don't mean that, Shane. You couldn't take a life," Lia gasped.

He was silent for several heartbeats. "Not like that. No," he said. "At that moment, I did feel regret, though.

I don't know. If I had stayed any longer, I might have been the one to take his life."

The certainty in his tone frightened Lia. He was so different from the abused teenage boy he'd told her of, but she couldn't comprehend what he'd been through. It was so tragic.

"Have you seen her since she's been locked up?" Lia was afraid to ask, but she needed to know.

"No. I don't have any desire to see that woman," he spit out, his body tensing again.

"Maybe you should, Shane. Maybe it would help you to heal and you could fully let go of the past. What she did was horrendous, but if you could tell her that, tell her how wrong she was, then you could let go of that burden."

"How would that help? She's mental," he snapped.

Lia knew he wasn't snapping at her. She knew he was in a world of pain right now. Having grown up with loving parents and siblings, she couldn't pretend to know what he had dealt with, but she loved him enough to get some glimmerings.

"It doesn't matter if you get through to her, Shane. It's about you. She stole enough from you, your childhood, your joy, your *love*. She took it all, and she doesn't deserve redemption, but you deserve to be able to let it all go."

"Well, I guess it really doesn't matter now, does it?" he said, shocking her as he turned toward her and smiled.

"Why is that?" she asked, completely confused.

"Because we're lost on a deserted island and may never be found again. It may be our sole responsibility to populate this land and start over," he teased.

"Mmm, that sounds like it could be fun," she said and rubbed against him. The frightening thing was the tug inside her heart at the thought of carrying Shane's child. It should terrify her. She didn't want to be a mother, not yet, but as she looked into his eyes, she could picture a little boy with his hair and eyes gazing back at her. She was also confused because of his earlier statement. Did he want kids or not? She didn't want them now, but she knew she would someday.

Shane drew her beneath him and easily slipped inside her body. She knew he was healing by losing himself within her. She was OK with that — more than OK, she thought as passion began building and thoughts of children evaporated as pleasure began enveloping them.

Lia knew Rafe would rescue them. It was only a matter of time. And so, in the meantime, she would enjoy every moment she was locked tightly in Shane's arms.

CHAPTER TWENTY-THREE

Ari

No worries here, Ari thought smugly as she walked up the steps to the huge library. She'd be safe, sound, and inviolable as Fort Knox. There was no way that Rafe would put the moves on her while in a public building. Well, he had in public before, but he wouldn't dare do something in a library, and they certainly couldn't have sex. *I mean, really!*

Since she'd done nothing but toss and turn the night before, she was quite irritated with Rafe. Had he been a terrible kisser, or had her body not completely betrayed her, then she would have been in a much better mood.

To top all of that off, the snore-worthy pig of a doctor had dared to call her at midnight to see if he could get her address and stop by. He wanted to have *dessert*. She'd just bet he wanted dessert...

She'd told him to lose her number, then hung up on him while he'd still been sputtering.

It seemed that Ari was doomed to end up in the

presence of the wrong men.

This last date wasn't really her fault, since her friend had set the entire thing up, but still… Some days, it seemed she'd end up as that person with ten cats, four dogs, three piranhas and a parakeet, rocking alone on her front porch. Not that there was anything wrong with that. And anyway, she was far too young to be thinking that way, but it still frightened her.

She didn't want to settle with just anyone because she was afraid of being alone. It was OK to focus on herself for a while. Being in a relationship didn't define you as a person. First, you had to be confident in yourself before you were capable of having a healthy, mutually beneficial relationship.

Ari had gained confidence over the last couple of years. She was just lonely, making it easier for Rafe to slip past her guard.

She'd have to put forth more effort in her attempts to keep him out of her pants.

She found a quiet corner table, and sat down. People were all around her, busy studying or reading for pleasure, but the point was that people *were* there. She felt secure. Her phone vibrated; picking it up, she saw a message from Rafe.

Have you arrived yet?

Yes, I'm sitting in the back. Meet me here.

I have a table on the third floor. Just come up the stairs and go to the right.

I have a great table. Why don't you come back down here? she replied. She'd been hoping to arrive before he did.

We can't eat down there and I brought a late lunch, he countered. As her stomach rumbled, she realized she'd forgotten to eat again. Food sounded fantastic. Even if she went up to the third floor, they wouldn't be in any less of a public place. She'd still be fine.

Picking up her bag, she didn't bother responding but made her way up the stairs. On the second level, she found the children's section, and she smiled as she watched a man with a circle of kids around him while he read. The boys and girls were fascinated with the variety of his storytelling voices. If only *she* could play her different parts as well when dealing with Rafe.

Continuing over to the next flight of stairs, she went upward, then frowned as she realized she was in the stacks section, the part of the library her classmates had said they would go to when they wanted to make out with their boyfriends.

Well, this wasn't a college campus, and if Rafe thought they were going to be doing any touching, then he had another thing coming. She was there to pore over the pages of his ancestor's journal, take notes, and learn all that she could. She wasn't there to get screwed on a hard table — both literally and figuratively.

When she rounded the corner and found Rafe sitting at a covered table with an elegantly presented lunch, she felt her heart speed up.

A smile crossed her face without her even thinking about it. Of course, Rafe couldn't just bring a sandwich in a brown paper bag. That would be too pedestrian of him. And too plebeian for that dyed-in-the-cashmere aristocrat.

"You look lovely, Ari," he said as he stood and moved to her chair, holding it out for her.

"Isn't this a bit much for lunch in a library?" she asked while trying not to enjoy his compliment.

"Nothing is too much for you. Not ever," he whispered against her ear, sending shivers down her spine.

"We're here for the journal and nothing else, Rafe," she reminded him in a breathy whisper.

"That's what you're here for. I have…other plans," he said mysteriously.

"Well, put those plans away…and anything else you might be thinking about taking out that should remain hidden. We're in public," she reminded him as she looked at the food — an out-of-the-ordinary chicken salad, artisan rolls, exotic fruit, and small appetizers. Yum. He'd even managed to bring in a bottle of wine.

She knew she shouldn't accept the wine, but she couldn't resist, knowing that because he'd chosen it, it would be spectacular. How her tastes had changed since meeting him. She used to despise alcohol, and with good reason, considering the trouble it had gotten her into on more than one occasion. She still avoided anything other than wine, and she now knew how to distinguish between good wine and rotgut. This definitely wasn't rotgut.

"We'll have lunch, and then I'll leave you alone for a while to study the journal," he said, and she looked at him with suspicion. *What was he up to now?*

"Hey, I'm trying to compromise," he told her as he held up his hands.

"I don't know if I trust you, Rafe. Scratch that. I *know* I don't trust you," she said, though the lifting of her lips took away some of the sting.

"You'll just have to learn how to trust me again," he said, then took a bite of lunch.

"Again? I never trusted you," she said.

He looked wounded and was slow in answering.

"I will just have to earn your trust, then. I want to earn it, and your respect, too. I want to be with you. You will soon realize how important this is to me. You will soon know I want only the best for you — for us."

"We can't turn back time, Rafe. I know that's not what you want to hear, but there isn't a magic wand available that you can just wave and — *abracadabra!* — the past is forgotten," she said, and the hurt in his eyes made her feel like a heel. She was close to apologizing when he looked down and the moment was over.

They finished their lunch, keeping the topics on anything but the two of them, and Ari found herself relaxing. When they were done, a man came in and quietly removed all traces of the meal, and then Rafe pulled out the journal.

Ari gladly took it, excited to get started again. Soon she was lost in the world of William and Saphronia, and she didn't notice when Rafe got up and left.

She also didn't notice when the floor was closed off and she was left all alone with Rafe.

Hours passed without Ari's notice. When most of the lights downstairs in the library went out, and they dimmed on the floor she was on, she kept on reading. She was oblivious to the rest of the world as she sank into the tragic love story between William and Saphronia.

The days creep by with an agonizing slowness, and now two full months are lost in uncertainty, nay, in terror. No word from you has reached my eager hands, and I do not know whether you are still among the living or — I cannot force my pen to write such words. Without you, my life is all confusion and woe. My father has demanded that I marry another, a man who is twenty years my senior, a man whose habits and tastes are utterly uncongenial, a man whom I could never love — even if you had not appropriated that most tender of feelings all to yourself. Father declares that this man will be able to take care of me and provide a secure life for my future children. I have expressed my love for you and you alone, but he says he would never sanction a marriage with a man who is a mere soldier and one who has cast his lot in with the North, among people who, in his words, would deprive his family and those around us of their rights and their freedom. He adds, so cruelly, that you will likely die on the field of battle or find another helpmeet with whom to spend your life, and that I am giving into silly and girlish ideas. Oh, if only a letter from you would reach me and tell me how you are and whether I am still the object of your devotion, just as you are of mine! I will never give up — not even with my dying breath.

Our rigid system of social laws should not allow me, a mere girl, even to ponder such an act as I am pondering — to leave one's home and one's connections is against all maidenly training. But should I come to you? Despite all the dangers of war, whither thou goest, I will go. If I hear nothing from you, then I must do just that.

I love you with a devotion that absorbs all else.

Ever yours,
Saphronia

Ari couldn't stop a tear from falling as she read a letter so fraught with suffering. The terror Saphronia was feeling — the pain and anguish of not knowing whether William was alive or dead. It would be too much for anyone to bear. If she were Saphronia, she too would have crossed enemy lines to find out.

"Are you enjoying the journal?"

Ari jumped as Rafe sat down on the table next to the journal. She quickly spirited it over, not wanting the delicate tome to get harmed.

"Oh, yes, Rafe. You really should read this. It's very beautiful," she said, although knowing he just couldn't appreciate it the way she did.

"I already told you that I would like for you to tell me all about it," he said, lifting his hand and stroking her cheek.

Ari lost all concentration on the book as she looked into Rafe's eyes. That was the point when she noticed the quiet. Of course, it *was* a library, but she heard nothing, not the turning of pages, or the rustle of books being removed from shelves.

She tore her gaze from Rafe and looked around, noticing how dim the library lighting was.

"Are they closing?" she asked, thinking it was probably a wise idea for the two of them to leave.

"They closed an hour ago. It's just you and me," he said.

Ari's head whipped back around to Rafe and saw the ardor in his eyes.

Oh, no.

She wasn't strong enough for this. It's why she'd chosen to meet him in public.

"How are we able to be here all alone?"

"I funded this library. They are more than accommodating when I have a special request."

She should have known he would somehow take a level playing field and "un-level" it to make it work completely to his advantage. She was dealing with Rafe, after all.

"I think it's time to go," she said as she stood.

"Not yet." He stood, too, and drew her into his arms. "I've been dying to do this all day."

With that, he pulled her against him and didn't hesitate to press his lips to hers. Ari resisted for all of two seconds before she gave in to him.

What would the harm be to feel pleasure for just a few moments? Would it really break her heart to be with him one more time? Maybe it would be good for her. Maybe she would finally get over him for good. It seemed the tender love story of William and Saphronia had weakened the walls of protection around her heart.

She didn't know whether she was just trying to convince herself or not, but she knew that she wanted this — wanted him so much, it was burning her entire body alive. She didn't have the will to resist anymore. She just wanted to be taken to another world.

And Rafe could certainly do that.

"I want you, Ari. Tell me no, and I'll stop." He leaned back to look into her eyes.

She didn't want to tell him no. She didn't want to stop.

"I should…" She hesitated as his hands made their

way down her back and gripped her hips, tugging her against his hardness.

"No, you shouldn't. What you should do is enjoy every second of this, accept what only I can give you and cry out in pleasure," he said, nibbling her neck.

Oh, yes, that was the right place.

"I need…" She didn't know how to complete that sentence. She needed so much.

"You need me," he said. He lifted her up and sat her on a high table, spreading her legs apart, wedging himself between her thighs, pressing his concealed hardness against her heat.

At that moment she was grateful that she was wearing a skirt, that she could feel the hardness of his arousal through the thin silk of her panties.

Though turmoil boiled inside her, she did want him, she did want the pleasure he could give. Her desire outweighed her guilt at betraying herself and her principles.

"Yes, I want you," she admitted.

Rafe stopped moving against her; he looked into her eyes, his body pressed tightly against hers. He'd been pushing and pushing, and now he hesitated. But she didn't want to give herself time to back out of this. She wanted him.

"You're sure?" he asked.

"Yes." As he gazed at her, she was more than sure.

"Once we start, we won't stop," he warned her.

"Then don't stop, Rafe. Take me," she said. She wrapped her hands around his neck and tugged him to her.

His head descended and he claimed her mouth hungrily, his hand reaching up to undo her blouse. He finished with the buttons in record time, and then tossed the garment somewhere behind her. Next, her bra came off and then his warm hands were cupping her flesh, holding up the weight as he leaned back and looked at her.

"Damn! You are even more spectacular than I remembered," Rafe said with whispered reverence.

He massaged her breasts, his thumbs tracing the edges of her puckered flesh. She wanted his mouth on them, but he didn't give her that; he just kneaded the flesh, then pinched her nipples between his fingers as he elongated them, sending heat straight to her core.

Finally, when she was about to scream in frustration, he bent his head and the feel of his tongue lapping against her skin had her crying out. Yes, it had been too long. She needed this.

He moved back and forth between her breasts, his hands kneading the flesh as his mouth ravished her peaked nipples. Somehow she'd ended up lying back on the table with him above her. She didn't know how. All her concentration had been on not exploding from just the attention he was giving her breasts.

Within moments, he had them both stripped free of clothing, and she was lying bare before him, feeling a sense of euphoria at the unrestrained lust in his eyes.

"I want to make this last all night, Ari, but I don't think I can," he said in apology as his finger drifted down her stomach and caressed the outside of her core.

"How about we just do it more than once?" she suggested, wanting him inside her more than anything else, but also wanting it to last forever. She didn't know whether it would happen again after tonight. She didn't know how she would feel tomorrow.

Rafe's eyes rounded, and he couldn't even speak for

a moment. He quickly sheathed himself before poising his body above hers. "You're coming back to my house when this is done."

There was the Rafe she knew, demanding, insistent, trying to get his own way, even when he was nearly delirious with passion.

"Right now, I would agree to anything," she gasped as he began slowly sliding into her.

"Now that is something I love to hear," he said. He surged forward, knocking the breath from her as his impressive erection nestled inside her body.

"Yes, Rafe," she called as he pulled back and then quickly began a rhythm that was thrilling for both of them.

"You're mine, Ari. I won't live without you. I won't lose myself that way," he cried as his body crashed against hers.

She knew she should shake her head, knew she should disagree, but she felt so right in this moment that she couldn't think of why. There was nothing but pleasure lodged in her brain as he continued thrusting inside her.

Two years was too long to go without this feeling.

"I'm sorry, Ari," he cried as he sped up, a thin sheen of sweat coating his chest.

What was he sorry for? She had no idea.

He pounded against her, and Ari's world shattered. She shook as her body gripped him, the orgasm lasting for an eternity.

Somewhere in the recesses of her mind, she heard Rafe crying out as he found his pleasure, but she could barely process it. All of her concentration was focused on the pulsing in her core, the pressure inside her breasts, and the fire shooting through her veins.

When she finally came back down from the mountain they'd climbed together, she opened her eyes, finding herself looking into Rafe's very satisfied expression.

"We were meant to be one, Ari," he said as he dropped down and gently caressed her lips.

"There has never been a problem with us in this department, Rafe. It doesn't mean anything," she replied. She didn't regret her decision to have sex with him again, but she needed to remember it was only sex.

"That's where you're wrong, Ari. What we have is beyond unusual, and beyond wonderful. I've never found so much pleasure with anyone else. I needed to change the sex, control it, master the woman to find any enjoyment. With you, all I need is one look, one taste, one touch. You turn my blood to fire, make me see only you and the starry night that you create. We *are* good together, and I will prove that to you."

Ari saw the truth in his eyes and felt a stirring of hope inside of her. Yet that was a dangerous emotion to be feeling right now. It could end up causing her to crash so hard that she'd never recover.

When he kissed her again, Ari thrust those thoughts aside. She would take her one night with him. She would enjoy it. Tomorrow, she would allow herself to think.

CHAPTER TWENTY-FOUR

Lia

"We need to go back to the beach. There are too many uninhabited islands out here, and there is no way that anyone will find us if we are hidden in this cave," Shane said.

Lia didn't want to leave their cave. They'd been there for two days, only venturing out to find food and materials for burning. Other than that, they'd made a lot of love and talked for hours on end.

She felt as if she knew Shane, as if he were a part of her now. She'd been so blind to the man he was, but then he'd been blind to her, as well. One could learn a lot about a person when no one else was around, and she was glad they'd finally opened up to each other.

A quiet confidence seemed to whisper to her heart that they would be OK. Maybe it was nothing more than feeling a kinship for the only other person on a deserted island, but she didn't think so. She was in love with him. But could she trust those emotions?

"I love our little paradise," she said while he packed the tent. She was too unhappy about having to leave to want to make departure more inevitable.

"Well, look on the bright side. It may take them several more days, or even weeks, to find us," he said with a laugh as he took a survey of their area, making sure he had everything.

There weren't a lot of supplies left, and they needed everything they had. He was acting flippant about how long a rescue could take, but she knew he was concerned. The island had an abundance of fruit and nuts, but still, they weren't used to living in the wild, and they didn't have enough to make them comfortable for long.

"I can always hope it will be a few more days, at least," she said with a smile. And she did cherish that hope.

"I have to admit that I'm shocked, Lia. I would have never taken you for a wilderness girl. You enjoy the spas far too much."

"Oh, I still enjoy the spas, Shane. I just love all of this time one-on-one. I've never felt this satisfied and this happy in my life. A spa definitely can't satisfy me in the areas you do." She walked up to him and pulled his head down, kissing him deeply.

When he came up for air, he smiled. "Well, not the reputable spas, at least."

It took her a second to understand his meaning, and then she burst out laughing. "Which ones have you been hanging out in, Shane Grayson?" she asked with mock anger.

"Well…"

"Shane Grayson!" she said, horrified.

"I'm just kidding. I would never even think of entering a house of ill repute," he assured her a bit too earnestly.

She glared at him for a moment before deciding he'd only been trying to get a reaction from her.

"You've been all over the world. I'm sure you have done things that would shock most people," she said, worried about the women he had been with. One of the reasons she'd been so leery of starting up with him again is because he was a known playboy. What if he did have women waiting for him in every port on every continent?

She knew she couldn't handle that. Lia didn't share well with others.

"Hey, it was a stupid joke," he said as he lifted her chin. "I promise you that my life is a lot more fictionalized than everybody believes. Yes, I've dated a number of women, but not as many as you might think. I've never been in love before — never even thought about getting married. That has always terrified me. Now, it doesn't so much."

Lia looked up at him in shock at his words. He wasn't actually proclaiming his love or offering marriage, but it looked as if he was setting the groundwork for just that.

It was too soon. She felt panic rise. What if he wanted too much too fast? She knew she didn't want to lose him all over again, but she couldn't just jump in blind. They needed more time.

"Lia, where'd you go?" he asked softly.

"I'm here. I just — this cave — well, yeah, the cave is starting to suffocate me," she said, her chest feeling compressed. Maybe this was her first panic attack. She hoped it was nothing worse than that.

"Lia…" She knew he didn't believe her, but she couldn't talk about this now.

"Let's just go, Shane. I'll feel better when we get back out into the sun," she said, her voice unusually high as she tried to mask her growing agitation.

He looked at her for several heartbeats, then gave her a soft, almost sad smile, before turning around and looking at the cave once more.

"I hate to leave, but I do want to get back to the beach. We need to prepare a large area where we can light a fire that can be seen from far away," he said in a falsely happy tone as he tried to hide his confusion. Then he walked over, bent down and nuzzled her neck.

"Thank you, Shane," she said. She was grateful he'd let the subject drop. This was where she needed to be with him for now, right in his arms, where she felt safe and cherished. They didn't need to worry about tomorrow or the next day — not yet. The sun would set and then rise again, bringing them a new day. It was inevitable. There was plenty of time to worry when there was something to worry about.

"I will cook you a spectacular seafood dinner on the beach with a nice fire and all-you-can-drink fruit juice," he said, trying to pull her from her funk.

"A romantic seafood dinner on the beach. Why, Shane Grayson, you just earned some extra brownie points," she said, giving him a kiss before moving through the entrance of the cave and walking outside.

Lia looked back, having to fight a slight tightening in her throat as the cave got farther away. She wasn't a crier, and she wanted to kick herself for feeling that weak emotion right then. It was just that she couldn't remember ever being happier than she had been during the past few days. Shane was incredible, and their time together — interruption free and distraction free — had

been just what her soul had needed. It felt different being with him now. But even as they moved toward the
beach, a little of that feeling was beginning to fade.

She was frightened that the farther they moved
away from their special place of bliss, the less chance
they'd have of making it together once they were saved.

She knew they needed to get rescued, but she really
did hope it would take just a little more time. Selfishly,
she wanted Shane all to herself. She'd been such a fool
to waste so much energy on fighting him. It was un-
believable that it had taken a shipwreck for her to see
what she'd been missing these last couple of years.

The two of them walked down the path back to the
beach, reaching the white sands in about half an hour,
since they were now familiar with the island, and knew
the fastest routes to take. The sun was high in the sky,
and as they scanned the water, there wasn't a boat in
sight. Lia felt a bit of relief, but a little panic as well.

Her feelings were seesawing wildly. What if they
weren't ever found? The past few days it hadn't seemed
so frightening, but she'd heard stories of people being
lost for ten years before a rescue, their families having
moved on, burying the memory of their lost loved ones
on the assumption they were dead, and continuing on
with their lives.

She knew her parents and her siblings wouldn't give
up, but the thought was rather daunting.

"They will find us, Lia." Shane wrapped his arms
around her.

"I know. It's just easier to forget we're stranded
when we're by that pristine pool of water. Being here
with the vast ocean before us makes our circumstances
that much more real," she said, holding on to his hands

as they rested on her stomach.

"You know your brother. He will move heaven and earth to find you. If he has to call out the Italian Coast Guard to search every island out here, he will. Hell, he'd try to hire the United States National Guard to do it. There won't be a single expense that he will spare. There's no way he will think you are resting at the bottom of the ocean. He can't give up. It's just not in him to do so."

Shane's words were helping to calm her.

"Thank you, Shane. I know I was teasing about us staying out here forever, but seeing the ocean is quite frightening. It just seems like it would be so hard for anyone to find us, especially since nobody knew you were coming here."

"That was stupid of me, and selfish. I'm sorry that I put you in so much danger," he replied, his tone full of remorse.

"If I hadn't been such a stubborn fool, you wouldn't have needed to go to such extreme measures," she told him, generously taking a share of the blame.

"I don't know how you originally fell for me, Lia, but I am eternally grateful," he said; he turned her around in his arms and kissed her lips.

"Me, too," she said when he pulled back.

"We won't get the fire pit built if you don't stop tempting me with your kisses," he said.

She just gazed at him with her eyebrow raised. Men! He was the one who'd been wanting to play. OK, she'd admit she wasn't doing anything to stop him.

They worked side by side the rest of the afternoon building a giant fire pit and getting their camp ready. As they settled in for the night, Lia lay in Shane's arms, wondering whether this would be their last night lost at sea — well, lost on a deserted island in the middle of the sea.

It would be good to be rescued, but the worry of what would come next wouldn't leave her troubled mind. She wanted to stay with him, get to know him, learn more about his life. But was she ready for what he wanted? Were they at the same place in their lives? Or were they bound to have only a day or a few days together, and then go their separate ways?

She just didn't know. Falling asleep wasn't easy, but finally she drifted off, Shane's heartbeat sounding in her ear.

CHAPTER TWENTY-FIVE

Rachel

"We're so very glad to have you here, Ms. Palazzo. I hope you will enjoy working for the embassy."

"Thank you. I've gone through all of the materials and feel I'm ready to do this job well. I'm excited to be here," she answered her new boss, Mr. Romano.

It had been only a few days since she'd slipped from Ian's room, and she couldn't believe the lingering ache that leaving him had left inside her. When she'd turned to look back at the room one last time, she'd paused, feeling an overwhelming need to run back to Ian's bed and wait for him for just a little bit longer. Knowing she was being foolish, she'd shut the door with a final click and walked away, not allowing herself to turn around again.

She'd been with the man for a mere week, but it was a week she'd never forget. There had just been something so magnetic about him. And the sex. Oh, the sex had been out of this world.

It was too bad she'd experienced something so

spectacular at such a young age. She had a feeling it would be hard to find it again. But she had no interest, really, in looking for it right now. She was on a mission — a mission to prove she wasn't a little girl anymore, to prove she was a responsible adult.

Her new boss left her in her cubicle, not even an office, with a ton of forms and documents that a monkey could take care of. It was almost ridiculous.

So here she sat at the U.S. embassy in Italy, behind a desk, wearing a respectable outfit, and she was bored out of her mind. She'd be handling a lot of paperwork in the back, not even getting to visit with people, but just stuck behind a desk.

That's what grown-ups do, she reminded herself. Not every job was full of glamour and mystery. She needed to accept that. If she were to run home just because she was bored, she'd be proving to everyone that she hadn't grown up, at all. That was unacceptable.

No. She would do her job, and on the weekends she would just have as much fun as possible. Explore the beaches of Italy, travel to nearby countries, and meet new people. It had been a while since she'd connected with people she knew in this part of the world, but she was sure a few phone calls would have her reuniting with longtime friends.

The only problem was that they were all upper-class friends, friends whose idea of fun was to attend lavish parties and rub shoulders with only the wealthy. At one time that had been enough for her, but she was bored with the very idea.

She had changed. She wanted to be just a regular person, live on her salary alone, and make a life for herself just as her brother did. OK, so he made billions, but who was counting?

Halfway through the day her phone rang and she picked it up with relief.

"How are you settling in, Rachel?"

Rachel smiled at the worried tone of her brother's voice. Even if he was slightly — OK, a lot — overbearing, she adored him.

"It's wonderful here," she lied, putting as much enthusiasm in her voice as she could muster.

"Then why are you lying?"

She'd never been a good liar. Rafe was thousands of miles away and could still hear the boredom in her voice. She'd have to work on her acting.

"I'm not fibbing, Rafe. I am just very busy now, and don't have time for personal calls," she said a bit haughtily, though she didn't really want to get off the phone.

"Have it your way. I'm making a trip that way in a couple of weeks. Make sure you pencil me in for lunch."

"Of course I will. We can swing over and visit with Lia," she said, excited at the thought. Her sister wasn't too far away, but on a nearby island while working on her resort project.

"I haven't heard from Lia in several days. I'm beginning to grow concerned," he said at the mention of their sister's name.

"I'm sure she's fine, Rafe. You know that Lia and I can take care of ourselves perfectly well," Rachel told him.

"It's not like her. She usually returns my calls. If I don't hear from her in the next couple of days, then I'll have to move up my trip."

Lia would kill him if he started treating her like a kid again. Rachel decided that she'd better change the subject. Lia would owe her big later.

"Have you gotten Ari to speak to you yet?" That would get his hackles up. Rachel loved Ari even more for her ability to resist her big brother. Rachel didn't normally like the women Rafe dated, but she'd bonded instantly with Ari, and she'd been sad when the two of them had broken up.

But she had supported her friend, especially knowing what an ass and a tyrant Rafe could be. Ari was too good a person to deal with that. Rachel did hope the two of them could eventually work it out, but the more time that passed, the more she doubted a happy ending was in store.

"Not that it's any of your business, but we have spoken," he replied smugly.

"From what I hear, you are stalking her in the classroom," she replied lightly.

"I just chose to take a history class. That isn't stalking," he said. "And how do you know? Are you gossiping about me?"

"Always, Rafe. That's what girls do best. Plus, according to Ari, you came in and asked her on a date in front of the whole class and then refused to leave. She also said your homework leaves something to be desired." Rachel loved having the upper hand with her big brother — a guy who always tried to be in control.

"That is nonsense. I don't fail at anything. My homework has been impeccable," he countered, making Rachel laugh out loud. Of course he'd ignored her other comments.

"OK. Sure. Fine. But I think I'll believe Ari on this one."

"When did you speak to her?" He was trying to

sound casual, but not quite pulling it off.

"We speak at least a couple of times a week."

"Since when?" Rafe blurted out.

Rachel knew he was surprised to be out of the loop with something that was going on in his family.

"Since forever. Just because you were a fool and broke her heart didn't mean that I was going to end our friendship. I really like Ari," Rachel said.

"I knew you still spoke to her, but I didn't realize it was so much. You could have told me."

"Ari didn't want you to know. I respected what she wanted," Rachel said.

"I'm your brother," he reminded her.

As if she needed reminding. Rafe wasn't someone you could forget, whether you were related to him or not.

"And I love you to pieces, but I don't think I could stand dating you, Rafe. You are arrogant, pigheaded, and domineering. I would have knocked you out on the first date," she told him pleasantly.

"I don't know why I bother calling if you are just going to insult me," he grumbled.

"Because you love me more than anything. Just like I love you. Don't worry; I have faith that you will someday pull your head out. I hope to have Ari for my sister-in-law. I adore her, which is really something because I've despised every other woman you've ever been with. They were nothing more than puppets for you to play with."

"I wouldn't go that far, Rachel. And I am considered a great catch," he told her stiffly.

"Ha," said Rachel, starting to giggle.

"I have a conference call in a few minutes, so I have

to run. If you hear from Lia, tell her to call me immediately," he said. He was obviously unhappy with what
Rachel had to say, but also worried about Lia. He might
be overbearing, but he did love his sisters.

At the genuine worry in Rafe's tone, Rachel softened. Was it really so bad to have a family member
worry so much about you? No. She and Lia were lucky
to have such a good big brother.

"I will try to get ahold of her today. I love you,
Rafe."

"Love you too, squirt."

Rachel hung up the phone and looked at the clock.
It was only one. She had four hours to go. She just
hoped she could make it. The worst part was that it was
Monday. Her week had just begun.

"Hi, Rachel, just checking up to see how you are
doing." Rachel looked up to find Harold standing in her
doorway, and it made her smile.

He'd only been at the embassy for a short time, too,
and seemed like a nice enough guy. It felt like he was
flirting with her, since he always seemed to be around,
but she just couldn't tell.

"It's another day," she responded, trying her best to
give him a positive smile.

"How about we grab a bite to eat after work? We
can compare notes about who has the more boring of
the jobs," he said with a wink.

It was too bad that Rachel wasn't attracted to him.
Still, she wanted to make new friends and this was a
great place to start.

"I'd love to, Harold. I'll meet you out front," she said,
trying to be friendly without being too friendly. She
hoped she was pulling it off. With a wave, he disap-

peared and Rachel looked back down at her computer. It was now only five after one. The day wasn't dragging out any less slowly.

As she began responding to an email message, she reminded herself once again that she was a grown-up. If she told herself this enough, maybe her day wouldn't drag on so painfully.

Somehow she doubted it.

CHAPTER TWENTY-SIX

Lia

LIA stretched her arms out groggily and smiled. As usual, the tent was too hot — the bright morning sun blazed through the open flaps, and Shane's body raised the temperature to supernova levels. But, she didn't care. She felt content, happy, and ready to face another day on their deserted island.

She slipped from Shane's embrace, getting away for once without waking him, and moved outside the tent, enjoying the warm rays shining down on her. Deciding to take a swim in the now calm ocean water, she stripped off her clothes and walked in.

By the time she emerged, she found Shane sitting on the beach with a smile and breakfast of fresh fruit and the last of their trail mix.

"Now that's a sight I could be happy to start my day off with for the rest of my life," he said as he stood and met her at the water's edge.

Lia's heart stuttered at his words. She knew he was simply flirting, but the thought of spending every morning with him until the end of time sounded like perfection to her. She didn't know how she was going to go back to the real world when this was over.

Her mornings would never be the same again.

"You're a pretty great sight yourself," Lia murmured as she came up to him and ran her wet hands along his bare chest.

Yowza. All solid muscle covered by tight, dark skin. She could touch and taste him every single day and still not get enough. Their bodies fit together perfectly.

At the instant lust filling Shane's eyes, Lia almost forgot about her hunger; only the growl of her stomach reminded her that it had needs, too. She decided that men shouldn't be allowed to have shirts. The only garment they needed to wear was low-slung trousers.

There was nothing sexier, in her humble opinion, than a man in only a pair of semi-loose pants. Bare chest and bare feet. Yum.

Looking even more delectable with his couple of days' growth of facial hair, he made her want to drag him to the sand. They'd made love so many times, it was almost ridiculous, but she wanted more and more and more no matter how much she was getting. She was becoming a nymphomaniac.

As his hands reached around her, she felt her nipples instantly harden in anticipation of his touch. The heck with food. She was hungry for something else entirely.

Shane dropped to his knees, the water lapping at her feet and soaking his thin pants. Lifting his hands up, he cupped her breasts, holding them gently as he gazed upon her.

"You are so beautiful, Lia. Seeing you come out of

the ocean completely bare is the most erotic sight I've ever witnessed — you are my Aphrodite, my goddess of love. No, don't laugh, my lovely Lia. I don't think I will ever tire of looking upon your perfection." He leaned forward and ran his tongue over one of her nipples, making her stomach drop and her legs shake.

She gripped his head to keep herself from falling over.

Moving to her other side, he circled her nipple with his tongue before sucking it into his mouth and gently nipping the sensitive peak. Gasping with pleasure, Lia wobbled before him. No problem. She wasn't going to remain on her feet for much longer.

Fire raced through her veins and her heart thundered behind her breasts. Fisting her hands in his hair, she tugged him closer, wanting more of what he was giving.

When he reached down and thrust two fingers inside of her wet heat, her body responded instantly, shooting her over the edge and making her shake with pleasure. As the last tremor died down, she sank into the sand in front of him, grasping his head and kissing him for all she was worth.

"Thank you," she whispered as her tongue traced the edges of his lips.

"It was my pleasure," he said with a sigh as he caressed her back, not in a hurry to find his own release.

"No, it was all mine. Now, it's your turn," she told him as she pushed him backward.

Catching him off guard, Shane fell against the sand, the gentle waves lapping at his legs. She grabbed the waistband of his pants and tugged. Shane lifted up, making the impossible chore easier, and soon she was looking upon his beautifully engorged erection.

"You are so breathtaking, Shane," she said in awe.

With the sun shining down on his perfect body, she lifted her hand and circled it around his straining member, rubbing slowly up and down, delighted when he groaned his approval.

"Ah, Lia" was all he managed to say.

Kneeling before him, Lia bent down and ran her tongue along his stomach, enjoying the touch of salt on her taste buds. Shane quivered beneath her open kisses, his stomach flexing as her tongue followed the hard planes of his abs.

"I could taste you all day," she sighed.

"Damn, Lia. I can't even think when you are doing that. What you do to me should be a crime," he groaned, his head thrown back as she continued rubbing her hand up and down his shaft, using its natural lubrication to help her glide more easily.

"We'll see exactly how far I can take you," she teased him as she moved further down his body, her head poised above his hardness.

"No, Lia," he said, reaching for her head.

"It's my turn, Shane. You just lie back and enjoy."

She didn't give him any more time to protest; her mouth descended and she covered the top of his erection with her warm mouth. His body jerked from the sand as her tongue ran along the sensitive head of his arousal.

He cried out when she dipped low, taking as much of him into her mouth as she could before retreating, then pushing back down again.

As the water lapped at their feet, she found her rhythm, gripping the bottom of his shaft tightly in her fist while her mouth moved quickly up and down him.

"Lia, you have to stop," he cried out, but he wasn't doing anything to stop her.

She quickened her pace, wanting to feel his pleasure explode on her tongue and slide down her throat. She'd never allowed another man to do that, somehow thinking it was too intimate, too much.

She pushed as far as she could, feeling his thick shaft enter her throat and fighting against her body's desire to push it back out. Then she felt warmth rush against her throat as Shane tensed.

"Lia!" he cried as his body shook and he groaned deeply. She pushed against him, taking him in just a bit farther as he released his pleasure inside her mouth, his erection pulsing between her lips.

When she couldn't breathe, she moved slowly back up his staff, taking just a moment to suck on the tip as he shuddered beneath her and she tasted his salty essence.

When she'd drained him of his release, she climbed up his glorious body and sat on his hips, sinking his arousal inside her folds. He was still hard, and she wanted to enjoy him until he wasn't.

"I can't…" he murmured as she began moving up and down his shaft, pressure and passion building inside her almost instantly. Feeling him let go so completely had turned her on beyond anything in her wildest imagination.

Knowing she'd been the reason that he lost control had made her feel powerful and sexy, and she needed to find release.

"Yes, you can," she cried as she moved faster, hitting his hips as she moved her body, glorying in the way he filled her so completely.

Shane groaned and his eyes widened in shock. He gripped her hips to steady her as he began thrusting upward quickly, pounding hard against her backside as he sank deep inside her.

"Yes, Lia," he growled, and his speed picked up. Sweat beaded on his chest and brow as he closed his eyes and thrust inside her. Pressure soared until she couldn't take anymore. Then with a cry together, they both shook with their own powerful releases.

Lia collapsed against Shane's slick chest, her breathing ragged, her body feeling torn in half from the pleasure.

"I can't believe…" he began.

"You are one hell of a virile, sexy man. I can believe anything," she said, kissing his damp neck.

"I hope to hell we never get saved," he murmured as his hands slid along her back.

She agreed with him. If she had this island with Shane for the rest of her life, she would be a very happy woman.

When they both regained an ounce of energy, Shane stood, then lifted Lia and carried her into the warm ocean where they cooled down before coming in for some much needed food.

They didn't know it, but their time was almost up.

CHAPTER TWENTY-SEVEN

Rafe

"Mr. Palazzo, it seems that Shane Grayson's ship got caught in a storm four days ago and he hasn't been heard from since. It appears that one of your sisters, Ms. Lia Palazzo, was onboard with him."

"What? Why in the hell am I just finding out about this now? Has a search party been formed? What were their last coordinates?"

Rafe's heart raced as he listened on the other end of the line. His sister and his best friend had been missing for four days and he was just now getting word. He barely contained his rage and fear as he tried to focus.

"We are just now receiving the information, sir. Apparently when the workers couldn't find them, it took a while before someone had information that Mr. Grayson and Ms. Palazzo had left on the boat to pick up supplies. They never showed up. The day they left, a large storm hit the area."

"Shane is extremely experienced on a boat. He would have seen the storm and gotten to shelter. I want a map of the islands, and I want search crews sent out immediately. I'm on my way."

Rafe hung up the phone and glared at it. After taking a calming breath, he dialed his pilot, then told his secretary he was leaving and to cancel everything. There was only one quick stop to make before he boarded his jet.

Pulling up to Ari's building, he sprinted to her apartment and hammered on the thick wooden door. He could have called, but he needed to see her for just a moment. She calmed him, and he didn't know how long this might take. It might be weeks before she was in his arms again.

She hadn't returned his calls since their night together at the library, and that was three days before — three very long and unsatisfying days.

Ari opened the door, and her eyes narrowed in irritation, but one look at his face and she grew worried. If he thought he had it together, he was clearly mistaken.

"What's wrong, Rafe?" Her tone filled with concern, she lifted her hand and placed it on his arm.

"Lia is missing. She and Shane were on his yacht when a storm hit. No one knows where they are. I'm leaving for Italy now, but I wanted to let you know what is happening. I may be gone for a while."

Ari looked at him for several seconds in stunned disbelief. He knew how she felt. He was still in shock. Then, to his surprise, she grabbed his arm and pulled him inside her door.

"Give me ten minutes. I just need to grab a few clothes."

"What are you talking about?" he asked.

"I'm coming with you. Lia is my friend, one of my best friends, and I won't be able to stay behind. It would kill me, Rafe. I need to be out there searching for her."

She left the room before he could respond. He didn't know if he could handle the distraction of having Ari there, but on the other hand, she might be the only person alive who would also be able to keep him from melting down.

If they couldn't find Lia... No! That wouldn't happen. If something were terribly wrong, he would feel it in his gut. His sisters meant the world to him, and he would just know if something weren't right.

Shane had gotten them to safety, and the two of them were just waiting to be rescued. He was sure of it. His best friend would never let something happen to his sister. He'd die first.

That thought made Rafe's stomach clench. The world would be a much sadder place without his best friend in it. Shane was one of the few people who knew Rafe inside and out, who could talk him down when he was ready to explode, and whom Rafe could trust with his life.

Rafe couldn't lose one of his sisters, but he couldn't lose his best friend, either.

"I'm ready."

Rafe didn't say another word as he looked at Ari standing before him with determination, holding a duffel bag and her jacket. He simply took the bag from her and walked out her front door, waiting as she locked up.

He sat silently by in the back of the car as she made the necessary phone calls to have her class covered and her mail picked up. He could see her fright, but she was holding herself together well — much better than he was, it seemed.

Just having her there in the car with him was somehow giving him the strength not to completely lose it.

"She will be fine, Rafe. I can feel it. If she's with Shane, he will protect her. There's no way he'd ever let something happen to her. Shane can be a fool, but I have no doubt that he truly cares about Lia. He's just not the wisest for ticking her off," Ari said with a crooked smile.

"Yes, you and my sisters can certainly carry a grudge," Rafe said, sending her a pointed look.

"Yes, we can. It's best you remember that."

"Believe me, I remember well," Rafe replied as they pulled up to his private jet.

Rafe escorted Ari up the stairs, then spoke to his pilot for a few moments before the doors closed and the giant machine began slowly moving forward.

He should be thrilled to have Ari all to himself, but as he leaned back, all he could think about was his sister, who was most likely lost and frightened. He found himself near panic, which was a state he never thought he'd be in.

He accepted a stiff drink from his flight attendant when they reached cruising altitude, but it didn't help much. There didn't seem to be anything that could at this point. Refusing a meal, he couldn't even muster up the energy to speak to Ari.

When he felt Ari climb into his lap and hold him, he didn't say a word. He just clung on tight and let her be his strength. His hands automatically came up and began stroking her back. The feel of her resting in his arms did the trick.

He felt his heart begin to slow its frantic beat, and his muscles relax gradually. He'd been wrong — it seemed he could be comforted. He'd just needed his other half — Ari.

He knew that Ari and his sisters were close, but until now, he hadn't quite realized how close. He was glad to have Ari with him, glad she was his rock in this moment. It just underlined what a fool he'd been to treat her so poorly.

Dammit, he would prove to her that they were meant to be together. Right now, he had to focus on his sister, but they would have a long flight back home — all alone — and then his focus would be solely on Ari, because Lia and Shane would be safe and Rafe would be able to breathe again.

"They'll find them both, Rafe. I know it."

He knew she was right.

CHAPTER TWENTY-EIGHT

Ari

Several hours into the flight, and more than a few drinks later, Ari looked up in surprise to find Rafe sending a glare her way. "Are you going to just pretend that what happened between us didn't happen?"

She hadn't really thought this trip through. All she knew was that Lia was missing and she had to be there to help find her. It never occurred to her that she'd be locking herself inside Rafe's jet for the next ten hours.

Maybe after the library incident, he was just assuming that everything would go back to the way it had been before. That she would just be his very high-priced call girl. If he was, he was going to be severely disappointed.

"Yes, that's exactly what I'm going to do," she said before turning away.

"That's not a very mature attitude, Ari."

"Rafe, with Lia and Shane not found yet, I don't want to fight with you. I want us to be there for each other. Can we do this afterward, after my friend is found?" she asked in exasperation.

"I need to get my mind off this, Ari. It's driving me insane to even think about it. I can't just sit here in this jet with you and pretend I don't still want you. I can't continue playing in my head all the scenarios of what could have happened to Shane and Lia, either. So, the bottom line is that we are in this jet for the next six hours together, so we need to hash it out. We need to come to a solution about us."

"There *is* no us, Rafe. Yes, I still want you. I'm human. I caved. That doesn't mean I want to dive back into a dysfunctional relationship with you. It just means that I haven't been laid in two years and my body went into meltdown mode."

Rafe froze, and she wondered what he was thinking now. She thought over her words and hadn't said anything too shocking. Yes, she enjoyed sex. Big deal!

"You haven't been with another man since me?"

Oops, that's what she'd admitted to. She hadn't wanted to do that. No, she hadn't been with another man, but not because she was in love with Rafe. Well, at least, she hoped that wasn't why.

It was just that after being with someone like Rafe, someone who knew how to please a woman so fully, she hadn't managed to find a man yet who could set off fireworks inside her. The men she'd kissed had stirred not a single atom of desire within her. Not even an electron.

If she could barely stand to kiss them, the thought of their hands touching her body was downright repulsive. There was no way she'd tell Rafe any of that, of course. He would have her on her back faster than she could blink. That wouldn't get the two of them anywhere — well, nowhere but immensely satisfied.

She had to remind herself that the pleasure lasted for only so long before she had to deal with the repercussions of guilt and longing for a man she couldn't keep.

"That's none of your business, Rafe. I don't ask you about your conquests, and I don't expect you to ask me about mine," she said sternly.

The grin spreading across his face took her breath away. Damn! When he smiled, he was spectacular.

"You haven't gotten over us at all, have you, Ari? All of this is just your way of protecting yourself. You are smart. I understand what you're doing. I treated you terribly. But I will admit that it pleases me that no other man has touched you."

"I didn't say that!"

Ari's cheeks flushed in her frustration. She knew speaking to him was a bad idea. She should have just taken a commercial plane to Italy, and not subjected herself to ride with Rafe across the ocean. She'd rather have been sitting in economy between a drunken fat guy and the nonstop snorer, with a screaming baby right behind her, to boot. It would be less torturous.

"Why are you getting so upset, Ari?"

"I'm not upset!" she shouted. At the stupid grin on his face, she made herself calm down, taking a few deep breaths. "I'm not upset," she repeated more calmly.

"Why don't you join me over here so we can speak without calling across to each other?" he offered, patting the couch he was leaning back on. "I need for you to climb into my lap again," he finished.

"I don't think so," she said with a huff.

"Don't you trust yourself, Ari?"

"Of course I trust myself. It's you I don't trust, Rafe."

"I can be a gentleman."

"Ha!" That was a good one.

"I brought the journal," he said as he pointed to his bag sitting next to him.

She should be worried about her friend. He should be worried about his sister. There shouldn't be this tension between the two of them.

"Now isn't the time," she said, though her eyes strayed to the bag.

"I've had it on me since the library. I just never took it out," he answered her unspoken question.

"Well, I'm worried about Lia. I couldn't concentrate on it," she told him.

"I'm worried about my sister, too, and my best friend. But, there's nothing we can do from up here. I have well over fifty boats out searching the water for them now along with several helicopters. They will be found. I guarantee it."

"What if you're wrong? What if their boat crashed and they are gone?" Though she'd been the one offering him comfort when he'd first shown up on her doorstep, now it was her turn to panic. She didn't want to voice the questions aloud, but her brain was firing on too many cylinders. Ari handled crisis excellently when it was first presented to her. But once she had time to think about it, she fell apart. It wasn't a trait she was proud of.

"I would know."

"How can you be so sure? You don't know, Rafe!"

"If my sister or Shane were gone, I would feel it. A piece of me would die with them. If they were gone, I couldn't help but know."

He was so self-assured, so confident, when just a

few hours earlier he had been the one tense and worried. She could still see the strain in his eyes, but she
also saw conviction. He had no doubt that Shane and
Lia would be rescued. Ari should feel a measure of relief
in his faith, but she was still afraid. She didn't have the
same faith as he did. After what she'd been through
with her mother — thank heavens Sandra was well
now! — she could never quite assume the best.

"I don't know…"

"They will be fine. I don't want to focus on that. I
can't do anything while we're in the air. So, I'd rather
focus on us."

"Do I have to repeat myself, Mr. Palazzo?" she asked
in her best schoolmarm voice. "There *is* no us."

"Oh, Ari, that is where you are wrong. There's been
an *us* from the moment you first walked into my office.
You caused my world to spin out of control, and it still
hasn't righted itself. I've just come to the conclusion that
I don't want it to be righted. I like it exactly the way it is
— with you by my side, spinning along with me."

"We're just going in circles, Rafe. I won't be a kept
woman ever again."

"Then how about you become my wife?"

Ari stared at him in confusion. She could have
sworn he'd just proposed to her, but she had to be hearing him wrong. There was no way he'd be such a fool as
to ask her to marry him — certainly not now.

"I must have misheard you," she said, sending a glare
his way.

"You didn't. You will become my wife. No, that
wasn't a proposal. When I propose, it will be done properly."

"You need mental help, Rafe," she said as she blew

out her breath in irritation.

"I only need you, Ari."

"I'm going to the bathroom."

She got up and practically ran to the back of the jet, where she locked herself inside the large bathroom, splashing cold water on her face. She couldn't go out there again. She couldn't face him.

Being with Rafe was like living in a tornado. Her world was flying out of control all around her, and she didn't know when she was going to land on solid ground again.

He was so sure of their future together — so confident. Could she be wrong? What if she caved in to him, and then things went back to the way they had been?

She wasn't normally this confused. She was strong and smart and could conquer the world. She needed to remember that or this flight was going to test her very sanity.

Finally walking back out to join Rafe, she looked in his eyes, and her heart fluttered and lurched. Oh, yes, this fight was going to be long.

CHAPTER TWENTY-NINE

Rafe

RAFE granted the poor woman a brief reprieve. Just as Ari returned to the cabin, dinner was being served, and his flight attendant acted as a temporary chaperone.

If Ari hadn't looked as if she were ready to fall over, he would have sent his employee away and resumed their discussion. But it was more than obvious that Ari needed food, and it wasn't fair of him to continue without giving her sustenance. It tore at him how tired she seemed — emotionally and physically.

He waited patiently while their table was set and hot food placed atop it.

"After you," he said as he stood and placed his hand on Ari's back.

She tensed, but allowed him to lead her to the table.

Pouring them each a glass of wine, he lifted his glass. "To the prompt rescue of Shane and Lia."

Ari hesitated only briefly before lifting her own glass and clinking it against his. Then she placed it to her lips and took a large swallow. "That is something I am more than happy to toast to," she told him with a slight smile.

She was quiet as she picked up her fork and began picking at her food. Anything she ate was better than nothing, he reasoned as he began working on his own meal. It wasn't the best he'd eaten, but it was something. Normally, he planned ahead and chose his menus. This had been an emergency, and he had to take what they kept at the ready.

Once the last of the food had been placed on the table, he dismissed his flight attendant, telling her to leave them for the rest of the flight. He wanted no more interruptions. The mess could be cleaned up later.

"I was at your graduation."

Ari looked up in surprise.

"My graduate ceremony?"

"Yes. You were glowing as you stood on that stage. I was very impressed, Ari. I knew you would do it, but it was still a thrill to see you standing there with such a smile of accomplishment on your face."

"I'm surprised you didn't approach me."

The look in her eyes suggested that she wouldn't have hated the idea. He had debated doing just that, but he had managed to stay back, just barely. He'd come because he'd had to be a part of her pomp and circumstance.

"I didn't want to ruin your special day. Your mother was there with her arm locked permanently around you, and I wanted you to bask in that. I thought my presence would take away some of your joy. Besides, I think my parents and sisters were on watch duty. They kept looking out at the audience. If I had tried to approach, they might have tackled me."

"They're your family, Rafe. Of course they wouldn't have," she said with a smile. It was such a relief for him to see it.

"You must not know them that well. My mother and sisters both lectured me endlessly about my losing you. They told me I was a fool."

"They are wise women." She smirked, but her cheeks were tinged with red.

"I told them I intend to have you back."

"That isn't your decision to make," she said, looking him deep in the eyes.

Her strength was an aphrodisiac. He could take her right there, and then do it again and again. Rafe knew he would never grow bored with Ari, never look at another woman after having her in his life. She was all he needed, plus some.

"You want me, Ari. It's in your eyes, in the way your body tenses when we are in the same room together. You want this just as badly as I do. I understand why you are suspicious of me, but don't let the past ruin our future. Yes, I made mistakes, and it's not easy for me to admit that, but I wasn't such a monster that I don't deserve your forgiveness. Isn't it clear that I've repented?"

He was laying his heart out there for her to do with what she wanted.

Ari looked at him for a long moment, as if trying to gauge whether he was speaking the truth or not. He had never been so honest, so open with anyone, and he hoped that she could see that.

"I think you mean what you say, Rafe. I believe you do care about me, but I don't believe you are able to change enough that we can make this work. You have chosen a lifestyle that is at odds with what I want. You choose to act in ways that aren't acceptable to me. Too much has happened that can't be fixed or forgotten. We can't make this work. We'd get back together, have some steaming sex, and then end up where we left off two years ago. My heart would be broken, and you'd be restless."

"Obviously, I haven't allowed you to know me well enough, Ari. I've told you before that once I make my mind up about something, though, I am sure in my decision. I've made my mind up that I can't live without you. I have tried force, and I have tried seduction. It seems neither is working. I will just have to find a better way."

To judge by the intake of her breath, he was getting through to her. Rafe leaned back but refused to release her gaze. She was his — she just didn't realize it yet.

* * * * *

Ari wanted to accept what Rafe was offering. Offering? Ha! Rafe didn't really offer anything. He demanded, he forced, he even cajoled on occasion. He didn't offer and he didn't ask.

Yes, he'd been better since coming back into her life, but he was still Rafe, still the domineering businessman with a kinky side that made her heart thunder beneath her breasts. The problem was that she did want him.

She'd been able to think of nothing else since he'd taken her in that dark library. Never again would she be able to study in any library without her heart racing and heat flooding her. One thing that Rafe would never be short on was charisma. He made her burn long after the passion had abated, long after she'd found exquisite release.

Was there any point in continuing this conversation? He wasn't going to listen to what she was telling him. He'd made up his mind that they'd be together, and he wouldn't accept anything less than that.

If she had still been angry, this would have been so much easier. She could have ignored him, or charged him with harassment. If she had felt nothing at all toward him, it would have been easier still. She could have pretended he was just a passing stranger — shrugged off the look in his eye, and the allure of his body.

But no, her traitorous heart and hormones had been all aflutter ever since he'd set foot inside her classroom. She wanted him with a desire that ran alongside the blood in her veins, and she still loved him, even after two years of trying to forget him, of trying to despise him.

"Right now, I'm so tired, I can't process any thoughts at all," she said, confusion seeming to hold sway among the myriad emotions she was feeling.

"I'm sorry. I know this has all been too much. I shouldn't push you right now," Rafe said as he reached out and took her hand, bringing it to his lips and gently kissing it before releasing her fingers.

Ari didn't know how to respond, didn't know what to do next. Her brain was too muddled at this point. The best thing would be for her to have a bit of time to rest; then, perhaps, if she woke up refreshed, she would be able to process all that he'd said, and figure out what she wanted to do next.

"I'm going to lie down," she said. She pushed the rest of her food away, stood up, and walked past him.

When he let her walk by, she was surprised. She'd

expected some kind of protest.

As she climbed beneath the covers of his comfortable guest bed, she shivered, the stress from the last week hitting her like a ton of textbooks. Thinking about the possibility of Lia being hurt only added to her body's tremors.

She was beyond the point of tears, beyond everything as she lay there in pain. It was all too much. When the bed shifted, she tensed, ready to flay Rafe alive.

"I just want to hold you, Ari. I can see that you're close to falling apart," Rafe whispered. He cradled her from behind, his hand coming over the top of her waist and pulling her against him.

She remained stiff as she tried to think of a suitably scathing retort. But she was so worn out, the words wouldn't come.

"I don't need you to hold me, Rafe. I'm fine." It would have sounded so much better if her teeth hadn't been chattering.

"We need each other right now. We can go back to a standoff when this is all over," he said, his breath rushing along her neck as he spoke. She'd sat there and comforted him when they'd first gotten on the jet and that had played havoc with her body. Allowing him to offer her reassurance and solace in this fashion didn't seem a particularly good idea.

Ari tried to resist his comforting, but as her body molded itself against his, the shaking stopped, and she began to relax. His hand gently glided along her stomach, making lazy circles on top of her shirt.

She felt warmth spread through her as his touch began to ignite a flame within. She didn't want that, even if her perfidious body had other ideas.

"Please, please don't wiggle your behind. I just want to hold you," he whispered, and she felt his hardness press against her backside.

Somehow, that relaxed her completely and she closed her eyes. It was insane, but she did feel safe in his arms; even though he was the one who'd caused so much of her pain, she still enjoyed the comfort only he seemed able to give.

For now, she couldn't think about it. For now, she just needed to sleep. When she woke, the day had to be better. It certainly couldn't get any worse.

CHAPTER THIRTY

Lia

"Do you see that?"

"Yes," Shane told Lia. Neither of their voices was excited — just accepting.

In the distance, they'd spotted a helicopter. Both of them had known it was only a matter of time before Rafe found them. They were sure there was an army out searching — literally. The two of them could have been missing for a year and Rafe still wouldn't give up. That was just who he was, and one of the reasons they loved him so much.

"Should we light the fire?" Lia asked with some sadness, a real question in her tone.

Shane looked at Lia with shock. Neither of them was ready to go, but they couldn't make their family suffer while wondering whether they were alive or dead. Pure passion had its limits.

"I love being here with you, too, Lia, but just because we're going back to the real world doesn't mean that anything will change." He placed his finger beneath her chin and lifted her head so she had no choice but to gaze into his eyes.

"That's exactly what it means, Shane. We've been relying on each other here. We won't have to do that when we get back to our lives. Reality will set in, and…" She didn't know how to complete her sentence.

"And I will still want to spend every waking second with you."

"It's not that, Shane. You hurt me. Out here, none of that mattered, but even now, as the helicopter draws nearer, it's jumping to the forefront of my mind," she said, not wanting to sugarcoat the words. He needed to know how she felt.

"I screwed up, Lia, and it cost me two years' time of being with you. Hell, I screwed up by resisting you so long before that. I'll earn your trust again. You'll see."

The chopper was now close enough that they heard a faint whirring and thudding in the distance. Shane released her and moved over to their fire pit. Looking back at her for only a second, he lit the dry tinder. It immediately went up in flames and the wood caught fire.

Once the blaze was hot enough, he threw on the greenery, causing a wall of smoke to lift high in the air. The search parties couldn't miss their signal.

Lia held out her hand as he walked back to her and they faced the chopper in the distance. It didn't take long for it to make a beeline in their direction.

As the machine approached their island and then began to set down, Lia had to fight tears. It was insane. She didn't cry. She wasn't one of those girls who broke down — she was strong and independent. She didn't need a man to complete her life.

When she wanted something, she wasn't afraid to take it. Coming from a loving home and having great parents and siblings, she'd learned to be strong and brave, and right now she hated herself just a little bit. She hated that she was surrendering to what she considered the ultimate in weakness.

Her happiness was not dependent upon anyone else. By allowing these tears, allowing this feeling of frailty, she was letting herself down — she was depending too much on Shane's love.

Her warnings to herself were doing her no good as the large helicopter landed, the propellers spinning, whipping up the sand around them. Neither Shane nor Lia budged from their spot. They just continued clinging to each other.

With a firm resolve, Lia pushed down the tears, refusing to let them fall as the chopper door opened and a man stepped out, sporting a huge grin as he rushed over to the two of them.

"Are you Lia Palazzo?"

She looked at him with a raised eyebrow. Seriously? Were there that many stranded women on these islands with a brother who would tear up the entire ocean to find her? Did he honestly just ask who she was?

"Yes," she finally answered when she knew she could do it with a straight face. The man's smile faded as he looked from her to Shane. He'd probably assumed they would be ecstatic to be found.

He'd assumed wrong.

"Um…well…if you want to come with me…" he said, obviously at a loss for words.

"Let me get the bag," Shane said as his hand trailed down her back, falling off at the bottom of her spine.

"Thank you," Lia said to the rescuer, who held out his arm, appearing afraid that she might turn around and run back into the safety of the island. No. She wouldn't do that. Rafe would have no problem sending the entire army after her now that he had her location. She was sure the pilot was calling in now, ending the search and notifying her family that she'd been found.

Her heart broke a little for Shane because he had no one to be notified or rejoice besides her family.

As she reached the helicopter, she turned back toward Shane as he jogged to her, and something inside her tore open. All of their talks, all that he'd said to her finally hit, and when it did, it hit with the force of a tropical storm in the waters around Italy.

She now realized why he'd done what he'd done, and she was filled with emotion as she once again fought tears.

Ah…yes…

Of course he had gone to Rafe. Shane had nobody he could count on outside of Rafe. He couldn't risk losing that friendship, not for anything, not even for love, especially a new love, an untested, unsure romance… Rafe was his family, his brother, the one person who had been there for him when the rest of the world had forgotten he was there, when his parents had done worse than abandon him — had made him feel he shouldn't even be alive.

As Shane reached her, she threw her arms around him, the wind from the chopper blades making the sand swirl around them and whipping her hair into reckless spirals.

"I'm sorry, Shane. I'm so sorry," she said, and she leaned forward and took his lips, trying to convey her feelings, her love for him, through the kiss.

He looked puzzled for a moment, but he didn't hesitate to pull her close and kiss her back. His tongue chased hers into her mouth, his hands spread across her back, and the two of them existed inside their very own bubble.

Why couldn't she have figured this out sooner? Why must they have an audience when all she wanted to do was please him, love him, show him that he could count on her?

"Um, Ms. Palazzo, we need to be leaving."

Lia wasn't happy about the interruption, but she reluctantly released Shane and turned to the pilot.

"Of course," she said, holding tight to Shane's hand as he assisted her inside.

She sat beside Shane and looked out the window as their piece of paradise disappeared. Neither of them said a word as the island became nothing but a dot on the horizon. Shane had lost his yacht, and they'd been stranded for five nights, but it hadn't felt as if they were. It had felt like a vacation, the best one she'd ever been on.

"This is only the beginning, Lia," Shane said as she leaned her head against his shoulder and fought the overwhelming emotions vying for a foothold inside of her.

Hope rose in her chest. Maybe he was right. Maybe it was a first step, just the beginning of a brand new chapter in their lives.

CHAPTER THIRTY-ONE

Rafe

RAFE rushed forward as Lia and Shane stepped off the helicopter. He might have appeared confident when he'd spoken to Ari, but he'd been terrified. When he'd climbed into the small bed and held her, it had been as much for himself as for her.

His sisters meant everything to him, and he couldn't imagine what the world would be like without them in it. It would be an unforgivable sin for life to go on as normal if something were to happen to either of them.

"Don't you ever do that to me again," he said as he pulled Lia into his arms and squeezed her tight.

"I'm just fine, Rafe. Thank you for finding us," she said, looking up with shining eyes. He was too relieved at having her safe to realize how off her reaction to being rescued was.

Rafe finally released her, then grabbed Shane and gave him a bear hug, surprising both himself and Shane. They weren't normally the type of guys to hug, but Rafe had been truly worried about his friend. Losing him was something else that was not to be borne.

"I thought I was never going to see you again!" Shane was barely able to brace himself for impact as Rachel came flying toward them, knocking him out of her way as she grabbed hold of Lia and held on so tight, he was sure Lia couldn't breathe.

Though the two got into their fights, and they might have wanted to rip each other apart on occasion, they truly did love one another. Rafe felt terrible that it had taken him so long to get to Italy, leaving Rachel all alone in her panic over her missing sister. He'd never once considered that Lia or Shane could be dead — well, maybe once — but he was afraid of how long it might take to locate them.

"I'm fine, Rachel. I promise."

"Don't ever do that again. Do you hear me?" Rachel gasped as she let Lia go, then turned toward Shane and wrapped her arms around him. "You either, Shane!"

"It wasn't like we had a lot of choice in the matter," Lia said with a laugh.

"How can you laugh about this? Are you crazy? Did you get hurt out there? Did you have anything to eat? Could you find clean water? Were there snakes? Poisonous berries? Wild animals? Rafe, we need to take them right to the hospital," Rachel insisted, not giving either Lia or Shane time to answer her rapidly fired questions.

"We're fine, Rachel. We had plenty to eat and drink," Lia said. "None of it fatal, as you can see."

"No. Rachel is right. I want you to be looked over," Shane interrupted, finally able to say something over the frantic voices of the two sisters.

"I'm fine. I don't need a doctor," Lia insisted, shooting a warning look Shane's way. Of course, he ignored it.

"You hit your head twice, Lia. I want you to go to the hospital."

All eyes turned toward Lia as if they were expecting to see blood shooting from her scalp at Shane's declaration. Her vicious glare let him know he was in major trouble for spilling those beans. Logically, she knew it couldn't hurt to get looked at, but she just wanted to lie down in a real bed — with Shane next to her.

She grumbled beneath her breath, but she knew she'd lost. If she refused to go to the doctor, they'd pester her to the point that she'd need a psychiatrist.

"Fine. But, let's get it over with. Are Mom and Dad coming?"

"Yes, I was able to get ahold of them, and they're on their way in now," Rafe answered.

Lia sighed with relief. Even as an adult, she found it nice to have a mom and dad when things went terribly wrong. No matter how strong she wanted them to all believe she was, she'd gone through quite an ordeal.

Rafe turned when he realized that Ari hadn't said a word. He found her standing back, a sweet smile on her face, but also appearing uncomfortable. He took a step toward her, wondering what was wrong, why she wasn't by his side. Before he had a chance, Lia yelled.

"Ari! I didn't know you were here!" Wasting no time, Lia rushed over to her friend.

"I didn't want to interrupt. You're with your family," Ari replied, as she put her arms around Lia, Ari's relief was obvious. Rafe saw the tears she was managing to blink back.

"You *are* family, Ari. You know that Rachel and I have claimed you for our sister," she said, her tone serious.

"And I have claimed you, but still…"

Rafe hated the longing in Ari's voice, hated that she had been lonely for many years. He'd so often taken his large family for granted, and Ari only had her mother.

Ari didn't know it, but Rafe had kept an eye out for Sandra these past couple of years. He'd genuinely liked her mother, and he hadn't been able to walk away pretending he'd never met her, known her, and grown to care for her. He hadn't bothered her…much, but he'd worried ever since she'd gone through her two major health scares.

Sandra was doing amazingly well now; she'd been dating the same man for more than two years, a man who treated her like a queen, and her floral business was thriving. Rafe had switched all his business orders over to her. He would have switched his personal ones, too, but he hadn't had anyone to order flowers for.

He would have to have a large bouquet delivered to Ari's apartment this week.

"I'm sitting with you, where I'll be safest," Lia said, wrapping one arm through Ari's, then the other arm through Rachel's. Rafe stood next to Shane as the three women made their way toward the awaiting limo.

"Are you really OK, Shane?"

Shane hesitated as he looked across the lot as the girls laughed together, their voices easily carrying back to the two men.

"Yeah, I'm good, Rafe. I lost my yacht, but it was worth it. Lia had no choice but to hear me out, and I think we're going to make it through all of this. I would have preferred for us not to get stranded on an island in the middle of nowhere, but it ended up being…well, not to sound too corny, but kind of magical."

"*Magical*? Really?" Rafe asked with a raised eyebrow. His lip twitched, but he restrained his snort.

"Yeah, whatever. You can shut up at any time," Shane said, his cheeks heating with embarrassment.

"You know I'm just razzing you," Rafe told him.

"Yeah, well, at least I did get Lia to myself. That's worth any razzing you can dish out," Shane said smugly.

"You didn't do this on purpose, did you?" Rafe gasped as his expression changed and he looked at his best friend with worry. Rafe knew he'd go pretty far himself to win Ari, but not risk her life. He didn't think Shane would either.

"No! You should know better than to even ask that, Rafe," said Shane, glossing over the truth of the matter only a little. "I wasn't paying attention to the weather and things got out of hand quickly. I'm just saying that being stranded on a deserted island with Lia for several days turned out to be pretty spectacular."

"I don't need details," Rafe said, deciding it was time to change the subject. "I am happy for you, though," he added.

"What about you and Ari? I notice she's here. That's a great sign."

"Yeah. She's here because of Lia, not me. However, I'm a little closer than I was a week ago. She's beginning to thaw."

Just then, the girls turned around and looked at them questioningly, wondering what they were discussing.

"She doesn't look like she's thawed all that much," Shane goaded him.

"Yeah, what do you know? You can't even keep a

boat afloat," Rafe replied.

"That was low, man, really low," Shane said, holding his hand up to his chest as if he were mortally wounded.

"We'd better hurry. They might just decide to leave us here," Rafe said as the women started climbing into the vehicle.

"I know Lia would leave me behind. That girl has fire," Shane said with admiration.

"Yeah, you're a brave, brave man, Shane. I will give you props," Rafe said while slapping Shane on the back.

"I need more than props when dealing with your sister, but I'll take what I can get."

The two men were still chuckling as they got into the limo and it pulled away from the heliport. What could have been a tragic day had turned to something miraculous and special in the blink of an eye. They would celebrate.

CHAPTER THIRTY-TWO

Lia

"We are never leaving again!"

"Mom, you don't need to be so extreme. Shane and I are just fine. As a matter of fact, we enjoyed ourselves on the island. The food was plentiful and there was even a spectacular cove of water," Lia said. She sent a wink toward Shane, who actually and unbelievably blushed. She knew exactly what he was thinking about.

Mmm, that was a great cove of water!

"I was so worried about the both of you. Your father and I couldn't get here fast enough," her mother said as she clung to Lia and then Shane and then back to Lia again.

"Let's all just be grateful they are fine and we found them. Now, we need to enjoy our dinner," Rafe said as he stepped in to try to help his sister. She looked over and mouthed *thank you* to him.

Their parents finally allowed them all to sit down at the beautifully set table for pre-dinner drinks, and Lia's shoulders relaxed.

"How have you been, Ari? I've been worried about you," Rosabella said as she focused her attention on Ari, who was quiet as the family spoke in a mixture of English and Italian. She knew a few Italian phrases, but was pretty much lost when they spoke in the other language.

"I'm doing wonderfully, Mrs. Palazzo. Thank you."

"I guess it has been too long if you are reverting to calling me by my last name again," Rosabella said with a raised brow.

"I'm sorry," Ari replied.

"No need to apologize, la mia piccola cara. We'll just have to go out together — no men, just women — so you are comfortable around me again."

"That sounds like a great idea, Mom. Let's do it tomorrow before you all head out again," said Rachel, obviously excited to have them all there, even though she'd been away from her family for only a couple of weeks.

"Your father and I have decided to stay in America for a while. I'm done with the boat ride," Rosabella replied.

"It's not a boat, darling. She is far too beautiful for such a simple title," Martin said with a smile.

"Yes, dear. But, still, we are done cruising the seas. I like to have my feet on solid ground."

"I know what you mean, Mama. I think avoiding the water would be a good idea for a while," Lia said with a laugh.

"I'm so sorry, my sweet daughter. Here I am complaining about being out on the water after all that you just went through," Rosabella said with a gasp.

"I really am fine, Mom. You need to quit worrying,"

Lia assured her.

Shane stood up and held his hand out to Lia. "Dance with me," he said.

"I would love to," Lia replied. She was grateful for the soft music coming from the string quartet in the next room. Melting into Shane's arms was the perfect relief after being grilled repeatedly by her family. She certainly didn't want to share everything with them about her time on the island with Shane.

That was for her and her alone. Of course, she loved her family, but she'd begun to build something real with Shane and she wanted selfishly to hold it tight against her chest, and not allow anyone else into their bubble. At least not right now.

The two of them moved away from the table, and Lia sighed and fell into Shane's arms, her stress evaporating in an instant.

"They mean well, you know."

"Yes, I know, Shane, but after our small slice of paradise, it's hard to come back to the real world. I want you all to myself, where I can peel off your clothes and have my wicked way with you," she said as her hand circled his neck, her fingernails lightly grazing his skin.

"If you keep talking like that, I will have to drag you out of here and shock your family," he warned her.

"Promises, promises," she answered.

"You are perfect in every way, Lia. There is nothing I don't adore about you," he said, his eyes becoming glazed with passion as he leaned down and gently kissed her.

"Even my stubbornness?" she questioned.

"Especially your stubbornness. I wouldn't change a thing about you, Lia. I love how alive you are, how independent, how loving. I honestly can't imagine my life without you by my side," he said with reverence.

"Don't you think this is moving too quickly, Shane?"

Fear clawed her insides. This was too good to be true, so the bubble would have to burst at some point, wouldn't it? Nothing this amazing could last for all time.

"I would say that wanting you forever but thinking you were off limits and fighting that attraction can be called moving at a snail's pace," he countered.

"You could have had me five years ago," she reminded him.

"The time wasn't right. You will always be my best friend's sister. But I now see you also as a woman, a beautiful, talented, kind woman. I see myself as spending the rest of my life with you."

Lia felt her heart swell. She wanted to grasp his words and clutch them to her heart, but a small part of her felt that it was too soon, rather as if they were still dealing with the honeymoon stage of being stranded together. What if he changed his mind in a week? They needed more time before making any big decisions.

"Is that a marriage proposal, Shane?" she teased.

"Not yet, Lia. I would never show you such disrespect by proposing on the spur of the moment. You are a queen and deserve to be treated like one," he said, no hint of teasing in his tone.

"I love you, Shane. I wasn't going to say that, I wasn't going to let my heart run away with my mouth, but I love you. I have since I was a young teenager, and though it was infatuation then, it has grown into a strong and complete emotion now, and it has overtaken my soul. Thank you for being good to me."

Shane slowly spun them in a slow circle, never breaking eye contact with her. The smell of his subtle cologne drifted around her, weakening her knees and making her shiver, and certainly surprising her that he still had such an overwhelming effect on her.

"Lia, there is no other woman for me. There is nothing I don't love about you. I think fate put us together long ago, and though I was a fool for years, I won't make that mistake any longer. The light in your eyes guides me, the rhythm of your heart keeps mine beating, and the touch of your hand awes me. I love you more than words could ever express, and I would die without you."

Lia felt as if she couldn't breathe. While they moved in time to the slow sound of the string band, Shane's hand gently caressed her back, his fingers moving beneath her camisole top and scorching her skin as he rubbed the sensitive spot that dipped in before her hips flared out.

As he pulled her against him, she felt his clear arousal pushing against her, showing her all too clearly that he was turned on, something he always seemed to be when they touched — which made her feel womanly and seductive.

She loved him because he was a wonderful man, but even more so because he made her feel special. He made her feel priceless. Yes, her family loved her and always encouraged her, but there was a difference.

To be loved by a man, truly loved, made a woman feel as if she could burst. Of course, Lia was strong and could face the world on her own, but it involved a deeper strength, she felt, to give yourself to another. To trust someone with your heart was a gift, and it was a gift she wanted to give Shane. It was a gift that he had earned.

Shane twirled Lia again, making her giggle. Instead of letting her complete the turn on the dance floor, he pulled her to him with her back facing his front. His arousal pushed into the soft curve of her behind as his arms wrapped around her middle, holding her tightly against him.

"Ah, Lia, what you do to me…" he whispered in her ear before he kissed her neck, his tongue trailing over her skin. "You smell and taste so good. Who needs food when I have you to taste?"

"We can always leave," she moaned as his fingers splayed across her stomach. She wanted to turn and devour his mouth, but she also loved exactly where he had her, with all of his hardness pressed into her curves.

"Please don't tempt me. Your family would kill us, and it's taking all I have not to drag you from here, caveman style."

Lia's mind instantly filled with images of him carrying her away, tossing her to a bed, and ravishing her over and over again. She couldn't wait to get him alone.

Shane released her, swinging her out wide, making her laugh with delight as her skirt flared. She felt pure enjoyment in their dance.

As he pulled her up tight against his chest and bent down, his eyes searing her with their desire, her laughter evaporated. Pure sexual hunger radiated through her. She pushed into his arousal, taking delight in the anguished gasp escaping his lips.

"We should go back now," he said. But his hands had other ideas. They were resting on her hips, but soon began climbing up her waist, slowly, reaching the side of her breasts, where his fingers briefly grazed the mounds before moving to her back and outlining her shoulder blades, pulling her tightly into him, making her beaded nipples ache as they rubbed against his solid chest.

Lia had all but forgotten her family sitting in the next room. Luckily, the other couples on the dance floor seemed just as entranced with each other as the two of them were, or the two of them would be making quite a spectacle of themselves.

The dimly lit dance floor was tucked into a corner of the restaurant, the perfect place for couples to work up anticipation for a night of scorching romance. Shane had built her desire into a frenzy, and she no longer wanted to be at the stiflingly decorous restaurant.

She wanted a bed!

The song " Fever" began to play; a vocalist had joined the string quartet, and her sexy voice only added to the throbbing in Lia's overheated body. The sultry rhythm automatically made Lia grind her hips against Shane's. She moved them in time to the music as her arms wrapped tightly around his neck.

"Later tonight, I'm going to push you down on the bed, unbutton your pants, set that beautiful arousal free, and take you deep into my mouth," she whispered, delighting when he shook in her arms.

"Lia…" he warned.

"Then I plan on stripping all my clothes off while you watch… After that, I'm going to climb up on top of you, and sink down on that thick staff of yours and ride you until the sun begins to rise."

"Let's go!" he said as his hands flew to her backside and he pulled her against him. If possible, he'd grown even harder at her words.

"Sounds good to me," she said, feeling triumphant. Her family would forgive her — she hoped.

They turned the corner and Lia ran right into a body, excusing herself until she looked up and saw the laughing expression on Ari's face.

"I didn't interrupt anything, did I?" Ari asked, not even trying to hide the mischievous expression on her face.

"Um…no…we…uh…" Lia couldn't complete a sentence; her brain was occupied with trying to figure out how to get around Ari so that she and Shane could complete what they'd started.

"Oh, you must be *so* warm after dancing for such a long time," Ari said, slipping between the two of them, making Lia want to groan in frustration.

She could take Ari out — no problem. Horrified at her own thoughts, Lia sent a pleading look over to Shane, who looked about as miserable as she felt as Ari looped her arms around both Lia and Shane and began leading them back toward the table.

"I have to use the bathroom," Lia said. Inspiration! She knew Shane would take the hint and follow.

"Great. Me too. We'll meet you back at the table, Shane," Ari said, pointedly locking her arm in Lia's, letting the wanton young woman know she wouldn't be allowed to get away.

"Fine," Shane mumbled as he walked away, shifting his body, obviously more than a little uncomfortable.

"Ari, I'm trying to get some time alone with Shane," Lia pleaded as she looked at her friend.

"Lia Palazzo, you have had plenty of time alone with Shane for almost a week. Your parents have been worried sick about you. Rachel, Rafe and I were terrified, too. I know you want to rip each other's clothes off, but you can't treat your family with such a lack of respect by rushing out. Your mother would be crushed. Family always comes first," Ari lectured her. "However, anticipation is half the fun. You could always see how much you can make Shane sweat through dinner," she added with a wink.

"Oh, that does sound like fun," Lia said as they slipped into the restroom. Hiding in a stall, she slipped off her panties and put them in her pocket.

She and Ari walked back to the table, where Shane's eyes drank her in as she sat next to him, scooting her chair just a little bit closer.

"When we get out of here, I'm going to release you from your tight pants and run my tongue all over your beautiful shaft," she whispered in his ear as her finger trailed over his arousal beneath the tablecloth.

Shane jumped in his seat, his knee slamming into the table, making the conversation stop as all eyes turned toward him.

"Is everything OK, Shane?" Rafe asked, looking at his friend with concern.

"Fine," Shane squeaked, then cleared his throat. "Sorry, thought I saw a mouse," he added.

Rafe looked at him as if he'd lost his mind. "A mouse?" he asked doubtfully.

"Um…yeah, don't know what I was thinking," Shane said, sending a glare Lia's way as her fingers rubbed over him again, making his brow break out in a sweat.

"You're all flushed, dear. Maybe you picked up an illness on that island," Rosabella said, her face a mask of concern.

Shane felt like a heel.

He gripped Lia's hand, trapping it against his leg,

the safest place he could think of with the eyes of all her family members on him.

"It's just a bit warm in here. I'm fine," he said. He picked up his glass of wine and downed it, not even tasting the exquisite liquid, just praying for a buzz so he could get through this agonizing night.

The family seemed unsure, but finally the conversation began again, and Shane turned toward Lia with a pleading look in his eyes. "Behave," he muttered as he let go of her hand and turned to speak to Rafe.

Less than a minute had passed when he felt Lia's fingers on his hand, then felt something in his palm. He turned it, trying to figure out what it was. Pulling it up on his lap, he'd barely managed to stop himself from lifting it to table height before he looked down and noticed the scrap of lace and satin in his hand. It was her panties!

Shoving his hand back under the table, his body went from hard to throbbing when he realized she was sitting next to him in a short skirt with no panties on. A small groan escaped his tight throat, and Rafe looked at him with concern.

"Are you sure you're OK, Shane? You really don't look well," his friend said.

Ari laughed, then quickly covered it up by coughing, and Shane was mortified to realize she had a pretty good idea of what was going on. The situation just kept getting worse and worse.

"Maybe I should go back to the room and lie down," Shane said, taking full advantage of their concern. When he got Lia alone, he was going to make her suffer as much as she was making him.

"Of course, Shane. You've been through so much,

and here we are keeping you out," Rosabella said, making him feel about two inches tall.

"You know what, I'm sure it's just that I'm too warm. I probably simply need more water," he said, looking down, not able to look in Rosabella's eyes and tell an outright lie.

"Are you sure?" she asked. She'd been like a second mother to him from the moment he'd walked into her home as a young man.

"I'm positive," he said, shooting a chuckling Lia a warning look.

Lia continued torturing him for the next two hours. But by the time they arrived back in the room, she wasn't laughing anymore, not when he pressed her against the wall and sank inside her, making her beg for more.

CHAPTER THIRTY-THREE

Ari

For two weeks Ari had been back at home, back to teaching, and back to her real life. Well, sort of.

She stepped inside the doors to her classroom, still getting that feeling of pride as she approached the desk she used when she taught history. The smell of jasmine enveloped her from a bouquet left for her in the departmental office; she had brought a few of the sprigs along with her when she went to teach.

Before every single class there was something waiting for her, in her mailbox or beside it — flowers, books, a bracelet, chocolates, candles — the list went on and on. And each time, a note accompanied the gift.

She'd told Rafe on the way home from Italy that she wasn't ready to jump back into a relationship with him; she'd warned him that she had to focus on herself first before she could consider attaching herself to another person — even him. But the man was persistent and she was wearing down.

She'd inhaled the sweet scent of jasmine as she

grabbed his latest note. Even her name was written beautifully in cursive on the envelope. Rafe had incredible handwriting, far better than hers.

> *Meet me after class. I promise it will be an evening you will never forget.*
>
> *Rafe*

Maybe she should just do it. Was she going to win this battle of wills with Rafe? She had every intention of holding out, but the thought of having him touch her, of having him make her heart race, was enough to make her think she was a fool for depriving herself of something she wanted with every fiber of her being.

Soon her class was about to begin, and as she looked out and her eyes connected with Rafe's, she was lost.

It was a fruitless battle. She desired him, wanted him on so many levels that it was insanity come to life.

Usually when she taught, the time flew and class was over before she knew it. Not so today. She couldn't erase from her mind questions about what he had planned for her.

Though she tried not to look his way, her eyes kept going to him involuntarily, only to find his gaze always centered right on her. Her blood circulation was rising, her heart beating as if she were in a marathon, and her clothes feeling like restraints on her overheated body.

She needed to decide what she was going to do. As her eyes connected with his again, she made her decision.

When the class ended, she sat at her desk, answered questions and waited.

When she looked up and found Rafe gone, her heart thudded dully. Maybe he'd given up. The disappointment that filled her made her angry. He'd left, given her what she wanted, so why did she feel so let down?

Leaving the sprigs of jasmine on her desk, Ari gathered her belongings and slowly walked from the classroom. It looked to be a long, achingly lonely night for her.

When Ari stopped and looked out at the curb along the building in which she taught, her heart picked up speed again.

There was Rafe, standing in front of his flawless silver Jaguar, a single orchid in his hand as he gazed at her with his sparkling eyes. She couldn't help but notice how debonair he looked in his sharp hand-tailored business suit, his crisp white shirt standing out against the black jacket and tie. When had he had time to change? Did it matter? No.

Slowly approaching, Ari felt relief and hunger all at once. She wouldn't turn his invitation down — not with the level of excitement filling her just at the sight of him looking so suave, so incredibly toothsome.

"I've thought of nothing but you today," Rafe said as she reached him.

"You look very handsome, Rafe," she admitted, not wanting to play games.

His eyes rounded in pleasure as he leaned in and brushed his lips across hers. "Words can't come close to describing how beautiful you are, Ari."

The honesty in his tone took her breath away. She felt beautiful in his presence. Her heart was already involved, so why punish herself any longer? There was no use in pretending she didn't want this, didn't want to be with him.

"Where are you taking me?"

At her simple words, his shoulders relaxed and he pulled her into his arms, the flower dropping to the pavement as he lifted his hand to her face, cupping her cheek and looking into her eyes.

"My place."

"That's a bit presumptuous, don't you think?" she asked on a sigh.

"Nothing will happen that you don't want to happen."

She knew he meant it. This gentler Rafe was nice, but she found herself missing the assertive, almost domineering Rafe she had known. What was wrong with her?

"I'll come on one condition."

He looked at her in surprise. She had always been strong-willed, but she had allowed him to lead their relationship. It seemed he didn't know what to do with this stronger personality that she was presenting him with.

"What is your condition?"

Ah, there was the fight she liked to hear in his voice. Rafe didn't like to be controlled. She'd test his patience tonight. Knowing what she had planned made desire pool deep inside her, made her feel emotions she hadn't felt for two years.

"I get to do whatever I want to you."

He looked at her with puzzlement.

"I don't understand."

"You're not supposed to," she said with a laugh. She felt powerful. It was freeing, and it was delicious.

"Why don't we discuss this over dinner?" he said, hoping for a compromise.

"No. Then you will just get your own way, as usual. I won't go with you unless you promise to give me control. Let me do what I want," she said, pulling back slightly against his grasp.

"What exactly is your idea of control?"

"I guess you will just have to trust me," she said, feeling a measure of triumph at the worried expression in his eyes.

They stood there at an impasse for several moments, but then she saw the reluctant acceptance in his eyes. She'd won this round.

"Fine."

Rafe didn't add anything further; he released her and opened the back door to the car, keeping his hands to himself as she got in. Just for added effect, she took her time, making sure to arch her back just a tad to accentuate her fabulous behind. At the gritted growl that escaped his teeth, she smiled, feeling on top of the world.

It felt good to finally feel that she was ahead of him, that she was the one with all the power. There was the very real possibility that it would prove short-lived — but for this moment, she was reveling in it.

"Would you care for a glass of wine?"

"Yes, please." She let him pour her a glass of red, then took a sip and enjoyed its complex savor.

There was no talking as they moved through town. Ari felt hunger and excitement. From the look in Rafe's eyes, he was worried, which only stoked the flames of her passion.

They arrived at his home, and Ari fought the immediate intimidation that she felt when entering his domain. Rafe was always the one in charge in his home — but not this time. He'd promised. One thing she knew about Rafe was that he was a man of his word.

Even if it killed him, he'd stay true to his promise. Wouldn't he?

He led her to an elegantly set table, and she sat gracefully, enjoying it when he pushed her chair in. She'd always appreciated what a proper gentleman he was when they were dining, but how he let go when they were in the bedroom. Pure bad boy!

When their first course was served, Ari had a hard time eating. Anticipation burned through her at what was to come. She had no idea what exactly she was going to do, but she knew she wanted to push him — and push herself.

There wasn't much conversation during their meal, neither of them being able to focus on anything except for the night to come. After they finished dessert, Ari was the first to stand.

If she was going to do this, she needed to have the confidence to see it through.

"Are you ready?"

Rafe's eyes widened in shock at her boldness. But fire clearly burned behind his eyes, now nearly all purple as his pupils dilated.

"Oh, yes, Ari. I am more than ready," he assured her.

Need was a constant pulsing sensation in her belly as she moved to the stairs, very aware of where his bedroom was. Walking with grace, she sashayed up the elaborate staircase, swinging her hips with each step, his heated breath on her neck, pushing her passion higher.

They stepped through the doorway and she walked

over to his bed, running her hand along the top of the black satin comforter.

Rafe stood in the center of the room, lifting his hands to undo his black tie.

"No. Stop."

He paused and looked at her in some confusion.

"I want to do that."

Looking downward at the clear arousal straining against his trousers, Ari slowly brought her gaze back to his eyes — fire leaping from their depths.

Leaving him standing there, Ari lifted her hands and undid the top button of her blouse. Slowly, she undid her top, then shrugged her shoulders to let the fabric fall from her body. Never breaking their gaze, she reached down and undid the button on her skirt, then unzipped it. With her slight wiggle, the fabric slid from her body, leaving her standing before him in nothing but a lacy white bra and thong, and a garter belt with white stockings and red heels.

Rafe had given Ari a love of sexy lingerie, and she was grateful now. She'd been wearing it ever since their time together, and here was a major payoff as his eyes stroked her body. Feeling ultra-feminine, she turned in a circle so he could get a nice glimpse of her shapely and uncovered derrière.

Turning back around, she slowly made her way over to him. "No touching," she whispered into his ear as she arched against him.

"That wasn't the agreement," he argued.

"The deal was that I'm in charge. You have to do what I say. If you can't play by the rules, I can put my clothes back on and walk from the room."

She hoped he didn't pick that option, because she'd

never be the same again. As it was, her body was in a constant state of arousal that only Rafe could sate.

"Fine," he said through gritted teeth as she lifted her hands and finished undoing his tie. She pulled it from his collar and ran the silky material through her fingers before lifting it and wrapping it around her neck, letting it dangle over her breasts.

"Mmm, I like this material," she murmured as she picked up one of the ends and trailed it across the mounds of her breasts. Her reward was Rafe's groan as he swayed toward her.

"Ari…"

"Yes, Rafe?" she asked, her eyes innocent.

"Please…" he begged.

"Not so nice to be on the other side of control, huh, Rafe?" she asked with a flirty laugh.

"Point taken," he gasped as she trailed her finger down his stomach and over the bulge below.

"Your lesson hasn't even come close to being learned, Rafe," she purred. She lifted her hands and began undoing the buttons on his shirt.

When the last one was undone and she'd parted the material, her nails trailed over his firm chest, and she couldn't resist leaning forward and running her tongue across his hard nipples, grazing them with her teeth and drinking in the musky flavor of his skin.

She left his cuff links in, then inspiration hit. She circled around him and pulled his arms tight behind his back.

"What the hell?" he gasped as she grabbed the ends of his shirt and looped it together, securing his hands in the cuffs of his shirt as she wrapped the rest of the material snuggly in place.

"Whatever I want — remember, Rafe," she said and gave a tug.

"I swear by all that's holy, Ari…" he cried out as he tugged back against her impromptu restraint.

"Would you like to stop, Rafe? Do you need a 'safe word'?" She mocked him, enjoying herself too much.

"You're a witch," he said as she circled back around.

"Name-calling, Rafe? That really doesn't become you," she said with a laugh.

"Paybacks are hell, Ari," he said, his eyes narrowing.

She leaned against him, her hands running along his sides. "I'm looking forward to it," she whispered, smiling as his whole body shuddered.

Lifting her hands again, Ari undid Rafe's belt, pulling the leather from his body, then running it through her hands. As she doubled it up, Rafe's eyes rounded at the clear intent in her eyes. "Don't you dare," he called out too late.

Ari lifted the belt and flicked it across his covered backside, not hard, but enough to make a smacking sound. When she circled back around, Rafe's eyes were large with shock at her audacity.

"Oh, Ari. You are in serious trouble," he said, but the excitement shining in the depths of his eyes had her stomach doing somersaults.

She'd just opened a door that she knew she could never close again. Instead of being afraid, she was elated beyond her wildest dreams. Yes, "regular" sex was great, but Rafe had shown her that adding a bit of kink brought about so much more.

He'd stretched her boundaries and made her see new worlds in the adventures he'd taken her on. She still wanted those amazingly slow moments of making love for hours with nothing but the two of them, but she also wanted other things. She liked the bonds, the contraptions he'd come up with. She liked the feel of fur striking her skin, making her come hard and fast, or slow and long.

She liked…more.

Instead of answering him, she let the belt fall, and she undid his pants, dropping to her knees so she could take off his shoes and then toss his pants away. She left him standing before her in nothing but a pair of tight black underwear, the front of which was wet from his obvious excitement.

She pulled them away from his hips, and his erection sprang free, standing thick and long in front of her face. She didn't hesitate, but leaned forward and took the wide head into her mouth, tasting him on her tongue as he shuddered.

"I'm going to fall, Ari," he said as his knees trembled.

She released him, looking up at his strained face, sweat beading on his brow.

Ari had done this. She'd made this big strong man tremble with need, made him weak. Euphoria surged through her at the power she had gained over him.

Standing up, she led him to the bed, where she had him sit down, then she kneeled in front of him and gripped his arousal in her hand.

"You taste so good, Rafe," she said as she swiped her tongue from the base of him, all the way to the head of his arousal before sucking him inside her mouth again.

Rafe leaned back, his arms trapped beneath him as she began sucking him deeper into her mouth, rubbing her hand up and down the bottom of his member and squeezing it to bring him more pleasure.

She was so wet, so turned on by the sounds of pleasure issuing from his throat.

"Please, Ari. I don't want to come like this," he gritted as his hips jerked.

"I don't want you to, either, Rafe. I want to be riding you when you release," she said as she reluctantly set his arousal free from her hot mouth.

Helping Rafe sit back up, she grabbed the tie from around her neck and began trailing the end over his body, running the soft material along his pecs, his abs, and his throbbing staff.

He jerked as her mouth followed, licking and sucking on his skin all the way from his neck to his legs, and then back up again, pausing as she kissed along his erection for several moments.

"Mmm, you taste so good, Rafe. I think I could enjoy doing nothing but licking your flesh all night long," she said as she circled his stomach, sucking on the tight skin there.

"I'm about done with this, Ari," he growled as he pulled against the shirt tying his hands.

"What's the matter, Rafe? Am I not satisfying you?" she teased as she ran her tongue along his moistened arousal, making him jerk.

"I want to taste you. Fair is fair," he said, the end of his remark a groan as she sucked his tip hard, scraping her teeth along the head.

"Yes, it is quite fun tasting you, devouring your body. I think I'll do this a while longer," she said with a smile before sucking him in deep.

"Enough!" he cried.

She looked up and smiled, loving it as she watched

him lose control. Ari was aching as she teased him, but it was so worth the pain.

Her eyes widened as she watched the muscles bulge in his arms. A glint entered his eyes as she heard the expensive material of his shirt begin to rip. Knowing he was about to escape, Ari jumped back, but it was too late.

Rafe was free, and his arms snaked out and grabbed her, lust and excitement gazing back at her.

"You've had your fun. Now it's my turn," he said as he flipped her over onto her back, laid her on the bed and kissed her with all the built-up passion of the last hour.

"That's not in the rules," she warned him when he released her mouth. But there was no heat behind her words. She was too turned on by the man molding his body to hers.

"The rules just changed," he growled.

Gripping her hands, he grabbed the tie that was still hanging around her neck and turned her over onto her stomach, stretching her arms above her head and quickly securing her to his bedpost.

Ari's blood felt as if it were boiling as he took hold of her bra straps and ripped them away, leaving her back bare before him. His hands pressed down on her back, kneading her muscles as he began kissing her neck, his tongue moving with a sweet roughness across her skin.

She cried out in pleasure as he sucked on her flesh, his teeth grazing her in the most devastating way. "Yes, Rafe, take me," she demanded. Now that the tables were turned, she wanted nothing but his strong, thick manhood inside her.

Right now!

"Oh, no, Ari. I want your taste on my tongue. I want to make you sweat like you did to me, tit for tat," he said as his lips moved down her back, causing goose bumps to spring out across her skin.

His tongue trailed down her spine, and his fingers ran beneath the elastic of her panties. Then he nipped the skin at the top of her buttocks, squeezing them in his hands as his mouth trailed down each side.

His hot breath nearly caused her to overheat when he lifted her hips, placing her on her knees before him, his mouth never leaving her skin.

Spreading her thighs, he ran his tongue down the seam of her thong panties, his hot mouth licking her core through the fabric.

"Take them off," she demanded, but he ignored her words. His mouth lavished attention on the outside of her core, sucking the swollen lips into his mouth before releasing them and running his tongue along the fabric again, then biting one buttock.

"I'm in charge now, Ari. You will do what I say," he said, authority clearly in his tone, making her stomach squeeze tight.

She felt the bed shift as he rose above her, then she gasped when she felt his thickness cradled in the cleft of her backside as he ran its head all the way down, then rested it on the outside of her core.

She jerked her hips toward him, wanting him inside her now. How had she ever thought she'd win this game? She'd known she wouldn't. This was what she'd wanted all along. She'd wanted him taking charge, owning her body.

His hand came down in a light slap on her derrière. "That's payback," he said as his fingers gripped her hips tightly while he pushed against her.

Even the slight sting excited her. She'd known the door she was opening, and she was more than willing to step through it. Rafe would never hurt her, never do more than she wanted. With a startling realization, she knew beyond a doubt that she trusted him.

"Mmm, I'll have my turn again," she promised.

Rafe laughed a pure, deep, beautiful sound. "I'm sure you will," he admitted.

Then the fabric of her panties tore, and there was no more speaking. His arousal was poised at her core, and she pushed against him, frustrated when he didn't thrust forward.

"Who's in charge, Ari?" he asked, his voice deceptively quiet.

"I am," she stubbornly answered, then groaned when he pulled back.

"Wrong answer, Ari. Who's in charge?" he asked again.

She knew this was a pivotal moment, a moment she could either go forward and have pure pleasure, or stubbornly defy him and be left aching. There was no doubt.

"You, Rafe," she cried, silently adding *for now*, then lost her breath when he slammed fully inside her.

So deep. He was so deep, stretching the swollen folds of her core with his thickness.

Before she could draw in needed air, he pulled out and slammed into her again, his hips hitting against her backside, rocking her forward with the force of his thrusts.

She came undone, her body letting go in releases of wave after wave of pleasure. He continued thrusting inside her, rocking forward slowly as he helped draw out her orgasm, which continued on and on.

When he felt her grip let go, he grabbed her hips hard again and began thrusting with new momentum, his hips slapping her ass as he groaned.

"So tight. Such a good fit. You are so hot," he growled as he thrust in and out of her, building her up to her second release. Yes, Rafe could make her come repeatedly, make her body sing until there was nothing left inside her.

Only Rafe.

When he bent over her, his hands coming around to hold the weight of her swaying breasts, Ari let go again, her body convulsing around him, making him stiffen as he cried out his own pleasure.

She felt him pulsing inside her, felt the strong stream of his release wash through her. Yes, this was what she wanted.

This pleasure — day and night — forever.

CHAPTER THIRTY-FOUR

Rachel

RACHEL looked at the stick again and then at the box. Not believing what she was seeing, she looked at the three other similar sticks.

"No. No. No. We were careful," she said to herself.

Looking down at the four different brands of pregnancy tests, she was horrified to discover that they were all saying the exact same thing.

She was going to have a baby.

"This can't be happening."

She knew that talking to herself probably wasn't the best idea in her current situation — she was already freaking out horribly — but she needed to say the words, needed to hear them.

Yes, she'd had an affair with a stranger, but they'd used protection every single time. Every time! How could she possibly have gotten pregnant?

In the back of her head, she could hear her eighth-grade health teacher preaching that condoms weren't foolproof prevention against pregnancy — that accidents could and did happen and you could get pregnant or catch a disease even when using them.

But she'd been careful.

It didn't matter that she knew the facts of life. She was in no way ready to be a mother. How could she possibly raise another human being when she wasn't grown up herself? She might be twenty-six now, but that was still young.

First, she was supposed to prove herself by having a dream job, which turned out to be anything but a dream. She absolutely hated it, which didn't help. Next, in her idea of what the future held, she was going to be on her own, no parents or siblings interfering in her life, and take some time to really live it up.

When all of that was finished, she would consider entering a serious relationship. She even had it written on paper. Nowhere in any of her plans did a baby enter into the picture. Especially with a stranger for whom she didn't even have a last name.

Oh, her parents were going to kill her. Rafe was going to kill her. She was going to murder herself!

Looking again at the tests, anger rose inside her, and then died down. There was no use in crying about it, or berating herself. The situation was as it was. She wouldn't even consider ending the pregnancy, and she knew she couldn't give the child up, so it appeared that she was going to be a single mother.

After the initial shock and disappointment wore off, she knew she'd have the full support of her family. They were always there for each other, even when one of them royally screwed up. Not that any of them had done something this foolish.

It was really going to suck to tell them she was

not only pregnant, but also had no idea who the father really was. Even thinking about the conversation hurt her head.

Knowing that she needed to have this confirmed, if for nothing else than her sanity, Rachel found a doctor and made an appointment for later that week.

Deciding it best just to go on with her days until she went in, she kept herself busy. It was hard not to think about the very likely fact that she was going to be a mother, but she went to work, tried to keep busy, and waited for the week to go by.

After the appointment, she waited for the blood test results to come in. A couple of days later, the doctor called.

Congrats. Single motherhood in only seven months.

Before the call could even fully register in her brain, there was a knock on her door. Almost in a trancelike state, Rachel opened it, then nearly fell over.

"Hello, Rachel."

"How…how did you know how to find me?" she gasped.

"I've had you followed for the last couple of months. There was no way I would leave the situation we were in without keeping an eye out for you. As soon as you were seen by a doctor, I made my way here."

Standing before her was Ian, but he looked different. He was wearing different clothes, powerful clothes. He didn't look like the man she'd met on the beach.

"You had me followed?" It was taking her brain a few minutes to catch up to what he was saying to her. Too many things had hit her at one time. Why in the world would he have her followed? She immediately became concerned.

She didn't really know this man — not at all. She'd spent a week with him, had great sex and then went on her way. If he was someone who would follow her afterward, she wasn't sure what he was capable of.

Her home was a small rustic cottage. Yes, she had neighbors, but before anyone could reach her, he could do whatever he wanted. Truly, she knew nothing about him, just that his name was Ian and that he was one hell of a lover — apparently he had pretty powerful sperm, too, if they could break through latex!

"Of course I had you followed. My good servant Harold has been working with you at the embassy. You made it very easy for me to keep track," he said with a smirk.

Rachel felt as if she had been punched in the gut. Her "friend" Harold had befriended her only because he was being paid to do it. It seemed she couldn't trust anyone. Before she had a chance to respond, his next words took her breath away.

"I discovered a broken condom. I had to make sure a child wasn't produced. Apparently we have created one," he said calmly as he looked down at her still flat stomach.

Raising her hand protectively without realizing it, she stared back at him through the doorway to her home. Though she hadn't wanted to be a mother, didn't even know where to begin in being one, she knew she must protect this child growing inside of her. Why would he care if she were pregnant or not, though? None of this made sense. They'd had a weeklong affair. That should have been the end of it.

"I…I'm confused" were the words she finally managed to get past her trembling lips. This was all too much.

"I guess it's time we formally introduce ourselves. Hello, Rachel Palazzo. I am Adriano, king of Corythia. The child you carry is the royal heir."

There was no fluctuation in his voice; he delivered a flat statement.

It took a few moments for his words to register, and then her hand lifted involuntarily and she slapped Ian straight across the cheek. He stumbled back a step and looked at her in complete shock.

Raising his hand to his face, he felt his cheek as if he couldn't believe what had just happened. Rachel had a feeling the so-called king had never been hit before. Well, it was long past time, she thought snidely.

"I am done with this conversation. You may come back when I'm not so flipping pissed off," she said, and she began to close the door in his face.

Her emotions had been over the top for the past week, and to have this man show up unannounced and tell her that he'd had her followed was sending her over the edge.

Ian regained his composure quickly. He put out a hand to stop her, then pushed his way into her small home, making the place seem even smaller with his six-foot-four frame invading it.

"Do you realize what could happen to you for such an offense if we were back home?" he said, looking cold-ly into her eyes. "You have assaulted the sovereign."

"Well, we aren't back at your home, *King Adriano,* so I guess I don't have to worry about it," Rachel said, em-phasizing his name with sarcasm. No, she didn't believe his cock-and-bull claim of being a king, but still, she was pretty ticked off at his audacity. *This* was the man who was the father of her child.

The poor kid didn't have a chance, not with her as a mother and a crazy man as a father.

"You obviously need to be taught how to respect your king." He looked around her modest home in disgust.

"You are not my king! I had an affair with you, Ian, which was obviously a very bad idea. It doesn't mean I'm willing to bow down to you, and it *certainly* doesn't mean I want you to remain a part of my life," she said, more than a bit offended by the way he seemed to be looking down his nose at her.

She might not be royalty — not that she thought he was — but she came from a very respectable family. That she had chosen to make it on her own didn't render her any less of a person. In fact, it made her stronger. She was quite proud of her home, the one he was sneering at as if it were a peasant's hovel.

"Because I have known your brother through business, I will give you some leeway. Had I known who you were that day on the beach, I never would have commenced with an affair with you. It's too late to have regrets now, though. We will obviously wed immediately. I think it's important to get back to my country right away so we can prevent the media from swooping in before you are my wife."

Rachel looked at him as though he had three heads sprouting. Her belief that he was crazy was beginning to lessen as horror took its place. The man could be telling her the truth. He just might be a king. Sheesh. That didn't mean she was his subject, or that she would bend to his rules in the slightest, but it meant a whole heck of a lot of complications for her child. Maybe she had indeed screwed up *royally*.

"Look, Ian, or whoever the hell you are, I have had a *really* long day — a long week for that matter. I can't take any more at the moment. We're going to have to continue this conversation at a later time. Don't worry, though. The baby isn't due for seven months, so there's plenty of time to talk later. I would appreciate it if you would just leave my home."

Rachel was proud of herself for staying calm, speaking like a sane adult, and not slapping him again. How had she been so attracted to this jerk two months earlier? He radiated command as if it were a part of his skin, and she couldn't stand men who thought they were lord and ruler of everything around them.

"I don't think you understand, Rachel. This matter isn't up for discussion. We *will* wed. My child won't be born away from my country."

The calmness of his voice frightened her far more than his words did.

"I won't marry you because of a child, Ian. You have got to be joking. It's time you leave before I call the authorities," she warned him as she moved toward the door.

The confident smile that appeared on his face made her stomach drop to her knees. What had she gotten herself into?

"You are still quite the wildcat, Rachel. I haven't been able to get you from my mind these last two months. It won't be such a hardship for me to have you as my wife." He leaned toward her and lifted his hand to her face.

Rachel raised her arm to slap him again, but he quickly grabbed it. When she lifted the other arm, he grabbed that too, then carefully pushed her against the wall. Pressing his body against hers, she felt his arousal pressing against her stomach as his head descended.

"Mmm, yes, being married to you won't be a bad thing at all," he said as he kissed the corner of her mouth.

"Get away from me," she cried, wishing the words were more forceful. As angry as she was, as confused, and frightened, she still felt a pulse of desire in her core at his nearness. The man had done things with her body that she'd never imagined could be done.

"For now, amore mio," he said, his lips taking hers for just a moment.

Ian released her and then walked through the door.

"I am not your love," she said, snapping out of the trance that he'd just put her in from a simple connection of their lips.

Just before she managed to shut the door in his face, happy to have the last word, he turned back around.

"My guard will keep an eye out for you until I return."

She knew he was telling her there was no need to run away — that he would simply follow her. Well, he could just stick it, she thought, slamming the door with extra emphasis.

Leaning against the cool wood, Rachel wondered what she was going to do next. The one thing she knew for sure was that it was time to go home. Making a phone call to her brother, she asked him send the jet for her.

She needed her family right now — it was time to face the music.

CHAPTER THIRTY-FIVE

Lia

"No. Please — stop!"

It was a rare day off from their work on the island and Lia felt pure contentment as she walked down the street of the market, hand in hand with Shane.

That was, until she turned to see a young boy taking off down the street with a woman's purse. It all happened so quickly, and the crowds around them turned to watch, but no one stepped forward to help.

"Stay here," Shane yelled to her as he began chasing after the boy.

Like hell she would.

After her initial shock, she bolted after him, but she lost the trail as he was swallowed up in the crowd. She slowed to a walk and looked around, searching for any signs of him or the boy. She had no idea where the two of them could have disappeared to.

She was getting ready to pass an alley when she noticed two figures standing tensely just inside the shadows. She looked again and saw that one of them had a knife.

And the other one was Shane.

He was in a face-off with the boy, and the situation seemed to be escalating.

Without thinking for a minute of her own safety, Lia ran into the alley, joining the two of them. Neither looked in her direction; their gazes were locked together. People were walking by the alley, but no one even glanced in the direction of the two apparent adversaries.

Were such crimes such a common thing that no one was going to help? Or was it that they were too afraid? This was something that Lia wasn't used to, and she didn't know what to do at this point.

"You don't want to do this. Just put the knife down. Let's have a chat," Shane said in fluent Italian, his voice low and firm, but not unfriendly.

"You're just another rich guy. You don't give a crap about me!" the kid yelled. He couldn't have been more than ten or eleven years old. His face was hardened, but there was still an innocent light about his eyes, even while he glared daggers at Shane.

"I know a lot, kid. I used to be just like you, stealing tourists' items to get by, sneaking food whenever and wherever I could, including from garbage cans. I've been there, but I got out. Let me help you. This world hasn't hardened you too much yet. You can turn this around."

The kid looked at Shane with distrust, but was unable to hide the flicker of hope in his eyes. He wanted a better life — Lia could see it. She wanted to step in and give him a hug, his dirty clothes, face, and all, but she knew better than to spook a wild animal, and that was how he was acting at this moment — like an animal with everything to lose.

"What could you know? Your clothes alone could feed all of us kids for a month," he snapped, lowering the knife slightly, but still making sure Shane could see it and that he wasn't afraid to use it.

"Have you stabbed someone before, kid? Seriously plunged a knife into real human flesh? It's not as easy as it looks. The flesh resists being stabbed, then makes a sickening sound as the blade goes in, quite possibly piercing a person's organs. Have you seen the light go out of someone's eyes? It's not a pretty sight to behold, especially if you know that you're the one guilty of taking a life. It's not easy to live with that knowledge."

"How would you know?" the boy screamed, his eyes filling with tears that he refused to let fall as he looked wildly at Shane.

Lia looked again toward the street, at the crowds only twenty yards away. At the screaming a couple of heads turned to look in, but the people didn't even slow down; they kept on walking, quickly deciding not to get involved. How could they be so oblivious and so callous? Why wouldn't anyone stop to help Shane?

Shane spoke simply to the boy. "Because I have taken a life."

Lia gasped at his words, making his shoulders tense, but he still focused on the kid, didn't turn in her direction. What was he talking about? He couldn't have taken a life. She'd known him half her life. He wasn't a killer.

The boy turned toward her, panic taking over when he perceived himself as being boxed in.

"Lia, this child is frightened. Can you please just back out from the alley and let us talk?"

He was so calm, so focused on the kid. Lia felt as if

she didn't even know this man standing before her. Yes, she'd known he was good with kids, that he helped get them off the streets, but this look in his eyes, this focus was something new to her. He'd seen some things in his life.

Questions were overwhelming her, but she didn't know where to begin.

"Who is she? Were you planning on attacking me?" the boy shouted.

"She's just my friend. We were walking together when I saw you take the purse from that woman. Lia followed us here. No one was planning on attacking you," Shane told him, not moving forward or taking steps back, but making a firm stand, showing the kid he wasn't afraid, but that he wouldn't threaten him, either.

"Why should I believe anything you're saying? You're just another rich guy trying to lie. Maybe you're another one of the sick guys who have wives at home but like to find street kids to fulfill your twisted fantasies," he snarled.

"I know you have no reason to trust me, kid. I get that, but I've helped others, and all I want to do is get you to return that purse you stole, and then help you to get off the streets. If the cops get you, they won't try to help. They'll just throw you in the system, where things can get a whole lot worse," Shane warned.

"How do I know you aren't one of those undercover pigs?"

"If I were a cop, I'd have to tell you, wouldn't I?"

"I don't know anything about the law," the boy said, looking at Shane as if he were an idiot.

"Well, I can't outright lie to you, kid. I'm not a cop. I guarantee that. I just saw you making a mistake. I watched you take that woman's purse. Let's just give it back to her and then have some lunch."

"Why should I? She can afford to lose a little bit. I can't," he cried.

"How do you know that? Maybe she has a little boy of her own who needs to be fed. Yes, it's easy to steal from people when you don't know who they are, but you never really know what you're taking. What if her last few coins are in that purse and you just robbed her of it? What if she can't feed her kids now? Do you want to be responsible for another kid who could be even younger than you going hungry? It doesn't feel good. We both know that."

The boy looked at him, obviously fascinated with what he was saying, but he was still so frightened.

"Lia, you need to leave us be," Shane said quietly as he waited for the kid's next move.

"But, Shane —"

"Please, Lia? I can't concentrate with you standing there. I'll meet you back at the hotel."

Lia could feel the stress emanating from him. She knew she was causing more harm than good at this point. She needed to back away. Besides, maybe it was time to get an officer. It didn't seem that's what Shane wanted, but she was very concerned with the knife the kid was holding. He might be young, but that didn't mean he didn't know how to wield a weapon with deadly force.

"OK," she finally answered and began to back away. That's when everything went wrong.

"Get down!" Shane shouted, but it was just a moment too late.

Lia heard a noise like a buzzing sound only seconds

before she felt extreme pain in her torso and then her body locked up and she was writhing on the ground. Her last thought before blacking out was to hope that Shane wouldn't do something foolish and get himself killed.

CHAPTER THIRTY-SIX

Ari

"The rest of the college is long gone, all students snoring peacefully in their beds, or more likely half drunk by now, and we've missed our dinner reservation. Do you think we can leave this library sometime in the near future?"

"You can leave any time you want, Rafe," Ari said in response to his snarky comment before grabbing the last book she'd been searching for.

"I want to leave with you. I just never imagined finding a certain book would take half a century," he grumbled.

"Well, aren't you being pleasant tonight?" she asked as she walked over to the desk and checked out her book.

"I had great plans for us," he said as he escorted her from the building.

"Well, they have to wait a few more minutes. I promised Professor Owens that I would water his plants. He won't be back until Monday."

"Where's his office?"

"In the Elson building, sixth floor."

Rafe was silent as they made their way across the college campus Ari was attending for her PhD. When they reached the older section, he looked around at the lack of lighting.

"Were you planning on coming here alone?" he asked grimly.

"It's fine, Rafe," she said with exasperation. "I've been going here for years."

"You told me a few months ago that you didn't like being out late because you were worried about your safety," he reminded her.

"I was just trying to avoid you then, as I should be doing now," she grumbled as they entered one of the oldest buildings on campus. She loved the architecture of the hundred-year-old building, with its faded red brick and large turrets. The building reminded her of a medieval castle, and she had princess fantasies of leaning from one of the windows on the top floor and calling down to her Prince Charming.

That wasn't Rafe.

As they stepped into the elevator, Rafe looked at the old doors with trepidation. "I think the stairs may be a wiser option here," he said as the doors closed.

"Oh, quit worrying. I've used this elevator a million times."

The elevator groaned in complaint as it ascended to the sixth floor and she promptly watered the plants before turning to find Professor Owens's stash of sweets.

"One advantage of watering his plants is that I always get good candy," she said with a smile as she snagged a few little bags and then a couple of sodas for the two of them.

Rafe reluctantly took his can before following her back out of the room and to the elevator.

They walked in and pushed the button for the ground floor. Too late, a loud screeching of metal alerted them that something was wrong, and the elevator tilted slightly to the side, causing them to lose their balance.

"What the hell?" Rafe shouted as he tugged her against him and grabbed the support bar on the wall.

Ari held on tight to Rafe, not too alarmed yet, but certainly eager to get out of the old contraption as it made its rickety decent.

After what felt like hours, but in reality was only a few seconds, the awful jerking motion stopped, but so did the elevator. There was no sound, no movement, nothing. Ari waited for the doors to open, but it didn't happen.

Rafe reached for the "open door" button and pressed it several times.

Nothing.

Then he began pushing floor buttons.

Nothing.

Next, he pulled the emergency stop, which confused Ari, as they were already stopped, but if it got them out, she could hardly complain.

Again, nothing.

"There's not an emergency phone in this thing?" Rafe asked Ari, as if she would know what was supposed to be in the danged elevator.

"Obviously, if you don't see one, then that would be a big *no*," she replied.

Taking out his cell phone, Rafe cursed. "It's like we're in the middle of nowhere. I have no service on my

phone. Check yours," he said, but he obviously didn't
hold out hope that it would be any different for her.

"No. Not even a glimmer of service," she said.

Ari swore that if he made one little comment about
being right, if he noted just once that they should have
used the stairs, then she was going to beat him with her
soda can. She glared at him as if daring him to do just
that.

"OK, we need to assess the situation. There has to
be a guard who patrols the floors. Even a cleaning crew.
We need to just get the doors open and call out when
we hear someone," he said as he moved toward the steel
doors.

Ari nodded and watched him take off his jacket.
She certainly shouldn't feel heat in her stomach as he
rolled up his sleeves and then gripped the doors and
began prying them apart, but she was mesmerized as his
back muscles flexed, making her want to run her fingers
over the solid man in front of her.

Though she'd continually tried to resist Rafe, she'd
just given up. Since they'd begun having sex again, she
couldn't seem to get enough.

All through her class this evening, he'd sent her
looks that had her body burning and her stomach quivering. She would think that having sex with the man
for weeks on end would satisfy her cravings, but it had
served only to awaken them in a whole new way.

She was hungry for him, and being trapped wasn't
helping her overheated body one iota.

"Dammit!"

Ari jumped as his voice echoed through the small
box. She noticed he'd managed to get the doors open
about six inches, but no matter how much he worked at

them, they weren't going any farther.

"They always make it look so easy in the movies," she said, making Rafe turn around with a look of exasperation at that comment.

"It's a safety feature. I was just hoping this contraption was so old that it wouldn't have it," he muttered as he gave up. "We're between floors, too. There's nothing more we can do at this point but wait."

He was resigned, but his frustration had seemed to fade.

"Want some candy?" she offered, pulling a couple of bags of chocolate from her purse.

For a moment she didn't think Rafe was going to ease up, which would be disappointing, since they were going to be there for an indefinite amount of time, and it would be even worse if he intended to be a bear.

To her great surprise, he grinned and accepted a bag.

"You know this stuff is terrible for you, right?" he said as he opened the package and took out a handful.

"Yep. I know exactly how bad, and I don't care," she answered happily as she took her own handful, popping it into her mouth with a satisfied sigh. She was very glad she'd swiped some on her way from the room. Her stomach was beginning to rumble because she hadn't eaten since lunch.

Ari slid down the wall, deciding she wasn't going to stand there all night. Rafe joined her as he began munching on his chocolate, making her feel quite smug, especially after his little health comment.

"I guess it's all right to indulge once in a while," he conceded.

"Oh, Rafe, it's OK to indulge *all* the time — in many things," she countered, giving him a flirtatious wink.

Looking at her incredulously for a moment, Rafe put down his chocolate and tugged her onto his lap, positioning her so her back was pressed against his chest, her backside cushioned on his thighs.

"You know, chocolate is an aphrodisiac," she said as she leaned back, content to sit with him with his arms wrapped around her middle, and her fingers full of chocolate gooeyness.

"Don't tempt me, woman. Hopefully, we're going to get rescued at any moment and I don't want anyone except for me to see you naked," he said and pressed his lips to her neck.

"What if we were really quick?" She wiggled on his lap.

Never before had she been this bold, this daring. Two years ago, the thought of having sex in a public place would have horrified her. Now, she was hot and swollen, and she couldn't think of anything better than to have him sink deep inside her.

Ari forgot all about the fact that they were trapped. It was almost as if she were sitting with Rafe in a quiet, though uncomfortable, room. As his hands made circles on her stomach, she felt only desire and warmth, no fear, no need to be rescued.

In that moment, she realized what she was doing. By focusing on her desire, focusing on her physical need for Rafe, she didn't have to focus on anything else; she didn't have to think about them as a couple.

That wasn't healthy. That's what got them into so much trouble the first go-round. Yes, she'd fallen in love with him, but it hadn't been enough. Why had she fallen in love with a man who had forced her into a situation against her will?

That said more about her than him.

She was already sliding back into that pattern, even though two years had passed. The thought of him fading back out of her life was almost unbearable. But why? What was it about him that made her never want to be apart?

"Tell me about South America."

Rafe stiffened, his hand stalling for a moment.

"What do you want to know?"

"Everything. Tell me what you did, who you met, why you say it changed you so much."

"I don't think this is the right time," he hedged.

"This is the perfect time, Rafe. We're trapped in an elevator with no idea when anyone will come around," she said.

"I can think of other things we can do to occupy ourselves," he said. His hands rose from her stomach and gripped her breasts.

"I thought you said we couldn't fool around," she reminded him.

"I've changed my mind," he told her, and he nuzzled her neck. His distraction technique was working quite well.

Ari felt herself melting, felt her body clamoring for the feelings he gave it, but she shook her head. They needed to talk — to really talk.

With reluctance, she grabbed his hands and pushed them back down to her stomach, her words a bit breathy when she spoke next.

"Please tell me, Rafe."

"I can't seem to deny you anything, Ari," he murmured. He pulled her even closer against his body, but his hands remained on her stomach and thighs, with his fingers drifting lazily across her skin, yet making no attempt to ignite her passion.

Of course, whenever he touched her anywhere, her desire was stirred up, but she did her best to repress it, knowing that when they did finally come together, it would be explosive.

Rafe pressed his nose into her hair and inhaled deeply, then exhaled and began, "You were right to leave me. I didn't think so then, but I know it was the right thing for you to do. After my wife left, I turned into a cold bastard. I think I figured that since she'd hurt me, it was OK for me to do the same to other women, that they were all cold and calculating, and only after what they could get. My ex-wife is that type of woman, but I shouldn't have lumped together everyone else. You are about as different from her as it gets — a polar opposite. My mother would never treat a man that way, and though my sisters can be brats, they aren't cruel, deceptive, or out for money and position. I had those examples in front of me, but I still thrust everything but my pain aside. I didn't want to feel again. I didn't want to allow a woman to have power over me."

Ari was surprised to hear him admit any of this. Rafe didn't often say he was wrong.

"I went a few years with relationships that were mutually pleasing. I had my needs met, and the women were provided for. Those women were happy. I wasn't what they were in love with; it was my money, my influence, my power. When I was done, I made sure they were set up for quite some time. I've only had a couple of them try to come back. I made it very clear that it wouldn't happen."

Right then he sounded so cold that a shudder passed through Ari. This was the man she'd met three years previously, the man who had frightened her, but also intrigued her. There was fire in this man's eyes, but also something that needed fixing. She'd been so naïve.

"Why me, Rafe? Why would you possibly choose me? I was nothing like those women you'd been with before. I had no clue what I was getting myself into when I went in for that interview. I honestly thought it was a real job."

"Oh, it was a real job," he said as he nuzzled her throat.

"I'm serious, Rafe," she scolded.

"I know. I knew from the moment you walked into my office that you weren't the right type of woman. I looked at you, and innocence was practically leaping from every pore on your body. You wouldn't cooperate, wouldn't fall into the type of relationship I demanded. I knew it was a bad idea from the start."

When he paused, she waited, then asked, "So why did you pursue me?"

"Because I couldn't stop myself."

"What?" None of what he was saying made any sense.

"I knew you wouldn't go along, blindly and unques-tioningly, with what I wanted. I knew it would be a constant battle, but even knowing that, I was drawn to you. I thought I wanted you so much just because you refused me, and that turned me on, but it was more than that. I couldn't get you from my mind."

"Are you saying you were in love with me?" Ari didn't believe in love at first sight.

"No. I was infatuated. I had to have you. I thought

if I had you even once, the appeal would fade, but the more I was with you, the more insatiable I became. You quickly turned into an obsession for me," he admitted.

"Is that what this is about? Obsession?" Ari felt as though her heart were being crushed.

"No! That was the way it was in the beginning. I fought the infatuation. I didn't like the control you held over me. I didn't like the free-falling sensation you inflicted on me, but I couldn't seem to function properly without you. I still can't."

"So, this is all because I said no to you, because I walked away? You can't handle that?"

"No, Ari. That was how it started. Now, I feel like I can't breathe without you, but it's not in a bad way. I was in South America and there was a couple. I knew better than to get attached, but I did anyway. The woman died during childbirth, and her husband was so devastated that he took his own life. That's how I feel."

"Like you want to take your own life?" she gasped.

"No. I would never do something so selfish. I am not that weak. What I mean is that I don't want to live my life without you. I realized while I was down there that it wasn't just obsession. It was love. I don't spout poetry, or admit to feelings too often, but I love you, Ari. Yes, this started as a desire to control you, to bend you to my will, to break you, I'm ashamed to say. But somewhere in the middle of all of this, it changed. I didn't want to break you anymore. I didn't want to hurt you. I wanted to see you fly. If I were a better man, I would walk away, let you live your life. But I am still selfish; I am greedy. I need you in ways you won't ever begin to comprehend. I love you."

Ari was left speechless; she twisted in his arms,

turning her body so she was straddling him and could look into his eyes. What she saw made her heart leap in her chest.

Raising her hand, she stroked his cheek. He lifted his own hand and covered hers, keeping their eye contact unbroken.

"I love you, too, Rafe." He smiled, but she continued, "But is love enough?"

He looked at her with so many emotions filling his unique eyes. "It's a beginning. It's a foundation. If you let me prove it to you, I'll show you that I will never hurt you again," he promised.

"I want that," she said, and then leaned forward and kissed him. Yes, her body was on fire, but that wasn't what this was about. This was about trust, need, emotional connection. There was more to life than just sex and passion — though those things were damn good.

She leaned her head against his shoulder while his arms wrapped around her. As his fingers rubbed up and down her back, one lone tear slipped from her eye.

Was love enough to overcome the pain?

CHAPTER THIRTY-SEVEN

Rachel

RACHEL sat at the small café, enjoying the spring breeze as she drank a cup of decaffeinated tea. What was the point of drinking it without caffeine? she wondered. Oh, this pregnancy wasn't going to be pleasant, not at all.

Having arrived in America only a few days before, she was taking the higher road and meeting up with Ian, who had asked nicely this time and had flown across the ocean to speak to her. For the sake of her unborn child, she could compromise — just a little. She was the one who had to carry the child, gain a million pounds and have strange cravings at all hours of the day, so she had her limits.

If anyone should be compromising, it should be Ian, but she knew it was more mature just to speak to him, to be an adult. She didn't want to have what ifs, and she wanted to be able to tell her child about his father, even if the man was a little bit crazy.

Still, the longer that she sat there, the greater her

misgivings and second thoughts about meeting with him. She was afraid of the turbulent emotions he caused in her, but then again, she knew she couldn't think only of herself. Though she didn't *feel* pregnant yet, there *was* a baby growing inside her, and whether she liked it or not, Ian would be a part of her child's life if he really wanted to be.

Her decision to have a weeklong affair with a stranger would forever haunt her now. She still hadn't worked up the courage to tell her family. There would be no choice soon, since she would be showing in about a month. She could probably hide it for a while longer with the right clothes, but then when she showed up for a family function holding an infant, she'd have more than a little explaining to do.

It was time she confessed. She wasn't a young girl who would get grounded or have her car taken away. She was an adult, and she had made an adult decision, and now she would face the consequences of her actions.

"Thank you for meeting with me, Rachel."

Rachel jumped at the rich timbre of Ian's voice as he sat down across from her. If only he weren't so devastatingly handsome. His nearly black eyes bored into her as he waited for her to say something.

At least today he was dressed in regular clothing. *Well, as regular as a wealthy man could wear*, she thought. His custom suit probably cost about fifty grand. Not that she had much room to talk, considering that her shoes had been ridiculously expensive — oh, and then there was her purse. Still, his expenditures left hers in the dust.

"Of course, Ian. We *are* adults and can discuss this

rationally. I think we both just needed a little time to cool down. I'm curious about something, though. Why are you so sure that the child I'm carrying has anything to do with you? Maybe I'm trying to scam you, take what I can get. You seem to have a low opinion of women, anyway, so what makes you think I haven't been a floozy, sleeping around with anyone and everyone?"

He sat there too stunned to utter words for a moment as she looked at him without emotion. Let him think what he wanted about her. She didn't care — well, not much, at least.

Finally, he must have decided on humor, because he laughed. "I have some very good reasons, Rachel. By themselves, each could be considered weak, but together, they satisfy me beyond any doubt."

"And they are?" She definitely wanted to hear how he'd come to his own conclusions. He was either very trusting, or incredibly foolish.

"The first is that you didn't try to deny it when I confronted you," he said.

Rachel almost snorted. "Maybe I wanted to pawn my child off on a king. Clever, no?"

"But you didn't know I was a king."

"Details, details. I could be one hell of an actress. You don't know me, can't possibly know me after only a week together. Maybe I just wanted any guy stupid enough to claim the child I carry. Maybe I simply don't know who the father is — for all you know, I could have torrid affairs with different men every week."

"But you don't, Rachel," he said smugly. "To be sure, I don't know precisely what you were up to before our week together, though my investigators didn't turn up any evidence of promiscuity, or even a serious boyfriend.

And after we were together? No one at all. Remember, I had you followed. In short, my sweet, *you* are not a wanton woman — or let me rephrase that. You seem to be very selective in your favors."

"Ha. Let me rephrase what I said earlier: *you don't know me*," she practically growled, not at all liking how thoroughly he'd had her watched. It angered and upset her. It also brought home the sad fact that she didn't have much of a life.

"I'm trying to remedy that now, Rachel. You're the one who is choosing to be stubborn while I'm putting myself out there," he scolded her, before adding, "Am I sorry that the condom broke? Who knows? It's impossible for me to form a decision either way because the reality is that it did break, and we can't turn back the clock now. I will emphatically say, though, that I am pleased that the mother of my child is an honorable woman. I would have expected that anyway because of your fine family."

Rachel decided to suppress her outrage; it wouldn't do any good. She'd just cut to the chase. "I'm sure by now," she said, "that you've realized how ridiculous your insistence on marriage was." Trying to act casual and unaffected, she picked up her cup and took a drink.

His eyes narrowed only the slightest bit, but she could easily see she'd irritated him. Well, too bad. He needed to realize that she wasn't some pushover, and he would have to learn very quickly that the baby she carried was in *her* body. When their child was born, he could help with decisions, but until then, it was all on her.

"I see you haven't taken time to consider the needs of our child."

"Maybe this wasn't a good idea, Ian. I thought by now that you would have come to your senses. Obviously you haven't," she said.

The waitress approached and Rachel sat there steaming while Ian placed an order, perfectly calm, even making the waitress swoon when he gave her his megawatt smile. She wanted to smack his face. That was the same smile he'd given her!

"This conversation would be much better held in private," he said when the woman departed.

"I don't trust myself not to stab you if we're in private," she told him pleasantly as she picked up her bagel and began to munch on it.

His eyes rounded before he laughed.

"Rachel, you are very refreshing. Do you know that? I am unused to women taking such liberties in the way in which they speak to me."

"Well, then, you haven't been hanging out in America long enough."

"No. I'm unable to be here for the length of time I originally planned. I have obligations at home, a country in upheaval since the death of my father, and a brother who is on a vendetta," he said, thanking the waitress when she set down his coffee.

"You lost your father?" she asked, her voice softening for a moment.

"Yes, about a month before I met you," he replied.

"I'm sorry, Ian," Rachel told him. That explained a bit about his desperation when they were together, maybe why he'd been so eager to be with a stranger. It didn't explain her own behavior, but it was obvious that he had been grieving and using sex as a way to deal with that pain.

If she hadn't been using him as well, she might have been offended, but as it was, she couldn't take too much of a stance.

"He was a great king," Ian said.

"I'm sure he was a great father, too."

"Yes, he did a good job of ruling his home and his country."

"That doesn't sound like a father. That sounds like a tyrant," she replied, even more worried now that this man was her child's father.

"You compare the king to a tyrant?" he gasped.

"Oh, come on, Ian. You are much too outraged over a little comment. I wasn't calling your daddy a tyrant. Sheesh." She blew out her breath, then returned to her bagel.

"It will do you good to be in my country. Obviously you need to have some manners taught to you," he said with a smirk, quickly recovering from his shock over her unrestrained tongue.

Rachel felt her blood boil.

"I can't believe you just said that. Seriously, Ian, I don't want to keep our child away from you, but I swear, if you make such insulting comments around him, I will chop off your head. My parents taught me that men and women are equal. I don't know what kind of archaic country you run, but you won't turn my child into a chauvinist pig," she said.

"I will enjoy taming you, Rachel. But I do hope you keep some of that fire — for the bedroom, of course."

"I'm done with this conversation. You're the man — pay the bill!" she snapped, and then rose from the table and walked away.

How had she thought they could have a normal

conversation? What had she gotten herself into by sleeping with a stranger? Her brother was going to kill her, kill Ian, maybe just throttle them all and call it good.

"We weren't done speaking yet," Ian said when he caught up to her on the sidewalk.

"You might not have been done, but I was," she informed him. She tugged against the hand he'd placed on her arm.

Suddenly, she was lifted in his arms and he was carrying her between two buildings, leaving them in a quiet alcove. She seriously thought about screaming bloody murder.

"Listen for two seconds," he commanded.

She was so shocked by his tone that her mouth fell open and no sound emerged from her throat.

"That's better," he said. "I can tolerate a certain amount of insolence because you do carry my child, but there are also some things on which I must insist. You will marry me — and I will play an active part in raising the future king. Once you accept this, it will be much easier on all of us."

His body was pressing her against the wall, and though she felt a small measure of desire, anger was quickly overriding it.

"If you don't release me right now, I'll have you arrested for assault and kidnapping," she snapped.

"As a foreign head of state, I have immunity under international law. Good luck with that."

His confident smirk sent her over the edge and Rachel struggled against him, ready to do damage to any part of his body that she could get her hands on.

Ian leaned down and closed his mouth over hers,

knocking her breath out from shock as his tongue slid along her lips. Before she could bite him, he pulled back.

"I won't leave without you, Rachel." By the look in his eyes, she could see that he was deadly serious.

"Well, then, welcome to America," Rachel replied. She'd finally got enough room to lift her knee, and she slammed it against his groin, making him double over in agony.

Before he had a chance to react, Rachel sprinted from the alley and hailed a cab. She was long gone before he emerged from the dark alley. That was probably a *really* good thing for her.

CHAPTER THIRTY-EIGHT

Shane

As the stun-gun prong plunged into Lia's delicate skin, Shane saw red. Time for talking was over.

Three men had approached, and of course, the maggots had gone straight for Lia. They were now circling around Shane, knowing he wasn't as easy a target.

"You need to get away from Andino," the largest man in the group said, menace clearly written on his face.

"You're going to pay for hurting my woman," Shane growled, taking a step back so he could have all of the men in his line of vision.

"What do you think you're going to do about it?" another of the men said and guffawed.

"Yeah, I think we're going to have a real good time with *your woman*. She seems like quite the little peach," the group's obvious leader said. He threw a leer in Lia's direction.

Their circling had pushed the group of men, including Shane, back farther into the alley, blocking them from the view of the passing people on the street — not that anyone had jumped in to help thus far. Shane didn't think anyone was planning to call the cops or come to their assistance any time soon.

Not that he needed help.

When the man turned toward Lia, taking his eyes off Shane, he made his first mistake. Never take your eye off the threat.

Shane rushed him, and the man turned back just in time to see Shane's fist slamming toward his jaw.

One hit. That was all it took for him to knock the burly man out.

His friends gasped in shock. Obviously, people didn't take down their leader so easily. They eyed Shane warily as they pulled out baleful blades.

Shane just smiled. He'd taken on far worse thugs than these pathetic wannabe gang members. He wasn't afraid of them; he was just seriously pissed off.

"Kid, I suggest you run like hell. Leave the purse," Shane said, keeping the boy locked in his vision along with the two more hardened men who were still standing.

"I…" The kid was obviously terrified, and he was at a loss for what to do.

"Don't listen to this piece of shit, Andino!" the other guy said. "This will be your first kill."

"No one is dying today, unless it's you," Shane told him. "It's your choice."

Shane didn't back down, and he noticed a glint of fear in the man's eyes. Of course he was afraid, as he should be. These street thugs were so used to using intimidation; they didn't know what to do when their usual tactics didn't work.

"You come into our territory, mess with our business, and then threaten us?" the man said incredulously.

"This isn't a business. This is theft and terrorizing. Real men don't go after innocent women. I lived on the streets. We never hurt women!" Shane thundered.

"Whatever. You haven't known a hard day in your life. But you're about to," one of them said as he braved up and charged Shane.

One kick to the man's throat and he sank to the ground, holding his bruised windpipe, gasping and gaping like a fish out of water as he desperately tried to draw air.

"Do you want to go, too?" Shane asked the third man, who looked properly afraid.

"Screw this," the last man yelled and ran from the alley, dropping his electroshock weapon to the pavement in his scramble to get away.

The kid, Andino, was left standing there in a stunned daze with the knife barely grasped in his shaking fingers. Shane moved quickly, removing the weapon from the kid's hand and tossing it in a nearby trash bin before he moved to Lia and carefully disconnected the probes that had probably sent two or three hundred thousand volts of electricity through her body.

"I need to get her to the hospital, but you have a choice to make, Andino. You can keep living this life, being a thug who goes after innocent women, or you can turn it around." Shane tossed his card at the kid before gently lifting Lia into his arms.

"The first step would be giving back the purse."

With that, he walked from the alley. From the terror in the kid's eyes, he thought he might have gotten through. It just depended on whether Andino walked away now or went back to the safety of his thug friends. Shane didn't have time to talk anymore. He had to get Lia help.

Coming out of the alley, Shane moved down the street quickly until he found a cab, then had the driver rush him to the hospital.

They got her in immediately, and the damage was minimal. The thugs had hoped to have their way with her, instead of committing murder. If they'd had a gun… Shane didn't even want to think about what would have happened then.

He never should have chased that kid, never should have put Lia in that kind of danger. He hadn't thought; he'd just reacted. He'd seen the fear on the kid's face when he'd snatched the purse, and he'd run like hell.

Shane knew there was hope for Andino, knew the boy could change his life around. Those were the kids he tried to help — the ones who could break out of the life they thought they were destined to live.

He hoped the boy would call.

"Shane?"

His head whipped around, and he saw Lia looking at him full of fright.

"I'm right here, baby. You need to rest."

"What happened? How did we get away?"

Shane sat there, not wanting to tell her about his life, not wanting her to know his secrets. He was trying to figure out a way around this. If she knew him, truly knew him, he was afraid he would lose her forever.

"They got scared, Lia."

She looked at him with her brow furrowed. Even Lia knew the dangers of gangs. They didn't often get frightened — at least not by one unconscious woman and one unarmed guy.

"Why did they get scared? They had weapons. We didn't."

Shane sighed.

"There are parts of my life that you don't know about, Lia. Some things I'm not at liberty to talk about, and other things I haven't wanted to share. I just…I just want you to know me — Shane. The same boy who showed up on your doorstep as a college student."

"What don't I know about you, Shane? What else could there be?"

"It doesn't matter right now, Lia. We'll talk more about it later," he promised, but he hoped it was a talk they'd never had to have.

The medication the hospital was giving her made her tired, and though he could see she was fighting it, her eyes closed and she fell back to sleep.

Shane leaned back, thankful to have some more time. He needed to figure all of this out. He was afraid that if Lia knew everything about him, she'd just give up and walk from his life for good. There was too much — far too much for any sane woman to handle.

Knowing he might not have much time left with her, Shane kicked off his shoes and climbed into her hospital bed, right next to her. He had to hold her, had to grasp on to what they had for just a while longer. Tomorrow, when the sun rose, his life might be much different. For now, he had everything he needed right in his arms.

Tomorrow.

Well, tomorrow might be another story entirely.

CHAPTER THIRTY-NINE

Ari

THE elevator lurched, and Ari looked at the door with trepidation. They'd been sitting in the cold metal car for about two hours and her bladder was full — darned soda! — and, even worse, they were out of chocolate.

Still, she didn't regret getting stuck. Thoroughly content in Rafe's arms, she experienced wonder and desire and a sense of safety. Yes, it was amusing that she felt safe trapped in a contraption that was on the fritz, but he'd opened up to her. Her overarching feeling was one of trust, both for him and by him.

Suddenly, the box began moving with the doors still open a few inches, and Ari and Rafe watched as they passed the different floors. When the elevator stopped again, the doors groaned before they opened halfway and then seemed to get stuck.

Rafe pushed Ari to her feet, then leapt up, wedged himself in the doors, and held out his hand.

"Let's get out of here before it decides to lock us in again," Rafe said.

Ari laughed and squeezed past him. The two of them made their way from the building, and Rafe made a call as soon as his phone got reception again, letting the school know the situation so someone else didn't get stuck in the wretched contraption.

"I have to say that was the best date I've ever been on," Ari remarked as the two of them moved through the empty campus toward the parking lot and Rafe's car.

He stopped and looked at her with puzzlement.

"Being trapped in an elevator?"

"You talked to me, *really* talked to me," she said, as if that was the greatest gift he could give. To her, it was. No subjunctive needed, she chuckled to herself.

"I'm sorry, Ari. I've been so terrible to you that just a moment of kindness is a shock." He pulled her into his arms.

"Yes, you have been terrible, but you have also done some pretty amazing things, Rafe. If you were nothing but a monster, I never would have fallen in love with you."

"If you're in love with me, then why can't that be enough?" he asked as he stroked her head, his fingers running through her hair.

"Sometimes love isn't enough, but the situation isn't hopeless. I just don't want to be a fool and make a rash decision because I'm all gooey inside," she said.

"Gooey?" he asked with a laugh.

"Yes, *gooey* is a word, a perfectly good one," she told him. She stood on her toes and kissed his jaw.

"I guess I'll take that as a compliment, then." He held her head and connected their lips, pulling her tight against his body so she could feel his solid heat pressing into her.

Ari couldn't get close enough to him as he deepened the kiss, his tongue tracing her mouth, devouring her. Her hands ran down his arms, then slid around his waist and came down to rest on his backside so she could pull him more tightly to her.

"I should have relieved the burn while we were in the elevator," he growled as he pulled back, desire clouding his vision.

"Yes, you should have. Then we wouldn't be nearly as desperate to remove these clothes," she said as she squeezed his hard buttocks.

"Oh, that's where you're wrong, Ari. I can take you one minute and be solid and ready the next. I can't ever get enough of you. Not your body — your mind — your soul — and certainly not your love. I want all of you, day and night, and it will never be enough, because the more you give, the more I want."

Ari melted at his words. She wanted all of him, too. That was the problem. Even though he was speaking of his love, she couldn't be sure he was giving all of himself. He was private and guarded, and he had built a wall around himself that he wasn't even aware of.

Would she be fine to settle for what he was willing to give? Or would it eventually rip her apart to only have the pieces of himself he could share?

What would be worse, though? To live with a piece of Rafe, or to have nothing of him at all?

"I know I can't change overnight, Ari. I know it will take time for you to trust me, but I promise you this. I promise that if you stay with me of your own free will, if you give us a real chance, I will forever love you, I will always take care of you, and I will listen to you. I won't ever try to change you again. I will be there for you, in sickness and health. I will support your career and carry you through storms. I will lean on you when I need to, and I will share my life with you. I want it all; I want forever. If you trust me, I will fix everything about me that is broken and I will give you happiness and…well, forever."

Ari looked into his eyes, saw the sincerity, the passion, the love. Rafe did have a way to go, but as he held her close, she also knew that they could both heal with each other. They could weather the storm if they held on tightly to each other's hands.

This wasn't the same man she'd met in his sterile office, the man who demanded her total submission. This man had been hurt, but he was willing to let go of the pain of his past, and was ready to give of himself to another.

To her.

"What are you asking of me, Rafe?"

She wanted to be very clear on what he wanted.

"I'm asking you not to run from me anymore. I'm asking you to stay by my side."

She didn't know if he wanted a mistress or a wife, and she wasn't going to ask. Maybe he wouldn't want to marry again after what his ex-wife did to him. Would she be content to be his permanent mistress?

As long as he didn't cheat, as long as he didn't hurt her again, it would be better to be with him than without, even if that didn't include a ring and a white wedding dress.

Disappointment coursed through her at the thought, but she tamped it down. This might be all he could give, but it was so much more than others gave. The bottom line was that she loved him, and to have this much of him filled her heart.

She ignored the small pang of wanting more. If it ever got to be too much for her to bear, she could make a decision then. Right now, none of that mattered. At this moment, she just wanted to feel the glow that was coursing through her without feeling guilty about it, without suffering as conflicting emotions tore at her.

"I don't want to be without you, either, Rafe. Not today, tomorrow or next year. I need you to love me. Please, just remember your promise. Please don't tear me down again," she said.

"I won't, Ari. Never again," he vowed.

The two of them began walking again toward his car. It was a silent ride back to his place, and that night, when they made love, it was truly lovemaking. She felt his desire, but she felt his love for her as he sank deep inside. He never broke the emotional connection, not even as their breaths rushed out in pleasure, not as he kissed her gently, and not when he separated their bodies.

CHAPTER FORTY

Shane

"IF you are ever going to get past this resentment, you have to visit your mother."

"What good would that do?" Shane asked in frustration.

The two of them had come to the States for a brief vacation, but there was only another week before they had to get back to Italy and the Gli Amanti Cove Project — though Lia didn't know he wasn't going back with her right away. He certainly didn't want to waste his time visiting a woman who had never wanted him. Why couldn't Lia just understand that?

"Shane, I know it's hard for you, but you need to know her story. You need to understand why she is the way she is. Do you know anything about your grandparents? Do you know anything about your family at all?"

"Lia, not everyone has a family like yours. As a matter of fact, most people don't. It's unusual for parents to be so great; hell, yours are still married to each other, and who else has parents like that? Most siblings don't get along as beautifully as you, Rafe, and Rachel do. It's why I was so drawn to you guys. I saw something in you that I thought was only on television. I didn't know real families still existed who actually loved each other." It wasn't easy for him to explain.

"I know your mother isn't mentally healthy, Shane. I understand that. But you wouldn't be alive today if it weren't for this woman, so you should at least talk to her, try to understand why she acted the way she did. Why she allowed your father to beat you and her. Obviously she'd had enough finally, since she killed him. Maybe she wants to tell you she's sorry. Maybe she doesn't. She may not even recognize you, but at least you can get some closure."

Shane looked into Lia's eyes, saw how much she wanted this. He didn't want to go, didn't want to visit with the person who'd given birth to him, but he also couldn't seem to tell Lia no. As it was, he'd gotten a call from his commander. He had to leave in a few days for a mission and this time he wasn't going to be able to pass it off as leaving for volunteer work.

He did do a lot of volunteer work, but most of the time when he was gone for extensive periods of time, it wasn't because he was building homes in Third World countries; it was because he was saving lives, fighting terrorism and protecting the people he loved — all without their ever knowing.

Well, Rafe knew, but that wasn't something he wanted Lia to know. She would be furious with him for once again shutting her out.

"I don't want to do this, but I will if it will make you happy," he said, and the smile of joy crossing her face made the upcoming visit with his mother worth it.

There was hardly anything he wouldn't do for Lia.

"Then let's do it now before you have a chance to change your mind," she insisted.

Before Shane had time to blink, Lia had hailed a cab and they were on their way to the psychiatric hospital that held his mother under lock and key.

Shane had been on some hairy missions before, but he'd never been as afraid as he was at that moment. Terror seized him at the thought of coming face to face with the woman who had nearly been responsible for his death.

Not his physical death. That he would have welcomed in those dark days. No, she had almost killed his very soul, turned him into a monster. As it was, he had to fight the demons that resided inside him, fight *not* to become a monster.

In his job, he did turn into that merciless beast, but he always got away before it enveloped him, always came home, where his best friend helped to ground him. This was also another reason that Shane volunteered so much. It opened his eyes to a world of good, where he saw that not all humans were disgusting, selfish creatures to whom heart, character, sympathy, forgiveness, and integrity were nothing more than meaningless words.

For a while, he'd thought only the worst. When he'd robbed people as a starving teenage kid, he'd never felt guilty. His victims were robots, nothing but dark souls on the inside. It had taken him a long time to realize that they weren't — that the people he was hurting were real.

He and Lia stopped in front of the hospital, and Shane was so caught up in his thoughts, he didn't notice

Lia paying the cab driver and tugging on his hand. He *really* didn't want to do this! He'd rather be in the desert somewhere with bombs flying at him.

"Maybe this isn't the best time," he said as the cabbie drove off. Lia must have paid the fellow extra to make a quick exit.

"You're not a chicken, Shane! Now, man up and let's do this," Lia said, looking at him sternly.

Shane snapped from his brooding thoughts and looked back at her. A slight smile parted his lips as he grabbed her by the hair and tugged her to him. Damn, she was good for him. A whiny, cajoling girl would have gotten on his nerves.

Lia's temper and attitude were the things that kept him grounded.

"Did you just imply that I'm a crybaby?" he asked in a menacing tone, one entirely counteracted by the light in his eyes.

"That I did, Mr. Grayson. Now put on your big-girl panties, and let's go," she said, grinning bravely at him.

"What if this only makes it worse?" he asked in a moment of vulnerability.

Lia stopped joking as she looked deep into his eyes. "Then she's forever the fool, Shane. She's missed out on your life — missed the amazing man you've turned into. It's all been her loss. If she can't apologize to you, then you are better off walking away. I think this can be healing for you, though. I wouldn't push so hard if I didn't feel that way."

He looked at her for several heartbeats before a small smile broke out on his lips.

"I guess I'm ready then. I'll never know if I don't walk through those doors," he said, sighing as he looked toward the front of the building.

"I'm always going to be here for you, Shane. Always. I think you need to do this, but if you can't, I understand," she told him, feeling guilt for pushing him so hard. She was trying to ease his pain, not make it worse.

Yes, he needed to do this. Maybe it would make a difference, and maybe it wouldn't, but either way, he would never know if he didn't at least give it a try.

"I can do it. I need to," Shane said. "Thank you, Lia. Thank you for being you, for being understanding, and for giving me exactly what I needed. Sometimes, all it takes is a little push. I guess I've just been too scared to move forward, too weak," he said, as if disgusted with himself.

"That's not true, Shane. You are strong, so very strong. You have faced obstacles that I can't even imagine facing and you've always come out ahead. You'll be fine no matter what happens from this day forward," she said as she lifted her hand and caressed his face again.

"I think we should just admit to each other than we are better people together than apart," he said, surprised by how much he meant those words.

"I can agree to that," Lia told him before reaching up and kissing him, feeling warmth all the way down to her toes. She was happy, unbelievably happy at that moment.

As they walked hand in hand toward the hospital entrance, Shane smiled down at her. Lia had effectively taken his mind off of the upcoming visit to the woman who had given him birth and little else but misery, and he felt relaxed, ready for this next step in his life. It had been a long time coming.

Once they walked through the doors of the institution, however, his shoulders tensed. This wouldn't be
easy — not at all. At least he had Lia by his side.

"It will all work out fine, Shane. I'll be with you the
entire time," Lia said, her hand rubbing along his back
in comfort. Miraculously, her touch soothed him again,
calmed his nerves as he approached the thick-glassed
windows.

"How can I help you?" the man behind the counter
asked.

Shane looked around the sterile lobby with plain
chairs and a counter that was protected by bulletproof
glass. He felt as if he were in a prison facility, but then,
that's essentially what it was. This was a place for crimi-
nals — like his mother.

"We're here to see Betty Grayson," Shane said, and
Lia realized she'd never heard his mother's name before.
Shane didn't refer to his parents by name, but only as
the people who had created him. It was a distinction he
made to remove himself from them further than he had
when he left their house for the last time.

"One moment, please," the clerk said, not showing a
reaction as he looked in the computer. "And how do you
know Ms. Grayson?"

Shane was quiet for a moment before finally speaking. "She's the woman who gave birth to me," he finally
said. It would be too much for him to say she was his
mother.

"Your name?" The man didn't even blink at Shane's
choice of words.

"Shane Grayson, and this is Lia Palazzo."

After a little more typing, the man looked back up.
"I need your IDs, please."

Shane and Lia passed them through a small dipped opening and then waited a while longer. Shane was hoping they would be turned away. Then he could honestly say that he'd tried but there was nothing he could do.

Of course, with his clearance, he could get in to see her if he truly wanted to, but Lia didn't know that. Yet.

After a few moments, the man handed them each a visitor's badge, then buzzed open a door next to the counter. "Go through to the left, and wait at the door there."

Shane sighed in resignation.

Shane and Lia walked through, then waited for another door to be buzzed open for them. Another staff member led them through a maze of hallways.

"If you'll wait here, we'll bring Ms. Grayson in to visit with you," the aide said before leaving them in a plain room with four chairs, a table, and nothing else.

After they sat there for several tense moments, the door opened again, and Lia had to fight a gasp when a woman was brought in. Stringy hair hung down, covering half her face and her reed thin body, wasted body was the picture of unhealthiness. But what shocked Lia the most was the vacant look in her black eyes — the same eyes as Shane had.

Dark, unhealthy circles adorned the area beneath her eyes, and her lips were just lax; there was no expression in her features. Her eyes traveled over both Shane and Lia with a complete lack of interest.

The aide led her to the chair across from them, and she and Shane locked gazes. He was surprised to feel pity for this tiny woman. He thought he would always have her image burned into his brain, but it had been nearly twenty years since he'd last seen her, and if he had passed her on the street, he wouldn't have recognized her.

He noticed that her eyes were the same color as his, but that's where the similarities ended. She looked washed out and vacant, her body just an empty vessel for a lost soul.

"Hello, Betty," he finally said, and she turned her head and she assessed him, a spark of something entering her eyes for only the briefest of moments.

"Do you know who I am?" he asked, his voice quiet, not harsh but not friendly.

She didn't do anything for several moments, then gave the slightest nod, so tiny a movement that if they hadn't been watching her steadily, they would have missed it.

Then she turned to look at Lia, and her eyes were puzzled for a moment, but quickly went vacant again as she turned back toward Shane.

"Do you talk?" he asked.

"Not much," she whispered.

Lia tensed at the childlike sound of her voice. This woman, who had caused so much trauma and pain for Shane, was clearly gone. Lia felt that some people who were locked up in mental facilities instead of prisons got off easy — got a free ride. This wasn't the case for Shane's mother. She was clearly in the right place.

"I didn't want to come today," Shane told her, again keeping his voice neutral.

"Why did you?"

"Lia thought I needed to get some answers from you. I don't think you can give me any," he told her honestly.

"I was bad to you," his mother said, looking right at him, her eyes unblinking, her hands motionless at her sides, as if they were just hanging there, useless limbs on an unused body.

At her words, Shane sat back in shock. Just the slightest tensing of his muscles betrayed his reaction, but Lia knew him enough now to know the words affected him.

"Yes you were," he said.

"That man. He was a bad, bad man. I killed him. He had to die," she went on, her eyes sparking for just a moment, but the emotion in them shocked both Shane and Lia. It was terror. Her hands twitched as if she was getting ready to move, but then she stilled again.

"Yes, you did. Why did you stay with him if he frightened you?" Shane asked, his body relaxing as he leaned slightly forward.

"Nowhere to go. My daddy said I was a naughty girl and I deserved to be with him. I was a sinner, a sinner! I deserved to burn in hell! A sinner!" she screamed as she looked at Shane, her hand suddenly shooting out and gripping his arm, her short nails digging into his flesh.

Lia didn't know what to do. Shane stayed oddly calm while his mother's fingers tightened around his flesh, her grip unyielding.

"No one deserves to be raped or beaten, Betty. No one deserves to go through the pain either of us went through," he told her, his voice still calm even with her growing hysteria.

"Hank hurt me so much. Hurt me all the time. He laid on me, pushed in me, hurt me. Then you were there. My belly grew with you, bigger and bigger. He told me I was bad. I was a slut. His slut. He was mad that you was in there, in the way of his grunts and groans. He hurt me."

"You hated me," Shane said. Still no inflection in his tone as he looked in her crazy, lost eyes.

"Yes, I hated you. I hated him being inside me so long. So long. He was inside me for too long. I thought it would stop, thought he would leave me, but then you were there, and then you came out, and he hated you, too."

Betty spoke with childlike honesty, her words tearing Lia's heart in two. She'd been so wrong to ask Shane to come here, so very wrong.

"Why didn't you give me up for adoption? Why not let someone else raise me if you didn't want me?" This was the one thing that Shane needed to know.

Betty looked at him in surprise and thought about the question. Maybe the idea had never crossed her mind. Maybe no one had told her that was an option.

"I was bad. I had to live with that. Live with being bad. You were my punishment. If you weren't there, I wouldn't be punished. I had to be made to suffer for being bad. Yes, I was bad."

Shane sat back, looking at her with pity. This woman was gone. She'd been gone for a long time. There was no use in staying there with her any longer. There was nothing she could tell him, no answers she would be able to give. Maybe she'd been lost from the first moment she'd met the man who had raped her and caused Shane's existence. Maybe it had been before that moment. Either way, she was just a shell, and he would never get any clear answers from her.

He rose, and Lia quickly followed.

"I won't be back, Betty. I'm sorry you've had such a

difficult life," he said as he looked down at the woman, who was now rocking herself back and forth, back and forth.

"Please, Shane, please," she pleaded, holding her legs as she rocked in the chair.

"Please, what?" Both he and Lia were puzzled.

"Please don't hurt me anymore. I was just bad once, just once. Please set me free," she begged, her eyes showing emotion as they teared up.

What Shane did next nearly dropped Lia to her knees.

He walked to Betty, and Lia was afraid he was going to hurt the woman, but she should have known better. This man would never hurt anyone — not even a person who had helped to ruin his early existence.

He kneeled down and put his hand on hers, which was resting on her legs. "You are free, Betty. Do you hear me? You've paid for your crimes. It's time for you to be free. There won't be any more punishment. You don't have to be afraid anymore," he whispered while looking in her eyes.

The rocking motion stopped, and she looked at him with wonder. The corner of her mouth turned up.

"I'm free?" she asked.

"Yes, you are free. No one will hurt you anymore. I won't hurt you. You've served enough time."

Shane stood up and moved to the door, knocking to be let out.

"Thank you," Betty whispered as he and Lia left the room. The last sound they heard before the door shut was the sound of laughter, a tinkling noise that made Lia think of a child, a very young one.

Shane didn't say a word as they walked from the

hospital, just took the time to process what Betty had said to him.

It was good that he'd come, good that he'd spoken to her. He could no longer hate the woman who had given him birth. All he could do was feel pity toward her vacant shell, once a person, perhaps, now mentally a child locked inside a useless body.

Now, maybe she would find a measure of peace. He meant what he'd said to her — she was free to end her punishment. He didn't love her, never could love the woman who had hurt him so badly for so many years.

He could forgive her, though.

"Thank you, Lia. It was good that I went there."

"I was thinking it was too much," Lia said as she faced him with tears in her eyes.

"No. I may have told her she was free, but I was also set free, Lia. How can I hold that lifeless woman responsible? She has punished herself far more than I would ever want to punish any person. She was wrong in what she did to me, but she's more than paid the price."

Shane pulled Lia into his arms and held on tight. Her freshness, love, and loyalty held him on the ground, kept his heartbeat steady.

With Lia, he could get through anything.

CHAPTER FORTY-ONE

Ari

SOMETHING woke Ari far too early in the morning. A noise? She didn't know what, but before she could open her eyes, she could smell the sweet scent of flowers. As she sleepily took in the room, she lay there with her mouth agape.

Looking around in shock, she couldn't see a single bare place on any of the tables in the room. They were filled with vase after vase of her favorite flowers, star-gazer lilies. The beautiful pink-and-white flowers were everywhere, mixed with roses, lilacs, carnations and delicate greenery.

The sight was so beautiful, Ari wished for a moment that she were a poet or a painter rather than a historian.

"Rafe?" she called, but there wasn't an answer.

She turned to glance at the clock on the night stand and noted that it was midnight. Not morning, at all. They'd gone to bed only a couple hours before. How had he managed to decorate the room while she was there sleeping?

Crawling slowly from his giant bed, she moved through the room, smelling the beautiful bouquets. On each one, there was a note attached. There had to be a hundred notes.

She opened the first:

Your smile is a beacon on a stormy night.

She rushed quickly to the next envelope:

My heart isn't whole without you.

She moved through the room, opening note after note.

Your beauty is unparalleled.

You make every day a delight.

Nothing makes me happier than to have you in my arms.

Your intelligence is breathtaking.

Ari clutched note after note in her hand, collecting them all, a shy smile splitting her face. When she entered the bathroom, more flowers awaited her, along with burning candles, their scent flavoring the air.

On the mirror another note was written in what appeared to be a permanent marker. His housekeeper wouldn't be happy, but Ari was thrilled.

Get dressed and come out the front door.

Ari didn't hesitate; she rushed back into his room

and found a stunning blue dress hanging in the closet, along with fresh lingerie and stockings, and a pair of heels she fell instantly in love with.

Dressing quickly, she then hurriedly put on a minimum of makeup, brushed out her hair and threw the bedroom door open.

Tears filled her eyes when she saw that the hallway was lined with more bouquets, all sporting notes, all in Rafe's handwriting. She wanted to rush out the door, but she took her time gathering the notes, opening each one and cherishing the words of his heart's confession.

Some were little quotes from texts and messages he'd sent her, some spoke of her beauty and talent, and some simply said, *I love you*. Each one she clutched in her hand, knowing she would forever hold on to them.

When she reached the stairs, she found large vases with more bouquets, and candles on every other step to guide her way down. Her collection of notes kept getting larger.

At the door, a man in a tux waited for her with a glass of champagne in his hand. She thanked him as she accepted the glass, then beamed when she saw the sparkling white limo in the driveway.

Another well-dressed man waited there. He opened the door for her, holding her glass while she got in. Expecting to see Rafe inside, she was disappointed to find herself alone. The man handed her the champagne, then gently shut the door.

When the engine started, a video began with the most tender piano solo playing in the background, and Rafe's face appeared on the large screen.

"There aren't enough words in the dictionary for me to express how you have changed my life for the better,

Ari. I was a fool for a long time, and yet you have given me a second chance. I promise you that I will never betray your trust again. I promise never to hurt you. I promise to do everything in my power to make you supremely happy."

He faded away, and her mother appeared on the screen, her face beaming. Ari felt as if she could reach out and touch her.

"My beautiful daughter. You have always brought me so much joy. I am so very proud of you and all that you do for those you love, and for those who love you. If more people in the world were like you, there wouldn't be war or hunger. There wouldn't be crime. You are gentle and kind, loving and giving. You are the child every parent dreams of having. I love you always. This is a special day, and I am so grateful to be a part of it."

The next image was of her friends from her old job, then Lia and Rachel, Rafe's parents, her favorite professors, a few of her students. So many people on screen telling her how wonderful she was.

Even though none of them could see her, Ari's cheeks heated with modest embarrassment at a video that was all about her.

The car slowed, and Ari's stomach tensed. When would Rafe appear? Was this a marriage proposal? She didn't want to hope, but suddenly that was all she could think about. Surely a man wouldn't do all of this just to express his love.

The door opened, and Ari stepped out onto a red carpet, one that led through a luxuriant garden. Softly glowing candles aligned the edge of the carpet to light the way. No one was around; the driver just gave her instructions to follow the path.

A few steps in, there were more vases of her favorite flowers highlighted by the glow of the candles. Suddenly a song started playing over speakers she couldn't see. Ari stopped as tears began cascading down her face.

"Bless the Broken Road" filled the air, surrounding Ari with Rascal Flatts's words of love, hope, and change.

Yes, Rafe had chosen the wrong path, but he was showing her in so many ways that he had finally chosen love over pain, that he had chosen her above anything else. The song finished as she went under an arch filled with stargazer lilies and finally found Rafe in the center of a large field.

Candles burned all around him; he stood there holding a single rose, looking unbelievably handsome in a sharp black tuxedo. She glided along the path toward him, not even sure whether her feet were touching the ground.

Somewhere in her brain, she registered Keith Urban's song "Making Memories of Us." All of it was too much, but oh, so perfect.

She reached Rafe and he kneeled before her, the dark of the night enveloping them both, all of which made Ari's knees shake and her tears fall.

"I'd rather die a thousand deaths than spend one more day without you in my life. You are the air that I breathe, the beat of my heart. You are the calm in a storm, and the only person who can take my pain away. I know you would flourish on your own; I know there isn't anything that you can't achieve for yourself. I am the one who will fail if you walk away. I would wither, crumple to the ground. You make me whole, Ari. Please say you will end my days of agony, my self-imposed prison. Marry me. Make me a better man."

Her throat closed, making it impossible for her to speak. Rafe didn't do anything by half measures. He loved her, really loved her, and he was showing her in the only way he knew how that it was forever.

Finally, her voice returned.

"You are wrong, Rafe. Both of us would survive without the other, but it would just be survival; it would be empty. Walking away from you once nearly destroyed me, and I don't think I could ever do it again. Yes, I will marry you. Yes, I would be honored to stay by your side. You have given me so much, and I only hope that I can show you how much you mean to me."

Rafe placed a sparkling diamond on her finger, the candlelight reflecting bursts of color in every direction. Yes, the ring was gorgeous, but only one thing, one thing alone, could keep her attention for long. Only the look in Rafe's eyes.

With a laugh filled with joy, Rafe stood and swept Ari into his arms, spinning her in a circle as she registered the sound of applause.

When he set her back down, she looked around, seeing their friends and family approaching them with large congratulatory grins and nodding in approval.

"Now, what would you have done if I had turned you down in front of all these people?" she asked with a laugh.

"I would have deserved the humiliation," he answered.

Rafe kissed her with so much love, she felt she would burst. Then they were surrounded, and Ari accepted congratulations from those she had loved her whole life, and from those who had recently become a part of her life.

How he'd managed to keep this all from her, she had no idea, but knowing that she'd get to fall asleep every night in his arms and wake every morning in the same place filled her with so much joy, she couldn't keep the wide smile from her face.

When there was a pause in the hugs, her head lifted and Rafe's gaze captured hers. He simply smiled back at her and Ari lost her breath. For the rest of their lives, he was hers.

CHAPTER FORTY-TWO

"This has got to be the world's shortest engagement," Ari said as Lia and Rachel danced in circles around her.

"What can we say? When Rafe decides on something, he goes forward at the speed of light," Rachel said with a forced laugh.

"Well, I expected it to last longer than two weeks, but I am excited to marry him. I really am," Ari told them as she tried on another gown.

Rafe had wanted one made, but Ari insisted that part of the fun of picking a wedding dress was to try on a hundred until she found the one that she couldn't live without, so she was at the bridal shop with her mother, Lia and Rachel.

The girls had already found their bridesmaids' gowns, and her mother picked out the perfect mother-of-the-bride gown. Now, Ari just had to find her own.

"Oh, Ari, that's the one!" Lia gasped as she gazed at her in awe.

As Ari turned around, she was reluctant to look in the mirror, sure she would hate what she was trying on now. None of them had been what she wanted, but she couldn't say what she wanted exactly, because she just didn't know. When she found *the* dress, she figured there would be no hesitation.

As she slowly spun around and looked up, her breath caught. Yes, this was the one. It had a flattering cut to the top that made it modest, yet showed off her shoulders and neck, allowing her to wear jewelry. The entire gown had intricate beading that formed small flowers from the neckline all the way through the flowing skirt. Hugging her tightly on top, the gown then flared at her hips, flowing down her legs, and easily fluttering as she turned in circles on the big stage she was standing on.

She swished her hips, making the silky fabric swish and the beads sparkle in the bright lights of the bridal shop. There was a lot of fabric, but it was so light that she didn't feel weighed down.

"Try this, darling," Sandra said as she came up behind Ari and placed a simple tiara on her head with a delicate veil that hung down her back.

"Yes, I agree, baby. This is the dress," Sandra said, her eyes filling with tears.

"Are you sure, Mom?"

"Very sure, Ari. You look like a royal princess."

"I feel like one, Mom. This is all so unreal. Do you think we are moving too fast?" That was Ari's biggest concern.

"If I thought you were making a mistake, I would tell you, Ari. You know that. I would never want you to be unhappy, not for any reason. You deserve the moon and stars, and I think Rafe will give them to you."

Sandra stood beside her daughter, leaning over and kissing her on the cheek. Ari wrapped her arms around her mother, thankful still to have her in her life. If the car wreck or the cancer had taken her mom from her, Ari had no idea what she'd be doing now. How did anyone survive the loss of one so dear?

She was strong enough now to make it through anything, but she hadn't been ready to let her mother go two years ago. She still wasn't ready, but few children ever were, no matter how young or old their parents were.

Lia and Rachel had stepped from the room to let the mother and daughter talk, but as the tailor walked in, they followed him, and they oohed and aahed some more while he put in the proper marks and promised to have the alterations ready in one week, just a few days before the wedding.

"OK. Now we have the dress and shoes. It's time to get the lingerie!" Lia said with a wicked smile.

Ari blushed as she looked toward her mother.

"I think I will leave you young women to do this part," Sandra said. She kissed Ari's cheek again, then gathered up her purse.

"You don't have to leave, Mom. We can shop for other things," Ari said, not wanting to make her mother feel unwelcome.

"I have a date with Marco tonight. I need to go and get ready," Sandra said with a smile.

"I'm so happy that he treats you well, Mom. Since you have been dating, you have a glow to your cheeks. When do you think I'll be attending *your* wedding?"

Sandra blushed and looked down. But then lifting her chin with a shy confidence, she smiled. "I think he may ask me very soon. He's been hinting a lot lately."

"We could always have a double wedding," Ari teased.

"Not on your life, Ari. Besides, I'm too old to have a big to-do if we do get married. It will probably just be the two of us in front of the justice of the peace," she said.

"That won't happen, Mama. You never got your dream wedding, and you deserve it just as much as I do," Ari said.

"Well, you just quit worrying about it, Ari. Your special day is in only ten days. We will focus on me later. I had to hire some help to complete all the flowers. Your future husband has insisted on a lot of arrangements."

"I should never have let him be in charge of flowers. I thought it was so romantic when he asked me if he could," Ari said with a sigh. She was thrilled he'd asked her mom to do all the arrangements, though. It would be good for Sandra's business, since a lot of Rafe's contacts would be at their wedding.

The event was going to be far larger than Ari had ever envisioned, but it didn't matter. All that mattered was that at the end of the night he would be her husband, and she his wife.

"You girls have a good time. I'm going to go and see my sweetie now," Sandra said, and she left.

"I love your mom, Ari. She's a beautiful woman, inside and out," Lia said while helping Ari get out of her dress.

"Yes, she is pretty spectacular," Ari remarked. She knew that some people didn't have such a great relationship with their mom. It was just one more thing she was thankful for.

She began fiddling with the buttons on her dress, but she didn't really want to take it off. Maybe she'd wear it for a week straight after the wedding. The thought made her giggle. But soon, it was being pulled off her, and she sighed as she began dressing in her street clothes.

"I feel kind of sad without the dress now," she moaned as the tailor took it away.

"You will get to wear it all day long in just over a week," Rachel told her.

"What's the matter, Rachel? You have seemed upset for most of the day," Ari asked, surprised when her friend blushed and looked down at her feet.

"There's nothing the matter. Besides, this isn't about me. The whole week is all about you, Ari," she said, a false smile on her face.

"We aren't leaving here until you tell us what's wrong," Ari insisted. Throwing on the rest of her clothes very quickly, she moved to the couch Rachel was sitting on.

"What is it, Sis?" Lia asked. "Ari's right. You've seemed depressed all day. I didn't want to say anything, but since Ari's brought it up…"

"I shouldn't talk about this right now," Rachel said slowly, but they could see that she really wanted to.

"Please, Rachel. I can't enjoy my day if I know something is upsetting you. You've become one of my best friends — and soon you'll be my sister-in-law," Ari said, leaning over and gave her a hug.

Tears filled Rachel's eyes and spilled over, shocking both Ari and Lia. She wasn't one to cry so easily.

"These flipping hormones are driving me nuts. Fine. I can't hold it in any longer, but please don't say any-thing to Rafe or our parents until after the wedding," Rachel said earnestly.

"You know that you can trust us," Lia said. Ari nodded her agreement.

"I'm pregnant." Rachel didn't work into it, give them time to absorb it, she just spit it out and waited for their reaction.

Ari was the first to say something, since Lia was sitting there with her mouth gaping open.

"I...uh...didn't know you were seeing anyone."

"I'm not," Rachel wailed, and Lia and Ari looked at each other with surprise and confusion.

"Well, it pretty much takes two people, Sis," Lia said with a gentle smile.

"Sheesh. I know that, Lia. I had a weeklong affair with a man in Florida. It was perfect. He was perfect. Oh, my gosh, was he ever perfect! We didn't even give each other last names, just spent the week in bed, making smoking-hot love," Rachel said, her eyes dilating as she spoke about it.

"And you weren't careful?" Lia gasped.

"Of course I was careful, Lia. We used protection every single time. One of them just must have failed. Either that, or he has some freaking smart sperm that managed to make a break for it and swam upstream."

"So you don't know how to get ahold of him?" Ari asked, fighting a grin that wanted to break forth at Rachel's choice of words.

"Well, that's the other thing..." Rachel said, with obvious reluctance.

"What's the other thing?" Lia demanded.

"Well, apparently, he figured out who I was and he had some of his men keeping an eye out just in case a pregnancy did happen. He showed up on my doorstep a few weeks ago."

"There is so much wrong with that statement that

I can't even figure out where to begin," Lia gasped in outrage. "He had men watching you?"

"Yeah, I wasn't happy about that, either. They must be really sneaky because I had no clue whatsoever," Rachel told them, irritation in her voice. "One of them, it turned out, was a co-worker at the embassy, hired by the guy with the wonder sperm."

"Does he want to be a dad?" Ari asked.

"Well, not exactly. He didn't want an unplanned pregnancy, but he insists on being a dad," Rachel told them.

"So, what are you going to do?"

"Well, I'm not going to marry him like he demanded I do!" Rachel said, with the color that had washed from her face now suffusing her cheeks in her temper.

"He insisted you marry him?" Lia asked.

"You sound like a parrot, Lia. Quit repeating everything back to me. Yes. He showed up at my door, told me I was carrying the royal heir and that I had to marry him."

At those words, both Lia and Ari just stared at her. Since Lia didn't want to repeat herself, it was time for Ari to step in after a short pause.

"Did you just say *royal heir*?"

"Yeah, apparently my one-week stand ended up being King Adriano of Corythia, and I'm carrying the royal heir," she said, her words thick with sarcasm.

"What if it's not a boy?" Ari asked.

Lia and Rachel both turned to her in surprise. Of all the questions, that one wasn't at the top of their list.

"I don't know. There's the queen of England, and the law of succession in England was just changed to designate the first child, male *or* female, as heir to the throne. Maybe girls can be queen there, too, or maybe she'd only be a princess, not Corythia's head of state. I don't know. He said future heir. The guy is arrogant and demanding. Maybe he's so pompous, he thinks he will only produce boys," Rachel said as she shrugged. "No blanks from King Smart Sperm the First."

Several moments passed in which none of them said a word. Finally, Ari broke the silence.

"And I thought I had problems."

Her words made both Lia and Rachel turn toward her. Suddenly the entire situation just seemed so absurd that the women burst out laughing. Five minutes later, when a clerk came to check on them, they were still guffawing noisily. The woman sneaked back out, assuming it was normal pre-wedding jitters.

"Well, Rachel, I will say this much. You know how to take away the nerves. I'm not even worried about the wedding anymore. I'm too busy trying to figure out what you are going to do next," Ari said.

"I have no idea, Ari. I really don't. I know I'm not getting married to that stuffy, self-important, arrogant, lying sack of sh—"

"Careful, Sis. You *are* speaking about a king," Lia interrupted with a laugh.

"Yeah, yeah. Get the jokes out of the way. And get ready to curtsy, because in about six and a half months, I'll be making you babysit," Rachel said.

"Oh, no. I know nothing about babies," Lia said with horror as she gazed down at Rachel's stomach.

"Well, I don't know anything either. I'm the baby of the family, remember?" Rachel said.

"Well, we'll all just have to figure it out together," Ari said.

"Please don't say anything to Rafe. Not yet."

"I promised I wouldn't. Besides, I want to be far away when you tell him," Ari said. Rafe was probably going to explode.

"Me, too. I think I'll call him while you're on your honeymoon, hopefully halfway around the planet."

"You wouldn't dare!" Ari gasped.

"You're right. I wouldn't do that to you. I may just chicken out and let my parents tell him, though. He scares me a lot more than Dad. I'm afraid he'll hunt the guy down and kick his ass or worse for daring to touch his baby sister."

"Yeah, I think he wanted us to be nuns," Lia said. "The thought of us having sex is just too much for him to handle. He even wanted to kill Shane."

"You're forgetting about the bigger picture, Rachel," Ari said, looking at her fondly.

"What's that?" Rachel waited for enlightenment.

"You're going to have this amazing little bundle in about seven months. This perfect child that you created. You're going to be a mother," Ari told her as she reached out and placed her hand on Rachel's stomach.

"I'm going to be an auntie," Lia gasped — the full knowledge was just hitting her.

"Yeah. I guess I've been so scared and dealing with this all on my own and haven't had time to really think about it. It's weird to think I'll be a mother. When I think of moms, I think of ours, not of myself," she said in awe as she placed her hand on her stomach, next to Ari's.

The women were silent as they thought about the near future, when a new baby would join the family.

"All right, we have to get moving," Rachel said. "I

appreciate that you both listened to me, and you've both made me feel much better, but enough talk about all of this. Today is Ari's day." She reached out and hugged them both, another tear falling. "Seriously, I hate these hormones," she grumbled, and she released the girls.

"They're only going to get worse," Lia warned her sister.

The three women walked from the bridal shop, arm in arm. Together they would get through this. They would welcome the new baby and they would be there for each other. This was a new beginning.

CHAPTER FORTY-THREE

Shane

"I can't believe my brother is getting married in just two days," Lia said as she lay in Shane's arms.

"I know. It's strange how things are changing," Shane replied, his fingertips gently trailing over her back. He had to tell her what was happening. He was leaving the day after the wedding. He had to let her know. With this mission, he wasn't sure when — or if — he would be back again.

It wasn't fair to keep her in the dark.

"I'd be happy to just lie here with you all day and night. I am looking forward to going back to the project. It's been nice to be home, but I've gotten used to it over there. I won't mind going back to our island for a while," she said.

Guilt was now eating him alive.

"There's something I have to talk to you about, Lia," he began.

"What is it? You sound worried," she murmured, her voice sleepy as she rubbed her hand along his chest. The touch of her fingers was mesmerizing him. He wanted nothing more than to just drift off to sleep with Lia by his side, but he had to say something.

Tomorrow was Rafe's bachelor party and then the wedding. He couldn't put this off any longer.

"I won't be going back to the island for a few weeks. I have another task I have to do."

She paused in rubbing his chest, and he was sorely tempted to end the conversation, have her stay relaxed in his arms while they held each other.

"Why?" she asked. She tilted her head, looking at him in the pale bedroom light.

"I can't explain, but I'm going to be gone on a task," he said, suspecting his answer wouldn't be good enough.

As she stiffened in his arms, he knew he was right. This would just feel to her as if he were dumping her. That wasn't it. For the first time since he'd been recruited for a special-operations agency, he hated his job — hated that he couldn't tell her the truth.

"I don't understand."

How could she understand?

"Do you remember when I was younger? I did my tour with the army," he began.

"Yes, but that was a long time ago. You served your time and quit," she said, her voice confused.

"Not exactly. I'm part of a team — I'm still in the military, but I can't talk about it," he said, almost loathing himself in this moment.

"What? I don't understand, Shane. I know you quit after four years," she said. He heard the mistrust in her voice.

"It's complicated, Lia, but I am still part of the military and I have to keep it private. I really can't talk about it," he said, his arm tightening around her when she wriggled against him, tried to pull free.

"Let go, Shane. I want to see your face," she demanded.

With reluctance, he loosened his grasp and she sat up, pulling the blanket with her to cover her chest as she stared down at him. Feeling at a disadvantage, he moved upward, sitting against the headboard.

"I'm sorry, Lia. I know I should have said something earlier, but I couldn't without going into a lot of detail. I…I don't really know how to explain this. My hands are tied."

She gazed at him as if trying to figure out whether anything he was telling her was the truth.

"If you don't want to be with me, Shane, you don't need to make up a story. I'm a big girl and can handle it. I've been broken up with before, but I have to tell you, this is the most original story I've heard yet," she snarled.

"It's not a story, Lia. I don't want to leave you. For the first time, I don't want to go, but I have no choice," he said and tried to pull her close.

She recoiled from him, not allowing his hands to wrap around her. Shane blew out a breath in frustration. Nothing with Lia was easy, but then he wouldn't love her as he did if she weren't such a strong woman.

"So, you want me to believe that you're some special agent with the military, and you have to go on a top-secret mission. You'll return when you can, but then you may just be swept off again when the time is right," she said, her words oozing with sarcasm.

"I don't expect you to be happy about it, but I've never lied to you, Lia. Not once," he said, looking her square in the eyes.

"I guess I wouldn't know that, Shane. You're doing a damn fine job of looking me in the face while you tell me this story right now."

"It's not a story, Lia. I have to leave for a while, but I shouldn't be gone more than three weeks tops."

"Wait! All those times you were supposedly in other countries building homes and helping the poor — were you on missions then, too?"

"Not every time, but yes, often," he answered.

"Then I guess you *have* lied to me, Shane, because I thought you were helping people," she snapped.

"I *am* helping people. Do you know the lives we save?" he thundered in frustration. He risked his life every time he suited up for a mission. She was acting as if what he did was wrong, was selfish.

"Well, I don't believe you, Shane. I think you are just freaking out because things have moved too fast between us. I knew this would happen. When we were on the deserted island, just the two of us, it was easy to believe that everything was perfect, that nothing else mattered. Now, we're back in the real world again, and you're getting cold feet. That's fine. I don't care. I'm a big girl and can take care of myself. However, I've known you far too long for you to disrespect me with a story like this. If you were in the military, I would know. Hell, Rafe would know, and that's something he wouldn't keep from me," she said.

He knew he must have a guilty expression on his face, because her eyes narrowed and she looked at him with dawning horror.

"He does know, doesn't he? You're actually telling me the truth!"

"Rafe and I go back a long way. He knew me when things were rough in my life. He's my brother, Lia," he tried to explain.

She threw her hands in the air, forgetting that she was clutching the blanket to her chest. It fell, exposing her perfect breasts to his view. He knew it wasn't a smart decision to stare at their beauty, not when she was so pissed off, but he couldn't help himself. He'd held their weight in his hands, tasted them on his tongue. It was impossible not to look.

The hard slap to his face showed him the error of his ways.

"Don't you dare look at me like that, Shane. I am so beyond mad at you, I don't think you'll ever have the privilege of touching my body again. And it's your loss!"

With that, she scrambled from the bed, not bothering to cover herself up as she stormed to the bathroom and slammed the door.

She just needed time to cool off. That was all. Everything would be fine. He could understand that she was mad that Rafe once again knew something she didn't know. It wasn't as if he'd *wanted* to keep it from her; it was just difficult always to have to think about what he could and couldn't say.

Everything was much simpler if people just didn't know. Of course, that wasn't an option when it came to Rafe. Shane had needed someone to talk to, someone who could understand when he needed to vent.

Some of the things he had to deal with gave him nightmares. He'd learned over the years to tune a lot of it out, to erase it from his mind, but some of it still got through. Rafe had always been there for him when those times came up.

Lia had been too young, and then when he started becoming serious about her, he hadn't wanted to burden her.

No. That was crap. He hadn't wanted to skate around the truth, think about what he could and couldn't say to her. He'd wanted to just be free to be himself, and to relax with her — just love her and have her love him.

Once she knew he had a secret life that she couldn't be a part of, then that's all that she'd ever think about, and it would always come between them.

When the door opened again, Lia was dressed.

She approached the bed, glaring down at him. "I'm going home."

She turned on her heel and began marching toward the door. Shane was fed up with what he considered her tantrum. He leapt from the bed and caught up to her before she made it to the door, pushing her against the solid wood as he blocked her with his body.

"We need to talk more, Lia. I don't want to leave with this between us," he said as she struggled against him, her arms trapped against the side of her body.

"I told you I'm through talking tonight, Shane," she replied through gritted teeth.

"Don't act like a baby. We're in an adult relationship, and couples fight. We need to face it, not run away," he said, wanting to lean forward and kiss her into submission.

That wasn't going to happen, and he knew it. He also knew he really should learn to think before speaking, because it seemed he was doing nothing but digging himself a deeper hole. He was sure she'd love to bury him inside of it when he was finished.

"Believe me, Shane, I am anything but a baby. I have claws, and if you don't let me go right now, I'll show you how sharp they are," she spit.

"Damn, you are stunning when you're pissed off," he gasped, his body hardening as he pressed against her.

He watched desire spark in her eyes as she felt his erection against her stomach. He also saw the determined glint behind the desire. He wasn't going to get to alleviate his hunger tonight.

"Let go now." Her voice was eerily calm. She refused to acknowledge his version of *you're so cute when you're mad*.

For him to keep holding her would be wrong. Taking a quick step back, he tried one more time.

"Let's just talk this out, Lia."

Her eyes drifted down his body, taking in his aroused state before coming back up and stopping at his face.

"Why don't you think about what you really want? I'm not just a quick and easy lay in the sack no matter how many times I've fallen all over myself to have you inside me. You've lied to me, kept information from me, and in the process treated me with disrespect. I'm a catch, Shane, a damn fine one. I won't be treated so poorly."

With that, Lia opened the door and walked through, shutting it with a final click behind her.

Shane knew he could chase after her, stand outside her door if he had to until she agreed to talk to him. But, knowing Lia, he would just be wasting his time. She needed to cool off, speak to her sister and realize that what he'd done wasn't so bad.

They had tomorrow. He could talk to her again. If

not, then they had the wedding. Didn't weddings make people all sappy? She'd surely want to make up before he left.

Shane went back to his now empty bed and lay down. As he looked over at her pillow and inhaled her sweet scent, he knew he wouldn't get any sleep.

Letting out a groan, he got up, threw on some clothes and decided to go for a run. He'd wear himself out to the point that he passed out, even if it took him half the night.

The only thing he knew for sure was that he couldn't leave on bad terms with Lia. She had to realize he was in love with her, wanted to spend the rest of his life with her. She would, he assured himself. She just needed to cool down first.

CHAPTER FORTY-FOUR

Ari

"This is ridiculous, Ari. I am too old to have a stupid bachelor party," Rafe said as he held Ari in his arms on the couch.

"Shane threatened to tie up anyone who got in the way of this ritual, Rafe. He pointed out that it's his duty as your best man to ensure that you have a smoking good time on the last night before the wedding. I did, however, threaten to hang him by his toes if you came to the ceremony with a hangover," Ari said, then kissed his jaw.

"I would much rather just spend the night with you in bed," he said, grabbing her head and kissing her.

Ari wasn't thrilled at the idea that Rafe would be hanging out with a bunch of rowdy men, drinking too much, and having women there to entertain them all, but Shane assured her they would keep the party PG. Still, she didn't trust Shane. He liked to have a good time just a little too much.

The thought of Rafe ogling half-naked women set

her blood to boiling. She trusted Rafe fully, but she still had to admit to some rather irrational insecurities.

"You're late, Rafe," Shane hollered as he walked into the house.

Ari had the sudden urge to grab on tight and not let Rafe go, but she refused to be one of those clingy, desperate wives who so justly earned the scorn of the world. There was no point in starting out their new life together if she didn't trust him enough to send him off to a simple bachelor party.

"This is so ridiculous, Shane," Rafe grumbled as he extracted himself from Ari's arms and stood looking down at her one last time.

"Time's wasting. We will see you tomorrow, Ari," Shane said with a wink.

Ari was concerned when she looked at Shane. He had dark circles beneath his eyes, and though he was smiling, it was obvious that something was wrong. She was about to ask him, but he turned and began leading Rafe away.

Soon, she was standing in Rafe's large living room all by herself, and she had to fight off a little anxiety before she got ready to head home. After all, it was bad luck to stay the night at Rafe's place, and with the bad luck they'd already had, she didn't want to jinx the wedding.

This was silly. She had the journal she could pore over, or she could call her mom and go out for dessert before heading home. She absolutely refused to allow Rafe's comings and goings to affect her this much.

As she moved toward the library, she heard the front door open, and her heart skipped a beat.

"Come on, Ari, we have work to do."

Ari turned to find Lia and Rachel standing in the living room, both dressed in tight skirts and revealing tops, and with their hair and makeup done to perfection.

"What's going on?" she asked with no little trepidation. They'd already had her bachelorette party the night before. It had been a great time, though she'd never admit to Rafe that they'd watched a performance of the Chippendales dance troupe.

He'd be furious if he knew that one of the dancers had basically given her a lap dance. After she'd had a few drinks, against her usual rules, she hadn't even minded.

Yes, she knew it was a double standard that she'd seen male strippers but didn't want him to have the same privilege with women dancers, but female strippers lost all their clothes. The male ones kept their "naughty bits" covered, leaving that for the imagination. So there, Rafe! And besides, men were always thinking below the belt, but did women ever do that? Hmmm. Never mind.

"We're crashing the bachelor party," Rachel said with glee.

"There is no way I'm doing that. I had to practically force Rafe from the house to go to his party at all. I don't want him to think I don't trust him," Ari said.

"Shane hired a stripper to jump out of a cake," Lia informed her.

Ari's eyes narrowed, and she glared toward the door. She hoped Shane felt the heat in his back.

"He promised me the party would be PG," Ari said.

"He lied. Apparently, he does that often," Lia said, and Ari had a good idea where Shane's dark circles had come from.

"I still can't…" Ari began, though she wasn't happy.

"Look what we bought. We're going to trade the stripper out for you. Then the only person dancing on your fiancé's lap will be you. Unless you don't mind some young, fake-breasted Barbie doll wriggling all over his…lap," Rachel said with feigned innocence.

She was holding up a tiny little skirt and sequined bra, plus a few other items Ari doubted she could fit into.

"I can't wear that in public," Ari gasped.

"Suit yourself. We can rent a movie and get fat on popcorn and chocolate," Rachel said, plopping down. The witch knew Ari was going to go crazy even thinking of another woman all over her fiancé.

"Fine, then," Ari said. She snatched the bag from Rachel and marched herself into the bathroom.

Fifteen minutes later, she was staring at the mirror in horror. The bra left her breasts half exposed. The skirt barely covered the lower part of her backside, and the garter belt made her legs look a mile long. She actually liked the way she looked — she would love to wear the outfit for Rafe in private, but there would be a lot of men at his bachelor party.

In fact, Rafe would kill her if anyone saw her like this, but desperate times took desperate measures. *Well, here goes nothing*, she thought as she opened the door and made her way back to the living room after dousing herself in her favorite perfume.

"Oh, my gosh, Ari, you look like a wet dream come to life," Lia gasped and made Ari do a spin to show off the outfit.

"Here's the final touch," said Rachel, holding up a

pair of five-inch red stiletto heels.

"I will end up killing someone with those," Ari said, eyeballing what she considered weapons.

"Well, then, the man will die a very happy death," Lia assured her.

"Unless *I'm* the one I kill with those monstrosities," Ari said. "It will be a miracle if I manage to stay upright."

"You probably won't stay upright for the *entire* evening in that getup," Lia joked. "Rafe will see to that." She sat Ari down and began putting her hair up while Rachel applied a thick layer of makeup.

When the two women were satisfied with their handiwork, they gave Ari a coat and marched her out the front door, pushing her into the car waiting for them.

As they approached the private club where the party was being held, Ari's nerves went through the ceiling. She really didn't know how Rafe was going to react, but the girls wouldn't let her change her mind.

They sneaked in through the kitchen, and paid off the stripper standing there.

"I need to check my makeup," Ari said, and she rushed toward the bathroom. The girls followed her, not giving her a chance to run away.

"Just breathe."

Ari looked at herself in the mirror and a blush stole over her cheeks. She couldn't believe she was about to step — no, leap — into a room full of men wearing practically nothing and give her husband-to-be a lap dance.

When she was almost ready to talk herself out of it, the door opened and a sharp whistle made her jump.

"Damn, girl! Too bad Rafe's blindfolded. You look hot. I can't wait to see his reaction when the blindfold comes off."

"Why is he blindfolded during a striptease?" Ari asked, puzzled.

"'Cause I called Shane and told him we were doing a swap," Rachel told her proudly.

"I can't believe he went for that," Lia grumbled.

"He's kissing your butt right now, Lia. I just told him that you insisted," Rachel said smugly. Lia didn't respond, just muttered something before turning back toward Ari.

"I'm trying to calm myself down, Rachel. You're not helping in the least."

"Oh, c'mon, you're a gorgeous sex goddess who makes him drool. I think you'll be fine," her friend replied with a roll of her eyes.

"It's not Rafe I'm worried about. I'm a bit terrified to shake my ass in front of his two hundred friends."

"Believe me, girl. They're all going to be wishing they could switch places with him. Hell, I'm thinking of switching teams. You are rocking that outfit."

"OK, I can do this. Thank you," Ari told her before adjusting her breasts, which were perilously close to falling from the skimpy top. Then she stepped inside the cake and the DJ immediately started playing appropriately sleazy music.

"Good luck," Rachel called right before the contraption was wheeled out. Ari wondered how she'd gotten herself into this mess. Trapped in another contraption. Her heart thundered as the crowd exploded in cheers. She couldn't see a thing, and she didn't know whether she'd be able to do this or not.

Taking a deep breath, she waited for her cue. She was committed now. She didn't have a choice but to follow through.

CHAPTER FORTY-FIVE

Rafe

"Come on, Shane! This is stupid."

"We can do this the easy way or the hard way, but it *will* happen."

Rafe looked into his best friend's eyes, trying to determine how serious he was. When Shane didn't back down even a little, Rafe knew this would be a battle to the very end. Though he was frustrated and more than a little bit sick of this bachelor party, he figured it would be better to get the event over with.

When it came time to deal with Shane, Rafe wouldn't hold anything back! That guy had gone beyond cruising for a bruising.

As Rafe sat down and felt ropes binding his arms to the chair, he closed his eyes and held on to the fact that the very next night, he'd be married to Ari and the two of them would be far away from all this nonsense.

"What in the hell are you doing?" Rafe's eyes popped open as he felt strong hands holding his legs against the bars of the chair and wrapping rope around them. He'd thought having his arms tied up was ridiculous, but he'd never agreed to being bound up so tightly, and on the legs, too.

"Just go with the flow."

"Like hell I will. This is no longer amusing. Untie me at once," Rafe demanded, letting his friend know he was finished. His tolerance for Shane had run out and he was leaving.

"Sorry, buddy — lights out."

Before Rafe could say a word, a cloth was stuffed in his mouth and quickly fastened around the back of his head. He was shooting a deadly glare at Shane before a dark cloth covered his vision. He was seriously going to kill Shane when this was all over.

Struggling against his binds, Rafe would have sworn out loud when the sultry music started and all the men whistled, but the gag prevented him from doing so. *Dammit!* He knew a stripper was coming. He had no desire to look at, touch, or come near a half-naked stranger. Why would he? Ari was waiting for him, and she was the only woman he needed. Who held a candle to her anyway?

When he felt a set of fingernails scrape along his neck, then undo the top button of his shirt, his struggles against his binds became frantic. When he got out of this, he was going to land a right hook straight at Shane's nose.

But he wasn't getting loose— his "friends" had tied him down too securely. Since struggling was getting him nowhere, he went completely still. He'd just wait them out.

As the woman straddled his lap, then rocked forward, her breasts pushing into his chest, Rafe felt the beginning stirrings of desire licking at his groin. Mortification filled him. He hadn't so much as looked at another woman since meeting Ari. Why in the hell would he desire a stripper?

It had to be the amount of booze he'd drunk during the evening, or maybe the blindfold. He tried tuning out the whistling men, the feel of the stripper grinding against him, and the smell of her sweet perfume. He pictured Ari in his mind, and without knowing it a smile appeared on his previously pursed and angry lips.

Wait. He knew that scent, knew it better than anyone. This wasn't just any stripper — this was Ari. He didn't know how she'd managed it, but she was here and giving him the best damn lap dance he could ever hope for.

The feel of her breasts pushing against his chest, her nails scraping his skin — it was all familiar, and it all turned him on beyond anything imaginable.

He groaned as she kissed his upper lip, wishing he weren't gagged so he could sink his tongue inside her mouth. At his groan, her body stiffened.

The realization hit him that she didn't know he knew who she was. Good. They'd tied him down, made him go through this ridiculous scheme, and tormented him — now it was his turn to torment his tormentors.

Throwing his head back he moaned a bit louder through the gag, and pushed his hips up, letting her feel his arousal. His moan quickly turned to a squeak as her nails dug into his chest.

His kitten had claws and they were definitely showing.

The crowd roared as they watched the scene before them, and that's when Rafe realized that Ari was most likely scantily dressed in a room full of horny men. His enjoyment was squashed flat.

As the blindfold came off and he looked into the fiery eyes of his very pissed-off fiancée, he glared right back.

"How could you be turned on by a stripper?" she snapped, still straddling his lap.

His eyes pointed down at the gag in his mouth, and it took her a moment to realize what he wanted her to do.

Finally, she got it and untied the knots. As soon as it was off, he looked angrily Shane's way, and saw that he was deriving way too much pleasure from the situation. Rafe definitely owed his best friend a solid right hook.

"Everyone out now!" Rafe roared.

One look at his face and the men decided not to argue. It had been all fun and games up to that point, but they could see that Rafe's mood was murderous.

The men began pouring from the room, Shane being the last to leave.

"Have fun, kids. Don't hurt him too badly, Ari," he said before firmly shutting and locking the door.

"Again, how in the hell could you get turned on by a stripper?" she asked, rage shining in her eyes.

"First off, I knew it was you as soon as I smelled your perfume. I'd know that scent anywhere. Secondly, what in the hell are you wearing?" he thundered.

Her eyes widened at his words, and then softened in pleasure.

"You really knew it was me?" she asked.

"Of course I knew it was you. I know everything about you, Ari!" he growled. His question still hadn't been answered.

"Oh, that's good then," she said as she pushed her hips against his and brought back to his focus the fact that he had an almost painful erection trapped beneath his jeans.

"I asked you a question. There's not much of your body that's covered, and every one of my friends just saw it!"

"Well, I couldn't let a strange woman grind all over you. I mean *really*! Your honor was at stake. As soon as your sisters told me there was going to be a stripper, we came down here. I didn't have much time to think about it, actually," she admitted as she looked down at her breasts, which were flirting with a major wardrobe malfunction.

"I will have to kill every man who looked at you," he said.

"I don't think that will be necessary. The room is pretty dark," she said. She began moving to the music, which was still playing.

Rafe was trying to concentrate on their fight, but he was quickly losing the battle. How could he stay angry when she was expertly pushing every button he had?

"Untie me, Ari," he said.

"Nope," she said. "But I will undo the rest of these nasty buttons for you." After she finished unbuttoning his shirt and parted it, her hands glided across his chest. "Mmm, you are so spectacular, Rafe."

He groaned when she bent down and ran her tongue along his lips, not quite connecting their mouths, but teasing him while her hands stroked his chest.

"Baby, I will make you sing if you just let me out of these ropes," he promised, wanting so much to reach up and unclip the bra she was wearing.

"It's your bachelor party, Rafe. I think I'll be the one making you sing tonight," she said. She stood up and turned around, wiggling her hips before bending over and touching the floor, giving him a nice view of her thong-"covered" derrière.

"Hot damn, Ari, I like that outfit," he gasped as she backed up and rubbed herself on his lap. "I really need to touch you," he moaned.

She turned around and smiled, glorying in the control she held. Rafe struggled more against the restraints, but he wasn't making any progress. The men had locked him down tight.

Ari turned back around and then undid his pants, sliding them down to the bottom of the chair and freeing his pulsing hard-on to her view.

"Yum," she said as she ran her finger from the tip to the base and then back, circling the wet head.

Then she stood back and reached to the front of her bra, unclasping it and letting it slide down her arms, releasing her beautiful breasts. She did another little twirl, making them bounce, and causing Rafe's mouth to go dry.

She took off her skirt and stood before him in a small red triangle of fabric that just covered her core, a black garter belt and fishnet stockings, and the sexiest damn red heels he'd ever seen.

Turning in a circle, she lifted her arms, dancing seductively to the music, making her breasts sway as she moved toward him. Leaning down, she rubbed one of her breasts across his mouth, and he quickly latched on to the nipple, sucking it inside his mouth and running his tongue over the hard peak.

Before he could do more, she pulled back, her eyes glazed with passion.

"Oh, that's good, Rafe," she said as she bent down and kissed him — just a fleeting moment of their lips touching.

Then she kneeled before him and quickly sucked his arousal into her mouth, making him cry out as she took him deep, then set up a seductive rhythm matching that of the music, making him nearly lose his mind.

Before he embarrassed himself and released in her mouth, she stopped, climbed back up his body and kissed him again, rubbing her luscious breasts against his chest.

He was going to explode before he got the chance to enter her.

His only salvation was in the fact that she was just as hot for him, just as ready to come.

Turning around, she backed up to him, sliding her panties out of the way while looking over her shoulder as she gripped him tight in her hand and guided him inside her from behind. Rafe looked down at her rounded behind, wanting so much to take it in his hands, squeeze the feminine flesh as she sank down on him.

Bending over so her hands touched the ground, she began moving her hips up and down his shaft, setting up a rhythm pleasing to them both, her buttocks hitting his legs as she slid all the way down his length.

"Oh, Rafe, this is good," Ari cried as she sped up, sliding up and down him in a frantic need to give them release. Just as he was nearing his peak, she stopped, pulling her body from his. He cried out his displeasure.

It didn't last long. She straddled his legs and then sank back down on him, continuing her breathless rhythm as her breasts mashed up against his chest and she grabbed his head, locking their mouths together.

Within a few minutes, she screamed as her orgasm overtook her, her tight heat gripping him while she continued to slide up and down. Rafe shouted out with her as he felt the pressure build, and sweet release finally overtook him.

When the last of their tremors fell away, she went limp against him; neither spoke while they caught their breath.

"That's one hell of a bachelor party," Rafe said with a chuckle. "Now will you untie me?"

"Oh, sorry. I completely forgot." Ari bent down and undid his legs first, and then his hands.

Rafe rubbed his tender flesh before picking up the ropes and looking at her with intent.

"Hey, I'm not the one who tied you up," she said, backing away. But Rafe could see the excitement in her eyes. She wanted this.

He made a move toward her and she ran around the pool table.

Perfect!

He caught her and then she was his.

The rest of the night he found out just how many ways he could make her beg for mercy. They barely had the energy to walk to their waiting car as the sun began rising in the sky.

CHAPTER FORTY-SIX

IT was her wedding day, and she couldn't believe it. After so much heartache and trauma, she was about to marry Rafe Palazzo. No second thoughts, no worries stared back at her when she looked in the mirror.

She was a little tired and had woken up alone in the early afternoon with circles under her eyes, but a make-up artist had worked magic. She was now dressed in her perfect gown, with her hair, makeup and nails done expertly, and she had about two minutes before her bridesmaids came in.

"You are stunning, Ari."

Ari turned to find Lia standing inside the door. Ari hadn't even heard it open.

"Thank you, Lia. Thank you for being here now, and for the last three years. I don't know what I would have done without you," Ari said as she moved forward and wrapped her arms around her friend.

"You would have been fine because you are beautiful, smart, talented and a real prize for any man. All you have to do is let me know if my brother isn't treating you right, and I'll come and straighten him out," Lia said with a twinkle in her eye.

"I have a feeling that you enjoy terrorizing Rafe," Ari said with a laugh.

"Oh, he well deserves it for the numerous pranks he played on me while I was growing up," Lia said.

"Where's Rachel? I thought she would be here by now," Ari asked; she realized it was getting close to time to walk down the aisle and yet there was no sign of Rachel anywhere.

"That's odd. I haven't seen her since this morning, when we dropped off the dresses here. She said she would be right behind me. I've been so busy that I haven't had time to think about it," Lia said, concern apparent on her face.

"Let's check her room," Ari said, sure that everything was fine, but with an undercurrent of worry because only she and Lia knew about the baby.

They stepped into the hall and made their way down to Rachel's fitting room. Ari knocked on the door and there wasn't an answer, so she tried the doorknob. It was unlocked.

The two women opened the door, calling for Rachel. Still no answer.

Ari felt her stomach heave with fear. She was afraid to look around, afraid they'd find Rachel lying on the floor bleeding. What if she'd had a miscarriage and had been lying there dying all day? She'd never forgive herself for being so self-absorbed that she hadn't noticed her dear friend missing for an entire afternoon.

"Oh, Ari," Lia gasped, making Ari turn slowly around. She was afraid to see what had made Lia's voice so frightened.

What she found was Lia holding a note. That wasn't so bad. Or was it?

"You'd better come here," Lia said, and Ari made her way over to her.

Ari didn't recognize the handwriting. It wasn't Rachel's.

When she read the words, she blanched.

This wasn't good — not good at all.

"What do we do?" Ari asked.

"We have to talk to Rafe," Lia replied with dread.

"He's not going to be happy," Ari said as she paced to and fro in the small room.

"No, he's not. Do you want to finish the wedding first?"

"Are you kidding me, Lia? Of course not. This is far more important," Ari said, and she walked from the room. Lia was right behind her.

Ari entered Rafe's room, stopping in her tracks when she saw just how breathtaking her future husband was. Shane and he froze in the process of putting on their black ties.

"You aren't supposed to see each other," Shane said, his mouth agape, the new shiner on his right eye not detracting from his looks at all. Lia was obviously taking a bit too much pleasure in the bruise left by her brother on Shane's face.

"You need to see something, Rafe," Ari said as she moved forward.

He read the note, and fire instantly entered his eyes.

"Is this a joke?" he asked, looking between the two women.

"No, unfortunately, it's not," Lia said, looking decidedly uncomfortable.

"Why wasn't I told of her condition sooner?" Rafe thundered.

Ari knew he was upset, but that was no reason to take out his temper on her or his sister. She sent him a warning look, and he calmed down, though rage was still brewing in his eyes as he passed the note to a very confused Shane.

"She wanted to wait to let you know," Ari told Rafe.

"You knew." It wasn't a question, just a statement as he looked from Lia to Ari.

"Yes, of course we knew. She didn't want to be yelled at for making a mistake, but she needed to talk to someone about it. So she told Ari and me about everything roughly a week ago," Lia confirmed. "She swore us to secrecy."

"I can't believe you kept this from me. Had I known, she wouldn't be in the situation she's in," Rafe said in exasperation.

"What? She wouldn't be pregnant?" Ari asked.

"There's nothing I can do about that, obviously. That's not what I mean. She wouldn't be gone," he said, running a hand through his hair.

"What do you want to do, Rafe?" Shane asked, his own eyes narrowed in outrage after reading the note.

"I'm going after my sister, of course," Rafe replied.

"I'll go with you," Shane told him.

"I can handle this, Shane. I don't want your ass hauled to prison for insubordination. We both know you leave tomorrow," Rafe said as he patted his best friend on the shoulder.

At the mention of Shane's departure, Lia cast dangerous and disgusted looks at both men.

"Lia, we need to talk," Shane said as he watched her stiffen.

"No, Shane. You go play G.I. Joe and leave me the

hell alone," she said, turning away from him.

"Sorry, Rafe, but your sister is a pain in the ass. I need to have a chat with her while you and Ari figure this out." Shane strode toward Lia.

Ari watched her friend take a step back, but she didn't look frightened. Excitement gleamed in her eyes. Shane followed, picking Lia up and carrying her from the room while she yelled bloody murder.

"It seems that both of my sisters are having man problems," Rafe said, running his fingers through his hair, mussing it up just the way Ari liked it.

"I will inform the guests that the wedding's been postponed," Ari said a bit sadly at the thought.

"We can still do this, Ari. I don't think Rachel is in danger. I just refuse to allow this man, this king, who I thought was my friend, to do what he's done," Rafe told her as he pulled her into his arms.

"Your friend?" Ari asked with confusion.

"Yes. Do you remember a couple of years ago — the business meeting you sat in on with me? Prince Adriane was there."

"Oh, my gosh! That's the man!" Ari gasped.

"Yes. We've worked on deals together. I never thought he'd be the sort to take such liberties with my sister," Rafe roared.

"Now I see why she couldn't resist him at the beach," Ari said, remembering well how handsome Prince Adriane was. Hell, *handsome* didn't capture his physical appeal. The man was magnificent.

"Excuse me?" Rafe said, his eyebrows drawn in.

"Let me explain…" Ari told him all she knew about how Rachel and Ian had met, and then how Rachel had found out she was pregnant.

"He still can't get away with this," Rafe said.

"I know. You need to go after her, Rafe," Ari told him.

"What about our wedding?" Rafe asked. He wrapped Ari in a hug.

"I can't have a wedding without Rachel here. It wouldn't be right," Ari sighed as she rubbed along his back.

"I love you, Arianna Harlow. I *will* make you my bride," Rafe vowed.

"And I love you, Rafe. But for now, you do whatever it takes to save Rachel. I'll face the crowd. You realize they're all going to think I'm a jilted bride?" she said with a smile.

"Ah, baby, they all know that I'm so in love with you, that could never happen," he assured her.

Ari knew it, too. She wasn't worried. She reluctantly withdrew from his arms and left the room. Informing all their friends and family in attendance at their wedding that the ceremony was postponed wasn't exactly her idea of fun.

As the huge double doors were opened for her, she found it quite amusing to be walking down the aisle on her own with no music. She should have them play a break-up song and really worry the crowd.

She stopped and gave Rafe's parents a brief run-down of what was going on, then stepped up to the stage to face the crowd while the two of them rushed from the room to find Rafe.

As she turned to look out among the audience, she saw a few sympathetic looks from people thinking that Rafe had gotten cold feet. She also saw a few hopeful looks from some of the women. Too bad, ladies! He was still taken.

"I'm sorry, but the wedding has been postponed. There's been an emergency in the family," she said simply before stepping down and exiting.

When she entered the room, Rafe was pacing, already on the phone. His mother was holding the note, her face grew pale as she read the words.

To Rachel's family,

I have taken Rachel to see my personal physician. After he clears her for travel, we will leave for Corythia, where I will be able to care for her and my child. Though Rachel is hesitant about the upcoming nuptials,

I will notify you of my plans for the wedding when they are final. You are welcome to join us, but I must inform you that I will not change my mind on this matter. She carries the heir to the throne of Corythia, and she will be my wife. Rachel will be well taken care of as the royal consort.

King Adriano of Corythia

EPILOGUE

Rafe should be married right now, slipping a piece of cake in Ari's mouth before he took her lips with his own. He should be holding her in his arms on the dance floor, then taking her off on a honeymoon, where they'd make love all night.

He shouldn't be waiting to talk to the king of Corythia.

Finally, Adriane came on the line, and Rafe didn't waste any words.

"Do you honestly think I'm going to just stand by while you kidnap my sister and take her off to a foreign country!" Rafe shouted.

The king didn't hesitate in giving his response. "She's carrying the royal heir. We will be married at once," he replied before adding. "It wasn't exactly kidnapping, Rafe. She was just…reluctant to come."

"You've crossed a line, Adriane. I won't stand for this."

"You don't have a choice, Rafe. Your sister is no longer a child, but carries *my* child within her womb. She is now mine to take care of. I left you the note out of courtesy, but there won't be any changing of my mind.

We *will* wed," Adriane said firmly.

"Over my dead body. I'll be there before night falls tomorrow."

"Good luck getting past my guards, Rafe. We've been friends up to this point and I don't want that to end, but you won't stand in the way of my being with my child."

"And you won't kidnap my sister and get away with it. Hand her over and we can walk away from this," Rafe warned.

"That I cannot do. I hope that you will come to your senses."

"No, Adriane, you are the one who had better reconsider."

Rafe hung up the phone before dialing his pilot. "Fuel up the jet; we're heading to Corythia immediately."

The End

See the conclusion in the Surrender Series, Scorched — Book Four — November 2013
Pre-orders available now on iTunes, Amazon and Kobo

Sign up for Melody Anne's Mailing list at www.melodyanne.com to be notified when a new book is available.

BOOKS BY MELODY ANNE

BILLIONAIRE BACHELORS
*The Billionaire Wins the Game
*The Billionaire's Dance
*The Billionaire Falls
*The Billionaire's Marriage Proposal
*Blackmailing the Billionaire
*Runaway Heiress
*The Billionaire's Final Stand
*Unexpected Treasure
*Hidden Treasure — **Coming Soon**
*Priceless Treasure — **Coming Soon**
*Unrealized Treasure — **Coming Soon**
*Wanted Treasure— **Coming Soon**

BABY FOR THE BILLIONAIRE
+The Tycoon's Revenge
+The Tycoon's Vacation
+The Tycoon's Proposal
+The Tycoon's Secret
+The Lost Tycoon — **Coming Soon**

RISE OF THE DARK ANGEL
-Midnight Fire — Rise of the Dark Angel — Book One
-Midnight Moon — Rise of the Dark Angel — Book Two
-Midnight Storm — Rise of the Dark Angel — Book Three

-Midnight Eclipse — Rise of the Dark Angel — Book Four — **Coming Soon**

Surrender
=Surrender — Book One
=Submit — Book Two
=Seduced — Book Three
=Scorched — Book Four — **Nov 2013**

To win prizes and more, visit Melody's Facebook page at www.facebook.com/melodyanneauthor
Sigh up for her mailing list at www.melodyanne.com
Sign up for twitter at @authmelodyanne and chat with the author and win more great prizes.

Thank you for reading the Surrender series. Please see her other great series, "Billionaire Bachelors" and "Baby for the Billionaire" Available at all retailers.

(This page intentionally left blank.)

Made in the USA
San Bernardino, CA
07 September 2013